SACRED RUSE

THE GUILD TRILOGY
BOOK TWO

SACRED RUSE

Emma K. C. Couette

ELGIN HOUSE
— PRESS —

ALSO BY EMMA. K. C. COUETTE

The Guild Trilogy

Silent Night
Sacred Ruse
Solemn Vow
Assassins Below

The Fidalian Chronicles

Summer's Revenge
Winter's Wrath

CONTENT WARNING

This book contains content/themes that may not be suitable for all readers, including: death, graphic violence, abuse, manipulation, alcoholism, loss of limb, mentions of torture, family trauma, and mental health issues, such as panic attacks. Please read at your own discretion.

Recommended Reading Age: 14+

CHAPTER ONE

Haven City, 06/2110

In the end, death comes for us all. Even assassins are not exempt from its cold, eternal embrace. I knew my time would come, but I never thought I'd die like this.

I don't bother to hold my breath; I let the water flood me. My lungs scream, expecting oxygen and receiving tidal waves. They rage against me, both inside and out. I've lost the feeling in my limbs. I've stopped fighting.

A part of me resents my choice, wants to live, but I don't remember what life is like. I don't remember anything. Death and frigid water are all I know and they carry me, slow but sure, into the dark.

Something is beating on my chest, a constant rhythm of stabbing pain tearing me away from oblivion. I don't know much about Hell, but it should be a lot more painful than this and if, by some twisted luck, I'd managed to slip into heaven, there should be no pain at all.

I should be dead.

Why am I not dead?

The pounding quickens, becoming more urgent, and I hear distant voices.

Get up, I will myself. *Life is a gift; you better take it.*

The next blow slams into me and my eyes fly open before fluttering shut again. The voice comes into focus. Someone is screaming.

I go to answer, recognizing they are calling for me, but instead, I choke on the water and bile that spews out of my mouth.

Someone rolls me onto my side.

"Oh God," they breathe. "Oh Guild, you're all right. You're going to be all right. Just get it out." I recognize the voice, but it takes me a second to place it.

Trey.

Trey is here. She saved me.

I throw up again and her voice is there to comfort me. My thoughts swirl in my head as my shredded brain tries to piece together the details of the life I almost lost. Tragedies play behind my lids as I continue to wretch. Darkness invades my thoughts; a life of horror takes up residence in my memories once more and then...

A face. A bright face and memories bursting with light and heat and love.

A name.

"Ajax," I gasp and then I hold back a scream.

My throat feels as though it has been skinned with rusty knives. The pain moves to the front of my mind and I lose myself to it. My lungs heave with the effort of drawing oxygen into their ravaged cells. My entire body shakes. Pricks of agony flare up in random places with no warning.

Oh God, I'm dying.

Finally, mercifully, the pain fades. It doesn't disappear, but it becomes something I can manage.

"Ajax," I say again, ignoring the fire it ignites in my throat. My voice is raspy and sounds nothing like me. I would laugh at myself, but that would only cause more pain.

"What?" Trey says.

"Ajax," I try for the third time. "Where…?" My words fail me.

"Safe," an unfamiliar voice replies.

I try to look up, but my head and eyes are both too heavy for the motion. I can barely focus on Trey sitting beside me, her face nothing more than a dark blur.

The voice belongs to a man, that much is certain.

Why is he here?

"We pulled him out too," the man continues, "but don't worry. Rest for a second."

I try to sit up. "No. I need…see."

White fire consumes my lungs and throat. I stay glued to the floor, my strength failing me. There is an ache in my bones, a deep exhaustion in every muscle. My eyes don't want to stay open, but I fight the urge to close them.

"I told you she was stubborn," Trey says.

The man shrugs and walks away, leaving my line of sight.

Trey pins her stare on me. "Relax, Night. You're going to hurt yourself even more."

I shake my head, the movement slow and difficult. The air around us smells like iron and mildew. I try not to throw up again as I remember the bodies that must still litter the area.

Trey sighs. "Fine. He's over there." She points to my left and I turn my head.

Ajax is propped up against the remains of the glass tank we were held in.

I muster all my remaining energy to focus my gaze on him and my heart clenches.

He looks terrible. His clothes cling to his frame, which looks thinner than I remember, and his head slumps on his shoulder. Chunks of glass litter the ground around him. If it wasn't for the rise and fall of his chest, I would've thought he was dead.

"Jax," I cry out, tears threatening to spill over my cheeks. I hold them back.

Ajax lifts his head and opens his eyes a fraction. "Silent?"

"It's okay. I… I'm...here." I try to prop myself up again, but Trey pushes me back.

"No," she snaps. "You're not strong enough. I practically raised you from the dead."

I slump to the floor in defeat, feeling exhaustion taking over. The floor is cold and I start to shiver. My still-wet clothes do nothing to help. "Trey..." I try. "How...did you...save us? How did...you...know?"

"Later," she replies. "What matters is you're safe now."

I bristle.

Why can't they give me a damn answer?

I hear footsteps and the mystery man enters the room a moment later. The torchlight doesn't reach his face, his features left in shadow. "The Charger's men are coming," he says. "We have to go."

My eyes widen as much as they can and Trey looks up sharply. "We can't," she replies. "The move might kill them."

"Well, we certainly can't stay here."

She looks torn.

"Trey," he snaps. "We have to *go. Now.*"

The man walks over to Ajax.

"Wait," I call out to him. "Who...*are* you?" My words are slurred, my focus fading.

The man glances at me and smiles. "They call me Kuen."

Kuen. *The* Kuen. The *legendary* Kuen is helping Ajax and I escape the Charger's clutches. What on earth has my world turned into?

I watch as Kuen picks Ajax up and slings him over one shoulder.

Jax tenses, but doesn't cry out. I can tell he's barely conscious.

I turn back to Trey as she reaches for me.

"This will probably hurt," she says.

"Doesn't...matter," I mumble. "Pain and I are...something like...friends now."

She doesn't laugh. She only picks me up and cradles me in her arms like I'm an infant.

I gasp.

Everything hurts.

"Ready?" Kuen asks.

Trey only nods.

The two break into a run and we soon disappear into a dark tunnel, leaving the Assassin's Guild behind. I surrender the battle to stay awake and let my exhaustion claim me. Maybe tomorrow I'll find this entire endeavour has been a horrible nightmare, but some part of me knows I'll have no such luck.

• • •

I must sleep for a while, because when I wake, I feel refreshed and the pain has faded to the back of my mind. I take a deep breath without a problem and can't help but smile. It's never felt so good to breathe before.

I open my eyes. Trey sits in a chair at the foot of my bed. She looks rumpled, as if she slept there, her black hair sticking up in several places.

"How are you feeling?" she asks me.

I shimmy into a seated position and shrug. "I've been worse, but I've also been better."

She smiles ruefully. "I know the feeling." Her dark circles almost match the shade of her eyes.

I take a moment to study the room and it doesn't take me long to realize I don't recognize the yellow walls. The bed is too big and the chest of drawers too ancient for us to be in the Resistance, but the window is the deciding factor. The Resistance is underground.

I narrow my eyes at the floral print drapes, feeling vulnerable with the outside world only separated from us by less than an inch of glass.

I push the window out of my mind and return my gaze to Trey. "Where are we?"

"We're in a safe house, somewhere in the west end of the city. We have to lay low until things settle down. It's not safe to travel."

"Why?"

She shrugs. "You know why. You planned it."

I swallow. "The attack didn't go so well, did it?"

She doesn't answer, but her eyes scream the truth. "Night," she says, "what happened to you? How did you end up in that tank? I thought you left."

I look at my feet. "I did leave. I ran, but then I realized running away from my problems has never solved anything and I still wanted my revenge, so when the bombs woke me up, I returned to my original plan. I went in search of the Charger, naturally, and I..."

I falter, remembering the horrible truth he revealed to me.

"Long story short," I go on, "I lost. Ajax came to help me and we ended up in that tank. How did you manage to get us out?"

"I had a feeling you would come back, but I knew you couldn't win, not alone. I went to Kuen for help and he showed me the secret tunnel that led to the Charger's private chamber. We arrived just in time, Night. Any longer and the two of you wouldn't have made it. Kuen smashed the glass with his axe and we dragged you guys out. You know the rest."

"Is Jax okay?"

She nods. "He has a will of steel, but the battle took its toll. He was asleep last I checked on him. It's the best thing for him, though, especially if he wants to heal that hand of his."

I nod and fall silent. I'm afraid to say what's on my mind, afraid talking about it will make it real. Truth sears through the comforts of life, sews despair and mistrust into our skin. Yet, I know I should ask her. I hid from the truth of who I was for years. I'm not going to hide again.

"Trey," I say.

"Yes?"

"The Charger he... He said that I... I didn't believe him, but..."

She looks at me curiously and I take a deep breath.

"He said he's my father."

She regards me with solemn eyes. "He finally told you then."

My eyes widen. "You...you *knew*? How? Why am I the last to know?"

Fire ignites in her eyes and she spits her answer out. "Because our father is a sadistic bastard."

Oh.

Oh my God.

"We're sisters?" I gasp.

She nods and tears build in her brown eyes. "I wanted to tell you sooner, but...it wasn't the time. You wouldn't have believed me."

"You're probably right."

I remember her reaction when we first met. She knew even then who I was, what we were meant to be.

I smile. "Even though it's the Charger that connects us, I'm glad you're my sister."

She smiles back, brushing the tears out of her eyes and I remember something else.

"*That's* why you were so upset when I almost died during the train attack."

She nods. "I couldn't bear the thought of losing you after finding you again, that you would die after finally finding yourself. It was too cruel. So, when I learned that you left on the eve of the attack, I knew I had to find you. You escaped death once; I knew you couldn't do it again without help and I didn't want to lose you. I came too close to that horror before."

It's hard to wrap my still-healing brain around this new concept. "Well," I say, "at least I know why you want to destroy him."

She shrugs. "Anybody with an ounce of heart would. It's not because he's my father, Night. You wanted to kill him long before you knew."

"I guess."

Something else clicks in my head then. Trey wasn't the only one who acted weird after the train attack. Avery had also come all the way from the Barn to see me and Trey... Trey had once said he was her uncle.

A memory flashes: the meeting with Avery all those weeks ago. What was it he said? Something about his name...

I asked him how he knew who the Charger really was and why he hadn't told anyone. He had answered cryptically, something about the how being the reason why and...

Avery Norin is not my true name either, but it's in there.

Oh.

Oh.

I rearrange the letters quickly in my head and have my answer in a heartbeat: Vyrin Aeron.

"Holy shit," I breathe.

"What?" Trey says nearly jumping out of her chair. "What's wrong?"

"Avery and the Charger are brothers."

"Guild, Night, you scared me half to death." She lets out a sigh and settles back into her seat. "Yes, they're brothers. So?"

"How come you never mentioned it? This is huge!"

"I was sworn to secrecy," she replies, "though I should've known you'd figure it out."

"It makes so much sense," I exclaim. "That's how he knew everything and why he wouldn't tell anyone. That's why the Charger said they went back a long way. Guild, what if they're working together?"

Trey looks at me, cocking her head as if to say, are you serious? When she realizes I am, she laughs. "Oh, Night," she gasps, "that's too good. Why the hell would

Avery be in league with the assassins? He renounced them, and his brother, decades ago."

"But how can we be sure? How can we trust him when he doesn't trust his agents with his true identity?"

"Think about it," Trey replies. "How would Jenson react to the truth? Look at how *you* reacted. No one would trust him. Avery wouldn't be able to run an anti-assassin organization with everyone worried he'd turn on them at any second."

"But—"

"But nothing. You worry too much, kiddo. Everything is under control. I should go. Let you rest. This conversation is doing nothing for your stress levels."

I scowl. "I don't want to rest."

"You don't have a choice, Night. You're not recovered yet."

"I'll be the judge of that."

Before she can react, I tear off my covers, swing my legs over the side of the bed, and jump to my feet.

In an instant, I'm writhing on the floor, screaming in blood-burning agony.

My leg.

My leg.

Oh God.

My vision blackens.

When I come to, I'm back in bed. Trey is standing over me, body tense and eyes frantic.

"What the hell happened, Night?" she demands to know. "Are you okay?"

"I..." I try. "Ahhh..." I gasp. The pain is still there. "I had a...run in with Hai...during the attack and he..." I take another deep, shaky breath. "He re-broke my shin or rather, he finished the job."

"Shit," she breathes. "We don't have a hospital to fix it. The Charger didn't think putting you in a tank was punishment enough?"

"Oh, this wasn't...his idea. Hai did it long before I reached the Charger."

Her dark skin blanches. "You mean you...walked on that? You fought for your life on a broken leg?" I nod and she shakes her head in disbelief. "How the hell are you still alive?"

"I don't know. Luck?"

The door swings open, slamming into the wall, and the mystery man flies in.

Kuen, I remind myself.

"What's going on? I heard screaming. Are you guys okay?"

"In a manner of speaking," Trey replies. "Night's leg is broken."

Kuen swears under his breath. "This isn't good. Go get the kit."

"She's not strong enough, Kuen," Trey argues. "She needs a doctor."

"Well, we don't have that luxury, do we?" I can hear the anger and desperation in his voice.

Trey sighs and leaves the room to retrieve the "kit", whatever that is.

I turn to Kuen, taking a minute to finally study his face. He's pale, but not nearly as much as I am and his hair is a dusty blond mop on his head. I can't tell if he's taller than Ajax, but he's definitely broader. He's not the type of person you would think to mess with on the streets.

He gives me a look, piercing me with his blue eyes. "Are you done staring?"

I blink. "I'm seeing if we have any similarities. Trey told me a while ago that you're her brother and I just discovered her and I are sisters. So you must be..."

He smiles sadly. "It's been a long time, sister."

"That's an understatement," I say coolly. "We've never even spoken, and you think you can walk into my life and call me sister?"

He frowns at me. "And Trey says you've changed. If this is the new you, I'd hate to see the old."

I scowl. "Watch it. I may be bed-ridden, but I can find a way to make your life miserable."

"Yes," he says to himself, "still the ruthless assassin I remember."

"I am *not*," I snap.

"Whatever," he says, waving a hand. "We don't need to discuss your morals right now. Who broke the leg?"

I'm surprised he can change the subject so quickly. Clearly, he wants to know more about my morals. I wonder what's holding him back.

"It was an assassin with an axe originally," I reply. "More recently...Hai, my—our brother."

"The bastard," he seethes. "I'll kill him."

I snort. "Good luck with that."

"What?" he snaps, clearly offended.

"He's already dead."

He narrows his eyes. "How?"

"I...shot him. In the head."

He doesn't say anything to that. I'm not sure either one of us would've broken the silence if Trey hadn't walked in, towing a large bag behind her.

"Oh, good," Kuen says. "What took you so long?"

"Well, first I had to find it and then I had trouble lugging it up the stairs. I could've used some help."

Kuen winces under the glare she sends him. "Sorry."

"Just get over here and help me. That leg isn't going to mend itself."

"Right." He walks over to her and they start pulling instruments out of the bag, instruments that look painful.

"Uh...Trey," I say, "what are you going to do, exactly? How much will it hurt?"

"We're going to try to reset the leg and then brace it," she replies. "Why does the pain matter? I thought you guys were something like friends?"

"I...um... I might have exaggerated a bit." Sweat drips down my back as I anticipate what's to come. "We're more like acquaintances," I go on, "met once on the street and made eye contact before going our separate ways."

Trey laughs then. "Only you could turn pain into a joke."

"Well, if you don't, then you let it control you."

"Lie back, Night," she says, ignoring my comment. "We better get started." She looks over at Kuen. "Hold her down."

Oh, this is definitely not going to be fun.

Kuen comes over to my side of the bed and leans over me, bracing his hands against my shoulders. The weight of his body presses against me, making escape impossible.

"All right," he says, "do it."

"Wait!" I gasp. "Trey, do you even know what you're doing? You're not a doctor."

"I did some training at the Resistance. Don't worry about it. You'll be fine."

"*Some*?" I try to rear up, but Kuen keeps me from moving. "How much does *some* entail? I swear, if you kill me..."

"Relax, Night," Trey says. "Honestly, you're not helping by raising your blood pressure."

"Just get on with it," Kuen says. He hands me a cloth ball. "Here, bite down on this."

The reality of the situation hits me then. They're going to give me mock surgery without any sort of sedative.

Oh Guild. Oh please, God, have mercy. I know I've done terrible things, I know I don't deserve your grace, but...

Trey doesn't give me a warning. One minute, I'm waiting for the axe to fall, and the next, something cold and metallic is beneath my skin, prodding at my wound.

I can't help but scream.

The sound is muffled by the cloth and my clenched teeth around it, but neither prevents the shriek from escaping.

"Hey," Kuen says sharply. "Look at me. Look at me!"

My eyes snap to him and I let out a shuddering gasp.

"You're going to be okay," he tells me. "You got that? You're going to be fine."

Trey digs further into my broken limb and I shudder.

I feel the bone shift.

I see white.

And then, nothing.

• • •

I drift on an endless sea of pain. How long I lay drowning in it, I'm not sure. Sometimes it fades enough that I can feel my senses returning. Voices poke at my eardrums, but never loud enough for me to discern what they are saying. Someone sits on a chair beside my bed; I can feel them holding my hand. Yet, whenever I try to squeeze their hand in mine, to tell them I'm okay, the pain pulls me back. Waves of agony crash over me and I am lost again.

CHAPTER TWO

This time, when the pain relinquishes me, it does not come back. I know it remains somewhere, waiting for the right time to attack, but I am free for now, which means it's time to get up.

It takes more strength than it should to open my eyes, but I manage it. The room is bright, sunlight sneaking in through the cracks between the curtains. There is a hand in mine. I squeeze it.

Beside me, someone jumps.

I look over and find Ajax sitting in the chair, which is now at my bedside.

"Gods above, Silent," he breathes. "You scared me."

I grimace. "Sorry?"

He shakes his head. "I'm glad you're finally awake. How are you feeling?"

I close my eyes again and groan. "Like death," I reply. "Thanks for asking."

"Well, you're alive," he says, "so look on the bright side."

"Oh shush." I would grab a pillow and smack him with it, but I don't have one. He must've removed them while I was out. I'm touched that he remembered my phobia.

"Seriously, though," he prods. "How are you?"

"Tired, agonized, and hungry. Not necessarily in that order."

He laughs nervously. "Having an appetite is a good sign. It could be worse."

"Says you." Then I take a good look at him.

He looks ragged. Dark circles lurk under his eyes and he seems drained, like he hasn't slept in days. Cuts and bruises still cling to his knuckles from trying to break out of the tank.

"Are *you* okay?" I ask him.

"Oh, yeah," he replies, "I'm fine, just worried about you."

He doesn't look fine, but I decide not to press it. "Well, you can quit worrying about me. I'm okay. I feel like I've been run over—twice—but I'm inching towards recovery."

He grimaces. "Does it hurt that bad?"

"Yeah." I don't try to deny it. I can't lie to him, not after everything we've been through. "What exactly did Trey do to me?"

He scratches the back of his head. "As I understand it, she, uh...reached inside your leg and pushed the bone back together. Then she and Kuen tied a flat piece of wood on either side to keep the bone in place. They hope it'll fuse itself back together now that it's set properly."

Now that he mentions it, I can feel the wood against my leg. The rhythmic throbbing in my shin must be from the constant pressure of the homemade brace.

"What happened to my other brace?"

"It sustained damage during the fighting and then the water ruined it. Trey threw it out as soon as we arrived here from what I was told."

Shame.

"How long was I out this time?"

He scrunches up his eyebrows as he thinks. "About four days," he finally says. "You were in and out of consciousness though, as far as we could tell."

I groan. Another four days lost. How many more will I spend like this or will death claim me next? What am I even doing? Do I have a plan for this "life"? I want a future, but like everything else in this damn city, I have to fight for it. Will the nightmare ever end?

I sigh.

There are so many cards stacked against me.

Ajax's voice pierces through my thoughts before I can dig too deep. "What's wrong?"

"What? Nothing."

He gives me a look. "No, it's not nothing. You have your brooding look on, as if you had the chance to save the world, but lost by a fingertip. What's going on in that head of yours?"

I sigh again. "I just… Oh, Jax, everything is a mess. My life has been turned upside down and shaken until the contents are scattered everywhere. I discovered things about myself that I never wanted to know and now I… I'm scared. I'm terrified. What if, after everything, he still wins? I can't…"

"Hey," he says, touching my arm as I trail off into silent tears. "It's going to be okay."

"But what if it isn't?" I counter, pulling myself together and wiping my eyes with the back of my hand. "What is the point of all of this anyway, of fighting back? Why are we here? What are we supposed to *do*?"

"The point?" He laughs. "Isn't that the question? No one knows, Silent, and I think that's why we're here, why we go through so many trials. We do it to discover the point, to find our purpose. We all have a place; we just have to get there."

I snort. "And where is yours?"

"Right now?"

I nod.

"Well, right now my place is at your side because after all those near-death experiences, I'm not letting you out of my sight."

"Even after everything I've done?" I want to smile at his words, but I remember our last conversation, remember where we stood before the Guild attack.

"Like I said in that tank," he replies. "It's not all forgiven. We both have healing to do, but I don't want to give up on us yet. In the meantime, I still care about you, as a friend, and I'm going to do my best to keep you from getting yourself killed, okay?"

I smile. "Good luck."

He laughs.

Silence surrounds us then and in it, I start to dwell on what happened at the Guild. I think about the secret I now carry, the burden weighing me down. I'm not sure how much Jax heard when he came to my rescue, but he deserves to know the truth and he deserves to hear it from me.

"Jax," I start, "there's something you should know."

He looks up at me. "What is it?"

"The Charger told me something, when I found him at the Guild. I think it was before you arrived. I didn't want to believe him, but it makes so much sense, ties up so many loose ends from my past that it has to be true. I *know* it is true, but I wish it wasn't." My stomach is a ball of nerves inside me as I talk.

Jax looks concerned. "What did he tell you, Silent?"

"He told me that…" I take a deep breath. "He's my father, Jax."

Jax goes white, his eyes widening in what I assume is fear and shock. He opens his mouth to speak, but no words come out. I know I've lost him, but I'm glad I got to see him one last time.

I look away, toward the curtains and the city beyond. "I understand, if you hate me now," I tell him, "but don't make this any harder. Just go."

"What?" he manages to say.

I turn back to him. "I said I understand if—"

He cuts me off. "No, no. I heard you, but I don't… Why on earth would I hate you, Silent?"

"Because the Charger is the darkest man to ever live and I have his cursed blood running through my veins," I choke out, feeling my chest tighten with the pain of the truth. "I am the spawn of that *monster*."

"That may be true, but—"

I ignore him. "And it all makes sense now, why I am the way I am, why it's so damn hard to let the assassin go. The bane of Haven City is my father." I put my head in my hands, squeezing my eyes shut. "This world is such a cruel place. Go now, Jax, before I beg you not to."

"Silent, you're not listening to me," he says. His hands wrap around my wrists. "Look at me."

I stay where I am, not wanting to see the disappointment in his gaze.

"Look at me," he snaps, yanking my arms away from my head so I'm forced to face him. There is more...frustration in his eyes than anger and something soft that might be...sympathy. "I don't care, Silent," he says.

I tilt my head as if to get a better look at him and narrow my eyes. "I... You what?"

He sighs and runs a hand through his hair. It's sticking up in more places than usual. "I don't give a damn that he's your father, Silent. You're not him. You've always been your own person. You stepped away from his influence. You started fresh. You changed and left him to deal with the consequences of his choices. You were always of his blood; knowing that now, why should it change things? He treated you like a servant, not a daughter. Don't forget that. Don't let him lay claim to you now because it suits him.

"You are your mother's daughter through and through. Sure, you might share some of his genes, some of his traits, but don't think for a second that means he owns you. You can make your own decisions and you have. Don't think about it for a second, Silent because it doesn't change things, especially not for me."

I blink back tears as I say, "Why are you so supportive?"

He shrugs. "Because I see the real you, the version of yourself that's never quite within reach. I see your potential, the amazing woman you can grow to be if you step out of your comfort zone. I see you, Silent. The Charger doesn't know the real you, not like I do."

I wipe my eyes again. "Thank you. You are more than I deserve."

He squeezes my arm. "I know you can't forget the truth, but don't let it control you."

I nod and take a deep breath to clear my head. "There's something else you should know," I tell him. "The Charger isn't the only relation I discovered. I also found two brothers and a sister, three half-siblings actually."

He raises an eyebrow. "The Master Assassin has more children? He doesn't strike me as the fatherly type."

"Oh, he's not," I assure him. "As far as I know, there are four of us and he killed all of our mothers."

"Oh my God," Jax breathes, "that's horrible. Does he have nothing better to do with his time?"

I shrug. "Apparently not. He makes deals with his mistresses: give up the child they conceive or their life. My mother refused him. The others must've done the same because he slaughtered them as well."

"He is so twisted," Jax replies, disgust evident in his face. "Why does he need the children anyway? Having him as a father is bad enough."

"He says he wanted an heir, someone to run the Guild after his eventual death. The first three grew up and he decided they weren't up to the task, so he tried again with me and I betrayed him."

Jax laughs a little. "So much for his luck. Who were the other three?"

I swallow slowly.

This isn't going to go over well.

"One was Hai, the guy who re-broke my leg and tried to snap your arm off."

Jax winces. "Well, *he* definitely inherited his father's personality."

I snort. "Tell me about it. Even the Charger wanted to be rid of him."

He raises an eyebrow. "Really?"

"I was ordered to kill him the day before I left the Guild."

Jax shakes his head. "Man, nothing like having your children kill each other for you so you don't have to get your hands dirty."

"I know."

"What about the other two? Another brother and a sister you said?"

I take a deep breath. "Please don't freak out."

He gives me a look. "Why would I freak out?"

"Because the other two are Kuen and Trey."

"What?" His voice is high and breathless. "Trey is your sister? That man is your brother? But he has to be like…"

"Thirty-one."

He narrows his eyes. "How do you know that?"

"He was somewhat of a legend at the Guild, a mystery. So naturally, we all knew everything about him." I smile. "He was the only assassin to walk out on the Charger without a single scratch or trace. He left one night and never returned. There was no explanation, no clues as to where he went or why. The strangest part was that the Charger didn't send anyone out after him. In fact, he ordered us not to look for him and the punishments for infractions on that order were severe. I never understood why the Charger would let him walk free, but I get it now. Kuen is his son and he trusts him somehow, the same way he once trusted me.

"So yeah, I know he's thirty-one. Trey is twenty-nine, I believe, and Hai was thirty, one of the older assassins. I'm so much younger than them because I was his last chance and still, he failed."

"Which means he can be beaten," Jax adds. "Silent, he's not invincible."

"He's the very definition of invincible," I counter. "I was this close to killing him," I hold my thumb and pointer finger a sliver apart, "this close. I had my knife against his throat and he still slipped through my fingers."

"But Silent, you got closer than anyone ever has. Who else can say they've done what you did, had the Charger anywhere close to being in their grasp like that? If Hai hadn't been there, the Charger would be six feet under right now."

"But Hai *was* there," I say. "There's no point arguing about what ifs. The Charger is still alive and I have to live with my mistakes."

"It's not your burden to carry alone, Silent. You—"

I hold up a hand. "Please don't. I know my burdens and I don't want to hear that wretched name anymore."

"What?"

"Silent. I'm done with that identity. It's full of dried blood—none of it my own. I no longer want to be associated with that monster. Black Death's servant is dead. My name is Quinn Marie Ballinger and I am a Resistance agent intent on bringing the Guild to its knees."

Jax claps. "Well said, Quinn. Well said." He smiles.

Goosebumps travel across my skin when he says my name. I want to kiss him, want to show him how much I appreciate his continued support, in a way words can't convey, but I know I can't. There is still tension between us, words we said and can't take back. That kiss in the tank was nothing more than the desperation of two people who thought they were going to die. We have a lot to fix before that can happen again, if ever.

"What does the aftermath of the attack look like?" I ask him, wanting to change the subject.

"Not good," he says, "not good at all."

I grimace. "What happened?"

"Well, for starters, the assassins have disappeared."

My stomach drops. "What?"

"There isn't a trace of them left in the city. Trey returned to the Guild while you were unconscious and she says they must've left and taken everything with them. You wouldn't know anybody had ever been there, if not for the bodies."

I shiver. "Well, that's wonderful. They could be anywhere by now."

"I know."

"Have you heard anything from Blake and Bast?" I'm afraid to ask the question. The fact that he hasn't brought them up yet suggests the news isn't good.

"No," he says, his face a mixture of sorrow and fear. "It's not safe to send messages to the Resistance, not when the assassins' whereabouts are unknown. Not to mention that Haven is a war-zone."

"What?"

"It's complete chaos out there, Si—Quinn. People don't know who to trust anymore, not that they ever did. They're terrified of both the assassins and the Resistance. Parts of the city are still burning from our bombs and the citizens are killing each other trying to defend themselves from a faceless threat." He wrings his hands. "Bast and Blake... They could be dead, or they could be okay, but they need me and your damn brother won't let me go out and find them." He spits out the last sentence and I bristle.

"My *brother* is trying to protect us. You just finished telling me it's chaos out there. What good would it do getting yourself killed? What would Blake and Bast think of that?"

He sighs. "I just want to know if they're okay. Your so-called brother might seem like he's looking out for us, but we don't know what his real motives are. We just met him."

"Don't judge him before you know him, Jax. Trey trusts him."

"Trey isn't infallible, Quinn," he reminds me.

"I know that," I reply, "but we want Kuen on our side and he *did* save our lives."

"Because Trey told him to."

I give him an exasperated look. "She *asked* him to help and he did. Can we drop this? I don't want to fight."

"We're not fighting," he argues. "We're discussing."

"But you're itching for a fight. You've contradicted everything I've said."

He throws his hands out. "Because I don't *agree* with anything you've said. I know you're excited to have found your family, Quinn, but you can't let that lull you into a false sense of security. Kuen is a stranger and an assassin. We have to be careful."

I tense, discomfort crawling across my skin. "So, what, he's guilty until proven innocent? He left the Guild years ago. We would be dead if he hadn't led Trey back into the Guild. If he hadn't known where that throne room was... I think we owe him a little bit more than this."

I can't believe him. What happened to his compassion?

"Exactly, Quinn," he breathes. "We *owe* him. That's what scares me."

I frown. "He's not going to—"

"You don't know that!" His voice isn't raised, but each word hits me.

I shrink back in the bed.

"You don't know, Quinn. I know that might be hard for you to believe, but you don't have the answers right now. He is a question mark we have to ponder carefully. We are a long way from the safety of the Resistance."

"Well, you don't know either," I point out. "Who's to say you have the answers?"

"That's not—"

I throw my hands up. "Listen to yourself, Jax. I might have reverted back to my old ways before I left the Guild, but so did you. You see an assassin and automatically see the worst. You see a killer, a monster, when he could be as much a victim as I was. You're a hypocrite."

His eyes darken. "That's not fair."

I cross my arms. "Isn't it? How is it any less fair than what you've said about him?"

He scowls. "Why are you defending him, against *me*?"

"I'm not," I reply. "I'm pointing out how ridiculous you're being."

Before he can retort, the bedroom door swings open and Trey walks in. She looks back and forth between the two of us, noting our defensive positions. My arms are still crossed and Ajax's fists are clenched. Our bodies are tense, leaning towards each other in frustration.

Trey clears her throat.

I manage to relax my stance. I can become business-like with a flick of a switch. Personality is just another weapon in an assassin's arsenal.

Yet, I'm not an assassin anymore.

I close my eyes.

God, what am I doing?

I open my mouth to say something, anything, but Ajax speaks first.

"We'll discuss this later," he says. "I'll give you two some time alone."

He walks out, letting the door swing shut behind him and I watch him go with a heavy heart.

Trey looks concerned. "Night, are you sure you guys are okay?"

I sigh. "We've been better."

"What happened?"

"We're not on the same page and he still hasn't forgiven me for killing his mother. That wound will take a while to heal."

She grimaces. "Is there anything I can do?"

"Not unless you can find Blake and Bast."

She sits down on the edge of the bed. "They'll be okay. They're tougher than Ajax realizes. He's just so used to them being by his side, so used to protecting them, that their absence scares him."

"I hope you're right."

"He'll come around, Night, I know it."

I sigh. "I don't think our situation is helping us any. We're all tense. Near-death experiences do that to people. Our emotions are on overdrive. The three of you are worried about me, I'm worried about you guys, Ajax is mad at Kuen, he and I are at odds with each other, and we're all afraid of what might come next."

"I know what you mean," she says. "This isn't at all easy. Never has been and I'm afraid it never will be."

We don't talk for a second.

Then she says, "Are you doing okay, Night?"

I shrug. "I've been worse and um... Don't call me Night anymore, okay? I'm done being the Charger's puppet. I want to be me."

She smiles. "Who are you then?"

"My name is Quinn."

She smiles wider. "Nice to meet you, Quinn." She gives me a wink, causing the slightest tug at the edge of my lips.

"Thanks."

"Well, Quinn, now that that's settled, I have to be on my way." She stands.

I frown. "Where are you going?"

"Scouting. You'll be okay with the boys?"

"I think so, but could you help me out of bed before you go, move me somewhere else for a bit?"

"Sure," she says, "I can bring you into the kitchen."

"How do you want to do it?" I gesture to myself.

She furrows her brow. "Well, take the covers off to start."

I throw the sheet off and then she helps me into a sitting position on the edge of the bed. It feels great to move again, but I'm ready for the pain that's bound to come.

"Good so far?" she asks.

"Yes. What now?"

"You'll have to stand up. Put your weight on the good leg and wrap your arm over my shoulder so I can support your bad side."

"Okay," I reply and then I do as she says. I keep my bad leg off the ground; there's a little pain in keeping it raised, but not much.

"Still good?"

I nod.

"Okay, then let's go."

She starts walking to the door and I hop after her, each bounce shaking my injured leg and sending dull fire through it. I clench my teeth.

I'm stronger than this.

Slowly, we make our way out of the room and down the hall.

We stop when the hall opens into the kitchen. Counter and cupboards line one wall and a table and chairs hug the other. Ajax sits at the head of the table and Kuen is fixing something in the kitchen. From where I'm standing, it looks like a rifle. Metal parts and tools are scattered across the stone counter.

Ajax looks up when we come in, but feigns disinterest.

Trey gives me an encouraging smile. "Kuen can get you something to eat if you're hungry. Right, Kuen?" She raises her voice for the last sentence and Kuen looks over, setting down his screwdriver.

"What?" he says.

"If Ni—Quinn is hungry, you'll get her something, right?"

"Oh," he replies, "yeah, sure. Don't you have somewhere to be?" He bends back over his work.

Trey shakes her head. "I'm going in a minute." She heads over to the table with me in tow and pulls out a chair.

I collapse into it gratefully and try to regulate my breathing. It's sharper after the exercise.

"All right," Trey says, "I should go. You'll be okay?"

"Yeah," I reply.

She leans closer and whispers, "Don't let the boys get you down. Kuen can be a real mother hen when he wants to be."

I laugh. "I can deal with them, but I do want to ask… What's with the rifle?"

"Oh, Kuen likes to collect broken things and fix them up, after tearing them apart even further to see how they work." She glances across the room at his current project. "I think he's trying to modify the scope on that one."

"Huh," I reply.

So my brother is a repairman. Cool.

"Well, I'll be seeing you then," Trey says. She leaves through a doorway on the other side of the room and I hear a door slam shut after her as she leaves us behind, leaves *me* behind with Kuen, who is mostly a stranger, and Ajax, who isn't happy with me at the moment.

I sigh.

Well, this should be fun.

CHAPTER THREE

"Hey."

I look up. Kuen is standing beside me. I didn't even hear him walk over.

So much for having impeccable senses.

"Sorry," I reply, "did you say something?"

He gives me a look, as if to say, *women*. Then he says, "I just want to know if you're hungry. I have soup or… Actually, soup is all I have."

"Soup will be fine, thanks."

He nods, but says nothing else.

I strain my ears as he walks away and just manage to catch the sound of his footfalls. They're so soft.

He used to be an assassin, I remind myself. *It's no wonder you can't hear him; no one can.*

The knowledge is unsettling.

Is this how people felt when they heard my name?

I shake my head and take a closer look around the room to distract myself from the shadows lingering behind my eyelids, echoes of a past I'm trying to leave behind.

The kitchen is quaint. The clock on the wall above the stove has a green tractor on it and the time reads ten thirty-five, in the morning I assume from the sunlight hiding behind the yellow curtains on the single window. The old cupboards squeak on their hinges as Kuen opens and closes them, not even trying to keep them from banging shut. I notice more metal in the cupboards than food or dishes. The wooden table is worn with scratches and creaks ominously as I lean my weight against it.

My chair skids across the linoleum floor as I attempt to slide it closer to the table.

Unfortunately, I slip and my bad leg smacks a table leg. I let out a muffled scream through my gritted teeth and this time when Ajax looks up, he doesn't tear his eyes away from me. His blue eyes look concerned, though he's trying to hide it.

Kuen runs over. "Are you okay?"

"Yeah, I'm fine," I breathe through my teeth. "Didn't realize...how close the...table leg was."

Oh Guild, the pain is like nothing else.

He winces. "You have to be more careful."

I give him a murderous glare as I try to steady my breathing. Each inhale through my nose beats in time with the pounding in my leg.

He doesn't shy away from my expression. "In any case," he says, "your soup is ready." He walks off and comes back with a steaming bowl and a spoon.

My mouth waters at the sight.

When was the last time I had a proper meal?

I scarf it back like it'll be my last and my tongue feels funny when I'm done.

"Hungry much?" Kuen says, taking a seat beside me and closer to Ajax. I don't answer and Kuen turns to Ajax. "Guess she's a quiet one, eh?"

I bristle.

I can see the tension in Ajax's jaw as he answers. "Sometimes."

I wince at his tone.

"She reserves the silence for people she doesn't trust or people she doesn't like," he goes on.

I frown.

Is he talking about me or himself?

"Which am I?" Kuen asks.

"A bit of both."

I scowl at him. "Could you refrain from sabotaging my relationship with my brother before it begins? That should be my choice, don't you think?"

Kuen frowns. "What is going on here?"

"None of your business," Ajax snaps.

I roll my eyes. "Oh, would you give it a rest? Honestly, you're so…" I stop myself.

"So *what*?" he echoes. "Say it, Silent."

My skin prickles. "That's not my name."

His words hurt and my first instinct is to run, to escape the pain.

I scrape my chair back so fast it nearly topples over and stand up, forgetting about my leg.

Kuen and Ajax don't react fast enough to catch me.

I hit the ground hard and let out a miserable whimper as unbidden tears stream down my face.

The pain is unreal.

My vision blurs around the edges, but I sense the boys dropping to their knees by my side. A hand touches my arm.

I turn my head and meet Ajax's eyes.

"Say something," he breathes, fear lacing his words.

As much as I want to hurt him, one look into his eyes and I can't. "That...hurt," I push out through clenched teeth.

Ajax lets out a breath, but can't help but crack a smile. "I bet it did."

I look to my other side, to find Kuen livid.

"It's not funny," Kuen snaps at Jax. "This is serious. She could be in big trouble after a fall like that!" His face is red.

Ajax's tone is even as he says, "You want me to cry? That's not going to fix the situation either."

"If you can't take her condition seriously..."

"Leave him alone," I try, but my voice is weak. My head hurts.

Kuen continues on as if I never spoke. "If she gets worse because of this—"

"It won't be my fault," Ajax counters.

"It would. You provoked her. You're the one who endangered her."

"Shut up!" I yell.

Silence falls.

My head pounds inside my skull, a steady beat.

"I endangered myself, okay?" I go on. "I always do. This injury is my own fault. If I listened to the nurses when it first happened, I wouldn't be in this situation, but I didn't. I made a choice. I have to live with it now, but I don't want the rest of you walking around on eggshells because of it or getting at each other's throats. I'm going to be fine, okay?"

And if I'm not, it'll be my own damn fault.

Kuen sighs. "Look, let's just get you back to your room." He reaches out a hand to help me up, but I latch my fingers around Jax's arm and pull myself to my feet.

Kuen looks affronted, but I've realized Jax is right. I can't trust him yet, especially after the scene we just had.

Jax wraps his arm around my bad side and together we shuffle out of the kitchen.

Kuen watches us go with unreadable eyes.

I hope I haven't made things worse, but bad luck seems to follow me, no matter where I go or how fast I run from it.

I limp back to the bedroom with Jax's help and ease myself onto the bed. He sits down beside me. I hear Kuen slamming cupboard doors in the kitchen again.

I sigh.

Jax takes in a deep breath.

"Jax," I say, at the same time he says, "Quinn."

We laugh nervously.

"You go first," I tell him.

"I'm sorry," he says.

"Me too."

"Our argument earlier was stupid," he admits. "We should be sticking together, not tearing each other apart. I can't blame you for wanting to trust Kuen. He *is* your brother, regardless of how long you've known him, and he *did* save our lives, but I'm not sold yet."

"I forgive you and I don't think you're a hypocrite. I was just…" I sigh. "It doesn't matter. I think you're right."

He raises an eyebrow. "What?"

"*You're right.*" The words burn in my mouth but I carry on. "We can't automatically trust him because he saved us, that *could* be exactly what he wants. We need to assess the situation properly."

He narrows his eyes. "What made you change your mind?"

"Did you hear him just now? He went from calm to furious in seconds, and he's scary when he's mad."

"So are you," he points out.

I scowl. "Are you even listening?"

"Yes, sorry. I know what you mean. His control is balanced on the edge of a blade."

I nod. "And I thought I was twitchy."

He shrugs. "You're not so bad."

I smile. "Thanks."

Jax's own smile fades as he looks at me and he hangs his head. "Listen, Quinn, I'm sorry for calling you Silent."

I bite my lip. "It's okay."

He shakes his head. "No, it's not. It was a low blow and I knew it."

"Oh, don't get all woebegone on me, Jax. I said it's fine."

"But—"

I give him a look. "Please leave it. We can't move forward if we keep recycling the same arguments. It wasn't nice, but I know you didn't mean it, not wholeheartedly. I forgive you. End of story."

He sighs. "Okay, but if I ever do that again…"

I smile. "I'll skin you alive, of course."

He laughs. "I wouldn't miss it for the world."

I shake my head and then lean it against his shoulder.

After a few minutes, he leans his head up against mine and says, "We're a hopeless mess, you know that right?"

"Yeah."

"What do you suppose people think when they look at us?"

I shrug. "Whatever they want; I don't particularly care about their opinion."

"Don't you ever wonder?"

"Sometimes, but nothing good ever comes from dwelling on it."

Jax sits up straight again and gives me a look, his eyes screaming at me to answer the damn question.

I roll my eyes and continue as if I never planned on stopping. "Though, if I had to guess, I'd bet people wonder how we came about and what you saw in me.

They'd want to know what it is about you that keeps me from killing you. They probably bet on how long it'll take before I snap."

Jax raises an eyebrow.

"But," I go on, "there are also those who don't know our backstory, those who saw us together and thought, 'Wow, aren't they adorable, I can't wait to see where they go from here.' Those people are still rooting for us. They believe in our happy ending, but it's up to us to decide what that looks like, I guess."

"Yeah," he says.

The tension of the morning has dissipated, though not completely. It is enough for us to be able to sit this close together. Guild, it is enough to know we are both still alive.

He pushes away from me then and stands up. "You need to rest."

"But I don't want to."

"I want you to."

Damn. I can't argue with that.

I sigh. "Fine, I'll rest, but... Could you stay?"

"I..."

"I don't want to be alone in this strange place and I hate that the world is just behind those curtains." I point to the windows. "Could you stay until I fall asleep?"

His eyes meet mine and he nods. "As long as you promise to sleep."

"I will."

"Okay then." He takes a seat in the chair beside my bed. "Close your eyes."

"Closing."

My fear was a bit of a stretch. The windows do make me nervous, but I mostly didn't want him to go. Despite all my injuries, there is nothing more painful than the distance between us, the distance that might never close again.

• • •

I sense someone near me when I wake and immediately let my guard down. "Jax?" I breathe. I try to force my eyes open, but I'm still groggy, sleep holding me under.

"No, not Ajax," a rough voice says, "just me."

I open one eye, my body tense. "Kuen? What are you doing?" He's sitting in the chair beside my bed—everyone's favourite spot it seems—staring at me.

He holds up his hands. "Sorry, I... I didn't mean to startle you."

I open my other eye. "Assassins don't appreciate surprise wake up calls. You of all people should know that. Do you have a death wish?"

"Sometimes."

"What?"

He looks me in the eyes. "Sometimes I want to die."

"Why?"

"I'm not exactly a nice person, Quinn. I turned my back on the Guild, but that doesn't mean it's ever truly gone. It runs through my blood, shooting its poison through my veins in a never-ending cycle of imprisonment. I've done things even you couldn't fathom in your worst nightmares. Not to mention my uncanny knack for running away from my problems."

I frown. "What do you mean?"

"I left the Assassin's Guild when I found it no longer suited me. I didn't try to fix things or help anyone."

"You needed time to plan," I say with a shrug. "No one can be ready to confront the Master Assassin on the flip of a dime."

"I had seven years to plan, Quinn, seven years to do something, but I never did. Trey at least joined the Resistance. I merely faded into the shadows, into legend, and hid. I locked myself in this bungalow and all I have to show for all that time is piles of random inventions and even more bad decisions."

"You're here now," I point out, giving him a small smile.

"And what good have I done?"

"You saved my life, and Jax's. That has to count for something."

He hangs his head. "Not enough."

"It's a start."

I don't know why he's telling me this now, where all this emotion is coming from, but I can feel his pain. This is how I once felt, and though I don't yet trust him, I can't help but want to ease his suffering. No one should have to go through the kind of self-loathing I subjected myself to.

"Kuen," I start, but he doesn't hear me.

He's already saying, "I just came to apologize for how I acted earlier. I… I should go now."

He goes to stand up but I reach out toward him. The action makes him pause.

"Don't," I say. "Kuen, listen. You can't take back what you've done, none of us can, but we can atone for it, we can give back and it doesn't matter when you start, so long as you do. I've made mistakes too, but I've chosen the right path now and every day I get a little closer to salvation. I'm not sure if I'll ever get there, but it can't hurt to try. So stop beating yourself up over it. The past is dead. Let it rest in peace."

He manages a smile. "You've really changed."

"Yeah?"

He nods. "Without a doubt. The girl I knew never would've talked about salvation."

I raise an eyebrow. "You say that as if you knew me well."

"I didn't really," he admits. "I just knew the impression I had of you. The last time I saw you, you were dragging an unfortunate soul to their demise in the Grand Cavern. As far as I could tell, you were a lost cause and the only thing on your mind was damnation."

"You remember that?"

He gives me a sad smile. "How could I not? That was the day I left. I was the Charger's right hand man for years, following his orders without thought, and you were the one who finally woke me up."

I frown. "How?"

"That unfortunate soul was the first traitor you brought in, your first day as the executioner. It was the smile on your face, the barely contained malice in your eyes… Our father had turned you into a monster, and I realized I hated him for it. To rob someone like you of their innocence, to turn a carefree child into a cold-blooded killer… It wasn't right. It took losing you for me to finally realize I didn't want that life, that legacy. I no longer agreed with the Charger's agenda, so I left. I thought I could better myself and give you a better future. I was coming back for you, but in the end, you saved yourself."

I smile, but my eyes are full of sorrow. Once upon a time, the Charger's children were full of life, but he broke every single one of us. I want to destroy him too, and then some. "Our father is the monster," I spit.

Kuen nods.

"He gave me a second chance, you know. He was willing to forgive everything, or so he said. You know what the price was?"

Kuen shakes his head. "I can only imagine."

"Originally, the price was Hai's life, but then Ajax showed up and it became his life or mine. Months ago, I never would've made the decision I did, never would've been willing to sacrifice my own life for someone else."

"Your point?"

"I'm not the person I used to be, the person he made me, and one day, you won't be either."

He frowns. "Who says I'm not changed now?"

I give him a sad smile. "My sense of self-preservation? Kuen, I want to trust you, believe me, but it's hard. We're still strangers."

I see anger in his eyes again, but he pushes it back and says, "I know. I understand your choice, even if I don't like it."

"When I can trust you, Kuen—and one day I will—you'll know."

He hangs his head. "I don't deserve you."

"Hey now, don't do that. This isn't your fault."

"I know." He sighs. "It's his fault. It always traces back to him."

I nod. "The one thing that's ruined all our lives, tainted all our spirits. We'll get him one day, I promise. Soon, if I have any say in the matter."

He smiles. "Judging from your spirit, I wager you will."

I smile back and he turns to leave again.

"I should go," he says. "Do you need anything?"

"Maybe something to eat?"

He nods. "I'll send Trey in."

I sit up. "She's back?"

"Yeah, she came in an hour ago. I'm going out now. Should be back before dark."

"Be careful out there," I tell him.

"Yeah," he says again. "We'll talk later?"

"Okay."

He leaves the room without another word. I can almost see the weight of his guilt pressing down on his shoulders. It's enormous. He shouldn't feel responsible for the lives his younger siblings ended up with, but I think he does. I can see it in the way he looks at me and hear it in the way he says Trey's name. He's constantly concerned for us, but I guess that's what older brothers do.

A few minutes later, Trey walks in with another bowl of soup. She closes the door behind her and says, "I know what you're thinking: is soup the only real food in this house? The answer is yes, but we have a bunch of different kinds so you won't get tired of it too fast."

She smiles at me and I laugh. "I'm not complaining."

"Ah, but you were about to."

I groan. "Am I that easy to read?"

"No, just sibling instinct." She winks.

I roll my eyes. "Of course."

She sets the soup down in front of me and I dig in, ignoring her warnings that it's hot. My tongue is still burnt from earlier anyway.

She takes a seat in the chair and watches me in silence until I'm finished.

"So, how's the leg?" she asks.

I set my spoon down. "Okay? I've tried not to think about it, to be honest."

"Well, as long as you're not in too much pain..."

"I can deal with it."

She grimaces. "How bad is it?"

"Seriously, Trey," I say. "I'm fine."

She sighs. "All right, I won't argue with you. Hopefully, we can go to the Warehouse soon. I won't be at ease until Shirley has taken a look at you."

"I've been through worse," I reply.

She shakes her head. "You're crazy, kid."

I shrug. "So I've been told."

"It's not a bad thing," she says. "Sanity is overrated. Most of us in Haven lost it a long time ago."

"So we're normal then?"

She pokes me. "You are. I, however, am firmly rooted in reality, which makes me unique."

I snort. "Sure you are."

She brushes her hands off on her pants and gets up. "Well, I'll leave you to rest."

I groan. "Do I have to?"

"You won't heal if you don't."

"But I'm bored."

"And you're going to stay that way. Get out of that bed and Kuen, Jax, and I will chain you to it."

I raise an eyebrow. "Violent much?"

She shrugs. "It gets the best results."

I shake my head. "I think you have it wrong, Trey. You're definitely insane."

She laughs and I join.

When we finally sober, she says, "Seriously though, sleep. It'll do more good than you realize."

"I know, I know," I sigh, "but I've slept more lately than I have in years."

She smiles. "Then you've never been healthier. I'll see you later."

"Don't..." But she's already slipped down the hall and out of ear shot.

I sigh and stare at the ceiling until I fall asleep.

CHAPTER FOUR

The days drag on, each more boring than the last. I do nothing but eat, sleep, and sit idle.

I hate it.

I can't stand being cooped up; I need to act, but it's barely safe enough for Trey and Kuen to leave the house, and with my leg the way it is, I wouldn't get far. It's infuriating, the waiting, the silence, the not knowing what's going on.

Jax's worry for Blake and Bast has him beyond agitated. When he's not sitting in the kitchen drumming his fingers on the table, he's pacing the floor or throwing himself into insane workouts until exhaustion dulls his thoughts. He wants to go out, but even he understands the dangers, despite his desire to find our friends.

Kuen fixes up an old radio for us, in the hopes of news, but Haven's two stations are silent.

The city is more lethal than ever. Trey says citizens parade the streets with pitchforks, that they set fires first and ask questions later, unaware the enemy is hidden away and they're doing the dirty work for them. A layer of smoke lays heavy over the city, dulling the senses and giving the darkness more places to hide.

Screams in the night keep us all awake and long silences during the day keep us on edge.

Still, the house is starting to feel like more of a prison than a refuge.

The worst part is how everyone keeps asking me if I'm okay, as if I'm a delicate flower that will be torn apart by the first wind that comes my way. I assure them constantly that I'm fine, but what I've gone through this time has been a hurricane, not a mere breeze, and I know, deep down, that I'm lying to myself.

I'm not fine. My leg is not fine. In fact, it's getting worse. A throbbing beat has started within it and it's getting more frequent and pronounced by the minute. I find myself afraid of what might happen, but I push the fear down. There's nothing we can do and I don't want to worry the others more.

The pain will go away. The leg will heal and then they need never know of its gradual worsening.

Another lie.

I'm not going to get better. Something terrible is happening and this time, they'll be hard pressed to save me.

I sit bolt upright in bed, screaming, a shooting pain in my leg tearing me from a dead sleep and…

Why are my sheets wet? What is happening?

Frantic footsteps echo down the hall and Jax, Trey, and Kuen stumble into the room. They fire what could be a million questions at me, but I'm not listening. I'm too busy rocking back and forth in an attempt to distract myself from the pain. I clench my teeth and breathe.

"Quinn, please," one of them shouts. "Talk to us. Say something."

"I can't," I gasp. I don't have the will to even cry. This is ten times worse than when I actually broke the stupid thing. Forget about a fire. I feel like I'm being held down in boiling water. I retreat into myself, closing my eyes against the unbearable agony.

Please go away.

My friends' voices are distant. Jax keeps muttering curse words to himself in between telling me it'll be okay in a soft voice. Trey and Kuen are arguing.

A cold hand touches my face. "Oh Guild, Kuen. She's burning up."

Someone ruffles the sheets.

"They're soaked. How long has she been lying here like this?"

"This is bad."

"Pull back the covers; we need to look at the leg."

I feel the wind of their passage as someone tears them off.

Someone gasps.

Kuen swears this time.

It must be terrible if they can tell without taking off the bandages.

Dammit, Quinn, I scold myself. *You knew this would happen. You should've told someone.*

What good would it have done? We can't get help. We're alone.

"Trey." It's Ajax and he sounds terrified. "She needs to get to a hospital."

Trey ignores him. "I'm just going to…" Her hand must touch my leg because I flinch, eyes flying open as I bite back another scream. A whimper escapes.

I reach forward and latch onto her arm. "No."

Her eyes meet my own. "Quinn, I have to."

"Please." I beg her to see reason, to recognize the agony in my eyes.

She turns to Kuen and Jax instead and says, "Hold her down."

I scream obscenities at them as Kuen grabs hold of my feet and Jax appears over my head. He leans over me and presses his hands against my shoulders, pinning me to the bed.

"Jax, please…" I gasp. "Don't let her…"

Her hand touches my leg again and I flinch again, but this time I can't move away.

"She has to, Quinn, just…try to relax."

"Relax? I—"

My protests are cut off as Trey peels the bandages and a scream tears free from my throat.

I thrash, but Ajax holds me firm. "Shhh… It's okay. You're okay. It's going to be okay." But I can tell from the tears glistening in his eyes and the broken, shaking of his voice that it's not. I can tell everything is far from okay, that I'm in trouble.

Trey is poking and prodding my wound and I keep screaming, try as I might to hold back the sound.

"Look at me, Quinn, just look at me," Jax pleads.

The trick has worked in the past to distract me from my suffering, but it's not going to this time. My vision is blurring and their voices are fading as the pain latches onto me and pulls me under. I resist, but it is futile. I have minutes left of consciousness.

Another cold hand touches my forehead. "Oh God, Trey, she's on fire."

"I know, I know, but I..." Her voice trails off into sobs. "I don't know what to do, Jax. I'm sorry."

"We can't leave her like this!"

"It's dangerous to move her." Kuen, I think.

"You think I don't know that? Yes, it's dangerous, but if we don't do something, she's going to die anyway. Do you want that on your conscience? I sure as hell don't want it on mine!"

"Oh, so you think I want her dead? Is that it? After all the trouble I went through to save her and your sorry ass? I haven't stepped foot in the Guild in nearly a decade. I went back to that goddamn hell for the both of you, so don't you dare say I want her dead."

"Then prove it! Make the right choice!"

"Guys! Please..." It's Trey. "Don't argue. Leave that for later, right now we need to make a decision."

"We have to, Trey," Ajax says.

"But..."

"Ajax is right, however abysmal that phrase is. You don't want her to die here, Trey. If she's going to go, let it be on her way to those who can help her. If she stays here, you're going to blame yourself and she won't want that."

"I—"

The voices cut off, turning into a mumble of incoherent sounds.

Pain flares and I see black.

• • •

I wake up to a world of smoke and ash. The world beyond my half-open lids is grey and washed out, as if fog hangs in the air. I can smell fire and gunpowder and...blood. The metallic tinge of it taints the air and I choke on my breath as the cloying smell envelopes my lungs.

"Oh my God," someone breathes, "she's awake."

I try to shake off the weight of sleep still pinning me down, but then I'm on fire. I thrash and someone swears and I can feel a presence behind me.

"Careful!"

"Drop her and I'll kill you."

"I'd have an easier job if she'd lie still."

"Can't you see she's in pain? She doesn't know what she's doing. Quinn...it's okay. I'm here."

"I doubt she can hear you."

The voices fade again.

Everything hurts.

I'm going to die.

I *can't* die.

Not now. Not like this. Not again.

My leg burns and my back arches with the pain of it. I feel someone struggling to keep hold of me.

A voice comes back, clearer than any of the others. "Quinn. Quinn. Don't go. Stay. Come back to me."

The last four words become my tether to the world and I latch onto them.

Come back to me. I'll wait for you.

It takes a great amount of effort, but I manage to still my thrashing limbs.

I will, Jax. I will.

• • •

I don't have the strength to open my eyes.

I can't feel my leg.

This is it. I'm going.

No! I scream into the void. *Don't take me! I have to go back! He… Someone...is waiting...for...for me.*

I can't remember who, and somehow that hurts more than anything. Forget the leg; this sets my heart on fire.

What is his name?

I can't remember his name.

I struggle against the mental bonds that hold me, claw toward the surface of consciousness.

Must go back. Must remember.

Hold on. Hold on. Don't let go. Don't give in.
Stay.

"Are...there yet?" a voice says. I can't identify it.

"...most," someone answers.

"Just...couple...streets..." says a third.

The voices are static, as if coming through a bad radio, but I know it's me. I'm lucky to hear even this. I should be dead, but I can't surrender, won't surrender. The voices need me.

There is silence for a while and it drives me crazy. I need something to hold onto or else I might slip.

His name, his name, his name. I have to remember.
Come back to me.

Then one of them cries out. "Here it is!"

Something explodes.

Screams.

A series of bangs.

Are we... Are they being...shot at?"

"Don't shoot! ...Please! It's me. It's Ajax Forrester! Oh God, don't..."

The gunshots cease, but I hardly notice. All I care about is the name.

Ajax Forrester.
Jax.

Jax is still trying to save me, is still waiting. I can't...let him down...

Something slams into me and I miss a breath.

I'm falling.

I collide with something hard and white hot pain comes flying back into me.

I scream and I scream and I...

Light comes back and my eyes open as my screams tear my throat ragged.

Someone is yelling. "You could've killed her!"

Moments later, strong hands close around my legs and back and the same voice says, "It's okay, Quinn. I got you. Hold on for a few more minutes, okay?" He lifts me up and my screams slowly die out as my eyes find his face.

"Jax..."

His eyes glisten with tears. "Yes. Yes I'm here."

"I...love...you."

A tear falls from his face onto mine. "I love you too, but you're going to get better, you'll see."

"Wait..." I clench my teeth as sheer agony rips at me, tries to drag me away, but I have to finish.

Then I can go. Then I can let go.

"Wait...for...me."

My vision blackens and I surrender.

Jax has me.

I'm safe.

I can let go.

So I tumble, willingly, into the dark.

CHAPTER FIVE

Time passes, in a myriad of black and white, dark and light, day and night. The pain fades away to nothing. Time passes and slowly I resurface.

I take a deep breath and open my eyes. The action is more difficult than usual, but that's to be expected. I shift into a half-sitting position, stretching my stiff limbs. I still can't feel my lower leg, but they must have me on heavy painkillers.

"I knew you'd come back," a familiar voice says, a voice that sounds like home because he's the closest I have.

My eyes search the room until I find him. He's sitting backwards in a chair at the foot of my bed, leaning against the back.

"Hey," I say.

He smiles. "We really have to stop meeting like this."

I nod. "I'll try to stay out of trouble."

He laughs at that, "You say that now, but I suspect you'll be itching to fight again this time tomorrow, so don't bother lying to me."

I smile sheepishly. "Well, when you put it that way…"

He shakes his head at me and gives me a look, as if he can't believe I'm sitting there before him.

I can't believe it either. I'm too lucky for my own good.

He sighs. "I'm glad you're all right, though I vaguely remember someone promising to never scare me like that again. Hmm?"

I wince. "Sorry?"

"If you weren't so stubborn, not to mention still recovering, I would try to knock some sense into you, but I know it'd be a waste of time. I trust you to stay safe next time, though I'm not sure what good it'll do me."

I grimace. "Was it bad?"

He nods. "It took us four days to get here, what with the chaos in the streets that we had to avoid. Kuen carried you the whole time and Trey navigated. I was too much of a nervous wreck to function."

"I'm sorry."

"Stop apologizing," he says. "I'm trying to tell a story here. We were exhausted when we arrived and were nearly shot on sight. Somebody's idea of security is a little too trigger happy. It took several minutes of me screaming for them to lower their damn guns. By the time

I got you inside, you were slipping away. Shirley said you were inches from death, Quinn. I almost lost you."

I reach out to him, forgetting he's at the end of the bed, and say, "But you didn't. I came back. That's all that matters."

"I suppose it is."

We stare at each other in silence for a while. I'm glad to see his hands are completely healed, the cuts on his face faded as well. If not for my injuries, the Guild battle could be forgotten.

Then I remember something.

"Blake and Bast!" I exclaim. "Did you find them? Are they okay?"

He smiles. "Oh yeah, they came out of the Guild battle with barely a scratch. Apparently, they're surprisingly hard to kill. Bast's words, not mine."

I roll my eyes. "Does his ego know no bounds?"

"Seemingly not, and speaking of them, they should be coming in to see you soon. They were both worried sick, though Bast assures us he knew you'd pull through the entire time, because he was pacing the hallway outside the room for some other reason."

"Aw... Sebastian."

He smiles. "It appears he's gone soft."

I laugh. "Could be worse."

"True."

I sigh. "I'm glad to be good as new again."

Jax's expression changes from happy to cautious in the space of a second. "Um... Well, not exactly," he says.

I narrow my eyes. "What do you mean?"

He looks at me with sorrowful eyes. "I'm sorry, Quinn, but they couldn't save it."

I feel cold. "Couldn't save..." I rip off my blankets, tear up my white hospital gown and... "Assassins below... My leg!"

Except that's not the problem. The problem is half of it is *missing*. Everything from below my knee is gone, replaced by a shining black prosthetic.

"Are those...bolts? In my knee?" I fight to keep my voice steady, but I'm starting to hyperventilate.

It's too much. It's all too much.

"Yes," Jax says, "they're in the bone, to connect the prosthetic to you properly. We don't want it falling off on you. It... Quinn?" He pauses and looks at me.

I'm finding it difficult to breathe. My chest feels tight, like someone set a boulder on it. My skin is prickly, tense.

"Relax, Quinn. *Relax*. Do you want them to come in and sedate you again?"

I take a deep shuddering breath. "But... Oh my God, Jax, they took my leg."

"The leg that was killing you," he points out. "Seriously, Quinn, you almost died. Again."

"I know and I'm sorry, but wasn't there another way?"

Did they have to take a piece of me?

"No and I asked, believe me. I knew you wouldn't like this, but the nurses said it was your only chance. The infection would have travelled to the rest of your body. They had to make sure they truly got rid of it."

"Okay," I say. I take another deep breath to calm my racing heart.

Half of my leg is gone.

How will I be able to fight like this?

"I'll be okay," I breathe, trying to convince myself more than Jax.

"Of course you will," he says. "You're tougher than this, stronger than this."

I look up at him. "How long will recovery take?"

"As long as it needs to and if you try to get up before you're ready, I swear on my life, I'll have you sedated and tied to your bed."

I give him a dark look. "You wouldn't."

He smiles wickedly. "Try me."

I search his eyes for some sign of a joke, but find none. "Great," I say, "you're serious. I must've rubbed off on you. I didn't think threats were your thing."

He shrugs. "They weren't, but when it comes to your safety, I'll do anything."

"I know."

There is silence between us then and a question hanging within it.

What now?

Are we going to go back to us?

He said he didn't want to lose me, but that's not the same as wanting to *be* with me. He saved me at the Guild too for the same reasons, but kept me at a distance.

Where do we go from here?

The door bangs open then, interrupting the silence and Bast and Blake rush in, nearly tripping over each other in their haste.

"Night!" Blake cries. "Oh my God, Jax told us you were going to be okay, but we had to see it with our own eyes. I'm glad you're awake. We were so worried!"

"Speak for yourself," Bast says, "but seriously though, Night, don't go dying on us again okay?"

I break into a grin. Oh Guild, how I missed these two. It feels like years since I last saw them, and our parting remarks hadn't been kind.

"Guys," I reply. "You have no idea how happy I am to see you. I'm sorry for what I said that last day..."

Blake waves it off. "Forget about it."

"Yeah," Bast agrees, "you were heartbroken. It's okay. We forgive you." He pauses. "Well, Blake does. I might need more convincing."

Blake slaps him. "Would you quit it?"

I shake my head. "Tell me something guys, do you ever not argue?"

"Occasionally," Bast replies.

"Never," Blake answers.

I laugh. "You haven't changed a bit, but I can't forget the way I treated you..."

"Yes, you can," Blake says, "or I'll have to break your other leg. How's that for an incentive?"

I raise an eyebrow. "Why is everybody so violent all of a sudden? One minute Jax is going to tie me to the bed frame and the next you're going to force me into needing a wheelchair. What gives? I thought I was going soft, but it appears it's you three who have sunk to my level."

Bast shrugs. "Not really. We were always this way, but we kept it on the down low. Assassins in disguise."

I roll my eyes. "Fine," I say, "I'll leave the past where it lies."

Blake sighs. "I guess I'll have to find another excuse to break a leg."

I give her an incredulous look.

"You could always become an actress," Bast suggests.

"Shut up," she says, laughing.

"Speaking of legs," Bast goes on, "what do you call this fancy contraption?" He pokes a finger at my prosthetic and I flinch out of habit, even though I can't feel a thing.

"It's a prosthetic leg," Ajax tells him.

"I know that," he says, his tone implying the phrase, *I'm not stupid*, "but it's cooler than any I've seen before."

"That's because I'm cooler than anyone you've met before," I reply.

He snorts. "Yeah right, we all know *I'm* the coolest person in the room."

Blake and I roll our eyes.

"He's right though," I say, looking at Ajax. "I've never seen anything like it."

"Well," he says, "I had it specially made to suit your needs. The metal is black so you can blend in and light won't reflect off of it, even though it looks shiny now. It's made with titanium, so it's lightweight but strong. You can still run around and do all your crazy stunts. The 'foot' has the best grip available so you won't slip while careening around corners or climbing walls. Last, but certainly not least, it can be easily fitted for weapon sheaths."

"Jax," I gasp, "you are an absolute genius."

He bows. "Thank you."

"Honestly, I just... How did they make it so fast?"

"Well," he scratches the back of his head, "I might have considered it back when you first broke the leg. I worry a little too much, so I asked them to start working on it anyway. Turns out I worry enough."

My eyes tear up. "I love you."

The words slip out of my mouth and I regret them immediately, covering my mouth with one hand. It was one thing to say it when I was dying, but it's much too soon to say it now.

His eyes look sad.

"I... I'm sorry," I stutter. "I shouldn't have..."

He waves a hand. "No, it's... It's okay."

Blake and Bast look between us with concern.

"Maybe we should leave you two be," Blake says, already making a move to get up.

"No," I say, grabbing her arm, "don't go yet. Tell me what we missed since the attack." I need the distraction of her voice right now.

"If you insist," she replies, settling back down on the edge of the bed.

Bast stays standing, still nearly bouncing with excitement, his long curls swaying.

"So," I say, "what happened after I stormed out and left the three of you with a far from heartfelt goodbye?" I don't look at Jax as I say it, afraid of what I might see in his eyes.

"Drop it, Night," Blake warns.

"Oh! That reminds me," I say, "you guys don't know."

"Know what?"

"I've decided to rid myself of my Silent Night persona. I realized after I left here that the assassin version of me was the disguise all along. I built Silent Night out of the ashes of my ruined past and I don't need her anymore. She'll always be there, but I don't need her to survive. I just need me. The real me."

Blake smiles and throws her arms around me. "I knew you could do it. I'm so proud of you." She squeezes me.

"Don't go soft and cry on me now, Blake," I say, fighting back tears of my own.

She pulls away and wipes her eyes, unable to stop smiling.

Bast's eyes light up. "Does this mean we get to learn your real name?"

I grin at him. "Indeed it does, Sebastian. Indeed it does." He scowls and I say, "Any last minute guesses?"

Blake and Bast shake their heads.

"All right then, so without further ado, I present to you, Quinn Marie Ballinger." I do a mock bow from my sitting position.

"Well, isn't that quite the mouthful," Bast says casually. "I'm surprised you could remember it all."

I glare at him. "You've been waiting all this time to say that, haven't you?"

"I had to," he says, "it was a brilliant comeback."

This manages to make me smile. "It was, wasn't it?"

"Your name is totally cool though," he says. "Nice to meet you, Quinby."

I scowl. "That's Quinn to you, Sebastiano. Call me anything else and you're toast."

"All right children," Blake says, "that's enough."

Bast and I grumble, but fall silent.

"So, Quinn," Blake continues, "I love it. You realize we match?"

"In what way?"

"We both have names that were traditionally meant for boys."

"Huh," I say. "My mother always said you have to be strong in this world and a strong name is a good place to start."

"What about the middle name then," Bast says. "Marie? Sounds pretty girly to me."

"I'll have you know, that was my mother's middle name," I retort, "and to insult it is to insult my mother. So, I'd shut up if I were you." My tone is scolding, but not harsh.

"Oh, honestly," Blake sighs, "you two could be siblings the way you carry on."

I point my finger at Bast. "He started it," I whine.

The four of us erupt into uncontrollable laughter.

When our laughter finally subsides, I say, "We are way off topic now. What have Jax and I missed? How was the battle? What's our plan now?"

Blake gives me a grim look. "Things haven't been good, Quinn. You've probably already noticed Haven has become a war-zone."

"I've been told."

"Well, citizens are killing each other and us. The assassins are still out there doing their dark deeds, though we haven't been able to find a trace of their whereabouts. Jenson is afraid to send us out anymore, because so few return. As for the battle, it wasn't a complete disaster, but it *was* a failure. We killed lots of them, don't get me wrong, but we were ridiculously outnumbered."

"How did you escape?"

"That's just it, none of us are exactly sure. One minute, the assassins were fighting us to the death with anything they could get their hands on. One of them even tried to bite me. The next minute, they all kind of froze and cocked their heads as if listening to something and then retreated. They fought their way out of our mass of soldiers, but nothing more and then they disappeared. As for us, we ran as soon as the coast was clear."

I frown. "I know what happened, but I'm not sure why."

"What?"

"The Charger called them off. Tell me, have you ever heard of a dog whistle?"

She nods.

"Well, this is the same kind of thing. He's trained us from a young age to be able to hear a specific noise and basically come when he calls us."

She scrunches her eyebrows. "How does that work?"

I grimace. "He tortured us with it, Blake. We hear it in our nightmares. We hear it whenever it sounds and we come because of the fear attached to it."

"Oh my God," Blake gasps. "That's awful."

I shrug. "It is what it is."

"Speaking of the Master Assassin," Bast says, "you didn't, by chance, end up killing him, did you?"

"No," I sigh, "and I'd rather not talk about that whole experience."

"Why?"

"Let's just say it might've involved Jax and me nearly drowning in a glass tank."

"Ajax!" Blake scolds. "You never told us that!"

He shrugs. "I guess it didn't come up."

"Didn't come up... Stop trying to spare us the pain. We need to know. We're your friends."

"Okay, okay," he says, throwing his hands up in surrender. "I'm sorry."

"You better be, Forrester."

"Oooooooo..." Bast says.

Blake turns her glare on Bast and he shuts up fast. He's definitely growing wiser when it comes to pushing her.

"If it wasn't for Trey and Kuen," I go on, "we would've died. Speaking of which, where are they?"

The three of them share a look.

"What?" I say.

"Trey's visiting Kuen at the moment," Blake replies.

"Visiting...?"

"He's in the dungeons, Quinn."

"What? Why? I need to get him out of there." I try to get up, but Jax pushes me back down. I resist the urge to scowl at him.

"Not a chance," he says. "He's fine."

"But why is he even there?"

It's Blake who answers again. "With everything that's going on, Jenson is more paranoid than ever. He doesn't trust Kuen."

I cross my arms. "Well that's ridiculous. He let *me* in."

"And look where that led him."

"Excuse me?"

She sighs, playing with the end of her braid. "Quinn, what do you suppose it looked like when you stormed out that night? Jenson thinks you're a traitor, that you gave our plans away to the assassins and that's why we fared so terribly in the battle. He's too stupid to believe the truth, that the assassins are so much more skilled than we can ever hope to be.

"When the four of you arrived last week, Jenson immediately ordered your execution and he was dead serious. He would've gone through with it too if..." She glances at Jax.

"If what?" I urge her.

"If Jax hadn't punched him in the face."

I whirl on Jax, eyes wide. "You did what?"

"I punched the bastard in the face," he spits. "No less than he deserved."

"But... Why?"

"Why? Quinn, he wanted to kill you. I wasn't about to let him."

"What if he decided to kill you too?"

He shrugs. "It was a risk I was prepared to take."

"That's just... You're an idiot."

He crosses his arms. "No, you're an idiot to think I'd let you die."

"And I think that's our cue to leave," Blake says. "Come on, Bast." She stands up and grabs Bast's arm.

He gives a little wave with his free hand. "See you around, Quinby, Jax."

I scowl and he grins.

I don't want them to go, but they probably have work to do and Jax and I need to talk about us.

They leave the room, closing the door behind them. It clicks into place, but I don't feel trapped. My fear of the world has lessened in the past few months, even though I've been near death on too many occasions. Maybe pain and loss make you stronger.

I turn to Jax. "I can't believe you punched Jenson."

He sighs. "To be honest, I can't either, but Quinn, do you think I'd do anything less for you?"

"No, I'm starting to realize that, but honestly, assaulting your—our boss?"

He shrugs and I finally manage to laugh over it, albeit tentatively.

"What did he say?"

Jax grins. "Well, one minute he was barking orders to the others, something like, 'shoot the girl' and as soon as he finished rubbing his jaw, trying to diffuse the agony, he said, 'just, take her in.' I could tell he was trying to hold back tears."

"Wow," I say, "who would've thought our dear leader was such a wuss."

"Such a coward as to kill you on the spot," Jax retorts. "He doesn't trust you. I shouldn't have brought you here."

"Don't be like that," I say. "If you hadn't brought me here, I'd be dead. So what if there's the threat of death still? I've always lived on the edge of a blade, Jax, one strong wind just itching to push me into oblivion. What's the difference now?"

"Well," he says softly, "now you have a reason to live. You have a cause and a future and friends and...and me." I feel tears waiting. "And I don't want you to die because of me, because of anything. I never thought I'd say this to anybody, Quinn, but I need you."

It's always been me that needed someone, that needed Jax. I never stopped to realize that maybe I hadn't been the only one who needed saving. Maybe I changed Jax as much as he changed me.

I don't know what to say and so I say nothing. I let my eyes speak and Jax has no trouble interpreting my wishes. In seconds, he stands up, walks around the bed, and sits down beside me.

I shift over to make room. "Does this mean you forgive me?"

"I guess it does," he says. "I realized, as you lay dying, that my mother's death was not your fault. You were a child. You were following orders. Disobedience would've gotten you killed, so I can't blame you for what happened. I certainly can't hate you. God, I tried that already and it ate me up inside.

"Things between us might be rough for a while, Quinn, but I can't stay away from you. I believe my mother would want me to be happy, even though she's gone, so I'm going to focus my hatred on the Charger, the real person who is to blame."

I nod, my eyes hard. "Sephtis Aeron," I spit.

"What?"

"Sephtis Aeron," I repeat, "that's the Charger's real name. We should start using it, to show we know the real him, that we won't give in to his whims. We won't give him the satisfaction of using the name he wants us to use, the name he's chosen for the tyrant he wants to be. He's not a master assassin, a charger, or Black Death. He's a regular person and a regular person can be defeated."

Jax nods warily. "Right, but I think his real name is more intimidating than his fake ones."

"All the more reason to use it, and get over the fear of it."

"I guess so."

"At any rate, Jax, I want to say thank you for saving me, for seeing more in me than I see in myself." I take his hand and he lets me. "I am still so sorry about your mother. It kills me that she's not here to see the man you have become. She would be so proud of you. I am willing to give you whatever space you need. I want to heal with you, to learn how to be better together."

He smiles. "This is what I love about you. You never give up."

I grin. "What can I say? I hate losing."

He lays his head against my shoulder and says, "Well then, here's to victory together."

I close my eyes and bask in the moment.

Neither one of us say anything else for a while, just content in each other's company. We don't go any further than his head on my shoulder either. It's a slow process, learning to love again, but I have no doubt we will find a way.

CHAPTER SIX

I'm not reminded I'm a patient until the next morning when I wake to a group of nurses bustling around the room. They cart a bunch of equipment in and that's when I realize I'm not hooked up to a dozen different machines, unlike after the train battle. I wonder why?

Then a nurse with a familiar attitude walks into the room. She's wearing her signature tight bun with not a strand out of place and her shirt has sunflowers printed on it. Sunflowers were my favourite when I was a child.

"Shirley," I exclaim. "How are you?"

She looks at me sidelong as she checks something on one of the new machines. "I'd be better if I didn't have to raise you from the dead so often," she replies. "I thought I told you to be careful?"

I wince and she tsks her tongue.

"You should've stayed away from battle. Then none of this," she waves at my now non-existent lower leg, "would've happened."

"You know that's easier said than done," I argue.

She snorts. "Apparently. Young people," she mutters. "No concern for their lives."

"That's not true," I retort. "It's *because* I care that I risked my life. It's no good living in this city when it's in this state. I'll gladly die trying to change it."

She raises an eyebrow. "Well, look who's gone and gained a heart."

I scowl. "I always had one, I just didn't...always use it. Shirley, I know I made mistakes. I'm sorry for not heeding your advice."

She shrugs. "Don't apologize to me. If you owe anyone an apology, it's yourself. Be grateful Mr. Forrester had the foresight to order you that leg, otherwise, I suspect you'd be learning to hobble around on the one for several weeks."

I look down at the prosthetic. "How does it work?"

"It's embedded into your bone structure," she replies, "so you'll be able to bend your knee and have the prosthetic bend with it."

"Won't that damage my knee?"

"It shouldn't. It's a tested theory, new technology that's guaranteed to work, or so Avery tells me, but I've seen the results. Everything heals well and the prosthetic functions like a real leg would within a few weeks."

I raise an eyebrow. "Avery?"

"He is our head scientist," she replies. "Has no one told you that?"

I shake my head.

"Well, he has a brilliant mind. It was one of the reasons he rose through the ranks of the Resistance so fast. The man didn't want to be a leader at first, such was his love of research, but we assured him he could be both. It's a good thing we did. Many more would have perished in this war without his inventions."

"I never would've expected that from him," I reply. "If we have advances like this in Haven, then how come everyone lives in poverty?"

She shrugs. "Because this city is a cruel place and no one wants to admit we can become more. It would mean facing the truth of what we are."

I fall silent and think about it for a moment. She's right; you have to want change in order to make it and most of the citizens have given up hope.

"You sound like you know a lot about these," I go on, gesturing to my leg. "How many times have you amputated?"

"More times than you'd think. There are as many injuries in war as casualties. You don't see it because people tend to hide their pain and imperfections."

"Is it difficult to do?"

"Yes and no." She sighs. "It's easy to operate, but the aftermath is difficult. People seem to think they're broken afterwards. It hurts to watch them, but I know that won't be the case for you. You'll be out of this bed as soon as I give the order, if not before then." She gives me a look.

I smile sheepishly. "You know me so well."

She rolls her eyes. "What I want to know is what you did to your leg to cause an infection like the one you got. Mr. Forrester wouldn't give us all the details, only bits and pieces, which made it even more difficult to help you, I might add. Your tests showed that your body has endured a good deal of trauma since I last saw you."

"Well, an assassin re-broke the leg," I tell her. "Then I ran on it and fought for my life on it. I was strangled to the point of blackout and almost drowned to death. After that, Trey messed around with my leg trying to help it heal faster and… Yeah, I think that's it."

She shakes her head in disapproval. "Remind me again why I bothered to save your life the first time?"

"Because it's what you do?"

"Mmmm… Maybe, but this better be the last time I find myself doing so. You hear?"

"Yes ma'am," I reply.

I do believe she's growing on me, but I'm also a bit different this time. She doesn't seem to hate me as much either.

Yet, we both must have reached our limit, because we say nothing more. She joins the other nurses in checking my vitals. They hook me up to several more machines and I grumble at the wires surrounding me and needles poking into me, but I don't complain.

As much as Shirley thinks I'm going to jump back into action, I've actually learned my lesson. This time, I'm going to focus on recovery. I know I can't go on missions or kill the Sephtis in this state. I have to be the best I can be, so I have to take this step by step until I'm healthy enough to resume my agent duties.

Life isn't all about gaining glory. Sometimes the best battles are won by convincing yourself you can get through one more day. The battle to recover from this injury might be the most noble battle I ever fight, so I better do it right.

When the nurses are done all their various checks, they unhook me from the equipment and cart it out again. Shirley orders three more days of bed rest before I can begin basic therapy. I agree, grudgingly, but I know I have to follow her instructions. I owe it to myself.

The nurses are only gone a minute when the door opens again.

I groan and close my eyes, flopping back onto the pillows. "What do you want now?" I whine.

"Just to see your face," Jax's voice replies, "but if now isn't a good time…"

I open my eyes. "Sorry, Jax. I thought you were the nurses again. I can only take so much of that in one day."

"I figured it was something like that." He smiles. "How did it go? What did Shirley say?"

"I'm doing okay physically, but she basically said I have no regard for my life and I'm an idiot. She's going to keep trying to fix me anyway though, because behind that stony facade of hers, she actually cares."

Jax laughs and then says, "A bit like someone else I know."

"Oh shush," I mutter. I pat the spot beside me. "Have a seat. What brings you to my humble abode?"

"Two reasons," he replies as he sits down on the edge of the bed. "One: I suspect you're bored out of your skull and will want company. Two: I've vowed to not let you out of my sight unless there's someone responsible in the room. And no, Bast doesn't count; he would go ahead with whatever schemes you concoct."

I frown. "Well, didn't you think of everything."

"I'm not going to let you endanger yourself."

"And I won't." I grab his hand. "I've learned my lesson, Jax. Nothing good comes out of trying to stay strong, trying to ignore pain. Sometimes, you have to stop and deal with it. You can't keep going or you'll end up pushing yourself too hard. I realize now that stubbornness can be deadly, and I don't want to die."

He squeezes my hand. "I'm glad to hear that."

"I'm surprised Shirley is leaving me alone, though," I go on. "I expected to be monitored all day and night this time around. I hardly feel like I almost died; this doesn't even look like a hospital room. Why am I not hooked up to a dozen machines?"

Jax winces, as if he was hoping I wouldn't ask that question.

"What?" I say.

He runs a hand through his hair. "Well, you've recovered enough to not need the machines. They're positive you're not going to die on us now."

I narrow my eyes. "But how can they? I've only been out for…" I trail off as I realize I don't know the answer. I give him a sharp look. "How long was I out?"

He braces himself as he answers. "We've been here for two weeks."

My stomach drops. "Two weeks?"

It's crazy. All that time lost…

It's nothing compared to losing it all.

"I almost didn't make it, did I?" I ask softly.

Jax nods, his eyes full of sorrow. "There were a couple times when…" He shudders. "When your heart actually stopped—along with my own—but they always got it going again. They were determined to save you. After the original surgery to remove the leg, you didn't regain consciousness for three days and then you lost it again during the procedure to attach the prosthetic. You've been in and out ever since, but they kept you sedated to help with the pain and trauma. They decided yesterday morning you were healed enough to cut off the sedatives."

"I'm sorry I caused you and the others so much pain," I say.

He merely squeezes my hand again in answer.

"Shirley said I have to stay in bed for another three days," I go on. "I know I have to, but it kills me. I mean, what do you think the assassins could do in three days?"

He shrugs. "Not much more than they've done in the past two weeks nor the past month since we escaped them."

I give him a look. "I'm serious."

"You tell me then."

"I know I was one," I argue, "but that doesn't mean I know the Master's plan. Guild, I couldn't even predict he was my father. I thought I knew how his mind worked, but I was wrong. The assassins could do anything in the next three days and I wouldn't be able to stop them."

"It's not your job to stop them."

"But…"

He sighs. "Quinn, you're not the only agent we have. Let someone else do the hard work for a change. Right now, your job is to stay alive and that's going to be hard enough without chasing after assassins."

"I can multitask."

"Try it," he counters, "and I'll go through with my threat from yesterday."

"You wouldn't."

He leans closer to me. "Try me."

I grin. That wasn't the smartest thing for him to say.

I reach behind me for one of my pillows and stop.

A slow shiver runs down my arms as I brush my fingers across the pillowcase.

Their presence hasn't bothered me until now, but I know this is just a side effect.

It's all in your head, I remind myself. *They can't hurt you.*

You control your fear.

I take a deep breath and let the grin settle on my face once more. Then I pick up one of my pillows and smack him across the face with it.

I never thought the action could be so satisfying. I laugh as the air flies out of him in a whoosh and his head whips to the side. He manages to stay sitting, which is impressive.

He scowls at me. "What was that for?"

I shrug and put the pillow down, not ready to hold it for too long. "Does it matter?"

"Aren't we a little old for pillow fights?" he asks me, giving me a scolding look.

"Never, and besides, this is my first."

"Your first..." Then it hits him. His eyes grow wide. "Sil—Quinn, I thought you were..."

I meet his gaze. "Afraid of pillows?"

He nods.

I glance at the pillow, making sure it is still all I see. "I never thought I'd be able to do it, but I overcame the fear."

"How?"

"I let go," I reply. "I renounced my guilt. I realized I *am* the kind of person that could make my mother proud." I pause. "I overcame it by letting myself become Quinn again."

He smiles. "I'm happy for you. That's a big step."

"Yeah," I say, echoing his smile. "I guess I've come a long way from that girl you held at gunpoint, eh?"

He laughs. "I guess you have."

In the silence that follows, I can feel that magnetic pull between us again, but I don't move an inch. I want him to be the one to initiate contact. I don't want to rush him into something he isn't ready for.

Someone knocks on the door then and Jax looks away from me, breaking the spell. "Who is it?" he calls out.

"It's Shirley, Mr. Forrester. There is someone here to see Ms. Night."

I frown at the name, but I'm sure no one has told her of the change.

"Who?" Jax asks.

"It is your superior," a familiar and unwanted voice returns, "and I should not be made to wait outside closed doors while someone else speaks for me."

Jax gets to his feet.

I look at the door apprehensively, expecting it to open at any second.

"All due respect, Jenson," Shirley fires back, "but the girl could be indisposed at the moment and should not have to suffer such surprises in her condition."

"You are testing my patience," Jenson replies.

"Open the door, Jax," I say. I sit up straighter and fold the bed sheet against my waist.

"Are you sure?" he asks.

"Just do it."

He pulls the door open and Jenson nearly falls into the room, his fist raised to knock again, albeit more forcefully than Shirley had. She stands beside him, hands on her hips, eyes revealing how displeased she is. Behind them, the chatter of other nurses and machines continues, a constant melody in the hospital wing.

Jenson regains his composure and nods at Jax. "Mr. Forrester," he says.

"Jenson," Jax replies. His stance is rigid.

"I would like to speak to the assassin," Jenson says. "You are free to go." He makes to push past Jax, but Jax doesn't move.

"Her name is Quinn," Jax says, "and you can speak to the both of us."

"That won't be necessary," Jenson replies. "The information I would like to discuss is confidential."

Jax snorts. "Is that the best you have? If that's the case, you *should* be talking to me, seeing as I rank higher."

Jenson scowls. "You are making this difficult, Mr. Forrester. I don't think you want to do that. I can diminish that rank of yours with the snap of a finger. Insubordination is an offense, after all."

I can taste the tension between them, can sense neither are going to budge.

I take a deep breath and say, "It's okay, Jax. Let him in."

He turns his head to me, but doesn't move from the doorway. "Quinn…"

"I'll be fine, Jax. He can't hurt me." I imagine Jenson rolling his eyes, but I keep my gaze on Jax, until he sighs and turns back to Jenson.

He jabs a finger into Jenson's chest. "If you hurt her, there will be hell to pay. I spent two weeks waiting for her to wake up. There will be more than insubordination if a hair on her head is out of place when I come back. You have ten minutes."

Jax gives me one last look and then pushes past Jenson and into the hall. Shirley follows. Jenson stands alone in the doorway as if in shock for a few moments before stepping in and closing the door.

"So, Assassin," he starts, "how are you holding up?"

I roll my eyes. "Oh please, Jenson, as if you care to know."

His gaze hardens. "I asked you a question."

"Fine," I say, fisting my hands beneath the sheets. "I am doing just fine. I am achy and tired and confused and I have one and a half legs. How are *you*? How's your jaw?"

He tries to look confused, but I can see the alarm in his eyes.

"Yeah," I say, crossing my arms, "I know you tried to shoot me on sight when I arrived here a few weeks ago, dying from a wound I received fighting for *your* cause, and yet, somehow, I'm still the bad guy. Explain that."

He walks closer to the bed. "I was hoping such an injury would've humbled you."

I scowl. "I am not an animal to be broken in, Jenson. I have been through hell and back, no thanks to you. I didn't do it for glory, but I certainly didn't do it to be dismissed like this. Jax gave you ten minutes, don't waste it being petty."

"Why did you do it then?"

"Excuse me?"

"Mr. Forrester said you fought with us during the battle and you just claimed the same. Why? Why risk your life for an organization you denounced not a day before? You led us on for months. You pretended to be reformed and then you attacked Ms. Roseanne, refused to atone for it, and left without a trace. You're lucky you're still here. If I had my way, you'd be hanging from the gallows. Why did you come back?"

"I mean, I didn't really have a choice in the matter. I was dying."

He waves a hand. "No, no. I meant the battle."

"Oh," I reply. "I guess you could say I snapped out of it. I wasn't pretending to be reformed all those months, but it's not as easy as it looks to turn your back on everything you know. I slipped that day. I made a mistake, but I found my way back."

"I see," he says, "and what's to say you won't slip again?"

I shrug. "Nothing. You either trust me or you don't. I can't promise you anything, but I believe in the Resistance. I will never stop fighting for it and my friends will never stop fighting for me. As long as I have them, your people should be safe."

He narrows his eyes. "Is that a threat?"

I hold back a smile. "Jax's promise goes both ways; the same goes for Blake Solarin, Sebastian Foster, and Trey. They have gone through hell for me and I will go back to it for them if I have to."

"Your friends are safe already," he retorts. "They have proven their worth over the years."

"Ah, but they have fallen from grace by associating with me and don't pretend that's not true."

"I'm afraid you're right," he replies. "Their standing depends entirely on you, not me. If you can gain favour, so will they. I am giving you another chance, Assassin, against my better judgment, I might add. Do not waste it."

"What happens if I do?"

He shrugs. "I am undecided. I can't throw you onto the streets, not with what you know, but life imprisonment might be too cruel, even for you."

The unspoken alternative hangs in the air.

I know he will kill me, despite his pleasantness now, despite Jax's threats. I can't let that happen. It would kill Jax too, both his spirit and reputation. He would fulfill his threat to Jenson and he would die a traitor to the Resistance, the organization he devoted his life to.

I can't let that happen.

"I will do everything in my power to not waste this opportunity," I tell Jenson.

"Then we are in agreement." He heads toward the door. "Rest up, Assassin. I will need you in the coming months. The war with the Guild has only just begun."

CHAPTER SEVEN

Jax returns moments after Jenson disappears and asks if I'm okay.

"I'm fine," I assure him. "He didn't even come near me."

He lowers his shoulders. "Good. So what did he have to say?"

I shrug. "He gave me a second chance. Other than that, there was a lot of posturing and meaningless words. The man can't be concise."

He smiles. "Well, I'm glad you're okay and the meeting is over with. Maybe we can avoid him now for a good while."

I nod. "At least until I recover. He assured me I will fight again in the future."

He sighs and rolls his eyes. "Of course he did."

"He's probably still hoping I'll get myself killed so he doesn't have to do it himself." I try to keep my tone light.

I don't want Jax knowing about Jenson's threat. That is my burden.

"He knows he'll never stand against me in a second round," Jax replies, bringing his fists up in front of his face.

I laugh.

"Hey now," a new voice interrupts. "You can't fight an injured person."

Jax turns around as Trey walks into the room through the still-open door. "Oh, hey," he says, "we were actually talking about Jenson."

"Ah," she replies, "in that case, carry on. He could use some humiliation."

I laugh again. "It's good to see you, Trey."

She smiles. "You too. Guild, I'm so glad you're okay." She looks at me as if she's afraid I'll fade away at any moment, as if she would blame herself for my absence. "Oh, and I promise to never perform mock surgery on you again. Shirley gave me quite the tongue lashing when I explained what I did or rather, what I tried to do." She shudders.

I shake my head. "Serves you right, but you did what you could. I appreciate the effort."

She gives me a small smile.

"How's Kuen?" I ask her.

She sighs. "He's certainly been better. He's already devised over a dozen ways to kill Jenson, refuses to keep quiet about his former assassin involvement, and didn't sleep a wink until I assured him you would live.

Stubbornness must run in the family because the two of you have a lot of it."

I resist the urge to roll my eyes. "Will he be okay though?"

"I think so. He has all the necessities to survive down there and he's not about to let his stubbornness be the death of him." She shrugs. "Personally, I think the dungeon is good for him. It keeps him out of trouble."

I smile. "I'm sure he agrees."

Trey laughs. "Doubtful. I'm working on getting him out though. I have petitioned for a trial, to decide his fate fairly. If the vote is against him, I'll smuggle him out somehow. I know Jenson will call for a death sentence, but I'm not about to let that happen."

The thought sickens me.

I'm sure he's done terrible things, but he doesn't deserve to die. I hope Trey too can escape the gallows.

I give Trey a small smile. "I think he deserves a second chance."

She beams. "I'm glad you agree. You two barely know each other, but we're family. We stand up for each other. He's saved all three of us in the past, so I'll be damned if I don't fight for him."

I reach out and squeeze her hand. "You don't have to convince *me*. Save that fire for the people that matter. Burn them to the ground."

She squeezes back. "It would be my honour."

"You two are crazy," Jax mutters.

"Look who's talking," Trey counters. "Didn't you punch Jenson in the face?"

He scowls and crosses his arms. "No one is going to let me forget that, are they?"

Trey slings an arm over his shoulder. "Why should we? It was brilliant. If I wasn't scared stiff, I would've laughed my ass off."

Jax cracks a smile.

"That's it, kid," Trey says. "Don't let the world get you down." She ruffles his hair and he wriggles out of her grasp before she can get him in a headlock and really mess it up. "Anyway, I should probably go. I just wanted to see how you were doing, Quinn."

"Thanks for stopping in," I reply. "Keep me updated, won't you?"

She nods. "I'll pop in at regular intervals to see how you're making out. Nice leg, by the way."

I smile. "Thanks. It's starting to grow on me."

"That's good," she says. "Well, I'll see you guys around."

She heads out and I turn to Jax. "So, what now?"

"Well, I brought cards."

• • •

The next few days are the longest of my life. I do nothing but lie in bed all day—talking to Jax, playing cards, and letting myself heal. The nurses check in on me each morning and Bast and Blake usually come in for a bit after.

On the third day, Shirley returns after lunch. Another nurse trails behind her, one I haven't seen before.

"Afternoon, girl," Shirley says to me in way of greeting, "boy."

Jax nods.

"You know, *woman*," I retort, "we do have names. It's Ajax and Quinn."

She purses her lips. "I seem to recall your name being Silent Night the last time you were here, or do you change your name with the wind?"

I flinch at the title. Now I know how Bast feels, though I doubt our hatred is caused by the same thing.

"I do not," I reply. "I've simply chosen to throw away my assassin persona. Quinn is my true identity."

"I see," she says, "how very...illuminating."

I scowl.

So much for the two of us getting along.

"Well, *Quinn*," Shirley goes on, "let me introduce you to Lana. She will be your physiotherapist for the duration of your recovery."

The new lady waves tentatively, stepping out from behind Shirley. "Hello," she says, her voice shaking a bit. "It's a pleasure to meet you." She has short blonde hair and mousy eyes. Freckles sprinkle her cheeks. She's wearing a light blue uniform with the letter N stitched on each shoulder. I find myself jealous of the colour. I find myself thinking of my mother.

I nod. "Likewise."

"Well, I'll leave you to it," Shirley says. "Good luck, Lana; this one won't be nearly as cooperative now that she's awake."

I choke back my laughter at the look on Lana's face as Shirley leaves, closing the door behind her, and at the fact that Shirley just quoted Jax. I can't believe she remembered what he said after the train battle. Back then, I was a challenge, and Shirley is now passing it on to Lana. I hope she's up for it.

She looks like a strong wind could blow her over, but strength isn't always shown on the outside.

"So, Lana," I start, "what do you want me to do first?" I try to sound kind, but I'm not sure it works.

"Um…" she stammers. "It would probably be good to…uh…begin with some…um… simple exercises. If you can sit on the…edge of the bed…that would be great."

"Sure," I say, giving her a smile. "You don't have to be nervous. I don't bite."

"Sure you don't," Jax says.

"You're not helping," I snap quietly at him. "Why don't you get ready to catch me if something goes wrong?"

He grumbles, but stands up, joining Lana at the side of the bed as she walks over.

I throw the covers off and spin into a sitting position on the edge of the bed. The sudden action makes the room spin and I sway a bit, blinking my eyes to regain my focus.

"How's that?" I finally say when the room comes to a stop.

"Good," Lana replies. "How do you feel about moving your leg?"

"Exhilarated?" That's an understatement. I can't wait to get moving. I mean, what kind of question is that?

She smiles. "Okay, so wiggle your toes on your good foot."

I frown. "What good will that do? I know it works."

"Quinn," Jax says softly, "just do what she says."

"Fine," I mutter, crossing my arms. Then I wiggle the toes on my left foot. I have to admit, they're a bit stiff.

"Good," Lana says, "now roll the ankle."

I do as she says without protest. I rotate my ankle clockwise and counter clockwise, as per her instructions.

"Point your toes to the floor, to the ceiling, and now bring your left knee up to your chest and hold it there."

That one is a bit more difficult; I've been laying in bed for a while.

"Okay, that's very good," Lana says finally. "You can rest the leg."

I let my left leg fall over the bedside.

Lana doesn't look as tense as she first did. "Now," she says, "you can only do one of those exercises with your right leg, seeing as you no longer have a foot to manipulate. That is one of the hardest things to adjust to for most people."

I nod. I can see why. It must be frustrating to have less control, simply because you have less *to* control.

"That being said," she goes on, "bring your right knee up to your chest, but don't hold it there. Take it slow."

I start bending my right knee.

"Oh," I gasp.

It feels so...weird. My leg is lighter, but the drop in weight doesn't make the action easier.

"I..."

Lana gives me a sympathetic smile and holds out her hands. "May I?"

I shrug. "Go for it."

She kneels down in front of me, placing one hand on my prosthetic and the other on my real leg, just above the knee.

I try not to flinch, but human contact still startles me.

"Tell me if it starts to hurt," she says.

"Okay."

Then she pushes my leg up and in toward my chest. I set my chin on my knee for a second before she pulls my leg back down into the resting position.

She looks up at me. "How was that?"

"Weird, but okay, I guess."

"Good."

She repeats the exercise four more times before telling me to give it another go.

I clench my teeth in concentration and manage to lift my knee and consequently my prosthetic up, but I'm not able to get the "foot" to rest on the bed. It hangs off, but I can't control the prosthetic, only my knee that it's attached to, which limits my options for movement.

"This is impossible," I groan as I let the leg fall again.

"No," Lana argues, "not impossible, just challenging and all challenges can be overcome with enough patience."

"Wonderful," I mutter. Patience isn't something I have in great quantities.

"You can do it, Quinn," Jax assures me. "I know you can."

I take a deep breath and give it another shot.

• • •

Lana returns each morning and afternoon for the next few days and runs me through my exercises. Along with bringing my knee to my chest, I have to bring my leg parallel to the bed and hold it there, which also requires my neglected ab muscles. I get better at doing them by myself and find it easier to roll over in bed as a result.

Jax is an endless well of support and so are Blake and Bast. Even Trey comes in to give me tips from when she broke her own leg. It's not exactly the same, seeing as she still had her leg when it was all said and done, but it helps. I no longer feel useless, but I'm still edgy.

No one knows what's going on. My friends can't tell me much when I ask about the war. The Resistance agents are only monitoring the situation right now. The biggest thing we've done since the Guild attack was put out the fires raging in the city. I'm told it took weeks, what with the citizens trying to kill our agents at every turn.

The assassins are still picking us off one by one. Half a dozen agents turned up dead three days ago, a few blocks away from the base, a week after they were due to return. Torture was evident in their bodies and Jax was in a rage telling me about it.

Jenson has Jax on stand down right now, but I know he'll be quick to go once given the chance, even if he is a bit rusty. He refuses to go train unless someone else is with me and Bast still doesn't count.

I want to get back out there too, but I know I can't. It's difficult to sit still, but if I injure myself again, we'll all be doomed. So, I have to keep going along with my therapy, as fast as I can without making it worse.

• • •

About a week into my physio, Lana enters my room with a huge smile on her face. "I have a surprise for you, Ms. Ballinger," she says.

She's taken to calling me that and it never ceases to make me smile. I think of my mother when she says it. I miss her, but I know she wouldn't want me to dwell on it. The blue streak in my hair must be almost completely faded now. I don't know if I should let it disappear.

I return to reality, where Lana is looking for a reply. "What's the surprise?" I ask.

She smiles wider. "Today we're going to start standing!"

My eyes light up.

Finally.

"Really?" I exclaim.

She nods. "You've been super cooperative so far and I think you're ready. You've earned it."

I look over at Jax. He's smiling too and it lights up his face.

"When can I try?" I ask Lana. My voice is high and excited, like a little kid.

"Right now, if you'd like," she replies.

I swing my legs over the edge of the bed and pause.

Can I really do this? Am I ready?

I have to be. I *am*. I can feel it.

Jax walks over and takes my hand. "I'll be here to catch you if you fall."

"Don't let go," I tell him.

Never let go.

"I won't."

I pull myself out of bed, putting my weight on my left leg first and setting my right "foot" on the floor. Then I shift my weight over...and feel myself falling.

"Jax!"

My fingers dig into his arms and he says, "It's okay. I got you. Easy." He guides me back down onto the bed. My breath comes heavy.

"Are you okay?" Lana asks me.

I nod, not trusting my voice.

"It's not going to be easy," she says, "but I don't think it'll take you long. The key is to possess the desire to accomplish it. Those who want to stand will stand; those who want to walk will walk."

For me, it's not a want, it's a need. I need to get up. I need to do something. I need to be free.

"Well, go on," she says, "give it another shot."

I set my weight down on my left leg again and then shift to my right, slower this time.

Again, gravity pulls me down.

Again, Jax deposits me on the bed.

I cross my arms. "What am I doing wrong?"

"Don't put all your weight on the bad leg," Lana replies. "You want to shift it over, but not fully. You need to balance yourself. Put both legs down at once, but gently."

"Okay…" I slide forward until both my feet are resting on the ground. "Jax, can you just…pull me up?"

"Sure." He moves in front of me and grips both my hands in his. "Hold on."

I nod.

I can do this.

He pulls me to my feet and this time I don't fall, but to be fair, he's keeping me balanced. The feeling of standing on my new leg is the weirdest sensation ever. I feel weightless and not entirely sure how I'm going to be able to walk like this.

"Good," Lana says, "now let her go."

What? No!

I clench my hands tighter around his.

"Quinn…" he scolds.

"I don't think…" Guild, it's such a small task but somehow, I've never been more afraid.

"Look at me," he says.

My eyes find his and they calm me.

"You can do this," he assures me.

"Okay. Okay, I can do this." I loosen my grip. Then I take a deep breath and he lets go.

I sway.

For a second, I think that's it, that I'm going to fall again, but then I stop moving. I'm balancing my weight evenly, trying not to think about the fake leg.

Pretend it is real and it will feel real.

I laugh.

I did it. I'm standing. I'm actually standing!

I grin and Jax laughs too. Lana claps for me.

I lean over as my laughter takes me and the sudden change in gravity ruins everything.

"Jax!" I shriek.

He reaches an arm out and wraps it around me. I cling to it, heart beating wildly in my chest. We stay like that for a minute while I catch my breath and then he helps me sit back down.

"I think that's enough for this morning," Lana says.

"No," I protest. "Please. Let me give it one more try."

"All right," she replies, "once more, but then you have to rest. You don't want to overexert yourself."

I nod, but my eyes are scowling.

Jax and I clasp hands again and he brings me to my feet one more time. He let's go sooner and I sway less before I'm standing still, free. It feels amazing.

I smile again. "I love this."

Who knew doing something as simple as standing could bring a person so much joy? People take things for granted when they have them. I will cherish everything from now on, because you never know when you will lose it, when it will be the last time.

I look down at my feet and consider something. "Can I...?"

Lana sees what I want and shakes her head. "Leave walking for another time. Don't get me wrong, you've done well, but let's not push it."

I sigh. "Fine." I sit down on my own and feel the proudest I have in a long time. Now that I've had this taste of freedom, they're not going to be able to leave me cooped up much longer. I want to go, go, go...

"Well, until next time, Ms. Ballinger, Mr. Forrester." Lana gives us a little wave and leaves us, closing the door behind her.

I flop onto my back with a loud, drawn-out groan.

"Something on your mind?" Jax says.

"Everything," I sigh. "I feel so agitated. I want to get out and do something. I want to help, but instead I'm stuck here in this room, on this bed, trapped in an endless dance of boredom."

He sits down beside me. "These things take time, Quinn."

"Which is something we're short on," I point out. "Sephtis has commissioned a new plan, one he's been working on since before we attacked. I know it. I can feel it. The longer we sit here and do nothing—the longer I sit here—the stronger he gets, the closer he gets to destroying us all, because that's his end game. He doesn't want glory.

He doesn't want domination; he wants decimation, and he'll get it if we don't do something soon to stop him."

"I know," Jax sighs, "but what can we do? What would *you* have us do? We can't fight an enemy we can't see."

"Then we'll have to find them, won't we?" I sit up and pin him with a stare. "We can't keep making excuses, Jax. We can't give up now. You were fighting them long before I came along and told you where they were. Why is it the end of the world that they've disappeared again?"

"That's not…"

"It is. Sure, things are bleak now, but it's not over. We've shaken the assassins, we've proven ourselves a worthy enemy. It is only natural they stepped up their game. We have to do the same. We can't curl up and pray we survive. We have to keep moving."

He smiles. "See, this is what I love about you. You're never willing to give in. You'll do anything, *be* anything to achieve your goals. You never give anything less than your best. That's part of the reason I fell for you. I knew when I failed to act, you would be there to remind me I have things worth fighting for. No matter what. I may have pulled you out of the dark, Quinn, but you keep us both from going back to it."

A part of me wants to cry, but I hold back. I have to be strong. "You were never in the dark," I tell him.

He looks down at his feet. "Not strictly true," he replies. "My childhood was better than yours, I'm sure, but it still wasn't easy. I fought a hidden enemy for years. To have finally found them and then watched them disappear again…" He clenches his fist. "It's devastating. It's hard to even look at the drawing board when you were sure it would be gone for good, let alone pick up the pen again, but I suppose drawing is what we're good at. We can do it for a little while longer, if we must."

"I know you can," I tell him, "and you won't have to do it alone. We can only triumph if we stick together because that is the Guild's weakness. All the assassins do is look after themselves. They won't work together because they refuse to die together. Whereas, if we work together, we will be able to tear them apart. There are already fissures in their ranks. Together we will conquer and divided they will fall. They may have numbers, but we have connections. We have a cause; all they want is misery and destruction. There will always be chaos, but we have to fight for harmony. It doesn't always last, but we have to try."

Jax claps. "Now *that* was a speech. We should have you rallying the troops. Hell, we should have you *leading* the troops."

I smile, trying to hide my blush. "Maybe. I doubt anyone would listen to me, though, given my history, but I'll join the fight again as soon as I'm ready. In the meantime, you should get back out there."

"What?"

I give him a look. "I know you're as bored as I am with no concrete reason. You don't have to watch me all hours of the day, Jax. You should be in the field, doing what you do best. The Resistance needs its greatest soldiers and that includes you. You don't need me to keep you from the darkness, you just need a way to keep fighting it."

"But what about you?" He squeezes my good knee. "You'll be okay here by yourself?"

"Of course," I assure him, "and I'll be by your side again as soon as I'm able, but we can't keep waiting for me. We need to act."

He runs a hand through his hair. "I'll have to think about it."

I frown at him.

"Quinn, it's not...an easy decision. There are a lot of factors."

"But I know your biggest concern is me. I'll be safe here; be grateful I'm not begging you to let *me* fight."

He sighs. "It won't be long, will it?"

"Not once I master walking," I admit. "My days in this hospital room are numbered."

"Well," he says, "I guess I better get a head start on those assassins for you, to ease your transition."

"You mean you'll do it?"

He sighs again. "Yeah, though if I live to regret it, I'm blaming you. I suppose it *is* my job. It's a miracle Jenson has given me even this much time off of active duty. I'd rather choose to go back on my own. It makes the action more noble."

I nod.

"Are you sure you're okay with it?" he asks me. "It's going to be dangerous, you know. I might come back to you in pieces."

I wince. "If you do, I'll find a way to raise you from the dead so I can kill you for being so careless," I reply. "Then, I'll find the culprit and cut them into even smaller pieces."

He grimaces, his face losing some of its colour. "Well that's...violent."

I grin. "It'll be nothing less than either one of you will deserve." My expression softens as I go on to say, "But honestly, Jax, you'll be fine. I've seen you fight. I almost died during the train battle and you came out with barely a scratch. The assassins will learn to fear you or they'll be dead. Simple as that."

He smiles. "I'll talk to Jenson tomorrow then, see what kind of missions he might have for me. Hey, did I tell you I was promoted to Level One?"

My eyes widen. "No! Really?"

"Yeah," he says. "Trey and I had to recount our activities during our absence to the council a couple of days after we returned and most of them agreed that I showed 'great valour and loyalty, especially when faced with a daunting task and certain death.' Some nonsense like that. So they voted to promote me. I'm now only about twenty spots below Jenson."

"Now *that* we have to celebrate. I'd suggest another Den party, but seeing as I'm practically bedridden..."

"I'll have Blake and Bast bring a cake over and invite Trey. We'll do it tonight."

I smile. "That sounds like my kind of party."

"Then it's a date."

I smile wider, mischievously. "A date indeed."

He leans in and plants a kiss on my forehead.

I want more, but I know I have to be patient. We still have barely touched since our kiss in the tank. It kills me, but losing him would be even more painful.

I pull him in for a hug instead, wrapping my arms tight around his chest. Despite what I said, the thought of him going out in the city to fight the assassins again terrifies me, but I know that's what I'd be doing if I could. So I have to let him. He needs to do something just as much as I do. I trust him to be careful. I want him back in one piece. If any harm ever comes to him, there will be hell to pay. I wasn't lying about that.

CHAPTER EIGHT

A week later, Jenson approves Jax for his first mission. He had to undergo physical and written tests first to prove he was still fit to enter the field after his time off. In between his tests, I learned how to walk again and I can do it now with minimal help. I suggest more cake to celebrate the both of us, but Jax says no, though he promises he'll make it up to me.

The next morning, he enters the room in his black field uniform. Guns, knives, a couple swords, and endless backup bullets hang from holsters and poke out of pockets. He looks dangerous; beautiful.

I smile from my place against the wall. I'm rarely in bed now that I'm not confined to it. Currently, I'm busy sharpening a dagger to lethal precision as only I know best.

"Going somewhere?" I ask him.

He smiles. "I'm just popping in to say my farewells. I should be back before nightfall, with any luck. Don't get into too much trouble while I'm gone, eh?"

"You don't need luck," I reply, "you have sheer will, and me, trouble? I never heard of such a thing." I grin.

He shakes his head and rolls his eyes, which then zero in on the dagger I'm holding. "Where did you get that?"

"Bast smuggled it in for me."

He sighs. "Exactly what I meant by trouble."

I laugh. "I asked him to grab me one, so it's not really his fault."

"I'm not going to argue. I just ask that you'll be careful."

"Don't worry about me, weapons are my brothers."

"That's why I'm worried."

I throw the knife and whetstone onto the bed. "I could be worried about you, but I know I don't have to be. I trust you."

He smiles. "I trust you too."

"Then come give me a proper goodbye and get going."

He walks over and I push myself off the wall to meet him halfway. I lose my footing after a couple of steps and stumble into him. He catches me, his arms wrapping around me, holding me tight. His embrace says the words his mouth won't.

I love you. Don't worry. I'll come back. And if I don't…

I hold him back tighter, burying my face into his chest.

I love you too. I won't. I know. You will.

After a minute, he lets go. He holds my gaze for a moment and then he leans in and brushes a soft kiss across my lips.

I close my eyes as the motion sends butterflies rocketing through me. When I open them again, he's gone and the butterflies fade.

I promised him I wouldn't worry. It's the first lie I've told him in a long time. Anxiety presses in on me as I stand alone, in the middle of the room, waiting for him to come back to me.

I jump a few minutes later when someone knocks on my door. "Come in," I call out, hoping it's Jax, but knowing it can't be.

He's barely been gone five minutes, for Guild's sake. Pull yourself together, Ballinger, honestly.

The door opens and Blake walks in, no Bast with her this time. "Hey," she says, smiling, but then her brow furrows in concern and she adds, "what are you doing standing in the middle of the room all by yourself?"

"I... I was waiting for Jax to come back. Stupid of me really, he just left, but..." I trail off and look down at my toes.

She comes over and puts a hand on my shoulder. "Hey, it's okay. Come on, why don't you sit down and we can talk about it?"

I nod and let her lead me over to the bed. I perch on its edge and she sits beside me.

"It's normal to be afraid, Quinn," she tells me. "I'd be more worried if you weren't. I'm scared for him too. I mean, it's a dangerous world out there, more so now than ever before, but I know he'll be okay. He's an amazing fighter; it'll take a lot to bring him down and that's what I base my hope on, the knowledge that he is capable of more than we can ever realize. He can do this."

"I know he's capable," I sigh, "but sometimes there are situations you don't plan for, where you can't do it. What if he misses something, what if something goes wrong? It only takes a heartbeat for a mistake to turn a battle. Even the best fighters can be thwarted, Blake. I had my dagger an inch from the Charger's throat when Hai sprang up and crushed my attempt to dust. If anything happens to Jax I'll... I was the one that put him up to it. I told him to get out there. I'll never forgive myself if..."

She squeezes my shoulder. "Stop. Thinking like this isn't going to help. What would Jax say if he knew you were this worried?"

I sigh. "He'd tell me not to."

"Exactly. So don't worry. It doesn't do any good for either of you. You need to relax and do something to take your mind off him."

I give her a look. "Like what?"

She shrugs. "I don't know. What would you like to do?"

I'd like to run after Jax and drag him back to me, but I know I can't and I don't tell Blake that. I think about her question for a minute before deciding on something. Jax wouldn't like it, not one bit, which is why I have to do it while he's gone.

"Could you take me to the dungeons?"

She frowns. "What? Why?"

"I want to talk to Kuen."

"What for?"

I shrug. "Why not?" I assume Jax hasn't told her he's my brother and I'm not yet ready to tell her myself. "He could probably use someone to talk to and he's helped save my life twice now, the least I can do is go see him."

"I don't know, Quinn…"

"Oh come on, Blake. What harm could it do? He's not the dangerous monster Jenson claims he is, and besides, he's locked up."

"It's not him I'm worried about." She gives me a pointed look.

It's my turn to frown. "I'm not going to *do* anything. I *can't* do anything, not like I am. Trust me."

She snorts. "Aren't those a pair of loaded words."

"Blake, please. This is important."

She's silent a minute before she says, "Okay."

"Thank you."

"Don't thank me yet. I'll be right back."

She leaves the room for a minute, and when I'm beginning to think she's ditched me, she returns with a wheelchair.

"No," I say, crossing my arms, "absolutely not."

She gives me a no-nonsense look.

"Blake," I try, "I'm not riding in one of those things like some…"

"What?" she says. "Like an injured person? An amputee? Because guess what, Quinn, you are both of those. There is no way in hell I'm letting you walk all the way to the dungeon and that is final. If Jax ever found out, he'd kill us both and, more importantly, I won't let you endanger yourself like that. I know you're almost recovered, but you can't jump the gun. So, get in the wheelchair or we're not going."

I scowl at her with as much frustration as I can muster but she doesn't react. "Fine," I mutter. "You win."

She smiles. "Good."

I get up off the bed and walk over to her, scowling the whole way. Then I sit down in the wheelchair, lifting my feet onto the supports like it's a bomb about to explode, and cross my arms again as I try not to think about it.

Blake smiles wider and wheels me out the door.

No one tries to stop us as Blake pushes me through the hospital wing. The nurses are too busy looking after countless other patients. It's then that I realize how serious the situation is in the city. I've never seen so many people in the hospital, but then again, I've only been here once before and this time around I haven't left my room. In fact, this will be the first time I've been out in the base for weeks.

It feels good to be free again, even if I am confined to the stupid wheeled contraption. Blake's probably right, though; my legs won't last long enough to get me to the dungeon and back. This is the best way, the only way, and if anybody says anything against me... Well, their death will be slow and painful, that I can promise.

I'm lucky Bast isn't here; he would never let me hear the end of this. Speaking of whom... "Blake," I say as we finally exit the hospital wing, "where's Bast?"

"That's a good question. I haven't seen him since last night at dinner."

Strange.

"You think he's okay?" I ask her.

"I don't see why not. I mean, he's Bast, a little reckless sure, but he can take care of himself. He's probably lying drunk somewhere after a trip to the Den."

"Did you check the Den?"

"I don't have time to look for him," she replies, "especially if he's drunk." She spits the words out, but I have a feeling the anger isn't reaching her eyes. I wish I could see her face.

Something tells me she's checked the Den and countless other spots, only to find nothing. She would never admit it, but I think she's worried. I don't call her out on it, though, and we continue in silence.

· · ·

It takes us twenty minutes to reach the dungeons, more than usual because of all the staircases we have to take as carefully as possible. A couple agents offer to help with them, but Blake assures them she can handle it. I'm sure she would welcome the help under normal circumstances, but she knows it would only wound my pride.

We reach the final stairwell that leads down to the cells and Blake comes to a stop.

Another agent stands at attention beside the doorway. He looks to be in his late thirties, a couple laugh lines on his face. "What are you ladies up to?" he asks us.

Blake holds her head high. "We're here to see the prisoner called Kuen."

The guard blinks. "He is not accepting visitors at this time."

I cross my arms. "You mean Jenson doesn't want anybody to talk to him."

"That's not for me to say."

I go to retort, but Blake places a hand on my arm. "Let me handle this."

I sigh and settle into the chair.

"I promise we mean no harm, George. Quinn here just wants to thank the prisoner for saving her life during the Guild attack. His incarceration is a huge misunderstanding that should be smoothed over soon. We'll only be a few minutes." She pulls her braid over her shoulder and blinks her eyes a few times.

After a moment, George lets out a long sigh. "Well, I suppose it's okay, but don't tell Jenson I let it happen, all right? I'll go let the guys know you're coming down."

Blake and I nod and he disappears through the door.

"Nice going, Blake," I say as I step out of the wheelchair.

"What are you doing?" she asks me.

"Just help me down this last staircase," I reply. "I'm not completely broken, you know. Besides, it saves you the trouble of having to manoeuvre that thing." I gesture at the wheelchair. "This staircase is rather steep, so it's probably safer to walk."

"If you say so," she says.

She comes over and wraps her left arm around my back and I drape my right arm over her shoulder.

George returns then and gives us a thumbs up. "You guys have ten minutes. I told the others to give you a respectable amount of space."

I resist the urge to raise an eyebrow.

Good thing I'm not up to something.

I turn to Blake. "Ready?"

"When you are."

Together we descend into the gloom, me hopping precariously on one foot and her supporting me so the shift in balance every few seconds doesn't send me tumbling. At the base of the stairs, we separate and walk freely side by side, boots scuffing against the dirt-strewn floor.

It doesn't take me long to locate Kuen. He's sitting against the wall in the same cell I occupied my first night here. It's oddly fitting. The dungeon's other two guards stand a couple cells down from his in either direction. They give us a nod before turning their attention back to him.

I walk over to the cell and wrap my hands around the bars, peering through them. The cold seeps into my skin and a shiver snakes through me. I forgot how damp this place is.

Blake lingers a few feet away, wanting to give me space.

"Kuen?" I say softly, thinking he might be sleeping.

He raises his head and looks right at me. "Hey." He drags himself to his feet and leans against the wall. "How's the leg?"

I shrug. "It isn't." I lift it up to show him the prosthetic, which doesn't shine at all in the dim light of the torches, just as Jax promised.

Kuen whistles. "I guess you really did do some damage."

"I would've died if they hadn't cut it off."

"Well, you look much better now," he says. "You're even walking."

"Yeah, I guess I am." I want to smile, but seeing him in that cell, I can't. He shouldn't be in there.

"What about you?" I ask him. "How are you holding up?"

He sighs. "I'm managing."

"You look like crap."

He rolls his eyes. "Thanks."

It's the truth. There are deep circles under his eyes and his hair is a mess, looking more brown than blond. His clothes are wrinkled and smudged with dirt and he slouches against the wall as if in pain but trying not to show it.

"You shouldn't have come with us," I say.

He shakes his head. "Don't even start. If I hadn't come, if I hadn't carried you here like a baby, you'd be dead. I don't regret my decision and neither should you. We can't take it back, and I wouldn't want to. I'm fine."

"But you shouldn't have to go through this," I protest.

"Yeah, well, your beloved leader thinks I should." He kicks at the dirt floor.

I snort. "Jenson is no friend of mine."

He looks up. "Is that so?"

"He treated me like dirt for months," I tell him, "still does. He tried to shoot me on sight when we returned and has wanted me dead since I first arrived here."

Kuen scowls. "He's definitely a bastard, but it's my own damn fault I'm still down here. I couldn't keep my mouth shut. He just... He talked to me like I was an idiot, like I was a child, instead of only ten years younger than him, and I guess… I guess I wanted to scare him, so I told him what rank I had as an assassin." He grins. "The man almost had a heart attack." He laughs and I want to laugh with him. I can picture Jenson's arrogant face...

I shiver. "You didn't tell him about your...relation did you?"

"Guild no," he says, eyes widening. "He'd shoot me on the spot, and besides, it's a lie anyway. I am *not* his son."

I know what he means, but denying it won't change the truth.

"Kuen, do you remember your mother?"

He raises an eyebrow. "Why?"

"I was just wondering."

"No," he sighs. "I don't. The Charger killed her before she knew me three days."

My heart clenches. "I'm sorry."

He shrugs. "It is what it is."

"Do you ever wish she was still alive, that you'd known her?"

I run my fingers across the bars, using the frigid metal to ground me, to keep images of my own mother at bay. I may have rid myself of my fear of pillows, but it doesn't mean the memories don't haunt me still, every now and then.

"What difference would it make?" he replies. "The Charger always gets what he wants."

I clench my fist around a bar. "Sephtis, Kuen. His name is Sephtis."

He narrows his eyes. "Who told you that?"

"I overheard him once. Who told *you*?"

"He did," he mutters. "It's my middle name."

"What?"

He lets out a heavy breath. "Sephtis is my middle name. He gave it to me, expecting me to be his perfect assassin…his prodigy."

I shudder, remembering how he had called me that too, the night I tried to kill him.

"Well, you're not," I tell him, "not anymore. Neither am I. Maybe we once were, but that time is over. We will destroy him, Kuen. I promise you that."

"Unless he destroys us first," he mutters. "Sometimes I wonder if one day I'll wake up back at the Guild, back under his fist, and regret everything I've done to get away. What if I lose myself?" He looks at his hands, as if blood is dripping from his fingers, and shudders.

"Trey and I will drag you back," I assure him, "dead or alive."

He smiles. "You promise?"

"On my life."

I think of something else then and I'm not sure if I should bring it up, but it's not like I can discuss it with anyone else, not anyone who would understand. "Do you think Hai could've had a chance?" I ask him.

"You're feeling guilty about killing him," he says. His eyes are sad.

I scrape my boot across the floor and nod. "I know I shouldn't, not after he tried to kill me, but…"

"Hai never had a chance in hell, Quinn," Kuen assures me. "He and Anane were too wrapped around their father's finger."

My stomach drops. "*Anane?*"

"Oh," he says, "I forgot you didn't know."

"Why didn't you tell me?" My skin is crawling at the news.

Kuen waves a hand. "It wasn't relevant."

I want to argue, but I bite my tongue.

Not relevant, my ass. Anane was the bane of my existence back at the Guild and now he's my brother.

That must be why he treated me like dirt.

"Unfortunately, it's true," Kuen goes on, "Why do you think Anane is such a suck-up? Not to mention his temper; that's completely inherited."

"Are there any others I don't know about?" I ask, afraid to know the answer.

"No," he replies. "It's just us five: me, Hai, Trey, Anane, and you. Well, I guess four now."

"I broke his leg."

He frowns. "Who?"

"Anane," I say. "When I fled from the Guild, the Charg— Sephtis sent Anane and Three after me. I shot Three and finally lost Anane on the iron bridge. He slipped and fell. I didn't look back, but Hai told me he got a broken leg for his trouble and a three-spot demotion. Anane deserved it, the bastard that he is, but Hai... Are you certain he was a lost cause?"

"Positive," Kuen replies. "You fought him; I'm sure you could tell where his loyalties lay. Anane might be cruel, Quinn, but Hai was psychotic. He was obsessed with you; he talked about breaking your fingers one by one or skinning you alive. He hated you, wanted you dead ever since Sephtis named you his heir. Hai never understood why Sephtis would give everything to you— you who didn't even know he was your father. Hai and Anane were the only ones who ever referred to him as such. Two sides of the same coin they were; unfailingly loyal. Trey and I, on the other hand, defected before it was too late. Hai would've never betrayed his father. Killing him, it was a kindness. He's free now and the world is free from him."

"But—"

"You need to stop worrying over it," he says. I have a feeling he would've grabbed my arms if he wasn't on the other side of the bars. "Hai wouldn't think twice about it if it was the other way around."

"But I'm not him, Kuen."

"And you never will be. So let it go."

I scowl. "You're not helping."

He scowls back. "That's what Trey keeps telling me. 'Shut up,' she says, 'you're not helping.' Well, I can't possibly be making things any worse." He crosses his arms, seeming to curl into himself, to retreat.

"Look," I say, "I'm sorry. I'm sorry you're in here. I'm sorry Jenson wants to kill you. I'm sorry I have such a short temper."

"Don't apologize for things you can't change," he mutters.

"Trey's petitioning for a trial," I tell him, trying to change the subject, "for your release."

"I know," he says. "I'm not sure what good it will do."

"Maybe it'll get you out of here so you can change your attitude," I snap. "I see my past self in you and trust me, it isn't pretty."

How can he give up already?

"Well, you know what I see in you?" he counters.

I glare at him. "What?"

"I see a scared little child."

Something in me cracks and I see a girl through the space, chasing a butterfly in a flower garden...

I shut that thought down.

"That child is not at home," I mutter. "She died a long time ago. I spent a great deal of time burying her and even more time trying to bring her back." I take my hand from the bar of his cell and look my brother straight in the eyes. "You have no idea what I'm like, Kuen, and if you don't change your attitude, you may never get the chance to learn."

I turn around and head back to Blake.

I'm almost to the stairs when Kuen calls out, "Wait!"

I pivot. "What?"

He's standing against the cell door, arms wrapped around the outside of the bars. "I'm an idiot, okay?" he says. "And I'm sorry. I just... I worry about what will happen if they don't agree to a release. If they sentence me to death, Trey will try to save me, but I can't let her get hurt. She risks herself all the time, I don't know if you've noticed. She has so many regrets, so much guilt locked inside her and she throws herself into impossible situations hoping she'll get hurt so the pain can distract her from her past." He squeezes the bars until his knuckles whiten. "Quinn, if I die, you have to look after her."

"You're not going to die."

His hand falls. "Promise me, Quinn."

Something in his eyes keeps me from hesitating. "I promise."

"Thank you." He slumps to the floor, energy leaving him, and I know it's time to go. I can sense when someone wants to be left alone with their thoughts.

I glance at the guards. Well, alone as he can be.

I grab Blake's arm and we head up the stairs, leaving Kuen to his misery...misery he must withstand on his own.

Blake pulls her arm out of my grasp when we reach the top of the stairs and grabs my shoulder. "What was that all about? Why is he an idiot?"

I grimace and walk down the hall a bit so George can't overhear our conversation. "I'm sorry you couldn't hear the whole story. It's probably for the best, but there's something..." I let out a heavy breath. "There's something I haven't told you, something I'm still having trouble admitting. Kuen and I couldn't even say it outright. A pair of cowards, we are," I mutter, the taste of defeat bitter on my tongue.

"No," she stops me, halting the narrative in my head before I can really get going. She gives me a sympathetic look. "Not cowards, Si—Quinn. Just human. It's human to feel these emotions, to want to hide things about ourselves that we don't like. I get it. It's still hard for me to talk about you know what."

"I know, but this..." I close my eyes and rub my temples. "It isn't even the same thing. I'm being ridiculous really. I don't want to be judged, but how can you be any more disturbed? You know the extent of my kills. I assassinated Jax's mother and he forgave me. Why is this so hard?"

She gives me a sad smile, her grip on my shoulder tightening, as if to steady me. "Because you're judging yourself, Quinn," she replies. "Every time I thought about telling the boys what I did to my ex, I would stop myself, not because I thought they would hate me. I stopped because I told myself I was worthless, stupid. I hated myself and a part of me still feels that way." She lets her hand fall. "Don't do that to yourself. It makes it worse."

I take a deep breath, her words settling the storm within me. She's right; I've been condemning myself ever since I heard the news. "I can trust you, right?" I ask her.

"Of course."

"Then you should know the Master Assassin is my father."

She nods. "You and Kuen were skipping around it and I couldn't hear everything, but I thought as much."

I tense. "You're not...scared of me, are you?"

The fact that she is still here is evidence to the contrary, but I still can't help but wonder.

I wouldn't blame her for it.

Sometimes, I scare *myself*.

She snorts. "Why should I be? You've always been his daughter, Quinn. Knowing it now doesn't change a thing. Sure, some things may make more sense now that you can trace the genes back, but you're not him. Parentage means nothing if you don't let them influence you. Don't let him change you now."

I can feel tears building up in my eyes, but I blink them back. "You're amazing, Blake. You know that, right?"

She smiles. "Thanks."

"I've been worried about it all this time," I go on, "but you're right. Why should knowing about it make any difference in my life?"

"It shouldn't," she says, "and nothing comes from dwelling on it either. I always wondered who I would be if my parents had raised me, but what good does that wondering do? I am who I am and I wouldn't have it any other way."

"What happened to your parents?" I ask her.

"They were assassinated while trying to save a family from a house fire some assassins had set. I was one."

"Did the family survive?"

She smiles. "They did. There were other agents on the mission and my parents were able to distract the assassins long enough for the family to get to safety."

"Do you…?"

"Ever wish my parents survived instead?" she finishes.

I nod.

"I used to," she admits, "but I soon learned that dwelling on what could've been does nothing." She sighs. "We should get back to the hospital before Jax returns."

"Agreed," I say. We head back towards George, thanking him for his hospitality, and I hop into the wheelchair. "Step on it," I tell her.

She grins like a maniac and grabs the handles. "Hold on," she says and then she starts running.

We race down the straight aways and careen around corners, almost colliding with a group of caretakers and a retired agent on our way. The latter waves his cane at us like a gun as we speed off, the closest he can get to it these days. We are laughing so hard by the time we reach the hospital wing that my sides hurt. We sneak past the nurses, trying our best to look innocent. As soon as we close the door of my room behind us, we erupt into giggles again.

Now *this* is life; I'm so glad I didn't lose it.

CHAPTER NINE

Hours spill into lifetimes when you're waiting for someone important to come home. Blake tries to distract me, but it only works for so long. She's worried too. Bast still hasn't come along and Blake's tapping fingers across the bedpost are starting to drive me crazy. She cares more about Bast than I think she'll ever admit. I'm beginning to wonder if the two of them aren't more than friends, and if I'm the only one who's noticed.

Finally, when I'm about ready to scream, the door flies open.

I jump to my feet. "Forget it, Jax," I snap, "there is no way I'm letting you out of my sight again. I've been sick with…" I trail off as I realize it's Trey standing in the doorway, not Jax.

She's covered in dirt, ash, and…

My breath catches in my throat, my heart stuttering in my chest.

"Please tell me that isn't *your* blood."

"Some of it," she admits, "but mostly it's..." She winces. "You guys better come with me."

Blake and I share a wide-eyed look.

Oh God.

"What happened?" I ask Trey. I can feel my blood pressure rising as I put two and two together.

"No time to explain." She pivots on one boot and heads out the door again.

Blake and I race after her.

My gait is a little bit awkward given our speed, but luckily, we don't have to go far. Trey leads us into the critical ward and over to a curtained section around two beds.

Two.

Oh please no.

Trey pushes past the blue curtains with Blake and I trailing in her wake and we finally see what I suspected.

Jax and Bast lie unconscious in the beds. Bast is covered in blood and Jax's arm is soaked. Both of them are cloaked in ash and dirt like Trey.

I freeze just inside the curtains.

The room is spinning.

Blake gasps, covering her mouth with her hands, and runs over to the beds, to Bast's side first. She sits on the edge of the bed carefully and, after a moment of hesitation, takes his hand.

I can't even smile at it. Instead, I whirl on Trey. "What the hell happened?" My heart is stuttering as if trapped in a vise.

Please let them be okay.

Trey grimaces under the weight of my glare. "We were ambushed."

"By who?" I fold my arms across my chest, as if to hold myself together.

She rings her hands. "Assassins, citizens, we don't know," she replies, "but I couldn't watch both of them and keep my own life intact too. Someone started another damn fire and one of the houses that caught had children trapped in it. A young couple came running, screaming for the kids. These two idiots," she points her thumb at Bast and Jax, "had to run into the burning building and save the day."

I take a deep breath.

Of course. Of course *they did.*

"Are they okay? The children?"

She waves a hand. "Yeah, they're fine, but these two... They never should've pulled a stunt like that."

"Trey," I argue. "It's their job."

"It's their job to stay alive too," she snaps, the stress of the morning getting to her. "We're already low enough on soldiers. We can't afford to pull them out of the field, but I think we might have to."

"Nonsense," a familiar voice says, interrupting my response, "they'll be fine." I turn to see Shirley pushing her way through the curtains. "You're way too dramatic, Ms. Trey. Mr. Forrester merely has a nasty gash on his arm and some superficial burns; nothing I can't fix. He's not in any danger of amputation or permanent damage." She gives me a look, watching as I visibly relax. "And

Blake," she adds, causing Blake to look up, "Sebastian's going to be fine."

I raise an eyebrow, surprised to hear Shirley addressing them—addressing anyone for that matter—by their first names.

"But there's so much blood," Blake protests, sniffing. Her eyes glisten with unshed tears.

"He hit his head," Shirley tells her. "Head injuries bleed a lot, but are rarely as dangerous as they look. He'll be right as rain in no time. You'll see."

Blake doesn't reply.

I worry she might be cutting off the circulation in Bast's hand.

"Now," Shirley goes on, straightening her shirt and rolling up her sleeves, "if the three of you would leave me to my job, the healing will get done a lot sooner."

"I..." My protest dies out as I see Jax's eyes flutter open.

"Quinn," he breathes.

"Jax," I exclaim. "I'm here. It's okay." I run to his side, pushing past Shirley who tries to pull me back.

His eyes meet mine and he smiles. "Hey."

I brush the hair out of his eyes. "We have to stop meeting like this," I say.

He smiles wider, but then closes his eyes again.

"Jax?" I whisper, worry creeping back in.

"He's fine," Shirley assures me. "He just needs his rest and the three of you need to get out. Now."

"But—" Blake and I protest.

Shirley gives Trey a look and Trey grabs me by the arm.

"Hey," I say. "Let go!"

She ignores me and drags me back to my hospital room, locking the door behind her as she leaves.

"Let me out, Trey!" I growl, throwing myself against the door. I feel a few things pop in my shoulder, but ignore the sensation.

Nothing happens.

I swing my foot at it next, mostly in frustration, but my metal appendage merely leaves a dent in the wood and I bite back a cry of despair as something twinges in my knee.

I am weak. Useless.

I blink back tears.

"Please, Trey," I mumble. "I swear on my life..." But my fire has lost its fury.

The doorknob clicks and the door opens again. I try to shove my way through, my last attempt, but Trey pushes Blake in and closes the door again.

A final click seals us in.

My anger sinks to the bottom of my mind and I fall back onto the bed.

Shirley said they'll be fine. Listen.

Blake leans against the door, forehead pressed into it, and says nothing.

I throw an arm over my eyes in worried exhaustion. "Was this what Jax was like back when I broke my leg for the first time?" I wonder aloud.

Blake sighs and comes to join me on the bed. We lie side by side in the small space and I find myself wishing I had found her friendship sooner.

"No," she says, answering my question, "he was much worse. When he wasn't muttering your name or 'please' over and over again, he said nothing. His silence almost drove me to madness. I wanted to hit him, see if he even noticed. He really loves you, you know."

"Yeah." I let out a resigned sigh. "I know."

His love is there every time he saves my life. It's there in the way he looks at me like I'm not a monster, a killer. It was there when he came back for me at the Guild, in the way he can't seem to let me go.

I think back to the soft kiss before he left this morning, a small promise that things were getting better.

I take a staggering breath, blinking back more wretched tears.

Please be okay.

"He came to me for advice back before you guys got together," Blake goes on.

Her soft voice shakes me from my thoughts and I turn my head to look at her. "He did?"

"Yeah," she says. "He came up to me one day and said, 'Blake, I know you don't like to talk about it, but what does love feel like?'"

I raise a curious brow. "What did you tell him?"

She looks at the ceiling as she answers, but there is a joy in her face I haven't seen before. "I told him that it's everything—even life itself. It's sunshine and rain, beauty and pain, a fullness and an emptiness all at once. It's feeling like you're jumping off a cliff into unknown waters and hoping they won't let you drown. It's terror at rejection and excitement at becoming something more. It's vulnerability and strength. Love is a miracle."

"What did he say to that?"

She looks at me, a smile lighting up her face. "He said, 'I think I'm in love with her.'"

I don't know how to reply. My heart feels so full. Blake has described love perfectly and now I know Jax and I feel the same, have always felt the same. He knew he loved me long before I could admit it.

I want to break down the door and run to him.

I want to tell him he is my strength, my miracle, that I care for him more than anything in this world and never want to jeopardize our relationship again.

Yet, I stay where I am, not because I'm scared, but because I know he has to heal and it'll be easier for the nurses if I'm not sobbing over him the whole time.

I can wait, and if I know Jax at all, he already knows these things. He knows my heart better than I do.

Instead, I look up at the ceiling and say, "Bast will be okay, Blake."

"What?" She looks at me sharply, clearly caught off guard by my statement.

"Bast," I repeat, making sure she heard me. "Bast will be okay."

"Oh, yeah," she says dismissively, "I know." Her tone is off and I know she's hiding something. "I can't believe he went on that mission with Jax and Trey. What was he thinking?"

I shrug, though she isn't looking. "Maybe he knew Jax couldn't do it alone. Maybe he was as tired of inaction as the rest of us."

She sighs. "I just wish they'd ask me to go too. Trey might not be able to watch their backs and her own, but that's been my job since day one."

I place a hand on her arm. "I don't think they'll make the mistake again. From the state of them, they wouldn't have survived childhood without you."

She laughs. "You don't know the half of it."

We lie there in silence until we hear yet another click and the door swings open a crack. Trey pokes her head into the room. "You can see them now."

"Oh thank God," Blake replies.

I follow her as she leaves the room to join the guys again, practically skipping in her haste. My steps are slow but sure, still getting used to the movement.

The curtains still hang around the beds, but Bast and Jax are sitting up in bed and two chairs are waiting at their bedsides.

Bast is the first to speak, as always. "So, ladies," he says, "how do I look?"

Shirley must've washed his face, but the rest of him is still caked in dirt and dust. He has a bandage wrapped around his head, half covering his left eye. His long brown hair is matted and sticking up in so many places.

"Honestly," I reply, "you look like crap."

Jax snorts.

"And I'd say it's an improvement," Blake adds.

Jax and I dissolve into a fit of laughter, which soon turns into a coughing one for him, due to the smoke inhalation. I run over and pat his back for him until he can breathe easy again. He's looking pretty rough too, his whole left arm lost to bandages.

"Seriously though," I say, "how are the two of you feeling?"

"Sore, but okay," Bast replies.

Jax nods. "My lungs feel like they're on fire, but other than that…"

I give him a sympathetic smile. "You'll bounce back in no time. I'm just glad that for once I'm not the one in the worst shape."

Jax shakes his head and Bast comes back with, "Says the girl with half a leg missing."

"I can easily make us match, Sebastian," I retort.

His eyes narrow to slits as he scowls at me.

I smile back.

"I don't think he needs more disabilities," Blake retorts. "He has more bandages on his head right now than he has brains in it."

Bast scowls at Blake instead. "You're just mad you missed all the action."

"No, I'm wondering what made the two of you so stupid as to go without me."

Jax winces, but Bast crosses his arms. "We don't need you to protect us."

"Says the guy covered in his own blood," she counters.

"It wasn't our choice to leave you behind, Blake," Jax says, trying to diffuse the tension. "Trey was the one who brought Bast along."

"Regardless," she replies, crossing her arms. "You should've told me what was going on."

Bast shrugs. "Quinby would've filled you in."

"About Jax, yes," I reply, "but I didn't know you had gone as well, *Seb*."

"Exactly," Blake interjects. "We were worried sick about you."

I raise a brow at the mention of we.

Sure, I was curious as to where Bast was, but I wasn't concerned, at least not until he came back bruised and broken.

Jax rubs his head. "Look, Blake, we're sorry. Isn't that enough?"

"It shouldn't be," she retorts, tugging at the end of her braid. She steals a glance at Bast and then takes a long breath. "Listen, the three of us are supposed to be a team, right?"

Jax and Bast nod.

"And when you're a team," she goes on, "you keep your members in the loop. I shouldn't have to find out about your whereabouts from Trey, *after* you've gone and got yourselves torn up. I shouldn't have to wonder whether or not you need me or if I should be somewhere I'm not. And I certainly shouldn't have been left with the guilt."

Bast cocks his head. "Guilt?"

"Yes, guilt," she snaps at him. "What if you two had died out there? How do you think I would've felt? We grew up together; you guys are the only family I have. I would've spent the rest of my life agonizing over it, wondering if you would've lived if I'd only been there to help you."

There are tears in her eyes and a tremble to her limbs.

I reach out to touch her arm, but then hesitate. If it was me, I would only shrug off the contact.

"I would've blamed myself," Blake finishes. "That's why I'm upset. You may not need me to protect you, but that's what family does. So please, don't keep me in the dark."

There is silence for a minute.

Blake sniffs and wipes at her eyes with the back of her sleeve.

Jax leans toward her, wincing at the pain of the movement. "I'm so sorry we put you through that, Blake. That was never our intention. If I had thought… Well, I guess that's the problem, isn't it? We didn't think."

Blake nods and I put a hand on her shoulder this time. She leans into me.

Bast scratches at his bandages. "Yeah I… I didn't realize you felt that way."

I roll my eyes at his attempt at an apology.

Poor Bast. Words are not his strong suit.

Blake takes another deep breath. "I'm not going to beat this argument to a pulp. I just thought you two should see it from my perspective. I'm glad you're both okay."

"So am I," I add, squeezing her shoulder.

The tension in the room dissipates.

I walk over and sit on the edge of Jax's bed. "All right, boys, why don't you tell us about your adventure then?"

I give Blake an encouraging smile.

She sighs and takes a seat on Bast's bed. "This had better be good."

Her words are harsh, but her tone is more lighthearted than before, a smile tugging at the corners of her lips.

Bast launches into the tale of their grand rescue, in his element now that the mood has changed.

I smile, glad my friends can settle their disagreements and move forward together. Their team has endured a lot of strife since my addition to it, but I know they will remain strong in spite of everything.

• • •

The four of us talk for a while until the nurses come to shoo us away again, telling us the boys need their rest.

I swear, if one more person mentions rest to me, they're going to experience the eternal kind. I kiss Jax quickly on the forehead and walk away. Blake gives Bast a long, yearning look while his head is turned and then follows me out.

I lead her through the hospital wing, away from the critical ward and back towards the long-term care section where I spent the last few weeks. We come to a stop and lean against a random wall, contemplating life's miseries and miracles. Joking aside, Jax and Bast are lucky to be alive. I chided Jax for watching over me like a hawk, but after this, I can't blame him.

Blake's voice interrupts my thoughts. "I should go. You need…"

"I swear on my life, if you say rest, I will end you."

Silence.

She crosses her arms. "I wasn't going to say it."

I scowl. "Sure you weren't."

"I wasn't."

I roll my eyes. "Uh huh."

"I was going to say you need…" She searches for words. "…to get back to your room…before the nurses start looking for you."

I snort. "Sure you were, and to hell with the nurses. I'm pretty much done with this place. A couple more days and I'll be leaving it, roaming around the rest of the base with you guys. Freedom will never feel so sweet."

"I bet."

Silence again.

"Can I ask you something, Blake?"

She looks over. "Of course."

I just go for it, and hope she doesn't hate me after. "How long have you liked Bast?"

"I... What?" she stammers.

"Bast, how long have you liked him?"

She hugs her arms to her chest. "I don't know what you're talking about."

"Blake, don't bother lying to me. I see the way you look at him."

"The way I look at him… Quinn, I barely tolerate his stupidity."

I give her a look. "Blake."

"No," she snaps. "I do not like Bast...not like that! It's a ridiculous question."

"Oh come on," I protest, throwing my arms out.

"No, you come on," she counters. "Are you walking around half-blind? You've seen the two of us together."

"I'm not the blind one here, Blake," I reply.

"I'm done with this conversation," she retorts, pushing away from the wall. "Our next one better make more sense." She storms off without another word.

I let out a groan and look to the ceiling, at the loose speckled tiles and bright lights.

Nice job, genius.

I know the truth now, even if she can't admit it to herself, but I can't help feeling it shouldn't have come out this way. Love is a sore subject for Blake, after everything she's been through, and after her argument with Bast and Jax earlier, it's no wonder she's afraid to act. She cares for Bast so much it's causing her pain. She's afraid that if she pursues him, she'll lose one of the only friends and family she has.

Guess it's easier to throw me away than admit I'm right.

Bast means more to her, but I don't fault her for it for a second.

If it was a choice between her and Jax…

Guild, it's a choice I hope I never have to make.

I want to help Blake, but I doubt she'll let me now. I'm not even sure I could give her good advice. Jax and I hated each other when we first met, and while Blake and Bast bicker constantly, it's not the same.

I sigh.

My life is a disaster. What's another mess?

Right?

Maybe tomorrow will be brighter, will bring another chance.

Sighing once more, I push off the wall and return to my room to get some *rest*.

CHAPTER TEN

Three days later, the boys are released from the hospital wing. Jax returns to hovering over me and Bast is free to roam again.

Despite our argument, Blake came back every day to see how they were doing, though she only spoke to Bast and Jax and half the time the curtain hung as a barrier between us.

I don't think the argument will ruin our friendship, but I hope it opened Blake's eyes. There's no use hiding your love; life is way too short for that. I tell myself she'll come around soon and we'll be thick as thieves once again.

Life is also too short to spend too much of it in a hospital, but the nurses say a couple more days. They've been saying a couple more days for a week. I'm getting restless, itching to do something—anything. If I stay here much longer, one of them is going to end up with an IV needle in the eye, and that's not me being dramatic.

Freedom comes earlier than expected, when Trey bursts into the room one afternoon.

"Night!" she exclaims, leaning over with her hands on her knees, trying to catch her breath. She finally looks up to see me scowling. "Whoops, sorry," she huffs. "I meant Quinn. I'm a little frazzled today."

"Why are you out of breath?" Jax asks her. His left arm is still in a sling to keep him from tearing his stitches.

"I ran all the way here," she replies. "Jenson finally agreed to the trial."

"Really?" I exclaim. "Trey, that's awesome!"

She crosses her arms. "Yes, well it would be even better if Jenson hadn't waited until the last second to tell me. He's holding the trial in fifteen minutes."

I stiffen. "For the love of... I'm going to kill him one of these days."

She straightens up. "I hear you, sister. He's trying to throw me off, make me flustered, in hopes that I'll screw up my case. Little does he know that I expected him to pull something like this and have never been more prepared in my life."

I grin. "Jenson hasn't learned his lesson yet."

She gives me a questioning look.

"Never underestimate an ex-assassin," I say.

"Too right. Anyway," she sighs, "I just thought I'd let you know. I better get down there, in case Jenson tries to start without me. You'll come, right?"

"Of course," I reply, shocked that she would think I wouldn't. "If anything will put Jenson on edge, it'll be my presence and we wouldn't want him to be at peace, now would we?"

It's her turn to grin. "Certainly not. Well, I have to run. See you in a few." She waves and then darts out the door again. Her footsteps echo in the hall as she runs off.

I stand up. "All right, how are we getting there, Jax? Does this outfit look okay? Am I even standing straight?" I lean over and brush some lint off my pants.

"Quinn," Jax says.

"You're right," I agree, "I'm being ridiculous. Even if I don't look okay, there's no time to change. We better get going. Oh I can't wait to see the look on Jenson's face when he…"

"Quinn," Jax says again, more forceful this time.

I turn around. "What?"

"You can't go."

I frown. "What do you mean?"

He hesitates a moment before saying, "You're not ready."

"Like hell I'm not," I retort. "I can *go* wherever I like." *Where is this coming from?*

He scratches the back of his head. "Okay, that's not what I meant. You are perfectly capable of going, but I don't think you should."

"Why not?"

He isn't making any sense.

"Because..." Again he struggles, as if he's not sure if he should tell me the truth. "Because I don't think it's worth your time or energy."

I feel the blood drain from my face at the shock of his words.

"Why would you say that?" My voice is cold, empty. "This is my brother's freedom we're talking about, his *life*. How is this not important?"

He shifts on his feet. "That's not what I'm saying. I just... Your presence at this trial isn't going to change the verdict. It's not worth the risk of injuring yourself again. You should stay back here and rest."

"I am sick of resting," I spit, resisting the urge to curl my fists. "I should be there to support my brother."

"Why?" he demands to know. "He was never there for *you*."

Silence.

Silence as I try to think of something decent to say, as I try to suffocate the urge to wrap my hand around his throat and shake him until he sees sense.

"Jax..." I take a breath, my body trembling from both rage and disappointment. "That's not fair."

My tone is uneven, my teeth nearly bared.

He better choose his next words carefully.

He throws out a hand, his other still bound by the sling. "Isn't it? He left you alone with a monster for thirteen years—both of them did—and now they want to be a part of your life?" His eyes darken. "They're cowards."

Irritation creeps under my skin, sending a prickly sensation through my veins.

"People can change, Jax," I say, trying to keep my voice calm. "Look at me."

"That's different."

"How?" I ask, throwing out my own arms. "How in the hell is it okay for me to change, but not them? I don't fault them for their past mistakes, neither should you."

"Don't tell me how to feel, Quinn," he snaps back. "Maybe in your world it's all right to welcome back those who abandoned you with open arms, but in my world, if people care, they stay."

"You're impossible," I growl. "I'm going to that trial and I don't care what you or anyone else says about it. Are you going to help me or not?"

He crosses his free arm over his sling. "I won't."

"Assassin's below... I can't believe you. I'll get there myself."

"Quinn..."

I ignore him and head for the door.

His hand closes around my wrist before I can grab the doorknob. "Don't," he says. "He's not worth it."

I can't bear to look at him. "And once upon a time, neither was I."

"Quinn, please."

"I'm going, Ajax, and you're not going to stop me. Now let go of me."

"I—"

"Let go!" I rip my wrist from his hand and fling the door open before he can reach for me again. I hear it bang against the wall as I half-run through the hospital wing.

He doesn't follow.

I veer around a corner and nearly trip over an abandoned stretcher, grabbing onto the wall to keep myself from sprawling across the floor.

There is a dull pain in my leg, but I ignore it.

I take a slower pace through the rest of the hospital, but break into a run again when I leave it behind.

Guild help whoever dares to cross me today. Jenson is toast and I can already smell him burning.

• • •

I remember exactly where the trial room is, despite the chaos of my last visit there. I arrive with five minutes to spare and I can feel the exhaustion in every limb. Still, I decide I'm not going to spend another night in that infernal hospital. It's too confining. Everyone tells me I can't fly, but they haven't given me a chance to spread my wings and try.

I'm tired of being grounded.

The trial room door is wide open and I cling to it for a moment as I catch my breath and survey the scene before me.

The tiered seats are nearly full; the trial must be open to everyone. Agents, young and old, lounge on the hard wooden benches. I even notice a young woman bouncing a baby on her knee. The room is a sea of grey against the white-washed cement walls.

I spot Jenson in the front row, directly across the room from Trey who sits in the front row below me. She's dressed in her all-black Resistance uniform with red cape, the outfit she was wearing when we first met at the Guild and her long black hair is pulled up in a high ponytail, making her look even taller. She and Jenson are staring each other down and don't notice my entrance; no one does.

Feeling secure in my anonymity, I slip onto the bench in the top row, glad to be off my feet. I have the best view in the room.

As I sit, my eyes flick to the person I've been avoiding so far.

Kuen sits alone in the middle of the room, chained to the same chair I occupied during my first visit here. I guess Jenson *has* learned from his mistakes. Kuen has no chance of escaping, unless he's as good as he says he is.

I watch him fidget in his seat, as much as he can with all the chains weighing him down. He doesn't look happy. He looks as if he's already given up.

Assassins below, Kuen, did you learn nothing at the Guild?

Watching him—seeing him defeated so easily—has my blood boiling.

I turn back to Jenson and notice a familiar face at his side. Nicholas Ross is wearing the same outfit as Trey and I realize they must signify their status as Avery and Jenson's Seconds. Trey wears hers better.

I glare across the room at Ross and notice something else.

Why, if it isn't her highness.

Natalie Sophia Roseanne sits on the bench beside her father, dwarfed by his shadow. She looks fragile, but in a way that makes her seem already broken. I study her closer and notice several things amiss. She's paler than usual, slouching in her seat, her head hanging down as if in shame. Her golden hair has even lost some of its lustre. Gone is the high and mighty princess. What happened to her?

For once, I feel sorry for her and...guilty.

Did I do this?

Jenson stands up then and I tear my gaze away from Natalie. The room settles into silence. He waits a few more moments before he speaks.

"We are gathered here today to discuss the fate of our most recent prisoner, who goes by the name of Kuen, though he held many titles as a 'former' assassin. Can we be assured he has left behind his old ways? At the moment, it is uncertain, but this trial will ensure the safety of the Resistance as a whole and all those who call it home."

Concerned murmuring fills the room and I cross my arms, a scowl taking up residence on my face.

Selfish bastard.

"Avery Norin's Second, Trey, will be forming the defense for the accused," Jenson goes on. "My Second, Nicholas Ross, will stand as the opposition."

Ross grins and I feel sick.

This does not bode well.

"Trey," Jenson says, "you may proceed."

Trey stands and it takes longer for the audience to quiet this time.

I can hear whispers about how dangerous Kuen looks, whispers wondering why Trey is offering a defence for the monster, whispers of why he hasn't already been killed.

My skin bristles at each one and I try to ignore them.

Trey sounds a two-note whistle and finally succeeds in rendering the room silent.

"Hello, everyone," she starts. "I thank you all for coming today. Most of you know who I am, but I will introduce myself for those who don't. My name is Trey and I am the right hand woman of Avery, our illustrious leader. Most of you know me as a strong, independent, responsible, and hard-working person. I have fought against our enemies like no other, earning myself a place as Avery's Second. You know me as a dedicated Resistance member." She pauses and takes a long look around the room. "However, none of you know about my past and I am sorry to have kept it from you." She fiddles with the hem of her coat. "The man chained to the chair in front of us is my brother and once upon a time I was an assassin alongside him."

The cries of outrage from the audience reverberate off the walls and my eardrums. They remind me of the citizens with their pitchforks and torches. Ready to condemn first and ask questions later.

"Hear me out, hear me out!" Trey yells, her voice carrying over the ruckus. "This has always been my past. Do not fault me for it now. I am not who I was. I changed and Kuen can do the same. Isn't this what we are all about?" Her voice is pleading and I can tell it pains her to reveal the truth about herself, but that she is willing to do whatever it takes to save our brother.

Silence falls and in it, Jenson speaks. "That is all well and good, Trey, but you have proven yourself. Kuen has not."

"It took me years to prove myself, Jenson," Trey points out. "Kuen has yet to be given a chance to do so. You cannot doom him without first seeing his potential."

Jenson ignores her words. "Is that the extent of your case, Trey?"

She shakes her head. "Kuen may have killed in the past, but I can also prove he has saved people. He has saved my life many times, though I know that is not a strong enough argument, considering my relation to him. Last month, however, Kuen led me into the Guild to save the assassin, Silent Night, and our fellow Resistance member, Ajax Forrester, who had been captured by the Master Assassin. Without him, they both would be lost."

"A...wise observation," Jenson says. "Do you have testimonies from the alleged rescuees?"

Trey hangs her head and Jenson smiles.

My stomach turns.

"No, sir," Trey says. "I do not."

"I see. Well, thank you for your words. You may be seat—"

"Wait," I yell out, jumping to my feet. I'm standing before realizing I want to do it.

Jenson's eyes lock on me immediately and the entire room follows suit.

I've never felt so scrutinized.

"Assassin," Jenson calls out. "What a...pleasure to see you. I trust you aren't trying to waste my time?"

A couple of the men around him laugh.

I take a deep breath to calm the rage within me.

No turning back now.

I hold my head high as I say, "My name is Quinn Marie Ballinger and I would like to stand as a witness to Trey's claims."

Jenson laughs this time, holding an arm to his chest. "You want to be her witness? Have you forgotten who you are? Your loyalty is as questionable as that of the accused."

I bristle. Guess our conversation a couple weeks back meant nothing. He's still going to let the other agents think I'm useless and untrustworthy.

Trey holds up a gloved hand. "Let her speak. Whether or not you believe what she says, she has the right to say it."

Jenson narrows his eyes at her, but says nothing more.

Trey nods up to me.

"During the Guild attack, I was captured by the Master Assassin," I start.

Whispers start up again and I can see the shock on the faces of the agents seated directly below me. I recognize one of them as the bartender from the Den. I wonder what he thinks of me.

"The Master Assassin made some demands in exchange for my life, but I refused, so he left me to drown in a glass tank. Kuen saved me with his knowledge of the Guild and the Master Assassin himself. And that is not all. I contracted a lethal infection from my injuries and Kuen carried me across Haven from our safe house to the Resistance so the nurses here could save me. I would not be standing here today without him."

Every face in the room seems touched by my words. I see a few people looking at Kuen with softer eyes, until Jenson breaks the silence.

"So you claim," he says.

I nod. "So I claim, but the great thing about freedom, is that you get to choose. Each person in this room gets to choose whether or not to believe me or you or Trey. Belief is an individual choice that you cannot control."

Jenson sets his jaw. "Well, thank you for your words, Assassin. We will now proceed with the opposition. Nicholas, if you will."

Trey and I remain standing as Nicholas gets to his feet. He walks past Jenson, down a couple steps to the trial room floor, and stops in front of Kuen, though facing the crowd.

"This man," Ross starts, "is an assassin. Before he 'left' the Guild, he was Assassin Agent One, right under the Master Assassin himself. Trey speaks of his *potential* and the other assassin speaks of his so-called good deeds, but I wonder about his potential to destroy us all."

The room takes a breath.

Ross turns to face Kuen, who barely looks up. "You stand accused of countless murders during your thirty-one years, both Resistance members and citizens alike. Do you deny these charges?"

Kuen stares at him. For a minute, I don't think he'll answer, but then he says, "I do not."

"So you admit you are a criminal, a murderer?" Ross goes on.

"I do," Kuen replies, no expression on his face.

"Then why do you sit here before us and ask to be pardoned?" Ross demands to know. He looks at Kuen as if he is a worm to be crushed underfoot.

"I ask for forgiveness," Kuen says. "I ask for compassion. I ask for a fresh start. I know what I have done. I don't pretend to be different than I am."

"And yet, you think your deeds can be forgotten? You expect us to believe it won't happen again?"

"I don't expect anything, Ross," Kuen drawls. "I only accept what I am given. If I am to die today, so be it, but I don't think that is what I deserve. I *was* once the Charger's right hand man, that is true. I was *once* a monster and it still lurks inside me somewhere, I know it does. I can never be free from the demons of my past; can anyone ever truly escape their history?" He leans back in his chair as much as the chains will allow. "I am not sure we can, but we sure as hell try, don't we? We all have monsters inside us; none of us are saints, not me, not Trey, not Jenson, not even you. Why should I be penalized because my monsters happen to be larger and more terrifying?"

Even Ross has nothing to say to that.

Everyone is hanging on Kuen's every word and I am shocked. He knows how to plead his case, how to appeal to the people. His motives and words are genuine, but I can't help seeing Sephtis in his ability to persuade. It unnerves me.

"So ask me this," Kuen continues. "Do I deserve to die or do I deserve to have a chance to beat my monsters back even further, to take more steps toward the unattainable goal of perfection? Does it matter that I, like all of you, will never get there?"

The air feels empty when he finishes.

Jenson looks warily at Kuen and then the crowd.

Trey beams at her brother.

Ross merely narrows his eyes at Kuen and returns to his seat.

Jenson clears his throat and says, "Both sides have said their piece. Does anyone else wish to say anything or may we proceed with the sentencing?"

Sentencing. As if it's already been decided that Kuen will die.

If I wasn't trying so hard to be good, I'd get up and call Jenson out on it, but I don't feel like arguing right now. Waiting for a verdict is exhausting me.

No one says anything and Jenson speaks again.

"Then we shall do the vote and confer. All in favour of conviction?"

Jenson and about three dozen others raise their hands, Ross included.

I notice Natalie's hand does not join her father's and the sight makes me pause. Doesn't she want to see another assassin crushed? Did I affect her that much?

I look away from her torn and tired face and back to Jenson as he says, "All those against?"

Everyone else in the room raises their hands and I feel a glowing flame of pride in my heart for Trey and Kuen. They plead their case well.

Jenson's face burns behind his cool facade as he realizes he has lost and Kuen will walk free.

Serves you right; this is karma.

He swallows back his anger and says, "Well, it seems we have reached a conclusion. Kuen will be given another chance, though he will be watched closely. I shall assign him an escort who will monitor his activity and report to me immediately if he so much as toes the line of what we deem right and wrong. Need I remind you what happened the last time we gave a 'former' assassin too much free reign?"

A few people nod and whispers start again.

I sizzle. He's talking about me, though I suppose it's my fault for speaking out.

"So, with that in mind," he goes on, "does anyone wish to volunteer for the position of escort? It will be a difficult one, but you will be rewarded for your efforts."

Across the room, halfway up the tier, a man stands up. He's in his twenties and is of average build, certainly not enough to take on Kuen if he decides to go rogue. He's perfect.

"And you are?" Jenson says.

"Callum Joseph O'Reilly," the man replies.

I cringe.

Oh Guild, we've gotten ourselves another Roseanne. *Lovely.*

"Level?" Jenson asks.

"Third, sir," O'Reilly replies, throwing his shoulders back in an attempt to seem bigger and more important.

I roll my eyes, glad I'm not close enough to see whatever stupid expression is on his face.

Jenson frowns. "Do you think you're up to the task?"

"Of course, sir."

"Well then, Callum, consider yourself hired, but I'll be watching you closely."

O'Reilly nods. "I will not fail you, sir."

"Good, then you can help Nicholas escort Kuen to his room. Nicholas will brief you on the way there. Guards!"

Ten guards dressed head to toe in dark grey and layered with weapons break away from the walls and walk toward where Kuen still sits in the centre of the room.

Nicolas Ross gets up from his spot beside Jenson to join them and O'Reilly makes his way down the tiered seats to the ground.

The guards unlock the shackles with a huge key ring and then handcuff Kuen's hands together behind his back.

Amateurs. As if that will hold him.

Kuen doesn't try to break free, though he could do so easily. Instead, he lets the guards, O'Reilly, and Ross escort him out of the room.

Trey gives Jenson one last look of contempt before she follows.

I wait until they're gone before taking my leave.

CHAPTER ELEVEN

As I head back to the hospital wing, I'm reminded of what happened when I left. Ajax and I had been arguing, again, and not like Bast and Blake arguing either. He had been so...selfish and cruel. I'm not as angry as I had been—the trial's verdict lightened my mood—but the fire still smoulders inside. I hope he isn't waiting in my room, because I don't think I can deal with him calmly yet.

No one pays me any heed as a walk through the hospital. I'm starting to feel a little strain on my leg, but not much. It's just from the exercise I haven't done in weeks. I need to get back to the training room before I lose my touch and all my well-earned muscle. I can't take down Sephtis in this weakling state. He'd crush me in a heartbeat, and that's coming from me. Guild knows I consider myself invincible.

Yet, after everything I've been through, I know I'm not. No one is. That's the only thing keeping me going. There *has* to be a way to beat him.

I finally reach my room to find the door ajar.

I groan.

Go away, Ajax. I can't cope with this right now.

I need time alone.

I kick the door in and it slams against the inside wall, revealing a boy sitting on my bed, a boy whose long brown curls and tan skin do not belong to Ajax.

I raise an eyebrow. "Bast? What are you doing here?"

"Waiting for you to get back. What do you think? How'd the trial go? Terrible, or did you kick the door in for fun?" He looks concerned.

"Never mind the door," I tell him, waving a hand. "The trial was okay. Jenson was an ass, but then again, when isn't he? Ross was even worse. It took some persuading, but Kuen's head is not on the chopping block, yet."

"That's good," he replies.

"Yeah," I say. "Where's Blake?"

"Oh, uh... She went to try to talk some sense into Jax."

"What? How do you...?"

His brown eyes are sad as he says, "Blake and I were just outside the door. We were coming for a visit, but then we heard you guys arguing."

I wince. "How much did you hear?"

"All of it."

"Assassins below," I sigh. "I'm sorry you had to find out like that."

He tilts his head. "Find out what?"

"That Trey and Kuen are my siblings. Half."

"Oh," he says, "yeah. I don't mind. I was kind of more focused on the fact that you and Jax were fighting." He brushes the hair out of his eyes.

I give him a sad look. He may constantly play the role of the jokester, someone who can bounce back from everything, but he gets hurt too. I often forget he's the youngest of us. He shouldn't be living in this world. He shouldn't be fighting battles and drowning his sorrows in liquor. He should be out on the town with his friends or playing video games in his basement.

"I'm sorry, Bast," I say.

"What for?"

I sigh. "For everything, I guess." For being an angry person, for keeping secrets, for the fact that life sucks, though that last one I can't really change. I *can* get rid of the secrets, though.

"I have to tell you something else, Bast, and you have to promise not to discuss it with anyone but Blake, Trey, Ajax, and Kuen, okay?"

He smiles, delighted with the surprise and the challenge. "Cross my heart, Quinby."

I scowl. "I swear, if you do not stop calling me that I'll..."

He crosses his arms. "You'll what?"

"I'm not sure yet, but it will be painful."

He wriggles his fingers. "Wow, I'm terrified."

"Oh shut up and listen, you insufferable person," I groan.

He grins. "Jeez, Quinnifer, lighten up."

"Oh, that does it…"

I lunge for him and he yelps as I curl my arm around his head, trapping him in a headlock.

He beats at my legs—er, leg—with his fists. "Let me go, you monster!"

"Not until you swear to stop calling me Quinby or Quinnifer or Quinton…"

"Oh, Quinton! That's a new one; I like it."

I squeeze harder, mussing up his unruly hair even further with my other hand. "Don't you even think about it."

Then, he laughs. It throws me off guard and I realize how ridiculous the two of us must look. I let him go and start laughing too.

"What is wrong with us?" I gasp between giggles.

"Well, you're a psychopath, obviously," he replies, "and I'm…"

"A child?"

"Sure. Wait, no. Take that back!"

I laugh even harder, holding my sides to keep myself together.

It takes a while for us to sober up, but when we do, Bast flops onto my bed and I sit down cross-legged beside him. The position is a strange one with my fake leg.

"So," Bast says, "Jax was being a jerk, eh?"

I pick at my nails. "You can say that again."

He gives me a sheepish grin. "Guys, am I right?"

I glare at him and he stops smiling.

"Okay…" he says. "Maybe I'm a jerk too."

I snort. "As if you would ever admit that." I heave a sigh and lay back on the bed beside him. "What should I do, Bast?"

"Well," he says. "You should start by asking someone who's more qualified for dating advice."

I roll my eyes. "I'm asking you for a reason, Bast. You know Jax better than anyone. Why was he so upset?"

He sighs. "It sounded like this Kuen guy has really gotten under his skin. Maybe he's jealous, maybe he's scared."

"That's a lot of maybes."

"Hey, don't shoot the messenger. *You're* the one that asked *me* for advice. *Maybe* you should let him fix it; he's the one being a jerk."

"He wasn't the only one who said some stuff... Ugh. Relationships are hard." I rub my temples.

Bast laughs. "Which is why I'm single; who's the smart one now?"

I roll my eyes again.

Blake is definitely in love with him, but I wonder for a moment if Bast feels the same and how you'd ever tell. He doesn't take anything seriously, but that's probably exactly what Blake likes about him.

That's one of the things that attracted Ajax to me in the first place, his ability to counteract my seriousness with his free spirit. I need someone carefree in my life and that's why I can't lose him. Bast would never fit the bill; he's not my type and besides, he and Blake are made for each other, even if they don't realize it yet.

"All right," I say, dragging myself to my feet, "I have to go."

Bast sits up. "To do what?"

"To fix things," I reply. "A relationship is a two-way street; both of us have to do our part. It's time to patch the holes in our road again. Relationships aren't perfect and if you can't argue, it's not real. As long as each person is willing to change because of it, no harm is done."

"Well, isn't that inspirational," he says.

I smile. "You'll understand one day."

"As if," he scoffs, "I'm going to be single forever."

"I'm sure you won't be," I reply. "Stop fishing for attention. I'm off now and you can tell the nurses I won't be returning."

He raises an eyebrow.

"If I stay in this place one more night," I tell him, "I'm going to lose it."

Bast cracks a smile. "Hate to break it to you, Quinton, but you lost it a *long* time ago."

This time, there is no mercy when I try to take him out.

• • •

I march down the halls, not exactly knowing where I'm going. I want to find Kuen before I talk to Jax, but I don't know where either of them would be. I doubt anyone will give me information on Kuen's whereabouts, given my past. I don't know what they would expect us to do together, though—form an attack plan and take the Resistance out, just the two of us?

Jenson shouldn't worry. If I was going to end his operation, I would've done it months ago. I don't particularly care about thwarting him anymore, not now that my eyes have been opened to my own horrors. The next time I go on a killing spree will be when I find the assassins again, not before.

I round a corner, lost in thought, and run right into someone coming from the other direction. I stumble on my new leg, but the person grabs my elbow and steadies me.

"Easy there, Quinn," Trey says, "you have to be careful with that leg of yours."

I scowl. "I know, I know, but I'm not as fragile as a teacup, okay?"

She holds out a hand. "I never said you were. What are you doing walking around, though? Shouldn't you be at the hospital?"

My scowl deepens. "I'm done with that place. I can walk fine on my own now. If I don't get back into routine, I'm going to break something, or someone."

She sighs. "So that's the mood we're in today."

I rub my forehead. "Look, I'm sorry. I've had a rough morning. Jax and I got into an argument before the trial and Jenson and Ross got under my skin. I'm glad Kuen is free, but I'm not in the mood to be bombarded with questions."

"Hey, I get it. We've all been there. I'll let you go blow off some steam." She makes to step around me, but I grab her arm.

"Wait," I say. "Do you know which room Kuen is in?"

"3672," she replies. "Why?"

"I need to talk to him."

She snorts. "Good luck; his guard is a real piece of work."

"I noticed, but I'm sure I can figure something out." If he's as much like Natalie as he seems, I shouldn't have a problem.

"Well, I have to run," Treys says. "Say hi to Kuen for me."

"Will do. See you around."

• • •

We go our separate ways and I weave through the Resistance halls towards where room 3672 should be. The stairs I encounter prove to be a bit of a challenge, but if I hold onto the railing and hop on my good foot, I have little to no trouble. Still, I'm going to have to work on it.

I reach the room fifteen minutes later at the end of an abandoned hall. All the other rooms are clearly vacant, doors thrown open to reveal empty floors. I guess Jenson couldn't house a 'dangerous' assassin anywhere near his precious agents, unlike he did with me. I might not have neighbours, but I'm still in the main residence section.

Honestly, I wish Jenson would make up his mind. Trust us or don't.

Callum Joseph O'Reilly stands at attention in front of Kuen's door, which has three bars across it and four padlocks.

Assassins below.

Jenson is pushing my limits.

It's as if Kuen hasn't left the dungeons. How is he supposed to change, supposed to prove himself, if he is locked in his room all day?

Oh, this ends now.

I march up to O'Reilly and he draws his weapon, a dainty-looking sword.

"Good luck doing anything with that butter knife," I tell him as I come to a stop a couple feet away. I cross my arms. "You'd have an easier time stabbing yourself with it. In fact, I'd be willing to help with that."

The grip on his weapon tightens. He's scared now, just how I want him. "Y-you shouldn't be here, Assassin," he stammers.

"That's Quinn to you, O'Reilly and you'll soon learn that I do what I like. I don't take well to rules."

"I'll inform Jenson you were here."

"Ooooooh... *Inform.*" I laugh. "Look at you with your fancy words. Tell Jenson if you want; he can't do anything to me. I'm untouchable."

His eyes narrow. "And how is that?" For a split second, he actually looks like he's my elder.

"I'm an asset," I tell him. "A secret weapon. The Charger is still out there, O'Reilly, and I will be the one to bring him to his knees. So, if you would be so kind as to let me in to talk to my dear friend, Kuen, I'll consider not punishing you."

I almost let the word brother slip out, but catch myself before it happens.

Callum's eyes go wide at the mention of punishment and he looks like a child again. "You can't," he breathes.

I raise a brow. "Can't I?"

"I am the escort," he says. "You can't threaten me or I'll…"

I roll my eyes. "Oh please, save it for someone who's actually afraid of you, though you'd be hard-pressed to find anyone." I push past him and he hits the wall with a whimper he probably doesn't think I catch, but my senses are sharp. "Don't whine, it's unbecoming."

His silence is a beautiful thing.

"Now," I say, brushing myself off, "which one of these lovely keys fits the locks?" I hold up a key ring with at least two dozen keys.

His eyes are like saucers. "How did you…?"

I pick-pocketed them when I sent him to the wall. It was a piece of cake.

I wave a hand. "Never mind how. All you need to know is that if you go running to Jenson, I'll tell him how easily I was able to steal these from you. You'd be out of a job before you could say…failure."

He hangs his head.

"That's right. You stay right where you are and I'll be back in a jiffy. Oh, and which key did you say?"

He sighs. "The one on the end."

I pat him on the chest. "See? That wasn't hard, was it?"

I grab the right key and proceed to unlock the bars and padlocks. I'm surprised they used one key for all seven. Amateurs.

The door opens and I give O'Reilly a little wave as I slip inside, taking the keys with me. I don't think he's smart enough, but I have no intention of being locked in here myself.

Kuen lounges on the bed, one arm thrown over his eyes. He groans when the door slams behind me. "What did I tell you, Callum? I want to be left alone!" He leans over and grabs something off the nightstand.

I drop to the floor instinctively, and whatever it was he threw at me hits the door and bounces back across the room.

"Hello to you too," I say.

"Oh," he replies, finally noticing me, "it's you."

"Yeah it's me, and you almost took my head off. Maybe next time you should check who it is before you try to kill them, hmm?"

"Oh shut up, Quinn, I'm not in the mood." He lies back down and I sigh.

"Well, neither am I. You're free now, so stop sulking and go do something."

"I would, if his highness Callum Joseph O'Reilly would let me."

I raise a brow. "Oh really? That's rich coming from you. You're going to let a spindly idiot like O'Reilly stand in your way? You're more of a coward than I thought."

He sits up and glares at me. "You're playing with fire."

I shrug. "I've been burnt before."

"You're insufferable."

"Says the man who's suffering when he doesn't have to. Look what I have."

I hold up the key ring and he squints across the dim room at me.

"Are those...?"

I nod. "I also have O'Reilly in my pocket now, so you have no excuses. Stop acting like a dead man; get out there and live."

He looks at me strangely. "Okay, I take back what I said before. You really have changed."

I throw my hands up in exasperation. "That's what I've been trying to tell you, but you were too caught up in your miseries to listen. You're welcome, by the way." I toss the keys at him. They miss his head by inches and I frown.

I head for the door.

"If I come back here, Kuen," I go on, "and you're still lying here, doing nothing, I'm going to put you on a stretcher. You hear me?"

"Loud and clear, Quinn. Now get out of my room, if you know what's good for you."

"Whatever," I reply and then I do as he says. Well, not because he said it; I was headed out anyway.

O'Reilly waits for me in the hall.

"I'll be going now," I tell him. "Kuen is free to walk around, to socialize, to eat in the cafeteria—with you following, of course. He is not to be locked in his room, and don't think I won't find out. If Jenson has any problems with the new arrangements, tell him to bring it up with me. I'd love to have a chat with him, catch up on what we've missed. You know."

O'Reilly nods timidly.

"Well, have a nice day." I start to walk away.

It takes him a moment, but he calls out, "Wait! Where are my keys?"

I stop, but don't turn around. "Kuen is looking after them for you. Don't worry, they're in good hands."

I can sense his anxiety.

"As I said, have a nice day."

Then I walk off without another word, leaving O'Reilly alone in the hall contemplating how exactly he managed to get so bamboozled.

CHAPTER TWELVE

I wander around the base for a while before my feet carry me to the cafeteria. It seems to be the right place to go. It's nearing evening and I somehow missed lunch. I haven't been to the caf in over a month. The Guild attack was on June thirteenth and tomorrow will be August first. I shake my head at the passage of time and at myself. The last time I was in the cafeteria, I bared my tattoos for all to see and told Bast and Blake our friendship was a lie. I had been horrible to them.

Now, as I step through the cafeteria doors, I tug on the monster's chain, ensuring it's still locked up tight. It growls down inside me and I shake my head again, to clear it of the nasty thoughts trying to rise to the surface.

The cafeteria is exactly how I remember it; loud and crowded. The noise does not deter me this time, though. I embrace it. I need something to drown out my thoughts.

I head over to the food line, more than eager to get my hands on some real food. The hospital food was...less than satisfactory to say the least. I'm looking forward to something with substance.

When I reach the front of the line, I grab a bit of everything: a bowl of soup, a piece of bread, crackers, a banana, a bowl of mixed vegetables, and an apple juice. I can't wait to dig in.

I carry the tray over to the usual table instinctively and take a seat. It feels weird sitting alone. I miss Jax's constant presence by my side.

I think back to our argument. He wasn't entirely wrong about Kuen and Trey. It's true; they *did* leave me behind with Sephtis. Kuen claims I was the one that spurred him to leave, but if he was truly looking out for me, wouldn't he have taken me with him? And Trey... I still don't know her whole story, but I can't expect either of them to be perfect. I'm certainly not. Sephtis' blood runs through all our veins.

Kuen was right too. All we can do is try to fight the monster. Jax and I have monsters of our own, but we can't let them destroy what we have. I see where he is coming from, why he didn't want me to go. He's worried Kuen might make my monsters worse and he's worried he might lose me. Lose me to the monsters.

I won't let them take me. I'll get Jax to shoot them first.

I look up just as Bast sits down across the table from me. "Evening, Quinby," he says.

"Bast," I reply, not even bothering to fight with him. "What brings you to my presence?"

"Blake's busy and I got hungry." He drops a laden tray onto the table, spilling peas onto the floor.

I cringe.

Wasting good food.

"You're a slob," I tell him. "You know that, right?"

"Of course," he replies, mouth already full of food.

I shake my head. "You'll never win a girl's heart like that."

He looks up. "Who says I would want to? I told you earlier: I am a single man and so I always shall be. Romance is great and all, but who can commit like that, to spend your whole life with one person? That would take a lot of love. I'm not sure I'd have it in me or if anyone else would be able to love *me* that much."

We eat in silence for a bit.

I think of Blake. I know she would be able to fulfill those requirements and I have a feeling that, when it came to the person he truly loved, Bast would lock himself up in commitment and throw away the key.

I questioned earlier whether or not Bast felt the same as Blake, but I think I can see it now. Bast doesn't think he's good enough for Blake. He wants her to have everything she can, and he'd be okay if that wasn't him, as long as she was happy.

Blake's busy, he said. He always follows her around, never Jax. It's always Blake and Bast and, now that I think about it, maybe Bast went on that death-defying mission to show Blake that he can save the world too. That he can protect her. And that time in the Dungeon, when he tried to kiss Blake… I have a feeling that wasn't just alcohol. I think drinking loosens our tongues, makes us say and do things we're too afraid to. Like me for example, I told Jax I loved him. It wasn't a lie then, just something my sober mind wouldn't let me say.

Blake has already condemned me for this, but I decide to dig myself another grave. "So you're not…interested in anyone?" I ask him.

Bast laughs to cover his quick blush, but I still see it. "Me? Quinton, I'm interested in everyone, and everyone is interested in me."

I raise an eyebrow. "Easy there, Mr. Ego."

"Shush, I just tell it like it is."

I roll my eyes. "Sure you do."

"Speaking of relationships," he says, "have you and Jax made up yet?"

I sigh. "No, we haven't, but we haven't actually talked yet."

"What? Why?"

"Well, the thing is, I don't exactly know where to find him." It's a poor excuse.

Bast gives me a curious look. "He's probably in his room."

"Thanks, tips," I reply. "The only problem is that I don't know where that is."

"You've never been to his room," Bast says, incredulous.

"Well, I have, I just…" I try to hide my blush. "Well, I wasn't exactly paying attention to where…"

Bast grimaces and holds out a hand, realizing what I'm implying. "Spare me the details."

"Lay off," I say. "Nothing happened. He found out about his mother a few minutes after we arrived and... Well, the rest is history, as they say."

His face falls. "I'm sorry."

I shrug. "Don't be. You had nothing to do with it."

"True, but I can still feel your pain."

I raise an eyebrow. "Feel my pain? Who are you, and what did you do with Sebastian?"

He scowls before saying, "What, just because I'm macho I can't have feelings?"

I snort. "As if. Are you sure that head injury didn't cause more damage than we thought?"

"Shut up," he replies, though he's smiling. Shaking his head, he stands up. "I have to go," he says, "you know, important things to do and such."

"Okay, have fun. I'll be busy doing nothing, again."

"No, you'll be busy talking to Jax," he says. "His room is 572, just so you know." He smiles at me and heads off.

Bast is a better person than he gives himself credit for.

I stay at the table for a few more minutes before leaving the cafeteria, in search of room 572 and a chance at redemption.

• • •

I recognize the hall as I walk down it, remembering the mad dash of Jax and I that night. The footsteps that echo now are not the same. The clunk of my boot and the tap of my prosthetic are in stark contrast to the slapping and skidding of our shoes against the floor last time.

When I reach the blue door, my anxiety levels send my heart into a frenzy. I feel sick.

What if he doesn't answer?

What if he does, but tells me to go?

What if we can't fix this?

I shake my head to clear it. Worrying about the possibilities never got anyone anywhere. I clench my fist and rap on the door three times, willing my heartbeat to steady.

Nothing answers, not even the sound of a creaking bed or pacing steps within.

I knock again.

Silence greets me.

My heart skips a beat as it clenches and then it's back, racing once more.

"Jax?" I call out. "Please answer the door. I just want to talk. I understand if... But... Please don't." I don't even know what I'm saying, all I know—as the minutes drag by—is that he's not answering and it hurts.

I knock one last time and when nothing happens, I flee, sprinting down the hall, away from the heartbreak and the pain, my feet going tap-a-clunk, tap-a-clunk on the floor as I leave the blue door and room 572 far behind.

• • •

Someone cleaned my room after I left. Whether it was one of my friends or other agents, I don't know, but there is no sign of my "temper tantrum" nor is there any sign of a new occupant. Room 2413 is still mine. A layer of dust covers the floor, the bed is made with six pillows, and the closet doors are ajar to reveal a rack of clothes neatly hung up.

There may be no sign of the dark memories, but I still remember them. They're there in every detail of this room that is not like me, everything that points to abandonment. The room seems empty, but it's full of everything I said, and everything I didn't say. The silence and the cleanliness unnerve me.

I sigh loudly to fill the void left by my thoughts. Then I make my way through the room, messing it up as I go.

I leave the door ajar and knock over the pair of boots sitting beside it. I shove all the pillows back under my bed except one. Who needs six pillows anyway? I rumple the sheets, untucking them from the mattress. Then I stalk over to my closet.

I grab an outfit off the rack, a black Resistance outfit with weapons loops along the waist. I wore this the day Jax and I went on our first mission, the day Silent Night threatened to kill him.

I clench the fabric in my hands and tear.

It's the sweetest sound I've ever heard, so I do it again.

And again.

I rip the outfit into shreds and move on to the next one.

I tear through my closet like a maelstrom, ripping clothes off their hangers and reducing them to pieces before discarding them in the growing pile at my feet.

Angry tears stream down my face as I destroy every outfit I wore as that hateful Silent Night. As I wrench my boots off my feet.

Boots that led me to so much death. Boots stained with the blood of every life I ended.

I try to tear them too, but the leather is thick, so I grab a knife. It doesn't help much.

My hand slips and the blade slices against the inside of my arm.

I hiss. "Damn you," I snap. "Damn you! Why won't you give up! *Why!*"

I chuck them across the room, knocking a vase off my dresser and it smashes on the floor, sending shards in every direction.

Sobs tear free of my throat, making it harder to breathe as I back away from the glass toward the wall.

I study my hands.

Is this all I am good for?

Destruction?

I look at my arm, at the blood dripping onto the floor, at the two ruined tattoos. Two names I might not remember now.

I remember the black zipped vest I wore on that final day. If I still had it, I would burn it. It deserves to burn.

It all deserves to burn.

I think there are matches in my dresser.

I walk over to it, kicking away the vase shards in my path, and rummage through the drawers, getting more hysterical by the second.

I need those matches.

It needs to burn.

I can't find them.

I slam the drawer shut, narrowly missing my fingers, and scream.

CHAPTER THIRTEEN

I'm still screaming, cowering against the dresser, gripping it for dear life when I feel arms wrapping around me.

"Quinn, it's okay," a voice says. "Just breathe. Breathe for me, okay?"

I flail about. "No," I gasp. "Let me go. It needs to burn. I need…"

I feel myself falling to the ground, feel a hand around my head, smoothing my hair, feel warmth seeping into me, a calm.

"Shhh…it's okay," the voice says. "You're okay."

I listen to the voice, listen to the person breathing, and try to see the light.

The vase shards around me remind me of the glass tank where I nearly lost everything. It had been the closest I'd ever come to death; the first time I actually feared it.

I was not afraid when I woke up chained by my uncle in that red brick bungalow. I knew Lincoln did not wish to kill me.

I was not afraid when that axe man brought me within an inch of life because, somehow, I felt like I deserved it.

Terror only gripped my heart when I could see the water rising, see my all-too-short life coming to a close, a life I had squandered. I realized then the mistake I had made in surviving, what Jax had been telling me all along. I needed to live, not exist, and it terrified me when I thought I would never get that chance.

I will never lose sight of that again.

I take a long, shuddering breath. I can feel the tear stains on my face now and the ache in my throat. My left arm is throbbing. I know now that it is Jax holding me and I make a point of relaxing into him, of letting the tension fall out of my limbs.

The knife I forgot I was holding clatters to the floor.

I survey my room and the carnage of my wardrobe. The place no longer looks like a tomb; it looks like a battlefield.

I shudder.

"Oh Quinn," Jax says, running a hand down my hair once again. "I'm so sorry."

I'm not sure what he means.

Sorry my life is a mess or sorry about what happened earlier?

Our argument seems so insignificant now.

We sit there in silence for several moments more until I take a deep calming breath and say, "I'm okay now."

"What happened?" he asks.

I grimace. "I really...don't want to talk about it."

"I think we should, Quinn. You've completed destroyed your closet, broken a vase, and cut yourself. You were screaming at nothing when I ran in here." I can't see his face, but I know the exact expression he's wearing. "I didn't mean to send you off the edge."

I wrap my arms around my knees, probably smearing the still-drying blood on my shirt, but I don't care. "You didn't do this, Jax. I did. I was perfectly fine when I walked in here and then… Well, I went a little crazy."

"You're not trying to...kill yourself, are you?"

I tense. "Of course not," I reply. "The knife slipped when I was trying to cut up my boots."

I can sense his raised eyebrow. "Your boots," he repeats.

I slouch down. "Yeah."

He lets out a breath. "I wish I'd come sooner, might've saved you some pain, not to mention a few outfits."

I shudder. "I don't want the outfits. They belonged to *her*."

"Ah," he says, "that's what this is about."

I tuck my wretched hands under my arms. "I just… I feel like I'm always destroying things. I worry she's not gone for good."

"I hate to say it, Quinn," he says, "but I think she was here today, making you suffer."

I sigh. "You're probably right."

Silence falls between us again and though his presence is comforting in this moment, my mind can't help but wander back to our argument.

Jax must feel the same because he says, "So about earlier… Can we…"

"Just tell me why."

"I was being…."

"Stupid? Ridiculous? Overly territorial?" My anger slips out and I grab for the leash.

It holds.

He sucks in a breath at each word. "Yeah, that," he says. "And as for why... I'm not even sure I have a good answer. I don't hate your brother, Quinn. I just… I don't trust him. I was worried you might act rashly if the trial didn't go well, that you might do something you'd live to regret."

"You thought she would come back."

"Maybe."

He could be right about that. I was seething at Jenson even with the verdict in Kuen's favour. Jax promised me once that he would save me from myself even when I couldn't. This was him keeping his promise, though he could've done it better.

"You said earlier that in your world, people stay when they care," I say.

"Yes," he admits.

"You know what happens in *my* world when people care?"

"What?"

"They come back." I take a breath. "Like how I came back to the Resistance and how you came back for me at the Guild. If we didn't care, we never would've bothered to return. If Trey and Kuen didn't care about me, they never would've saved our lives at the Guild or brought me back to the base. When people don't care, they stay gone. Like my father."

"I think you're right," he says. "Distance tests our bonds, but the true ones don't break."

I raise an eyebrow. "So you're admitting you were wrong?"

"I don't pretend to be perfect, Quinn."

"And you think I do?"

"No! That's not it at all. I think you believe you'll never be perfect, but no one ever will and that's okay. You're perfectly you; attitude, sass, impatience, strength, intelligence, beauty and all. You're perfect to me, but what matters is that you see that too."

"So you're saying...?"

"That I know sorry doesn't cut it, it never does, but I'll say it anyway and that I hope we can move on, though not necessarily forget. I want to learn to change, not on my own, but together. I want to change with you, even if I'm the only one who needs changing."

I shake my head. "It's not just you. My past is something that still haunts me and I don't want to use that as an excuse... I need to change too. I know that. I'm not perfect, Jax, and I *know* I can never *be* perfect, but I want to get closer to it. I would like to learn to change too, together."

I get to my feet and straighten my clothes. He follows me and I finally turn to face him.

He stares at me, his blue eyes etched with relief and lets out a breath.

I let him read my emotions through my eyes. Sometimes words aren't enough; sometimes eyes are too much. That's why I didn't look at him until I had my emotions in check. Foolish really. Somehow, he can always tell.

"I forgive you," I tell him.

"I forgive you too," he replies.

We sort our thoughts out during a moment of silence. Then he takes his eyes off of mine and regards the room. "Guess we should clean up this mess. Honestly, Quinn, you're going to need a maid at this rate."

And, despite myself, despite everything, I smile, because life's too short to hold grudges and he makes me happy.

"I think there's a broom somewhere in the closet. You can get started right away." I manage a grin and he reflects my mood with a smile of his own.

"I'm glad you decided to come back, Quinn."

I shrug. "Didn't have much of a choice did I? What with me dying and all."

"That's not what I meant," he says. "I meant I'm glad you decided to come back to our side. I'm glad you decided to leave Silent Night behind."

"I'm trying my best," I reply. "Today was a big step in the right direction. There's nothing physical left to remind me of her, but I still feel like she's watching from the shadows, waiting for the right moment to pounce."

He takes my hands. "I won't let that happen."

"I know, and that's why I can't stay mad at you, because you keep me sane. You are my anchor to the world of good, the world of what is right. You keep me from the dark."

He smiles. "And you remind me there are people who need our help still, that just because my life has light, doesn't mean others' do. You keep me down to earth. I will always be grateful for you and how you opened my eyes to the fact that just because assassins are the 'enemy' doesn't mean they're evil or that their case is hopeless. Maybe... Maybe you won't be the only one we save."

I sigh. "That would be nice, but the chances are low."

He frowns. "Why?"

"Because I think, after what happened with me, Sephtis would've had any possible deserters executed." I shudder as memories flash behind my open eyes. Rachel's screams echo as if distant.

Dead, I remind myself. *She's dead.*

"He wouldn't..." Jax tries.

"He would," I reply. "Trust me."

"Okay, let's say he did then. That would be horrible, but it doesn't mean the assassins are a lost cause."

"They are the very definition of a 'lost cause.'"

"Quinn... Stay with me." He tugs on my hands, pulling me closer.

I tremble, but don't move away.

"What's wrong?" he says. "You can tell me."

And it's the way he looks at me, the concern in his eyes, his desire to understand, that makes me forget our fight. It reminds me why I fell for him in the first place. Why, when everyone else lays dead at my feet, I can forgive him.

So I refuse to hang my head down. "All those people..." I say. "If Sephtis truly did kill possible deserters... All those people are dead because of me, because of my choices and what I did. Because... Because I killed my brother instead of you."

His eyes widen at the last sentence. "What?"

"At the Guild," I tell him, "when Hai was trying to break your arm and I pulled a gun on him. Remember how the Charger appeared behind me? He... He told me that everything would be forgiven, that he would take me back if only... He told me he would let me live if I killed you. I shot Hai instead."

"You... You what?" Jax chokes out, sounding pained. "You were willing to sacrifice yourself...to save me?"

Those can't be tears building up in his eyes... Can they?

"Yes," I reply, barely above a whisper.

"Why? Quinn, you could've... He was going to kill you and you threw away life..."

"It wasn't life I threw away," I gasp. "I threw away survival because if I had gone back to the Guild, to Sephtis, I would've returned to mere existence. That's not what I wanted. I wanted to *live* with you and if you weren't going to be there, I didn't want to live. I couldn't let your light go out. I knew there were too many people out there that needed you. And I knew you'd move on, you'd find someone else and I... I would retreat back to the darkness with no one left to drag me out. So yes, I was willing to sacrifice myself for you, no one else, but you... There is no doubt."

He blinks his eyes to deter them, but still one tear escapes. "Come here," he says, holding out his arms.

I step into his embrace.

He holds me tight, crushing me into him and I return the favour.

I feel so safe and he feels so vulnerable at this moment. Never before have I considered Jax to be as breakable as the rest of us. He's always been so strong.

We don't say anything, we just hold on, becoming an anchor for the other in the storm of emotions raging around us. To think, we've gone from anger to this.

We finally pull away far enough to see our faces.

"You're wrong, you know," he says, brushing away that stray tear with the back of his hand.

"Wrong?" I ask.

"I wouldn't move on," he tells me. "I wouldn't find somebody else. How could I, after how much you morphed my world? Quinn, no one can ever live up to you, *ever*, and I wouldn't want them to."

I can't stand it anymore.

The magnetic pull is tearing me apart.

I look into his eyes, my gaze burning into him. "Jax, can I...?"

His lips are on mine before I can finish the question, but I guess that's my answer.

I wrap my hands around him and pull him closer as I kiss him back, fast and fierce like I'll never have another chance.

A moan escapes him and his hands tangle in my hair, holding me captive.

I press against him.

I missed this. I missed him.

We would've stayed that way for a long time if I didn't have that single ounce of self-control. It's enough for me to break the kiss before we get too carried away.

He leans his forehead against mine. "Must you tease me so?" he asks, his breathing haggard.

I ignore his question and say, "I missed you."

He smiles. "I missed you too."

"Let's agree to never take a break like that again, okay?"

He laughs. "Okay."

"I love you, Jax," I breathe.

"I love you too."

"It's late," I say after a moment, hinting that he should go. I don't want him to. Guild, how I wish he would stay, but he can't. It's not the time... He needs to go before my self-control slips.

"So?" he replies.

I take a step back, removing myself from his gravity. "So...I should...rest."

He raises an eyebrow.

"Alone," I emphasize.

He grins and concedes. "As you wish, Quinn," he says. "I'll get out of your hair." He tugs at a couple strands as he says it.

I scowl. "You better. I don't want to have to throw you out."

He snorts. "As if you could lift me."

"I could try."

"I couldn't let you; I know how much of a sore loser you are."

"You take that back!" I gasp, but I'm trying not to laugh.

"Not a chance," he replies. He walks towards the door, stepping around the glass. "Night, Quinn."

"Goodnight, Jax."

He smiles at me and disappears into the hall, closing the door behind him.

I shake my head.

Guild help me.

CHAPTER FOURTEEN

Someone is knocking on my door.

I groan and roll over. "Go away."

The knocking comes again, accompanied by a voice. "Come on, Quinn. Rise and shine."

I suppose someone chose today to die.

There's a long silence and then… "Quinn Marie Ballinger," Jax barks. "Don't make me come in there."

I roll my eyes and kick off my sheets. "Fine," I call out. "Give me five minutes."

I yawn and stretch as I sit up. Then I ease to my feet and amble over to my closet.

I cleaned my room last night before I went to bed. All the shredded fabric is under my bed, stuffed into my extra pillowcases. The only clothes left in the closet belong to Quinn.

What to wear today? I wonder. *Grey outfit number one or grey outfit number two?*

I decide on number three, though there isn't any difference between the ten hanging in there.

I pull the outfit off the hanger and begin the fight to put it on. Getting dressed is a nightmare, less so every day, but it's still one of the most challenging tasks I've ever done. I have to be careful the fabric doesn't get stuck on a part of the prosthetic and rip. The number of outfits I've ruined since I got back here...

"You okay in there?" Jax asks. I can almost see him leaning on the door outside.

"Yes, just a minute. You know...how...difficult...this is."

Finally, I get it on and I straighten it out, breathing heavier. I feel the fabric pressing against the scab on my arm from last night.

"Do you need...assistance?"

"Not in the slightest." I fight to hide my blush, even though he can't see it. The day I let him dress me...

Oh Guild.

"One more minute," I tell him.

I walk over to my mirror and take myself in. I look smaller, but still strong. The grey outfit is anything but flattering. I frown for a second, a familiar expression on my face, and head over to the bed, lifting the mattress and pulling out the dagger I stashed there eons ago. Then I grab my right pant leg by the knee and, holding it out, begin to rip it with the knife, more systematic than what I did last night. When I'm done, my pants are cut to just below my knee, showing the entire prosthetic.

I smile.

Much better. Now, I look totally badass.

"Okay, I'm ready," I call out.

"About time," he replies.

I shake my head as I walk over to the door, pulling it open a foot and leaning against it. "So," I say, "to what do I owe the presence of your gorgeous face at such an early hour?"

He smiles at my compliment and returns it with his eyes alone. "Early? Quinn, it's eight o'clock. Unless you want to miss breakfast…"

I step outside and close the door.

He starts walking down the hall.

"So, it's back to the old routine then?" I ask as I fall into step beside him.

"Well, yeah," he replies. "If you don't want to be a patient anymore, we're not going to treat you like one."

I sigh. "You're going to make me regret my decision, aren't you?"

He grins. "I'm certainly going to try." I shove him playfully and he laughs, raising an eyebrow. "That's all you have?"

"Shut up," I say, but my scolding tone turns into a laugh and I can't help but smile.

We walk down the halls to the cafeteria and I can feel people watching us, watching me. I wonder how many of them heard about how I left, how many heard or were there when I returned. They probably despise me.

Then I take a closer look. Their eyes aren't angry; they're shocked, concerned, wondering.

What?

I follow their gazes and realize what they're all staring at. It's not me, well, not exactly. They're eyeing the prosthetic and probably wondering how the most feared assassin in Haven City managed to lose her leg. I shift a bit under their eyes, but for the most part, I could care less what they think.

I'm not going to cover up my injury. I'm proud of my scars; they show I've lived, that I've fought for life and even after everything, after losing my leg, I'm still standing. I wouldn't even be ashamed to bear my tattoos now, but not to show them off as trophies. I want to show that I acknowledge them, that they are a part of me, but that I've moved on.

Jax also notices the people staring and takes a better look at me. "What did you do to your pants?" he asks.

"What? You don't like it?"

"No, it's good, different. I just wondered why."

I shrug. "I see no point in hiding it. Besides, the fabric bulges a bit in places, and how can I use the weapon sheaths properly if they're stuck under my pants?"

"Good point," he says, "though I was hoping—stupidly I might add—that I could keep you away from fighting."

I laugh. "You're right; that *was* stupid."

He shrugs. "It was worth a shot."

"Not when I'm this good at dodging bullets." I grin at him and he rolls his eyes.

"Hilarious."

"Oh shush," I tell him. "Hey, speaking of fighting, I need to get back to the training rooms after breakfast. I'm rusty and we can't have that."

"I'll come with you."

I smile. "I wouldn't have it any other way."

• • •

We enter the cafeteria and the sounds of the usual ruckus make me smile wider.

This. This is home.

We grab some grub: cereal for me and a full-course meal of eggs, toast, and bacon for Jax.

Blake and Bast are already at the table when we arrive, sitting side by side I notice, but I guess that's probably because they figure Jax and I will want to sit together.

I'm still trying to piece together what little information I've gleaned from the two of them. Blake has definitely fallen for Bast, but I still can't be certain he likes her back. He likes *someone*—I didn't imagine that blush last night—but whether or not that person is Blake... I wish I knew, but maybe I should keep my nose out of their business. Guild knows I wouldn't want anybody in mine.

"Morning, Quinby, Jax," Bast says, without looking up from his massive plate of food.

"Sebastian," I reply evenly.

We scowl at each other.

Blake shakes her head and Jax laughs.

"Good news," Jax says as we sit. "Quinn has decided to get back into the swing of things today."

"Bravo," Bast exclaims, clapping with his fork still in hand. "Proud of ya. What's it going to be today?"

"Starting back with training I guess." I turn to Jax. "I'm done with lectures, right?"

He nods. "I'd say so; no way I'm torturing you with them anymore." He picks at his food. "Oh, that reminds me. Bast, we have a meeting this afternoon with Jenson."

Bast frowns. "What for?"

"He wants to discuss our next move," Jax says, "regarding the mission we went on with Trey." He takes a couple bites of food.

Blake looks up sharply. "You're continuing that?"

Jax nods.

"You can't be serious," she says.

"I am," Jax replies. "We've sat idle long enough. Bast has been cleared for action again and my stitches come out tomorrow. We have to get going."

She shakes her head. "What's the point of going out there and risking your lives? It's too dangerous."

"We have to find the assassins, Blake," I tell her.

"To what end?"

"To the destruction of them forever," Jax replies. "We're the Resistance. We resist the darkness; we fight the assassins; we protect the people. We can't let fear rule us or we're going to be right back where we started and our enemy will get ahead."

She picks at her food. "Well, I better be going with you this time."

Jax gives her a sympathetic look. "I'm sorry, Blake."

She drops her fork. "Am I being punished for something I don't remember doing?"

It's a good question and I wonder for a moment if Natalie finally used her blackmail or something.

"No, Blake," Jax replies. "You have nothing to answer for, I promise you. Jenson wants to keep the team small, just Trey, Bast, myself, and a few agents from other teams for a fresh perspective. I'm not even the leader; Trey is."

She crosses her arms. "So Jenson is throwing perfectly good agents aside for ex-assassins?"

"Hey now," I protest, "that's a bit harsh."

"Stay out of it, Quinn." She doesn't look at me when she says it, but at least she called me Quinn without stuttering.

"Jenson made a decision," Jax says in answer to her question. "He wants Trey on the team *because* she's an ex-assassin. He figures that, like Quinn, Trey will be our best chance at finding them."

"Then why don't you bring Quinn? Both you and Bast prefer her over me anyway."

"Whoa," Jax says, eyes wide.

"That's not true," Bast adds.

"I am sitting right here," I remind her.

"Nobody is at the bottom of this team, Blake," Jax goes on. "I told you guys I believe in equality and that still stands. Quinn is not ready to re-enter the field. If I could include you in these missions, I would, but it's not up to me. I thought you could look out for Quinn and help her train while Bast and I are gone, keep our team strong for when it can reunite."

"I am not a babysitter," she snaps. "I am a soldier and last time I checked, Quinn can look after herself."

I would take that as a compliment if it wasn't for her tone.

I shift in my seat. "Blake might be right, Jax. I don't think I need to be watched."

Blake throws out her hands. "See, even Quinn doesn't need me."

I look over at her. "That is not what I meant. Don't twist my words. Don't act like you know what goes on in my head better than I do. I still value our friendship."

She laughs, a cold, dark sound. "Oh, you don't like it when someone assumes something? Strange."

The conversation was three days ago, but I still know what she's talking about. I could apologize. I could let it go, but my ego gets the better of me.

"I can't assume something I already know," I tell her.

"Oh, you are so self-centred," she snaps. "My business is none of your concern."

Her words sting, like a thousand tiny paper cuts. "I am trying to help you, Blake. I'm trying to be a good friend. I just… I want you to be happy."

She raises an eyebrow. "Yeah?" she says. "Then you'll leave me alone." She gets to her feet and looks across the table at Jax. "I'll stay out of your stupid mission, but Quinn is on her own." She storms off then, her dark braid flying behind her.

Bast and Jax alternate between gaping at me with silent eyes and where Blake disappeared.

People at the surrounding tables stare at us. I send them a glare that says, "Mind your own business or I will *end* you." They can't scramble to look away fast enough.

"Quinn." Jax reaches for me and I brush his arm away.

"I'm just…" Bast says. "I'll go after her." He doesn't look in my direction.

Jax nods.

Bast gets up and moves like a robot through the tables, following whatever trail Blake left behind.

Blake.

Where the *hell* had that come from? She leapt at my throat, and I returned the favour.

Assassins below.

I take a breath to calm myself and unclench my fists. Then I let out an enormous sigh and lay my head on the table.

"Well, that was great," I mumble.

Jax sets his hand on my shoulder.

I tense, but let it stay there.

"It's…" he tries.

"It's a mess," I tell him, raising my head again.

His arm falls. "But it's not unfixable."

"Says you."

"Quinn, look," he says, "people get into arguments all the time; it's part of life, not the end of the world. It will get better. People are meant to forgive." He scratches the back of his head. "Could you imagine if the two of us stopped talking after our first argument? Hell, when you got mad at Blake that one time, you threw daggers at a door you were pretending was her. She forgave you then."

"I didn't tell her about the dagger throwing," I point out.

"Okay, but you get what I'm saying," he replies, "and just for the record, it's not all your fault. I got her going and today… Today is a rough day for Blake."

"Why?"

He looks uncomfortable. "I'm not supposed to say."

Ah.

"Is it...about the baby?"

He lets out a breath. "So she *did* tell you. I wasn't sure. Today is the two-year anniversary of her daughter's death."

"Oh Guild," I breathe, my heart seizing in my chest. "Now she has to spend it alone. That's terrible, we never should've…"

He puts a hand on my arm. "Hey, it's okay. You didn't know. You can't blame yourself for something out of your control."

I massage my temples. "But what do I *do*, Jax? How do I fix it? I'm the kind of person who constantly tears things apart. I don't know how..."

I clench my fists.

They never taught us how to put our shattered hearts back together at the Guild, just how to keep from slicing ourselves on the fragments.

Jax pulls my hand away from my head and squeezes it. "I can help you, when the time is right," he says, "but right now, she needs space."

I sigh and let the warmth of his hand sooth my anxious thoughts.

As much as I hate to leave Blake alone today, he's right. Trying to fix it now will only make it worse. She's in no state of mind to listen to me.

"I suggest we go train like we planned," Jax goes on. "It'll take your mind off it for a bit."

"I suppose that's as good a plan as any."

"Well, I came up with it."

I roll my eyes. "Shut up and lead the way, you crazy idiot."

"Don't mind if I do." He stands up, dragging me with him. I let him pull me to my feet and into a future that—while uncertain—may lead to something better.

CHAPTER FIFTEEN

The training room looks smaller, less impressive than I remember. Shadows line the walls. The weapons rack looks down on me, as if it knows the wrongs I've dealt.

Stop judging me. I didn't mean...anything.

I look over at Jax and he gives me an encouraging smile. "So, where do you want to start today? Your choice."

I scan the weapons rack. Where to begin? Part of me doesn't want to pick up a weapon ever again; the other part yearns to have the comfort of a blade in my hand once more, to tear apart all those who wronged me.

I push against that second part.

My instinct is to choose a knife or dagger of some sort because it is small, and I should work my way up to bigger weapons, because it's where we started at the Guild.

I ignore that instinct and stamp down on the inferno of that other life trying to roar toward me. It will stay ashes. I won't follow in my old footsteps.

"Hand me a bow," I say.

He raises an eyebrow at my choice. No doubt he expected me to choose a sword or gun. "Cross or long?" he asks.

"Long," I reply.

"Any particular preferences other than that?"

"Surprise me."

"Can do." He marches over to the weapons rack with me trailing behind. He studies his options, hands on his hips, a frown on his face.

I study him. He's just so irresistible.

Finally, he grabs a light brown bow, most likely made of yew that looks as if it survived many more battles than Haven's twenty year war had to offer. It's ancient. Scratches mar its limbs, along with dents and other questionable defects. The pure white colour of the string tells me it's new though, so the bow might not fall apart when I put it to use for the first time in centuries.

Jax holds it out to me. "What do you think?"

"To be honest, I think it'll turn to dust the moment I let go of the string," I tell him, but I take it anyway.

He rolls his eyes. "It's not that old."

"Says you."

He shakes his head. "Just give it a shot," he says, grinning at his "joke."

"Arrows?" I ask, refusing to acknowledge his lame attempt at humour.

He hands me a quiver and I sling it over my shoulder, before making my way over to the target area. I set my feet—or my foot and the metal contraption of the other one—and then I reach for an arrow and set the notch against the bowstring.

Breathe, I remind myself. *Focus. No distractions.*

I pull the bow up and back once to get a feel for it. The draw weight is heavy, but not unbearable. I lower the bow, keeping the arrow nocked, and look over at Jax. "Target?"

"Um... It's right over there." He points to the target stand across the room from us, while looking at me like I've lost my mind.

"No, I know that," I say. "Tell me what I should hit. Give me a target on the target."

He frowns. "Aren't you supposed to aim for the centre?"

I glare at him.

A grin creeps back onto his face.

"Oh my god, stop messing with me."

"Left outer ring," he says, ignoring my comment...

I raise the bow again and my arms shake from the force of holding it back. Maybe I shouldn't start with a longbow.

Or maybe you shouldn't have stayed bedridden so long, I scold myself.

Shut up.

I steady my limbs.

Breathe in, I remind myself.

Aim.

My eyes squint, focusing on the white ring.
Breathe out.
I let go of the string.
The arrow flies out with a *twang* and lands with a *thump.*
I take in the target and the arrow still quivering from its impact in the left outer ring.
Score.
I grin at Jax. "Beat that."
He gives me a look that melts me to my core and barks out, "Second ring, top right."
I suppress my blush and raise the bow.
Breathe in.
Aim.
Breathe out.
Fire.
Twang...thump.
Another perfect shot.
"Third ring, touching the edge of the centre ring."
Breathe.
Aim.
Fire.
Twang, thump.
"Bull's-eye."
Breathe, aim, fire.
Twang, thump!
Jax whistles. The arrow is dead centre, an inch of it lost to the eye. "Not too shabby," he says.
"Not too shabby?" I reply. "I'd like to see you do better."

He crosses his arms. "My superiority would only embarrass you."

"Oho," I breathe, "watch it there, wise guy, or one of these arrows might go clean through your heart."

"Oh please no, anything but that. Cupid already hit me there once…"

I resist the urge to kiss the smirk off his stupid face, and focus on the task at hand. I unsling the quiver of arrows and hold them and the bow out to him. "Daggers," I say.

"So we're moving on?"

I nod. "Bows are nice and all, but they're not practical."

"True," he agrees. "Daggers it is." He takes the bow and quiver from me and returns them to the rack.

I peruse the dagger options and my eyes zero in on a set of six sleek black blades. "Those ones," I tell him, pointing to them.

"You sure?"

"Positive."

He reaches up and grabs them for me. "There you are, milady," he says, bowing as he hands them over.

I smack him on the arm. "Cut it out," I say, but I'm smiling, blushing.

I whirl away from him and face the target once more. The blades find homes in my belt and I palm one in my right hand, feeling the grooves in the hilt. I switch hands for a second and wipe my sweaty palm on my pants. Then I plant my feet on a slight angle and lean back, pulling my arm with me.

I take a deep breath, closing my eyes for a second to centre myself. Then I focus on the target and shoot forward, my weight transferring from my back foot to my front, the force racing through my body.

My elbow and wrist snap forward as I release the dagger.

It spins in the air, the thump of my heart matching each rotation until...

Thump.

Bull's-eye.

Come on, Quinn, you can do better than that.

I take the second dagger in my left hand. It lands to the right of the first blade, scraping along it. The sound sends chills down my spine.

"Right," I say.

The third dagger goes right-handed into the rightmost circle.

"Left."

The reverse becomes true.

I study the target and the fifth dagger in my left hand. "Dead centre," I say.

I take a deep breath, lean back, aim, and...

Thump.

Perfect shot.

I smile. "Again."

Breathe, lean, aim...

I close my eyes.

Thunk.

"What?" Jax exclaims. "That's impossible!"

I open my eyes to see my last dagger stuck into the hilt of its predecessor, which is now embedded an inch into the target. I smile wider.

I turn to Jax and bow low. "World's best knife thrower, at your service," I tell him.

"I'll say," he replies. "That was an amazing throw."

I raise an eyebrow. "You're actually giving me credit?"

"Well, after witnessing something like that... I'd be crazy not to."

"Thanks."

"You're welcome," he says. "Next request?"

I smile. "Guess."

He heads over to the weapons rack once more and I amble over to a training mat. He returns with two wooden practice swords.

I groan. "Wooden ones?"

"I don't want you to trip and hurt yourself."

I scowl. "Oh someone's going to get hurt, but it's not going to be me."

He grins. "Come and get me, Ballinger."

"It would be my pleasure."

I catch the sword he throws at me and we sink into fighting stances before rushing each other.

He lunges for me and I dodge.

My sword scrapes his hair as he ducks the blow I aimed at his head.

I feel the passage of his sword by my ribcage as I whirl away.

Parry, dodge, and thrust.

Our swords smash against one another as we attempt to gain the upper hand. He doesn't budge and neither do I.

Our arm muscles strain.

My foot slips.

My sword begins to fall. I try to fix my stance, but my right knee gives out and...

I'm falling.

Jax throws his sword away and lunges for me.

I end up in his arms.

He ends up on the floor.

He looks at me with a ridiculous grin on his face. "Fine pair aren't we?" He's breathless.

Well, that's not about to change.

I lean in and kiss him. He returns the favour and soon we're gasping for air, stealing each other's limited oxygen supply. He's the first to pull away.

I lean my head against his chest as we both regain our breath. I can feel his heartbeat going a hundred miles a minute through his sweat-soaked shirt.

I smile.

He looks at me. "What?"

I smile wider. "Nothing."

"Well it has to be *something*."

"Don't you like not knowing?" My smile turns into a grin.

He groans and leans back to the floor. "You're going to be the death of me, you know that right?"

"I'll make it quick."

He chuckles. "Thanks."

"No problemo, friend."

He frowns. "Friend?"

"What, you want me to call you sweetheart or honey bunches? No thank you."

"Aw babe," he replies, squeezing his arms around me, "*come on.*"

I burn beneath the surface as his words catch me off guard. "God, you're so beautiful," I tell him.

I reach over to pull him back to me, but then I hear the door scrape open along the tiled floor and I stop mid-motion.

"*What* is going on here? Seriously guys, get a room."

I roll my eyes. Trey. I give her a scathing look before peeling myself off Jax. Then I stand up and adjust my outfit.

Jax sighs and follows suit.

My right thigh is pulsing a bit after my fall, but at least I don't have a shin to bruise anymore.

"Better?" I ask Trey.

She narrows her eyes. "Fractionally."

I cross my arms. "What do you want?"

"Jeez, don't sound so enthused. Wrong side of the bed this morning?"

"No, I just don't like interruptions."

"Well, if you weren't in such a public place," she points out, "you wouldn't have to worry about it."

"Spare me your logic and answer the question." I'm not angry, just trying to be the irritating little sister. Sort of.

"Jax's presence is required in the council room," she replies.

"Oh yeah," Jax says. "I didn't realize the time."

I give him a confused look.

"I have to go to that meeting I was talking to Bast about this morning."

"Oh right," I say.

"Do you want to come?" he asks.

I shake my head. "It wouldn't be a good idea, especially if Blake heard about it. I don't want to push her away any more than I already have."

Trey looks relieved. "I'm glad I don't have to fight you on that."

"Why would you?" I ask her.

"Jenson told me that I am, under *no* circumstances, to allow 'the assassin' to come."

"I'm going to kill him," I spit. "One of these days I'm just...going to kill him."

"I'm sorry," she says, genuine sympathy in her voice and eyes. "I don't agree with him, I just pass on the message."

"He's lucky I already decided to step back, but he can't exclude me forever. I may be injured, but I'm still important."

Jax touches my arm. "He'll come around, Quinn. Jenson just... His mind isn't easily changed and he's been under a lot of pressure since the Guild attack. Deep down, he knows you're crucial to our success. You and Kuen both, seeing as you're the only two people the Charger—Sephtis, rather—has ever trusted."

"That's no longer true," I reply, "not for me anyway."

"Maybe," he says, "but even so, you still have a lot of inside knowledge from years of experience. You got us into the Guild, something no one has done since...ever."

"Yes, but how much did we accomplish?"

He squeezes my hand. "A lot more than you think. We showed them our might. We forced them to scatter and now they're worried. They know we have potential. We've sharpened an edge and they're still stitching themselves up. They don't have a base—"

"That we know of."

"We found it once. We can do it again. Someone smart told me that." He winks and I can't help but smile.

"That's why these missions are so important," Trey adds. "Besides, just because you're not in the meetings or on the missions right now, doesn't mean we won't be working with you or telling you everything."

"I guess that's true."

Trey gives me a smile. "It won't be forever, Quinn. I promise you. Jenson just needs more time."

I sigh. "I'll try to be patient."

"And I'll try to hurry the old man along," she promises. She and Jax start heading for the doors.

Jax turns back. "You're not coming?"

"Well, not to the meeting," I reply. "We just discussed that, but no. I'm going to stick around and practice some more. And don't worry, I'll be careful. Honest. I have no interest in restarting my recovery. I'd rather jump off a building."

He gives me a look. "Promise me."

"I promise. Cross my heart and hope to die." I draw an "X" over my chest.

"Okay," he says.

"Go bug the hell out of Jenson for me," I tell him.

He smiles. "I will. See you later, though I'm not sure what time."

I shoo him away. "Get going will you?"

He sighs and follows Trey out of the room.

I smile at the door as it closes behind them. Jenson might have thought he was being clever, but we'll show him who is the best fox in the base. If he wants to play at being cunning, that's fine. I'm game, but he's going to lose.

CHAPTER SIXTEEN

I practice for at least another forty minutes. Several people come and go: a few individuals and one group of about five. I try my best to ignore their presence and focus on my training, to ignore their stares. I figure I probably look pretty haggard, sweat-drenched and disgusting. Not to mention my torn pant leg and the prosthetic that is still a goddamn beacon.

I can just imagine all the stories circling around.

You hear about the crazy assassin girl?

They let her back, eh? Only now, she's a cripple.

I heard she almost died.

I heard they were going to kill her.

I wish they had.

Yeah, and then where would they all be? If I go, the rest of them don't stand a chance. Even *with* me…

It takes a lot of effort to keep up hope in this day and age. Guild, I contemplate death too often, but I'm not a believer in false hope. I hate disappointment.

I resist the urge to glare at each person who walks through the training room door and throw myself into my training. I bring out a couple different kinds of guns to work on balance with the kickback and I continue doing sword drills by myself.

When I hit the ground for the fourth time, I call it quits for the day. I pick myself up and brush the dust off my uniform. Then I gather the array of weapons scattered around the targets and my training mat, and return them to the rack. I'm breathing pretty heavily by the time I finish.

I notice I'm limping as I head for the door and vow to take it easy for the rest of the day, and a bit of tomorrow. I don't want to push it. I haven't even been walking that long; sword drills are another story entirely. I sigh and step into the hall. Will the torture of recovery ever end?

I make it to my room without incident and I don't know if I'm relieved or frustrated. I lock the door behind me and hobble over to my closet. I reach for my weapons to disarm myself, before I remember I don't have any to my name anymore. It's a weird concept. For a moment, my chest feels empty, but then I shake it off and get changed.

I don't need weapons to complete myself. It's probably a good thing they're gone. It will help me move on from that life. It'll keep Silent Night six feet under where she belongs.

I shudder and tug on my second outfit of the day. Grey uniform number six. I grab my knife from under the mattress again and cut the pant leg so it matches my first outfit. Then I pull all the outfits off their hangers and take a seat on the floor where I proceed to fix them all to my new standard.

There's a pile of fabric in my lap when I'm done and my remaining eight outfits lack lower right legs, as they should. I'm remaking myself in a new image. I'm not going to hide anymore. Silent Night wouldn't have wanted to show any kind of weakness. Quinn doesn't believe the leg is a weak point, and even if it is, I don't care. Let others see that I'm not invincible, that I'm human too. For me, the leg is proof I walked through hell and back and managed to stay standing. I'm so lucky and, with any more luck, I'll live through the battles still to come. The chances...

I shake my head and stand up, taking the pile of fabric with me. I shove the pile into one of the emptier pillowcases still tucked under my bed. I should get rid of them soon, throw away the memories.

Soon.

I sigh and walk over to the bed, shoving the knife back under the mattress.

I'm not sure what to do next; I'm used to my days being filled with physio and nurse visits. It's odd to have free time once again. Eventually, I decide it's probably late enough in the day for lunch, so I head to the caf. I ignore the stares this time, keeping my head held high, without being condescending. It's a fine line, I discover.

It really is too early for lunch; I can tell by the amount of people in the caf when I arrive. I can count them on one hand. However, this also means the lineup doesn't exist. I practically skip over to the counter and pile a plate with food. I'm starving after my training session. I take a look at my plate and shake my head. Bast is rubbing off on me.

I wince at the thought of him. Bast and Blake. I haven't seen either one of them since breakfast. At least they have each other. Maybe it'll make them realize how much they mean to each other. Maybe it'll be a good thing. I hope so.

I could have the pick of any table in the caf at this hour, but habits die hard and loyalties once cemented, even harder. So I take a seat at our regular table and dig in. I need to cut back on food though, honestly. It's getting a bit out of hand. I eat every meal like it's going to be my last.

It might be.

I sigh. Here comes the thoughts about death again.

Mercifully, my dark thoughts are interrupted by shouting in the hall outside. Angry voices penetrate the doors of the caf, but not enough to make out any words. I stand up, cautious and then the doors burst open.

A man storms in, every muscle in his body taut. I'm so used to seeing depression on his face that I don't recognize him at first. Then, his gaze sweeps around the room and lands on me.

Kuen?

Assassins below, what has he done now?

He looks away from me and marches over to the food counter.

O'Reilly comes tearing into the room after him, giving off the pathetic aura of a drenched cat. "I do believe that is an infraction of your sentence, Assassin!" he yells at Kuen.

The term doesn't have as much of a ring to it as it does when aimed at me.

"And I don't particularly care, Callum," Kuen retorts. "Look at me. Does. It. Look. Like. I. Care." His voice isn't raised, but it carries across the room nonetheless.

O'Reilly is totally out of his element, I can tell by the way he stares at Kuen without saying a word. He has no idea what to do. If I was him, I'd back off. I can sense Kuen's kill vibes from here. Hell, I'd be able to sense them from halfway across Haven.

Kuen wants nothing more right now than to rip O'Reilly's head off his shoulders, but he's holding back. The killing instinct is telling him to decimate and he's staying in control. That takes an incredible amount of willpower. Kuen would be a formidable foe indeed.

"Nothing to say?" Kuen asks. His voice leeches contempt.

O'Reilly remains silent.

Amateur.

Kuen would chew him up and spit him out in seconds, before O'Reilly ever knew he was in danger of being eaten.

"Good," Kuen says through clenched teeth, clenched against the monster that wants *out*. "Now go stand by the door like the good little guard dog you are."

I wince as I remember referring to Jax as such when I first arrived. I was awful, wasn't I?

O'Reilly chooses this moment to stand up for himself.

I want to melt into the table.

He puffs out his chest and says, "I am in charge here. You can't order me around. I'll report you to Jenson before you can even blink an eye, so—"

Kuen punches the wall beside O'Reilly's head, missing O'Reilly's skull by millimetres. O'Reilly must have felt the wind of its passage for he sways a fraction.

Kuen brings his bloody knuckles in front of O'Reilly's face. "I can put an end to your pretty little life before *you* can blink an eye. Don't you dare tell me what to do."

O'Reilly can barely breathe.

"Go. Stand. By. The door," Kuen repeats.

O'Reilly does as Kuen says.

Kuen slams a plate onto an empty tray and fills it with food, the entire caf watching his every move. Even the table of giggling children has lost interest in their meals.

"I take back what I said about you being a guard dog," Kuen calls out to Callum as he walks away from the food counter and over to me. "You're more like a puppy, too pathetic to do anything but follow exactly what your master says."

The room is silent as a tomb when Kuen finally looks away from O'Reilly—as if dismissing his existence entirely—and back at me.

He smiles at me and says, "Morning, Quinn. Lovely day, isn't it?"

I shake my head at his quick turnaround of emotions. The guy has to be a psychopath. Maybe I shouldn't have given him the tools to roam free.

"Hi," I reply, a bit wary of what I should say after what I just witnessed.

Kuen sits down across from me and sets his tray down, his right hand dripping blood onto the floor.

I wish I picked a different table.

He doesn't say anything else and I follow his example as he starts eating. I can feel every eye in the room watching us. The freak-shows. I've never felt more uncomfortable in my life, and I've been in some interesting situations.

After about five minutes, I finish my own lunch and sit up straighter. I gauge Kuen's face and, after deeming it to be safe, I say, "You know, Kuen, when I told you not to let O'Reilly hold you back, I didn't mean you should terrorize him to the point of shortening his lifespan." Despite myself, I tense, waiting for his reaction.

"Ah, but then again," he replies, "you didn't say *not* to." He is trying to lighten the mood, but this situation isn't funny.

"Kuen, I'm serious," I say, leaning closer to him. "What were you thinking? Do you *have* a death wish? If Jenson didn't like you before, he surely won't now."

"I slipped, okay?" I can hear the control in his voice wavering again, but I ignore it.

"Slipped? *Slipped?* You can't slip, Kuen, ever." I clench my fist on the table. "You can't afford to. They *will* kill you, without question, without another trial. Trey won't be able to save you and that will kill *her*."

His eyes harden. "Don't bring her into this."

"Oh, I will. I'm not going to sugar-coat it. You might think it's funny to go all scary assassin on O'Reilly, but it's not. It's serious. This isn't the Guild."

He scowls. "You think I don't know that?"

I lean back. "No, I don't think you do. If you did, you wouldn't be so blatantly violent, so blatantly stupid."

He points a bloody finger at me. "You watch it."

"No," I snap. "*You* better watch it or one day they'll stick a syringe in your throat and you'll wake up chained to that chair in the trial room and they'll decide exactly how they want to kill you."

I grow quiet and he lets go of anger long enough to study me. "You say that as if you know what it's like."

I bite my lip. "I know exactly what it's like. The day before the Guild attack, I... I messed up. I lost it on somebody, let anger and killing instinct take over and I... I attacked a girl, for no more reason than the fact that I couldn't stand her. Trey was the one they sent to come get me; she was the one who sedated me with that awful needle... I realize now, how hard that must have been for her, but that's not the point of this. I woke up in that trial room and if they'd chained me to the chair, instead of tying my hands to the arms, I wouldn't have been able to escape their punishment.

"The point is, Kuen, that they've learned from their mistakes and you won't have a chance in hell, if they choose to end your time on this earth. So don't you dare throw it all away because of hatred for one person. O'Reilly is not worth your anger, let alone your life."

And Natalie was never worth mine.

I take a moment to breathe and Kuen stares at me as if he's never seen me before. "I never would've thought…"

"What?"

"I never thought it would be you saving me. I thought I'd get to be the hero, but instead, I'm the damsel in distress."

I smile. "Serves you right."

He snorts. "I can't promise you anything, Quinn, but I'll try to be better."

"I know," I sigh, but trying might not be enough.

"It would be a lot easier if those damn 'initiation lessons' were even remotely interesting," he goes on.

I give him a look. "You lost your temper over *that*?"

"Not entirely." Again, he's trying to lighten the mood, but this time it works.

"What," I reply, "you don't like listening to the teacher repeat herself over and over for an hour?"

He laughs. "Honestly, I'd rather smash my head into a telephone pole."

"I often contemplated returning to the Guild so I could throw myself into one of those underground lakes and end the torture on the rocks," I admit.

He tries to hold back his laughter and fails.

When he finally sobers, he says, "I have to go back to them, don't I?"

"The lectures?"

He nods.

"Yeah, you do."

"For how long?"

"Until they've decided their doctrines are cemented in your mind. Until they think they've tamed you."

He groans. "I'll be going to them until I die. *They'll* be the death of me."

It's my turn to laugh. "I'm sure there are worse ways to go."

"Like what?" he snorts.

"Nothing I can think of off the top of my head…"

"That's what I thought."

Neither one of us says anything for a while. He finishes his lunch and I just sit there, lost in thought.

Then he stands up. "I guess I should go then, drag Callum along with me."

"Yes," I reply. "You better stop by the hospital too and get that hand checked. I wouldn't doubt that it's broken."

He lifts the hand in front of his face, dried blood staining it. "Oh, I'm sure it is." He gives it the once-over, rotating his wrist, and then shrugs. "I've had worse, though."

"Doesn't mean you have to suffer now."

"I'll think about it."

"Don't forget what I said," I remind him. "This isn't a game; if you lose, there's no starting over. So please, be careful."

"I will," he assures me. "Thanks for the, um...pep talk. We'll call it that."

"You're welcome."

He walks away. At the door, he says something quietly to O'Reilly and then leaves. O'Reilly follows after him, more like a servant than a guard now. When the door shuts behind them, I stand up.

As I head for the door as well, my eyes drift to Kuen's blood decorating the floor. It sets me on edge. I hope to God it doesn't stain because something tells me it'll be an omen, one of even worse things to come.

• • •

My feet carry me halfway to the hospital wing before I remember I don't have to go back there. What do I do now then? I need a goal to work toward; I need to go out and do something, but I'm not ready.

Will I ever be, though? I consider jumping back in the action now, but I know that's the impatience talking. It's certainly not the logic, if I even have any.

I should go find Blake and talk to her, but she might kill me if she sees me again today. She needs space. I'm not about to deny her that right, but I wish I had someone else to talk to. I wish I wasn't such a loner.

I groan.

Why does life suck? Why aren't there ever any answers for all the constant pressing questions? Why?

I feel like screaming to release all the pent-up energy packed inside me, but I don't. Instead, I steer my legs back toward my bedroom, hoping to find something interesting to do along the way.

Fate must be smiling on me, for once, because I turn a corner halfway to my room and run into someone.

I stumble, but the person grabs clumsily for my arm, just managing to keep me upright.

"Sorry, Quinby," he says. "You okay?"

I step back and brush myself off. "I would be better if you looked where you're going."

"Except you were the one who walked into me," he replies.

"I was not!"

Bast holds up a hand. "Look, Quinby, I'm going to be nice and forgive you this time, but you should pay more attention next time, okay?"

I go to take a swipe at him, but he is already leaping out of range when I raise my hand.

He grins. "Missed me."

"Oh you are the most insufferable person I know," I exclaim, clenching my fists.

He smiles. "Why thank you."

I shake my head. "What are you up to, Bast?"

"Just came back from that meeting with Jenson. He kept us forever."

I snort. "Anything useful?"

He shrugs. "I tuned most of it out to be honest. I'm sure Jax will update me on the important stuff when it's needed."

"Which means I can't get any intel from you then."

"Sorry to disappoint."

There is a pause in our conversation and I have to ask.

"How is Blake?"

He sighs. "She's been better, but I think she's stable enough."

I bite my lip.

Bast must notice my distress because he adds, "She'll come around."

I wrap my arms around my chest. "You can't know that."

"But I know Blake. She doesn't hold grudges, Quinn. If she did, she and I would've stopped talking the day we met. She throws up walls, but she hates being alone. She always comes back."

"But what if she doesn't?"

He pokes a finger into my sternum. "You, my friend, worry too much, which will only make everything worse. Blake will resolve the problem when she's ready. You need to relax. "

I sigh. "I wish there was something I could do."

"Well, Jax and I could help, if either one of you would tell us what the problem is exactly." He's fishing for information, but I'm not going to take the bait.

"Nice try, but I'm not going to betray her trust, especially now. You'll find out anyway, if things work out."

He raises an eyebrow, still oblivious.

"And that's all I'm willing to say, Sebastian. So get your nose out of my business."

His brows knit together in a scowl and he sighs. "Fine, I won't pry, but I'm on the hunt. So tread carefully."

"Oh, I'll definitely keep that in mind," I tell him. A plan is forming in my mind, but my smirk gives me away.

"You're going to drop false hints aren't you," he says.

"I didn't say that."

"But you're thinking about it."

"Maybe."

I start walking down the hall and he falls into step beside me.

"Where are we going?" he asks.

"I'm not sure. What do you suggest?"

He thinks for a moment and then he says, "Have you ever been to a library?"

I give him a quizzical look.

"Oh, you poor girl," he gasps. "It isn't as exciting as the Den, mind you, but every decent person needs to experience the library."

"What is it?" I ask.

He answers with another question. "Do you like books?"

"Sort of? I mean, my mom used to read me fairytales, but I have never read any books on my own. The Guild taught us how to read for mission purposes, not leisure. We weren't taught anything for leisure." Which explains why I'm always so fidgety if I don't have something I'm supposed to do.

"Well, if you even remotely like books, you'll love this. Come on." He grabs me by the hand and basically tows me along as he starts running down the hall and towards this mysterious "library."

CHAPTER SEVENTEEN

By the time we reach the library, I can feel the strain on my leg. I rest my bad foot on my good one and lean against the wall as Bast regards the large double oak doors at the end of the hall.

He looks at me. "Blake and Jax consider this to be heaven on earth."

"Should be interesting to see then," I say, "considering I'll never enter the real heaven."

He shoves me playfully. "You're getting there, Quinn, even if the three of us have to drag you along."

"My weighted sins will only drag you down," I argue.

He gives me a look. "Stop being such a pity party."

"Whatever, let's carry on, shall we?"

Without further ceremony, he leads me into the library.

I've never seen so many books in all my life. They line the walls in rickety shelving units from floor to ceiling. The room is dimly lit by light bulbs hanging from the ceiling, and pockets of darkness linger throughout. Hardwood floors run beneath our feet, an attempt to give it a homey feel, I guess. The wooden shelves themselves are knotted and bowed, dilapidated masters of the books they hold. I can't tell at first how big the room is, but the shelves continue beyond sight, disappearing into the gloom.

Bast spreads his arms out, turning in a small circle. "What do you think?"

"I'm not going to lie, this place is a bit creepy," I tell him, "but I like it."

"I assume you'd like a tour?"

I smile. "Of course."

"Then let's get going."

He leads me down the corridors between the leaning stacks, showing me the sections where different genres of books are kept. He tells me they are organized further alphabetically by the author's last name. I ask him who wrote the books and why.

"No idea," he says. "They're from before the war. I guess people had time to write back then and motivation. Nowadays, we're too focused on survival to sit down and write something that will likely never be read. Maybe one day we'll find that headspace again."

I smile. "I'd like to see that day."

"It's what we're all living for, a time when survival isn't on the top of our to-do list."

I nod. "So, where did you guys get all these books?"

"We take them from the abandoned houses we come across and bring them here."

"Who's allowed to read them?"

"Anyone. They're free. You can take your pick." He spreads his arms out towards the books, as if offering me the greatest gift of all time.

"What?"

"I'm sure you're bored out of your skull being out of the action. This will give you something to do while you recover. Grab one and it's yours. Well, I mean *technically* you're supposed to bring it back one day, but…"

I smile, taking a few steps away. "I'll be back in a bit."

He nods.

I drift through the stacks, brushing my fingers along spines and tilting my head to read the vertical titles. I'm drawn to the fantasy section, wanting to lose myself in another world, escape from this harsh reality of a nightmare we are living.

I stumble across a book with a familiar figure on the spine, familiar in the stance. I would know an assassin anywhere.

I tug the book off the shelf. A white-haired girl with a fitted suit and countless weapons stares back at me. Her eyes are a mixture of despair and hatred, but perhaps there is a flicker of hope there too, in the way she stares down into my soul. It's as if she is telling me to keep going, to never surrender.

I won't. I promise.

I don't bother reading the back cover. I tuck the book under my arm and continue on.

Several rows later, something else catches my eye. A once-shiny, now-faded cover faces me, a cover I recognize.

It's Snow White.

Mom.

A tear finds its way down my cheek. On the floor, a speck of dust washes away.

Oh Guild, I miss her so much and to find this story once again... It is a piece of her.

I take it gently in my hands, as if it's in danger of disintegrating at any second, as if it's not real but only a figment of my imagination and rapidly deteriorating mind. It looks real, feels real. I cradle it in my arms. Then I turn and start heading back to Bast.

At least, I think this is the way. In this labyrinthine library, there's no way of telling where you are, let alone where you are going. I don't mind, though. It's my kind of place—enough dark to shelter me, yet enough light to keep me standing.

In the end, Bast finds me.

I turn a corner and there he is. My heart skips a beat and I jump back.

He laughs. "Did I scare you?"

I snort. "Scare me? I am fearless, though a little warning next time would be nice."

"What," he says with a grin, "you'd rather I made all the floorboards creak so you spend five minutes biting your fingers down to nothing, wondering if it's me or an axe murderer?"

I shudder. "Great, so now I'm not going to sleep."

He waves a hand. "Meh, sleep is for sissies."

I roll my eyes. "You're crazy."

He snorts. "Look who's talking."

I ignore his comment, noticing the book tucked under his arm. "Who's that for?"

He shifts it into his hands, flashing the cover for a second. "Oh, this? It's Blake's favourite. I thought it might cheer her up."

I fight to keep my expression neutral.

Somebody pays close attention.

Before I can say anything else, a muffled siren sound shatters the silence.

I jump again.

Bast swears under his breath.

"What is that?" I ask.

He sets the book on the shelf beside him and reaches for something on his belt. I realize it is some sort of walkie talkie as he holds it up to his ear. He presses a button and the siren stops. "Hello? No, I'm with Quinn. What's up?"

I furrow my eyebrows.

Who's he talking to?

"Are you sure?" His voice is excited, nervous, and cautious all at once. "And you want me to...? Okay, I'll be ready in ten."

Ready? Ready for what?

"Yes...Of course I can...Yes, I'll tell Quinn you said hi...See you soon."

It has to be Jax. I set my books on the shelf.

There is a click and I know he's hung up.

"Jax says hi," Bast says, returning the device to his belt.

"What's happening?" I ask him. I can hear the trepidation in my voice.

For a second he looks as if he doesn't want to tell me, but he takes a breath and says, "A pack of assassins was spotted a couple blocks from here. Jenson wants our team to intercept them. If we go now, we might catch them; it'll probably be our only chance."

"And Jenson is sure they're assassins?"

Bast shrugs. "How should I know?"

"It's too dangerous."

He frowns. "Again with the worrying."

"You know what, Bast? I—"

"Bast? Quinn? You guys in here still?"

Jax!

"Over here, man," Bast calls out. "Follow the knocking." He raps his fingers on a shelf in a steady rhythm and a few moments later, Jax rounds the corner.

My heart feels lighter at the sight of him.

He smiles. "Thought I'd say hi myself."

"What's the plan?" Bast asks him.

"You go on ahead and get your gear," Jax replies. "I'll be along in a minute for the briefing."

Bast frowns. "Isn't Trey supposed to do the briefing?"

"She is, but Jenson had her pull an all-night watch at the entrance. She isn't in any shape to face assassins."

Nerves bubble in my stomach. "Is it safe to go without her?"

"It'll have to be," Jax says. "We can't miss this opportunity."

"So do I get to be the leader next time or…?" Bast starts.

Jax gives him a look. "Didn't I tell you to get going?"

"All right, all right," Bast says. "See you around, Quinby."

"Thanks for showing me this place."

He smiles. "Anytime."

Bast heads out and Jax takes his place. "So, the library, eh? What do you think?"

"It's amazing. I didn't think something like this was possible and I'm surprised Bast was the one to show it to me. He doesn't seem like a reader."

"Oh, he's not. He keeps a stash of whiskey in a back corner somewhere. The place isn't frequented, so he comes here when he wants to drink alone. Don't tell Blake."

I shake my head. "Typical. How does he come up with these ideas?"

Jax shrugs. "I wish I knew. Anyway, the team is waiting for me."

I grab his hand. "Please be careful."

"I will." He goes to pull away—I can see the agitation in his movements, he wants to *go*—but I hold tighter to his hand.

"Ajax Forrester," I say, "I'm serious. *Don't* underestimate them. Watch your back. Keep your eyes and ears peeled."

He nods. "I know. I've got this."

"I know," I echo. "I just don't want to lose you."

He locks eyes with me and lets me see the words he can't form, that he won't sacrifice anything in vain, that I can trust him. "I don't want to die today," he tells me.

"You better not; I'll kill you."

He laughs at that. "So, don't do anything you wouldn't do, right?"

I smile. "Right."

"I better go." He tries to walk away again.

"Hey," I protest. "Aren't you forgetting something?"

He grins and my feet are swept from underneath me as he pulls our still-joined hands toward him. He dips me towards the floor and his lips dance across mine. There's barely enough time to kiss him back before he's set me on my feet again. Still, I'm breathless.

"How's that?" he asks.

I can only nod.

He smiles and says, "Love you, Quinn. I'll be back as soon as I can." He kisses me quickly on the forehead before he leaves me.

By the time I find my voice again, he's gone.

"Come back to me," I whisper to the silence. "I'll wait for you."

When I regain my senses, I reach for the books I set on the shelf. I cradle them in my arms once more and start heading back to the entrance. Now, a *gentleman* would've led me out before he left me. However, I've been trained to find my way in new places, in the dark, so I have no problem in the dimly lit library. A few minutes later, I'm slipping through the oak doors and back into the main base.

I make my way to my room, but the going is slow. I worked my leg too much today. I have to be careful. I'm lucky to have this leg at all; I don't want to lose it.

For once, I don't get stares from everyone I pass and it's a relief. I like being in the spotlight, but it can get overwhelming. I didn't realize how much attention the prosthetic would draw. I didn't realize how much that attention would make me doubt myself.

But I have other issues to worry about. I reach my room and close the door behind me. Then I sink onto the bed, setting the books down on my bedside table.

I can't believe assassins were spotted this close to the base. They wouldn't be that stupid, or would they? Maybe it's a trap.

Oh God, I have to warn Jax.

I jolt to a sitting position before I remember the Guild has no idea where the Resistance is. I'm the only assassin—ex-assassin—who's ever found the place, and I haven't told a soul. So the assassins have no idea how close they are to their enemy base, how close they are to their lifetime goal...

Maybe that's the point. Maybe they're trying to sniff us out and we fell right for it.

We...

I shut down my thoughts. Guild, I'm overthinking this. I need to slow down and take a deep breath. I never worried before.

Yeah, and look where that took you.

Shut up.

I'm being ridiculous. Being alone isn't helping. I need someone to talk to. If only Blake...

Blake.

Oh God. She doesn't know.

I think of the book Bast grabbed for her, but left behind. I should've taken it with me. I should've made him tell her before he left.

Damn idiot.

I forget my leg, promising myself I'll rest all day tomorrow, and fly out of my room, barely managing to close the door in my wake.

I rush down the halls and it takes me a moment before I realize that, like with Jax, I have no idea where Blake's room is. Blake was right; I am a terrible friend. The only room I know about is Bast's and I wouldn't even know that if I hadn't gone with Jax that night when Bast was drunk out of his mind.

I wonder briefly how that habit started. Bast is too young to be chained to an addiction, but that doesn't change the truth. Maybe that's why Blake is so scared to admit her feelings. She doesn't want to let herself love someone who is slowly killing himself.

I wonder if Bast knows what he's getting himself into. Do any of us? Everybody has one thing that brings them down. We're all addicted to something—with some of us, it kills our bodies, and with others, it's our minds that die. If I had to guess, I'd say I'm the second, but enough of that, I'm supposed to be finding Blake.

If I were Blake, where would I go? Where would I feel safest after emotional trauma? The thing is, I don't even know that. What kind of friend am I? To not even know...

Wait. Maybe...

It's worth a shot.

I change direction and head for Trey's room. I pray she's in the same one as before, or else I'm screwed.

It doesn't take long to reach the guest wing. I knock on the door and wait. If you ask me, she should get her own room; she's been here too long to be a guest.

Take your coat off, Trey, make yourself at home.

I'm laughing at my own joke when she opens the door. "Quinn? You okay?" She gives me a weird look.

I sober up. "I'm fine, I was just wondering... Does the Resistance have a place where I can buy clothing? I mean, we have a tattoo parlour and I always get new clothes when I ask. So I thought..."

"Of course we have a clothing store," she says. "You think we can shop anywhere in town without the assassins noticing?"

I scowl. "Okay, I get it. The assassins suck, I'm well aware of that. Where is this clothing store?"

She crosses her arms. "Why do you want to know?"

I shrug. It's none of her business about Blake. "No reason in particular," I reply.

"Quinn," she says.

"I'll tell you if it works."

She gives me a look. "What are you planning?"

"Nothing, I swear to you," I tell her, "and even if I was, what are you going to do about it? You don't control me."

"I'm your sister."

I cross my arms. "That didn't make a difference before."

"Well it does now. I'm supposed to be concerned about you, Quinn. It's my job."

"Why though?" I ask. "Why act like a sister now, after everything? Just because it's convenient? That's not how this works."

She sighs. "I know. I know. I'm sorry. I just... I feel like I need to make up for the time we lost."

I sigh too. "Don't apologize, Trey. None of it is your fault and I don't want you pretending, lying to yourself to fill the gaping wound *he* left. I don't want you to feel like you owe me. You and Kuen both. I don't need your apologies. I don't blame you for anything and if you guys need my forgiveness or something, you can have it. Stop trying to atone for something you never did. So what, you abandoned me? I didn't know you had and you were saving yourselves. I would've done the same thing."

"It's down in the Den," she says.

"What?"

"The clothing store," she replies. "Follow the bar to the far side of the room. You can't miss it."

"Thank you," I say and then, "it's about Blake."

She nods. "Then do what you must."

CHAPTER EIGHTEEN

I hear the music pounding through the walls as I approach the Den. I forgot how loud it is and I'm not even there yet. I shake my head. This place is crazy, but I love it.

I reach the first door and, not having Bast's key to unlock it, I pull out my trusty bobby pin. I haven't broken in somewhere in a long while; it's disgraceful. I slip the pin in the slot and only have to twist it around a couple times before it clicks. Nice to see I'm not out of practice.

I take the steps slowly. My leg aches. I need to sit down soon.

The music intensifies as I descend. I push the last door open and am immediately immersed in the chaos that is the Den. It often reminds me of the Grand Cavern, just cooler and less hostile.

Okay, so they don't have much in common, but... Whatever.

I navigate the crowds as I make my way across the dance floor and try not to be pulled in by the beat. Thankfully, they're not playing dubstep, so I think I'm safe. My eyes flick to the tattoo parlour door as I pass by it.

I think about the thirteen letters inscribed on my ankle: Lincoln McColl. A false name. It should read Jacques Ballinger. Maybe I could get the tattoo artist to change it for me...

That's when I realize it's not there anymore. The tattoo is gone forever, along with the leg it was written on. I had it on my right ankle, the one I lost.

Somehow, I feel lighter, knowing that is one less burden to carry. Somehow, I know he wouldn't want me to carry it. I walk a little straighter and finally reach the far side of the club.

There are two doors on the far wall, but one is painted a vibrant blue. I figure that's what Trey meant by, "you can't miss it." I push it open and slip through. As soon as it closes behind me, the noise of the club cuts out.

Impossible.

I spin in a circle, anticipating an attack before my senses tell me I'm safe.

Damn Resistance and their innovations.

Different music is playing in the store, quieter and more relaxed. I look around. The place is packed with clothes, outfits ranging from dangerous to debonair. I spot a floor to ceiling rack of shoes and have to force my eyes away. I wander further in, scanning each nook and cranny for a glimpse of long, braided brown hair or Blake's face.

I find her in the back corner, looking through cloaks. She holds up a black one in front of a mirror and I approach so my reflection doesn't join hers.

"I like it," I say, "goes well with your eyes."

She jumps and whirls around, hand going to her heart, but her terrified expression morphs into a scowl when she sees me. "Oh," she mutters, "it's you."

"Yeah, just me."

She crosses her arms. "I thought I told you to leave me alone."

"You did, but I…"

She cuts me off. "What do you want?"

"I want to talk," I reply. "It's about…Bast."

She goes rigid. "I thought we've been over this," she all but spits. She tries to brush past me, but I grab her arm and push her back.

"Blake, please, just hear me out."

She narrows her eyes. "Or what, you'll kill me?"

"Oh, for God's sake," I snap, "save me the drama. I'm trying to do something nice."

"For once."

I ignore her comment. "Jax got a call from Jenson," I tell her. "A pack of assassins was spotted a couple blocks from here and his team was ordered out. Bast went with them."

She drops the cloak she's holding. "What?"

I grimace. "He didn't tell you he was going, did he?"

The pain in her eyes is answer enough.

I crouch down and pick up the cloak. Then I replace it on the rack, giving her a minute to compose herself. Still, she stares at me and says nothing.

"Blake? Are you...?"

There's an awkward moment of silence and inaction where neither of us are sure what to do. Then tears build up in Blake's eyes and she says, "I'm sorry."

Next thing I know, she lurches forward and wraps her arms around me, her entire being begging for forgiveness. I hold her as she starts crying.

"It's okay," I tell her.

She clings to me and sobs. All the fear and insecurities of the past little while come pouring out. I remain her rock as the oceans around her rage.

I run a hand down her hair. "It's okay. I forgive you. Just let it all out. You'll be okay. Let go."

And slowly, painfully, she does.

"You were right," she gasps when she finally resurfaces. She wipes her eyes. "You were always right. I love him. I love him so much it hurts. I'm sorry I couldn't face the truth enough to tell you. I just... I never thought..."

I squeeze her hand. "Don't apologize; I understand why you did it. You have to accept it on your own before you can share it." I shake my head. "It's the ones you don't see coming that shake you. Hell, did I ever tell you how it happened with Jax?"

"No," she sniffs.

"It was the day we went to the Guild together to see if my tunnels would work. I ordered an assassin outfit for him so he would fit in and as soon as I saw him in it... Guild he looks hot in black." The image flashes in my head and I blush.

Blake manages a laugh.

"I knew then I had fallen for him," I go on, "but I didn't know how hard. Not until we both almost died and it was only him that kept me on this side of the grave. He saved me, in more ways than one and I knew... I knew I couldn't go back."

"At least he told you how he felt," she sighs.

"I'm not going to tell you Bast feels the same—that would be cruel—but I'm not going to tell you he doesn't either. He took me with him to the library earlier. Do you know why he went?"

"Why?"

"To get you your favourite book. He thought it would help you feel better. He left it in the library in his haste to leave for the mission, but it's the thought that counts. I think you have a chance, Blake. Don't give up before you try."

Her brown eyes meet mine, muddy from the tears. "If he truly does remember my favourite book, then maybe you're right, but it's not going to matter if he gets himself killed."

"Hey now," I chide, "that's no way to think. I'm sure he's fine. He knows what he's doing."

"I know, but he worries me sometimes. He acts before he thinks. He's so... Sometimes I think I've fallen for a child, but then other times… Well, you know how it goes."

I nod.

"I can't help but think though that if he liked me at all, he would've told me he was going, *especially* after the last time."

"Maybe he was afraid that if he said goodbye, it would be forever."

"Maybe," she allows.

"Do you want to talk about it? We can go somewhere else. Jax also told me what today is. Whatever you need, Blake, I'm here for you."

She smiles somehow. "Thank you, Quinn, but if it's all the same to you, I'd rather stay here and try to take my mind off things. I think I will honour her more by having a good day instead of spending it in misery."

"I think you're right," I say. I pull the black cloak off its hanger once more and hold it out to her. "First order of business: trying this on."

"Okay fine," she replies, "but if I do, you have to promise to try on this dress I found."

I frown. "Dress? You know I hate those."

She puts her hands on her hips. "Don't make that face before you've seen it. You'll like this one, trust me."

I sigh. "I suppose I can give it the benefit of the doubt."

"Good, then give me that." She takes the cloak from me and whirls it around onto her shoulders. The fabric ripples in the light like obsidian waves.

"You look astounding in that," I tell her. "If black wasn't *my* colour, I'd say you should wear it more often." I grin.

She laughs. "Colour hog."

I shrug. "Hey, I can't help it if I look good."

· · ·

We shop around for forty minutes, trying on several pairs of boots, cloaks, and shirts. Blake keeps the first cloak and I have a pair of boots. Eventually, she drags me over to the dress section.

"Do we have to?" I whine.

"You promised," she reminds me, pinching my arm.

I flinch away. "But..."

She gives me a stern look, her brown eyes burning into me. "I swear to God, Quinn..."

I step away. "Okay, okay. Don't get your cloak in a twist."

She takes me to the far wall and points upward. "What do you think of *that*?"

My eyes find what she's talking about and they widen.

Now that *is a dress.*

The bodice is in corset style with a heart shaped neckline, though still modest. The skirt flares out a little and will go just below knee height when on. It's cut up a little on the ends, so it looks ragged, but enticingly so. The skirt is a dark—almost black—grey and the bodice is the same, with a touch of deep crimson. I love it.

"Wow," I breathe.

Blake laughs. "That's what I said. You will look amazing in it. Come on, you *have* to try it on!"

She grabs it off the hook and leads me over to the dressing room where she hangs the dress up inside. "Go on." She gives me a soft push and I step into the room, closing the door behind me.

For a moment, I just stand there. I don't know why, but it's hitting me that Jax might be facing certain death and I'm...shopping.

What is wrong with me?

My eyes are drawn back to the dress. It's gorgeous. Jax would love me in it, I know he would, but if he... It would only serve as a reminder.

You're not allowed to buy it, I tell myself. *You can try it on, but buying it would be a mistake.*

I pull it gently off the hanger and slip it on without another treacherous thought. The mind is a terrible thing—a human's worst weapon, a monster's greatest arsenal. I'm still not entirely sure where I stand. I'm not sure I ever will.

I tug the dress into place, smoothing the front and adjusting the skirt. My eyes can't—won't—find the mirror.

Why am I here? What am I doing?
You're helping Blake, I remind myself.
But what if that's harming me?

That's what friendship is about, Quinn, sacrifice. She'd do the same for you, so pick up your chin. Take it like the strong person you are.

I stand up straight and look myself in the eye. The mirror in front of me reflects my determination and the absolute glory of the outfit Blake discovered for me. I look like...not a princess. No, I look like a dark queen. For once, the colours and connotations don't remind me of my past. I don't look in the mirror and see Silent Night, Queen of Assassins. No. I see Quinn Marie Ballinger, Warrior of Worlds.

I love it and I hate it.

The assassin has lost her hold, but at the same time, so much responsibility has been placed on my shoulders. I don't want it; I don't know if I can handle it.

Can I save this city?

Not alone.

Blake knocks on the door then, reminding me I have friends, allies, people who will aid me. I'm not alone. If we work together, we never will be.

"How's it look, Quinn?" Blake asks.

"You want to see?" My tone is light and it surprises me.

"Of course! Come on out."

I open the door.

"Oh, Quinn..." she gasps. "It's perfect. You look amazing."

I smile. "I know."

She returns my grin. We're like a pair of school girls in our barely contained excitement. "So," she asks, "are you going to get it?"

I sigh and look down, my smile fading. "No."

Her face falls. "What? Why not?"

"I just... I can't. Maybe later when..."

Sorrow flashes in her eyes as she finally understands. "Oh."

I grimace. "I'm sorry I brought us back to that."

"No, it's okay. I can't ignore the truth forever. It helped though, for a bit."

"Well, I'm glad of that. I'll take this off."

She nods and I close the door again. I shed the dress before I get attached and change my mind.

I rejoin Blake outside the changing room, leaving the dress where it hangs, and we walk up to the front. Blake approaches a counter and we place our purchases on its surface.

"One ten," the girl behind the counter says.

Blake slaps some copper coins down.

I wonder how she earned them and why the Resistance even bothers with currency after the war collapsed our economy. The Guild and most of Haven trade in goods and bribes these days.

We grab the cloak and boots and leave the shop. The music of the club slams into us as soon as we enter it. Usually, I welcome it, but this time it's a shock to the system and my eardrums pound in protest.

"Let's get out of here," I say to Blake.

"Agreed." Her eyes flick to the stools in front of the bar as we navigate the crowds. No doubt she's imagining Bast there, almost hoping to see him lost in his cups, instead of out in the dangerous city fighting against deadly enemies. I don't blame her. Drunk is better than dead.

Until being drunk kills you.

I shake those thoughts out of my mind. That's an entirely different problem for another time. Bast has to come back alive first.

He will. He has to and Jax will be with him.

I tell myself this, chant it inside, but my heart won't let myself believe it. It prepares for the worst.

CHAPTER NINETEEN

"So what do we do now?" Blake asks once we leave the Den behind. I realize that I have no idea where we should wait for the guys, how long they might be gone, anything. "Do you know if Trey went with them?" she adds.

"She pulled an all-night watch, so Jenson kept her here. Maybe we could…" My leg spasms and I tense up, switching weight immediately to my left leg. "Ah," I gasp.

Blake grabs my arm. "Quinn? Are you okay?"

"Yeah, I…" I hiss in pain as I try my right leg again.

Not going to work. Not right now.

"I just... I need to sit down." I hop over a couple feet to the wall and brace myself against it as I lower myself to the floor.

Blake comes over and keeps my right leg from hitting the tile. I'm taking quick breaths to relieve the pain when she joins me against the wall. "What did you do?"

I wince. "Too much...strain today." I pull up the ragged end of my pant leg, exposing a red and swollen knee. The skin looks angry.

Blake sucks in a breath. "Look how irritated it is. You have to be more careful, Quinn."

"Ugh," I sigh. "You sound like Jax. Tell me something I don't know."

"It'll get better," she says.

"Yeah, sure, and by the time it does, we'll all be dead and gone." I yank my pant leg back into place.

"Positivity is the root of success, Quinn."

"And hope is a death sentence," I mutter. "It just leads to disappointment."

She gives me a stern look. "That sounds an awful lot like someone I *used* to know."

"Who?"

"Oh, you know, she was a broody, woe is me, the earth is doomed, and we're all dead anyway kind of person, a legendary assassin in the second position at the Guild. I'm sure you've heard of her."

My eyes turn dark, exactly like the person in question, but then I sigh and my expression softens. "Sorry," I breathe.

She pats my thigh. "It's okay. Everybody has relapses."

"But I can't afford to, she'll latch on and drag me back in." I think about the pillowcases of shredded clothes under my bed, the shards of broken vase scattered across my floor, and wince.

"And you'll fight back," she assures me. "You won't let it happen. I know you won't."

I look at my feet. "Thanks for the confidence."

"That's what a best friend is for," she reminds me. "Helping you find what you're missing. I help you find confidence in yourself and you help me find courage."

I give her a look. "Blake, you're the bravest person I know."

She looks away. "You're just saying that."

"No, I'm serious. You've been through a lot, losing your child and your first love, but you didn't give up. You picked yourself back up. You face it every day and keep going. On top of that, you argue with *me* and don't give a damn that I used to be an assassin."

She cracks a smile. "I'm not sure if that's bravery, more like stupidity."

I smile back. "It's something."

We sit in silence for a moment and then she says, "Do you think you're okay to move now?"

I grimace. "I'm not sure if I should risk it."

"I could try to carry you," she suggests.

"And what if you drop me? I'll be in worse shape than before."

She scowls. "What makes you think I'll drop you?"

I raise an eyebrow. "What makes you think you won't?"

"Touché, but we can't just sit here and wait for the boys to come back."

"Help me up then," I say, "and I'll use you as a crutch."

"Oh you will, will you?" she says, standing up.

"Yeah, I will, and you're going to be happy about it."

She puts her hands on her hips. "Is that any way to treat your elder?"

I grin. "Shut up, you old prune."

She laughs and then sighs. "You sound like Bast. It's hardly fair."

"Sorry."

"It's okay. It hurts, but it's also...comforting. You know?"

I nod and reach out my arm. She takes my hand.

I brace myself as she takes my other hand as well and drags me up to my feet, slowly but with enough force to get the job done. I take in a sharp breath as my right foot brushes the floor and the impact reverberates up my leg.

"Sorry, sorry!" Blake gasps.

"It's okay. Ah…" I wince, leaning against her.

She holds me up, wrapping an arm under mine and around my back. "You are going to be on bed rest for the next week," she says.

"But Blake…"

She gives me a sharp look. "No excuses."

"It's not that—"

"Bad? Not that bad," she repeats, shaking her head. "Quinn, you can barely stand. Actually, scratch that, you *can't* stand."

"I just... I worked too hard today, obviously."

"Which is why you need to rest," she replies, "at least for a few days. Then you can go again, but as soon as you feel even the slightest pain, stop and rest. It's not supposed to be rocket science." She throws her free arm out in exasperation.

I look at my feet. "I know, I know, but I'm tired of sitting around."

"Well, you'll be doing it a lot longer if you don't take it easy," she points out.

I sigh and gaze around the hall, glad it's empty and no one was there to witness my weakness.

"Let's just get me to my room," I say.

She nods. "It'll be painful. Don't move too fast or you'll lose your balance."

I give her a look. "I'm crippled, Blake, not stupid."

"Right," she says. "Sorry."

"Should we get going then?"

"We better," she replies, "or we'll be here for eternity. One foot after the other, right?"

"More like one hop after another," I mutter and we both laugh.

I slow my breathing and take a hop forward, about half a foot.

Blake steadies me and shuffles forward.

I groan. "This is going to take forever."

"It has to be done. Does it hurt at all?"

"Aside from the leftover throbbing from before, I don't think so."

"Good. Give it another go."

I make another hop, then three, and soon we make it halfway down the hall. We have a good rhythm going now and we keep it up. At each corner, we stop and take a break, so I can catch my breath. It takes three times longer than usual to reach my room, but we finally make it, just when I'm about to lose hope.

I see the door with the numbers 2-4-1-3 on it and say, "Thank the Gods. I thought we'd never get here."

"Me neither," Blake says, a little out of breath. It can't be easy supporting me.

I lean against the wall as Blake opens the door and then she helps me inside. I finally collapse on my bed, letting out a huge sigh.

Blake falls beside me. "I hope you don't mind?"

"Not at all. Make yourself at home."

She rolls over onto her stomach. "Did Jax ever make himself at home?" she asks with a sly grin.

"Maybe...?"

Her eyes widen. "Oh my God, he didn't!"

It's my turn to blush.

"Spill," she demands.

"It's not what you think…"

She grabs my pillow and smacks me with it. "*Spill.*"

"All right, all right, stop pressuring me. So it was the night after...? No." I wave a hand. "Forget what day it was; my memory was shot then. It was the day I was released from the hospital after breaking my leg, the night actually."

"Go on," Blake says.

I scowl. "You're insufferable, you know that right?"

"Of course, now continue."

"Well, the nurses had to sedate me in order to put the brace on and when I woke up, it was dark and Jax was there, lying beside me, in my bed."

"Oh my God, he wasn't."

"He was and well, we said a couple words and both fell back asleep."

"That is adorable," she says, grinning.

I fight back a smile. "Shut up."

"You don't have to be defensive about it."

"Speak for yourself."

She sighs. "You're right. Quinn... What do I do if—when he comes back?"

"Whatever your heart tells you to do."

"I know what my heart wants—to just tell him—but my brain is telling me that would be a horrible idea."

"Yeah, brains can be bitches."

Blake laughs. "Seriously though, what am I going to do?"

"I can't tell you that, I'm afraid. As your friend, I can support you, but I can't make decisions for you."

"I want to tell him, but at the same time, I don't," she sighs.

"What are you afraid of?"

"What?"

"You're a smart person, Blake," I tell her, "so the only thing that could be holding you back is fear. You have to ask yourself what that fear is and then conquer it. Or else, nothing good will ever come out of anything."

"I..."

"You don't have to tell me. I'm not the one you have to convince."

"I suppose you're right."

"Of course I am. Now quiet; I'm trying to sleep." Exhaustion is creeping in.

She rolls her eyes as I close my own. "Sweet dreams, Quinn."

"You too," I reply groggily, sleep already taking me.

• • •

We awake to the sound of pounding footsteps in the hall. I bolt upright in the bed and accidentally elbow Blake in the face as she does the same.

"Ow."

I wince. "Sorry."

"What's going on?"

"Hell if I know, but I'm going to find out." I reach under the mattress and pull out my dagger.

"Nice hiding place," Blake says.

I shrug and roll off the bed, landing in a ready stance. Most of my weight is on my left leg, just in case, but my right is feeling much better.

Blake follows me as I prowl over to the door. She pulls her own dagger out of a boot sheath, standing behind me as I slowly turn the doorknob and pull.

We look out.

A dozen Resistance agents dressed in full gear are running down the hall, harried looks on their faces. I grab one by the collar as he rushes past, pulling him to a stop.

"Hey! What are you...? Oh."

I sigh as I realize he's recognized me, but return swiftly to business. "What's going on?" I ask him. "Where are you headed?"

"The dungeons of course," he says. "You'll never believe it. We did it... Agent Forrester did it actually."

I raise an eyebrow. "Jax? Did what?"

"He caught an assassin."

CHAPTER TWENTY

The agent grins like a maniac. I drop his collar and he runs off without glancing back.

Blake and I share a look.

"We have to get down there," I say. "Now."

"Quinn, we can't just…" she starts. "And your leg."

I shake my head, yanking on my boots as fast as I can. "It doesn't matter. If we don't move fast enough, they'll either all be dead or we'll have lost the only lead we might ever get to a suicide note."

Fear flashes in her eyes, bright and lethal. "What?"

"If they haven't dealt with the assassin properly—which I doubt they have—he or she will either try to kill them all or commit suicide. Or both. We have to get down there."

"Okay," she says, "but I'm carrying you."

"What?"

"Get on my back, Quinn. Like you said, we don't have all day."

I scowl. "Fine, but don't tell the boys, *ever.*"

She smiles. "Cross my heart and hope to try."

"You're insufferable," I tell her as I scramble up into piggyback formation.

She doesn't reply as she heads off down the hall, incredibly fast for someone carrying a person on their back, I might add.

• • •

We reach the dungeon sooner than expected, but we have to take it slow down the stairs, so Blake doesn't drop me or trip and send the both of us tumbling. We can hear a jumble of voices below us.

Thank the Gods; that means most of them, at least, are still alive.

Finally, we reach the bottom and Blake sets me down. A couple dozen agents are crowded around the cells.

I hobble over and push my way through them, ignoring their protests. "Jax," I say. "Jax!"

"Quinn?" I hear him reply.

"I'm here, I'm..." And then I break through the crowd and see him, standing a foot away from the bars and the person lying on the dirt inside, unconscious. For now. "Thank the Guild, you're okay," I breathe.

He steps towards me. "What's wrong? Are *you* okay?"

"I'm fine, but Jax, you need to..." I trail off as I recognize the assassin in the cell.

Assassins below. How did Jax manage to...?

"Quinn?" Jax says, worry creeping into his voice.

I'm frozen where I stand and my mouth is too dry to speak. Still, I try.

"Jax..." I'm finding it hard to breathe. "You didn't..."

Hard footsteps on the stairs interrupt me along with someone yelling, "What in the Guild is going on here?"

I recognize the voice. Trey.

Oh hell.

She breaks through the crowd, causing twice as much ruckus as I had, and whirls on Jax when she gets through. "Jenson sent you off without me, eh? Thought he could pull the wool over *my* eyes? I..." She trails off as she too notices the prisoner. "Shit, kid," she says.

"*What?*" Jax demands to know, his voice raised. "Would one of you please tell me what the hell is going on and why you both look like we're all about to die!" I've never heard Jax talk like that before; it's kind of scary.

"You..." I try again, but Trey comes to my rescue.

"Jax," she says, "I love you like a brother, but not bringing me was the stupidest thing you could've done. I would have told you to leave that one," she points at Anane, the unconscious prisoner, "well enough alone."

He crosses his arms. "Why? What's so bad about him?"

I sigh. "His name is Anane, Jax. He's Agent Six at the Guild—at least he was the last time I checked. He's also the Charger's only remaining son."

Jax swears, his eyes wide. "What are we going to do?"

"First we're going to put him in a different cell," Trey replies, "*before* he wakes up."

He frowns. "What's wrong with the one he's in?"

"We kept Kuen in that cell," she reminds him, "and if I know him at all, he would've fashioned some kind of weapon, in case he decided to either kill himself or whoever came to get him."

"What could he possibly have made a weapon with?" Jax asks.

Trey gives him a severe look.

"Trust her, Jax," I say. "Please." We need to get Anane secured as soon as possible.

Jax takes a deep breath. "Okay." Then he points at a pair of agents. "You two, bring the prisoner out and move him to Cell Four." He looks at Trey. "Any more requests?"

She nods. "Search him again for anything he could use to make a weapon; nothing is off the table. Then I want him in a strait jacket, hands tied behind his back. Chain his ankle to the floor with a foot of wiggle room."

"Yes, ma'am," Jax replies.

I take a deep breath, glad Trey is here to get the ball rolling. It pays to have an ex-assassin the agents actually listen to. I envy her position as Second.

Jax turns to his men. "You heard the woman; see that it's done."

"Yes, sir."

Most of them leave to accomplish their various tasks. The two assigned drag Anane's limp body into the cell across from the one he was in. Another walks in after them and pulls a needle out of his coat. He jabs it in Anane's neck.

I wince, but Anane doesn't so much as flinch.

A hand falls on my shoulder. I turn to see Jax standing behind me, Blake on his other side. I give her a questioning look and the answer isn't good. He's not here.

"Jax," I ask, "where's Bast?"

He waves a hand. "Oh, he's fine, don't worry."

I sigh and watch as ninety-five percent of the tension leaves Blake's body.

"Speaking of which," he continues, "I have something else you'll probably want to see. Trey?"

"What?" She's standing over by Anane's new cell, back to us.

"Do you want to come?" he asks her.

She shakes her head, but doesn't turn around. "That's okay, kid. I'm going to keep an eye on this guy. I don't care how far I can throw him; I don't trust him for a second. It would be the second I die."

Jax looks at her like she's lost her mind, but I understand her completely. Anane's a snake. I trust him about as much as I trust Sephtis, which is not at all.

Jax shakes his head as if to clear it and then walks deeper into the dungeon, Blake and I following.

"Where are we going?" Blake voices the question in my head.

"You'll see in a moment," he says.

I sigh.

Why does he do that? He knows I have no patience.

Finally, Jax stops and I see Bast, guarding another cell with two others.

Blake breaks away from us and flies at him, nearly knocking him over. She squeezes him tight and he pats her back as if he's not sure what to do. "Thank God you're all right," she gasps. Then she pulls away and points a finger in his face. "Next time you go out on a dangerous mission, Sebastian, you tell us. I thought we went over this. Quinn and I were worried sick. Again."

I snort when she mentions my name.

Nice cover.

He winces. "Sorry?"

"You better be."

Blake steps away from Bast and I focus again on the cell. "What's going on here?"

Jax looks over at me. "I caught Anane, but he wasn't alone. Bast got the other one." He gestures to the cell.

I walk over and Bast steps to the side so I can get a better view. A young man is slumped against the far wall, not much older than Jax and Blake. He has dirty-blond hair and streaks of blood across his face. His clothes hang off him, as if he hasn't eaten well in a while, if ever. I don't recognize him.

I turn back to Jax. "Who is he?"

He scratches his head. "We were hoping you could tell us that."

"Sorry," I say. "He's not familiar. He's either new or ranked low. I tended to ignore any agent below thirty unless they got in my way when I was at the Guild."

"I guess it's hard to know everybody," Jax replies, but it's clear he was hoping for a better answer.

I wish I could give it to him.

"We should go back," I say. "Anane will be waking up soon."

"Yeah, you're right. Bast?"

Bast looks over. "Yeah, Jax man?"

"We'll switch the shifts in half an hour," Jax tells him. "You good until then?"

Bast grins. "Never been better." There's dirt on his face too and a smear of blood, but he's in much better shape than the last time.

Blake looks at him. "You're telling me *you* caught that assassin?"

"All by my lonesome," he replies, still grinning. "Little bugger thought he could sneak up behind me and not get punched in the face. Idiot."

Blake rolls her eyes. I guess she's forgiven him for leaving without warning. Good thing we're going because they'll likely be arguing in a minute.

Blake and I follow Jax back to the front of the dungeon where we find an interesting scene. Trey is standing right where we left her, stance rigid and eyes focused on Anane, propped up on the dirt floor of his cell. Beside her stands Kuen and he's even more tense than she is, if that's even possible. I notice his right hand is in a splint.

So he did take my advice after all.

Out of the corner of my eye, I spot O'Reilly, leaning against the wall by the stairs. The smell of fear leeches off of him and I cough pointedly.

Jax's men stand in a semi-circle around Trey and Kuen.

In the cell, Anane is wrapped in his new jacket, hands tied tight and his ankle chained to the ring on the floor.

I walk over to Kuen. "What are *you* doing here?"

"Watching your stupid backs apparently," he mutters. "Trey sent for me. When I heard what, rather *who*, your idiot boyfriend brought back, I came as quick as I could."

I cross my arms. "Jax is not an idiot."

Kuen stares at me, pale blue eyes chipping away at my confidence. "The fact that I have eyes on Anane right now makes me beg to differ."

"He didn't know," I say.

Kuen shakes his head. "Ignorance is the root of disaster."

"So is negativity."

I pretend I don't notice the glare he sends me and instead look to the cell. Anane is stirring.

Well, isn't this going to be fun.

Everybody puts one hand to their weapon, but I don't bother, neither do Trey and Kuen. We know full well that our presence alone will strike more fear into Anane's heart than steel ever would. He's an assassin. Death follows his every step, but his family… He won't be expecting that.

Anane groans.

I shift my weight again, resting my left leg for a second before solidifying my stance.

Inside the cell, Anane tenses up. "What the hell?" he mutters. He must've noticed his bindings.

I smile a little.

Anane's head snaps up and he studies the scene before him. After a moment, his eyes lock on his three siblings and not a trace of fear lingers in their dark depths. "Well, well, well, what do we have here?" he asks us. "A little family reunion? Father would be so horribly upset not to be invited." He smiles, but it's broken, twisted.

"Shut it, Anane," Kuen snaps.

"Oho, big brother trying to assert his authority. Well, it's not going to work, not on me. I don't answer to traitors." He spits on the floor of the cell.

Anane grins malevolently at Kuen, who looks about ready to snap his arrogant neck.

Trey puts a hand on Kuen's shoulder, digging her fingers in to ensure he understands her meaning.

Don't let him get to you.

Kuen sets his jaw.

Anane laughs. "That's right, Kuen, listen to little sis, she probably knows best."

"Glad to know you haven't changed," I drawl. "You're still the same arrogant ass I knew and despised."

"Speak for yourself, Silent Night," he spits, "or do you go by something else now?"

"That's none of your business, Six."

At my final word, Anane tugs at his bonds, murder clear in his soulless eyes.

It's my turn to laugh. "Don't bother. You're not going anywhere. And yes, I know all about your demotion. Must've broken your poor, pathetic heart to be dragged back to sixth, but I guess that's what happens when you fail the Charger on such a *simple* task."

He frowns. "It was supposed to be simple, but father underestimated you."

"*You* underestimated me," I retort. "The Charger knew exactly what he was doing. He always does." I scowl at my own words and so does Anane.

"Fine, maybe I was in over my head," he admits, "but it looks like you were properly punished for *your* arrogance. Did karma pay you a visit, *sister*?" He gestures to my right leg.

Despite myself, I smile. "Maybe," I reply, "but I'd do it again in a heartbeat."

He raises an eyebrow. "Is that supposed to scare me? You didn't break my leg, not really. The fall did. I wouldn't be proud of something that happened accidentally."

"The next time I get my hands on you, there will be nothing accidental about it."

"Still waiting to be terrified," he says. His hands are tied behind his back, but I can imagine him crossing his arms nonchalantly.

The image infuriates me.

"I was the Charger's executioner," I tell him, "but I'm going to delay your death as long as possible. You tell us what you know, and we might let you die. Might."

Anane shrugs as much as he can with the straightjacket. "Try me."

Kuen tears away from Trey's grip. "This is a waste of time," he snaps. "The bastard isn't going to talk."

Jax speaks up for the first time. "Why not?"

"Because he always has been and always will be his Master's perfect puppy dog," I answer.

"At least I'm not his favourite bitch," Anane retorts.

I'm glad we're on the outside of the bars or Jax would've punched him in the face. I would've strangled him.

"Shut your mouth," Kuen barks, kicking the cell bars hard enough that they shake.

Anane actually flinches, but he shakes it off saying, "I don't think I will." He looks away from Kuen to me. "You know he still considers you his prodigy? Top Dog. You're still Agent Two, Agent One now actually, since you killed Hai. Father's still waiting for you to return and when you do, he'll forgive everything. *Everything*.

"Tell me, One, why are you so damn special to him? All I did was lose you in a chase, and I earned a demotion and the title of scum beneath his boots. You betrayed him, betrayed all of us, and he gives you the world. Why?"

"I don't know!" I snap.

It's the truth. I have no idea. I can't believe I lost my temper, though, can't believe I let him get to me.

"Good to know you're perfectly useless," Anane spits.

"Actually, it would seem the Charger thinks I'm the exact opposite of useless. He doesn't keep people who have lost their value to him, like you."

He pulls at his bonds. "That is a lie. I am invaluable to him!"

I raise a brow. "Is that so? The way I see it, you have three options going into the future. You either betray him and live, stay true and die, or escape and get to tell your dear father how you were *caught*. Ask yourself, Anane, is he still going to value you? Is he going to be proud? I don't think so."

The light dims in his eyes. "I…"

Finally, I've caught him.

"Oh, you don't have to tell me the answer. You have to tell yourself. The Charger is done with you no matter what, so you decide now what's best for *you*, not him. He never cared anyway. Trust me on that one."

He scowls. "What would you know about that? He certainly cares about *you*."

"When I brought the Resistance to the Guild, I had to fight him," I reply. "I risked everything I was, my life and my soul, in order to end him. I failed, obviously, but he gave me a choice. He told me either to die, let him kill me, or shoot Hai. You know what choice I made."

For once, Anane is silent.

I don't tell him that the Charger later tried to trade Hai's life for Jax's.

"Anane, he wanted Hai dead, because he'd outlived his usefulness, because he's a sadistic bastard, and because he doesn't give a shit about any of us. Whatever his grand scheme is, he's in it for himself, no one else, and whoever gets in his way has to go, regardless of who they are to him. We are like every other face in the crowd, exploitable and, ultimately, replaceable. He's not going to save us, Anane. If we want salvation or glory, we have to do it ourselves."

"I'm not looking to be saved," he says, "but I'll get the glory, don't you worry your pretty little head over it." He sends me a malicious grin and this time I shake my head.

"You know what, Anane, as much as I can't stand anything about you, as much as your very presence annoys me, I feel sorry for you."

He laughs. "So the executioner finally grew a heart, eh?"

I ignore his jab. "I feel sorry for you because you've spent your life worshipping this image of a person you will never actually know, and you don't even care. You've always been alone and you always will be. You'll die that way and that is why I feel sorry for you."

I turn away from him and Trey squeezes my shoulder. "You mind if Kuen and I take a stab at him?"

I shrug. "Be my guest; I've had enough."

She nods. "Jax, assemble whatever guard you want, but he'll need at least five at any given time. Kuen, let's see if we can't get him to talk."

Kuen grins. I pray he is strong enough and smart enough to keep his monster in check. Guild knows I wouldn't be.

I don't glance back as I make my way through the crowd again, trying not to limp too much with my audience.

Blake follows after me, wrapping an arm around me as I start on the stairs.

Jax stays behind to sort out his men.

I'm not sure exactly what Trey and Kuen are going to do, but I don't want to witness it. I gave them free reign. It's going to get messy and violent, quickly. I suppress the shudder that wants to shake itself free and square my shoulders against the shame as I leave Anane to his fate.

You are a monster, my mind screams at me.

I know. Assassins below, I know.

And yet, that doesn't change a thing.

About fifteen minutes later, Jax joins Blake and me in my room. Blake is sitting on the edge of my bed. I'm lying down, face buried in the pillow. We haven't talked since the dungeon; I don't *want* to talk. I don't deserve friends, especially not someone as caring as she is. I don't deserve *anything*.

"What's wrong?" Jax says to Blake. "Is she okay?"

"I have a name," I mumble into the pillow.

"Are you okay, Quinn?" he asks me.

"Do I look okay?"

"No. What happened?"

"I unleashed Kuen and Trey's monsters is what happened. What are they doing to Anane?"

"I..."

"No, don't tell me. I don't want to know. It's too horrible. I shouldn't have done this. I'm the *real* monster."

"I don't think..."

"I *am*."

"No, Quinn," he says, "just listen. I don't think Kuen was going to wait for permission. He doesn't take well to authority at all, let alone his younger sister telling him what to do. If you told him to leave Anane be, do you think he would have listened?"

I scowl into the pillow. "This is just your hatred for him coming out."

"No, I don't... Quinn, I don't hate your brother, as much as I want to. I just don't like how he carries himself, the things he says, or his complete lack of obedience."

"Didn't notice."

"What I'm *trying* to say, is that this isn't about my so-called 'hatred' for him. I'm making an observation based on what I know of his personality. He wasn't going to listen to you, and the sooner you realize that, the sooner you can come back from your guilt trip. It isn't your fault, at all."

I pull myself up into a sitting position and look at him properly. "Okay, but I still didn't try to stop it."

"You couldn't have, Quinn," he says and Blake nods. "If he let his monster out, he wouldn't care who you were. If you stood in the way, he would have gotten rid of you, in whatever way he could. You can't afford any more injuries."

"I also can't afford to do nothing, not when this world is full of darkness."

"Quinn…"

"Don't 'Quinn' me, *Ajax*. I'm not some delicate flower. I've known and seen things you could never *dream* about, and they're not pretty. I don't need you to tell me what I can and can't do. I'm certainly not going to sit back and relax while the rest of you do all the work. This is my battle too, maybe more than anyone else's. I will choose how it will end. So don't 'Quinn' me; it'll get you nowhere."

Jax sighs. "Okay."

Blake looks back and forth between the two of us with one part unease and one part surprise.

You'll have this one day, Blake, I tell her mentally. *I know it.*

"So what do you want to do then?" Jax asks me.

"Do you think you could get me an audience with Jenson? It's about time we had a discussion, whether or not he welcomes my counsel."

He nods. "I'll see what I can do."

"In the meantime, I'm going to give my leg as much rest as I can, and see what I can do about Kuen and Anane."

"Anything I can do?" Blake asks.

"Keep an eye on Bast," I tell her, "and don't let *me* do anything stupid."

She smiles. "Fair enough."

"We'll have the Charger before he knows what hit him," Jax says.

"Oh, when it's his time," I say, "I want him to know who deals the final blow, and that blow will be mine."

Jax only nods, as if he never questioned it in the first place.

CHAPTER TWENTY-ONE

The next morning, I return to the dungeon. I can smell the despair as I descend into its depths, and certainly the iron—the blood.

Oh Gods, what have they done?

I am alone. Ajax is vying for an audience with Jenson, as promised. I'm not sure what Bast and Blake are doing, but I know they're together. Blake offered to come with me, but I told her to focus on Bast for once, get to work on the courting. I'm not sure if she actually will, but it's her choice. My only company in this pit of pain will be the guards and Anane himself, or what's left of him.

I'm afraid to keep going, afraid of what I'll find, but I square my shoulders and push the fear back. Fear is for the weak and I have to be strong to defeat my enemies, to protect those I love. Fear is for the weak, and I will not fall prey to it.

Finally, I step into the dungeon, and I'm surprised by what I see or rather, what I don't see.

The guards are gone and I realize that George was absent from his post at the entrance.

There's someone in Anane's cell, looming over his crumpled form.

Oh hell.

Even from ten feet away, I can tell he has at least one broken limb and is that a dislocated shoulder? I walk over to the cell, my approach deathly silent. The smell of shame and anger in the enclosed space is overpowering. I choke on my next breath and cough.

The person in the cell whips around at the sound.

What in the Guild?

"Trey?" I gasp. There is a chill in the air and I wrap my arms around my chest.

"Quinn?" Fear shines bright in her eyes.

"Trey... Assassins below.... What the hell are you doing?"

Her expression becomes guarded, the fear disappearing. "You shouldn't be here."

"The hell I shouldn't!" I snap. "What are you thinking? If Jenson finds out... You should be ashamed." I expect her to understand, to hang her head, but she doesn't.

She stands taller, rigid and unmoving. "Get out."

"What?"

"Get out, Quinn, or I'll have to throw you out myself." She throws her dark hair over her shoulder. "Trust me; you don't want this."

"I'm not going anywhere," I retort, crossing my arms. "What has gotten into you?"

"Quinn... I'm warning you."

I square my shoulders. "And I'm not going to listen. I'm not afraid of you."

"This is one battle you won't win," she insists.

"I don't think so. I was under the Charger's tutelage for much longer. Try me, Trey. See how well it goes."

On the ground, Anane groans. Then he says, "You should listen to sister, Silent Night. Run away while all your limbs are still intact—well, those remaining."

"Shut it," Trey snaps at him, giving him a swift kick in the ribs.

Anane's scream is cut off by a gurgle as he coughs up blood. He heaves, his entire body seizing as he tries to pull oxygen into his ravaged lungs. I know what it's like to drown. To hell if I'm going to let him meet the same fate.

"Trey... Step out of the cell."

"Quinn, just go. Please."

"Get out of the damn cell!" I snap. I move before I finish the sentence.

I'm standing in the cell beside her, the door shut behind me, before she has time to react. Then I trip her with my good leg.

She hits the floor and lets out a pained whine before she jumps back to her feet, aiming a punch at my head.

I duck and grab her hand, twisting her arm until it starts to protest. I can see her holding back her screams with every ounce of her will. Her other hand tries to claw at my face.

I dodge it and send a right hook into her stomach, hard.

She doubles over and I release her arm. Then I slam her to the ground once more.

Again, she tries to get up, but I set my left foot on her neck.

She stiffens. She knows that one wrong move on her part and I will snap her neck, no second chances. So she lays there, heaving in the oxygen her attacked body forgot she needed. My breathing is ragged too, but I don't let it show.

Off to the side, Anane lets out a dark, wet chuckle. "Look at us. Wouldn't father be so"—he coughs—"proud."

"Shut—" Trey tries, but I dig my foot in and her words cut off.

"That's enough," I say, "and I mean the both of you. Anane? I hate you, make no mistake about that, but I'm sorry this happened."

"Don't apologize," he mutters. "Apology is weakness. I deserved this. It's what happens when you're a sadistic bastard." He flashes a grin, and it would've been menacing, if not for the blood coating his teeth in crimson.

I shake my head. "Whatever. Trey? I want you to listen to me, and listen well. This will not happen again."

She squirms and I grab her arm and twist again, eliciting another scream.

"It will not happen again," I repeat.

"Okay!" she gasps. "Fine. I won't do it again, just let me go!"

I drop her arm and she heaves a sigh of relief into the blood-smeared floor.

It's Anane's turn to shake his head. "Pathetic," he mumbles, "a complete waste of energy. No wonder you betrayed us. So weak, so susceptible to fear."

"Anane, please. Shut up." I struggle to keep my voice even.

"Or what? You'll gut me?"

No, I'll skin you alive, is what I want to say, but that's what *she* would say. In fact, that's exactly what Silent Night once said to him. I'm taken over by this intense feeling of déjà vu.

I've been in this situation before, but this time, I don't smile.

"I don't know, Anane, just shut up."

He doesn't have a comeback. Instead, he falls silent, sinking back to the floor.

I return my focus to Trey. "I'm going to let you up now, and when I do, you're going to head straight out that cell door and you're not going to look back. Understood?"

"Yes." Her voice is defeated.

Good.

I take my foot off her neck, and step to block Anane from her sight.

She eases to her feet and catches my gaze. Her eyes try to tell me something, but I ignore it. I'm not going to listen to her side right now. Her shoulders drop, a sign of submission, and she shuffles out of the cell. The door swings shut behind her, creaking softly.

"Well, you've done it now," Anane coughs.

My eyes snap to him. "And what would you know about it?"

"More than you think."

I say nothing else and follow Trey out, locking the cell behind me.

I find Trey leaning against the wall beside the dungeon entrance, nursing her arm. She looks over at me, nothing but despair in her gaze.

What the hell happened back there?

Part of me doesn't want to know, but I have to ask.

"You probably hate me right now," I tell her, "but I need to know what happened and why. Where are the guards? Anane's probably going to be incapacitated for a while, but still..."

She looks at the floor as she says, "I told the guards to come back in an hour. I give them ten more minutes."

I swear, using one of Jax's choice words. "Assassins below, Trey. What were you thinking?"

She wraps her arms around her chest. "I... I don't know."

"Can I have a straight answer?"

"You don't want to know."

"I don't care," I reply. "Tell me or I will tell Jenson what happened and you will be down there with Anane, in your own cozy cell."

She sighs, as if this is the hardest decision she's ever made. "Okay, but let's go back to my room. I don't want an audience."

I nod and we walk off.

. . .

Trey sits down on her bed when we reach her room.

I perch on the arm of one of her chairs. "Tell me."

"You're going to hate me after this, I know it," she says, hanging her head, "so I want to start by saying I'm sorry. Assassins below, I have never been more sorry. I wish I could take it all back... But what's done is done. I can't erase the past."

I give her a sympathetic look. "Just tell me, Trey."

"Anane is my mortal enemy," she says, "and he has been since I left the Guild, since the night my life changed forever. There's something I've been...keeping from you, Quinn." She wrings her hands in her lap. "The real reason I left the Guild was because I disobeyed a direct order from our father. I tried to prevent an assassination—your mother's assassination. Except, she wasn't just your mother, she was mine too."

My heart skips a beat.

No.

"You... We have the same mother?" I breathe.

She nods, tears in her eyes. "I didn't know she was alive. I was taken from her at about a week old, but the

Charger told me her name once. I didn't particularly care, not until…"

She swallows.

"The night before she was supposed to die, I was hanging out in the Grand Cavern with Kuen, Hai, and Anane. We were all pretty close then, or as close as the children of Haven's most feared assassin could be. Anane brought up his next assignment. I remember it as clear as day. He told us father had assigned him to a mistress kill. We all knew what that meant. Some unfortunate young woman out there was going to meet death, all because the Charger found her amusing enough to sire a child with."

She shudders.

"The Charger, as always, would do the killing, but Anane would get to witness everything. We knew that by morning, the four would be five and there would be a newborn in our midst that would one day try to take us out. None of us knew how old you were... But that's not important." She looks up at me. "What's important is that Anane was told the mistress' name and when he said 'Ismae Ballinger,' I forgot how to breathe."

"So what," I say, "I'm supposed to believe you changed sides because the Charger was going to kill your mother? Two seconds before you knew who it was you didn't give a damn about the poor innocent woman's life."

"It wasn't because it was her," she argues, "not completely. I just... I couldn't believe she was still alive, that the Charger had let her live, and I don't know, something told me I *had* to be there. So I found out everything I needed to know about the mission. That night, I arrived at the house undetected, or so I thought at the time. I climbed up the wall and slid through a second-story window... It was your room, Quinn."

I forget how to breathe.

Trey was in my room that night. I could've... I *should've* heard her. So many opportunities to change my mother's fate... But what would I have been able to do against Trey, against any of them? I was five years old; they would've killed me too.

"Quinn, I was expecting a baby," Trey goes on, "and instead I found you, not even a toddler anymore, sound asleep in your bed, in a room full of all the things you had collected over your short years and I... I was horrified. You had a life. You had a bright future ahead of you, a normal future, and he was going to take it all away."

I narrow my eyes. "So, you're saying I changed your life?"

"Yes," she exclaims. "In so many ways. I still don't understand it. I didn't know you, I shouldn't have cared, but we had this unspoken connection. I thought to myself that I'd already lost my mother, that you shouldn't have to go through the same thing. I promised myself I would save you and I failed. I left the room—I'm not even sure what I planned to do, but Anane was waiting in the hall. He wrapped his arm around my throat before I could even shut the door behind me.

"Then he pressed something cold and metallic into my hand and said... Well, he told me I had two choices. Either I tried to save you and would be brutally murdered by the Charger himself in front of the entire Guild or I could take the syringe Anane gave me, sedate you, and disappear into the night. You know what path I chose."

My heart stutters in my chest. "You... You sedated me?"

She nods grimly.

I feel cold.

"Do..." I clench my fists. "Do you have *any* idea how long I've kicked myself for not hearing anything that night?" I choke out. "Do you know how long I've wished desperately that I'd had a chance to save her? That's what you took away from me, my one chance..." I shake my head. "You should've taken me and run, screw the consequences. Why did you leave me there? Do you know what I woke up to?" Tears, unbidden, run down my face. I hate them. Assassins below, I hate each droplet of pain.

"I—" Trey tries, but I cut her off.

"No," I spit. "No, you don't. I woke up to sunlight and nothing but silence. I found her body—they waited until after I did to take me away. I entered her room to a snow globe of feathers, my mom's empty pillow covered in blood. It pooled on the floor and my mother was dead. Dead! You left a five-year-old to witness all that horror..."

A reel of images plays behind my lids, the memories I can never be rid of. Blood and feathers and pain.

I may have forgiven, but I'll never truly forget.

Trey regards me with wide eyes. "I didn't know."

"You didn't know?" I scoff. "Well, here's another interesting piece of information: I had nightmares for a year and the first time I slept with a pillow on my bed since that day was the night before the Guild attack. No child should have to go through that. Where was the unspoken connection all those years while I lived in constant fear of waking up with a bullet in *my* head? Where was the sisterly love then? Oh wait, you *left*. You left me in hell, all because you were too attached to your own life to spare me the horrors of mine. You were a coward!"

"I know!" she yells back, tears streaming down her own face. "I know I am! Doesn't change a goddamn thing! What would you have done? Look me in the eye and tell me you would have behaved differently, when a death by our dear father was staring you in the face. You'd save yourself, don't even try to deny it. I know."

I want to argue, but she's right. All the hot air leaves me and I feel like a deflated balloon, pointless.

Trey sighs. "What I was trying to explain is that I regret it. I have regretted it every second since I left, but I couldn't go back. The Charger would kill me on sight and when I saw Anane in that cell... I don't know what came over me. I just... I wanted him to *pay*. I wanted him to pay for the decision I had to make."

"You let the coward take over, Trey," I tell her, "and that's exactly what the Charger wants. Don't fall for it. Don't let him win."

She narrows her eyes. "Wait... Are you saying the Charger *wanted* Anane to be caught?"

"Of course he did," I reply, crossing my arms. "We're all pawns in his game, Trey. What happens happens because he allows it. The sooner we all realize that, the better off we'll be." I stand up. "I better not catch you in that dungeon again because I won't keep quiet about it a second time. I'll go straight to Jenson."

She hangs her head. "I understand."

"Good."

Then I leave her to her memories, memories of a past she could have changed, if only she'd tried. If only the Charger had turned his back for a *second*. If only.

CHAPTER TWENTY-TWO

Several hours later, after lunch with the gang for the first time in months, I'm lying on my bed, dreading the thought of what I must do next. Lunch was surreal; it was like everything—all the horrors of the past few weeks— had never happened, as if the Guild attack was but another nightmare. Then I had to go to bed to rest my leg and everything came rushing back.

All the secrets that came to life these past few months, all the problems still holding me back. I keep replaying my conversation with Trey...

And there is always that lingering anger that Sephtis still breathes, that I failed my one mission and my mother still lay in her grave, un-avenged.

I sigh.

The past can never be the past, can it? It always has to haunt us. How can we believe in a bright future when what once was still cloaks our world in shadow?

Maybe I'll never know. Maybe I won't live long enough to see it.

I roll out of bed.

It's time to face the inevitable. I was the one who asked Jax to get me a meeting with Jenson; I can at least follow through with it. I guess I didn't expect it to be so soon; I want more time to prepare myself, but I might as well get it over with.

I straighten my outfit before I leave the room, flattening out the wrinkles and adjusting the torn leg. Then I slip my dagger into my left boot.

I practically drag myself to the council room. I don't want to go, but it has to be done. We have to start making moves or Sephtis will have us surrounded before we even lift a finger. He has been playing his game far longer and he's good at it. In order to beat him, we have to get ahead, but I fear it's already too late. If Anane's presence is any indication, Sephtis is already closing in for the kill, like a cat hiding in the long grass, waiting for the right moment to pounce.

I shake off the shiver that wants to claim me and walk a bit faster.

I'm not afraid.

Oh, but who am I kidding? I'm terrified.

• • •

I enter the Council room and am greeted by thirty pairs of eyes. Jenson has increased the number of guards present, as if I'm even more dangerous with a missing leg.

I snort.

Jenson can forget it; I'm not here to hurt him. I'm here to reconcile, something he isn't man enough to do.

From the head of the table, Jenson nods to acknowledge my arrival. "Assassin," he says.

At the other end of the table, I see Jax's fists clench.

I leash my own annoyance and reply, "It's Quinn now actually, Jenson, but I'm not here to argue with you."

"Then why are you here? Ajax said it was important, but wouldn't share the details. It better be worth my time or you will have an even more worthless place in my books."

I pull out the chair meant for me and lean on it for a moment. "Jenson, I don't particularly care what you think of me. Not anymore. It doesn't matter. What *does* matter is what we're going to do about the *real* assassins. You know, the ones still killing people and attempting to destroy the right way of life in this city."

Jenson purses his lips. "Go on."

I sit down. "Let's start with the elephant in the dungeons. The assassin in Cell 4 is called Anane. The other assassin's identity is yet unknown. Anane has been interrogated by both Trey and Kuen. As former assassins, I assure you the job was thorough."

Jenson doesn't so much as flinch at my words. He doesn't even ask why Kuen was out of his room.

I shift in my chair to suppress my own shivers.

"And?" Jenson prompts. "What did we learn?"

"Nothing. As much as Kuen and Trey are trained in the art of torture, Anane is trained in the art of withstanding it. He's a high-ranked assassin and won't be easily persuaded to betray his master."

Jenson frowns. "Surely there is something we can offer him?"

"Aside from mass Resistance suicide? No. He wants us all dead."

"We could always threaten to kill *him*," someone else at the table suggests.

"And what good would that do?" Jax replies. "That's what he wants. He knows the Charger will kill him if he says anything. He would rather die than say a single word. We kill him and we lose our chance."

I smile at Jax. It seems he *does* listen to what I say. "Jax is right," I jump in, "at best, we use him as a bargaining chip, but there's no guarantee the Charger would take the bait. Though his subjects are deathly loyal to him, the sentiment isn't mutual. They are pawns in his deadly game."

Jenson massages his temples. "And at worst, Assassin?"

I look at him. "What?"

"You said he would be a bargaining chip at best. What's the other end of the stick?"

I take a deep breath and say, "At worst, he's the Charger's secret weapon and is planning to kill us all."

"Wonderful," someone mumbles.

"So you're saying the Master Assassin has an inside man now?" Jenson asks.

"Yes."

Jenson crosses his arms. "How much of a threat does this Anane pose? What is his background?"

I hesitate, wondering what I should tell them, but I decide on the truth. They deserve to know. It might be the only thing that saves us.

"He was Agent Four at the Guild when I left," I tell them, "demoted to Sixth after my escape when he failed to drag me back to the Charger."

Several of Jenson's cohort's eyes widen at that.

"He's been under the Charger's influence fourteen years longer than I was." I take a deep breath before I light the match underneath them all. "He's also the Charger's youngest son."

Silence.

I notice the clock on the left wall for the first time. Each tick reverberates in my eardrums, reminding me our time is running out. The Charger shakes the hourglass, coaxing the sand to fall faster.

Finally, mercifully, Jenson speaks. "You're telling me the monster has children?" He looks sick.

I nod. "He doesn't much care for them, but they are his ultimate weapons."

I remind myself the worst of them is dead, that if I could kill Hai, I can take Anane, but I can't quite convince myself. My confidence has wavered ever since that glass tank and I wonder if I'll ever get it back.

"Let me get this straight," Jenson says, holding up a hand. "The Master Assassin's *son* is in our dungeons?"

"Yes."

Jenson swears. "I assume you already have a plan for him?"

I shrug. "I suggest we leave him in the dungeons. We let the Charger think his plan is working. We don't kill Anane and we don't release him. We let him rot away in his cell, but we can't get complacent. He will be waiting for an opportunity, so we must exercise constant vigilance."

"Your suggestion has merit," Jenson says, "but I wonder at your true motives for this meeting. We haven't spoken since the trial. What are your plans, outside of the boy?"

"He's not a boy, Jenson," I retort, ignoring his other comment. "He's a grown man and a killing machine."

"I seem to recall you having a similar past," Jenson counters.

"I have moved on," I assure him. "Anane...will never have the same chance. He is chained to his demons, and the Master Assassin didn't throw away the key, he destroyed it. There is no hope for Anane."

Jenson rolls his eyes. "I wasn't planning on saving him, Assassin. I was simply stating parallels."

I set my jaw. "I am *not* like Anane."

"I never said you were."

I stand up, pushing my chair back hard, yet mindful of my leg. "This is a waste of time."

Jax reaches for me. "Quinn..."

I flinch back, but then I stop and take a deep breath.

There is more at stake here than Jenson's and my ego. I can't afford to walk away from this meeting right now. The *Resistance* can't afford it.

I sit back down. "We've been over this, Jenson," I say. "I decided to come back; you decided to let me stay. We both made a choice and now we need to work together to fix the mess we're in, okay? Quips about the past will get us nowhere. Believe me when I say Anane is a bigger threat to this organization than I could ever be. Can we unite against a common enemy for the sake of your agents and this city?"

He looks surprised. "Very well, Assassin, I can try, but you are not in the clear yet."

I shrug. "I don't suppose I ever will be, but I'll do my best."

• • •

We talk through several strategies and plans and the tension has almost left the room entirely when Nicholas Ross walks in.

All eyes turn to him and the room goes quiet.

Jenson does not look up. "You're late," he says.

"I was tied up with some disputes in the residency," Ross replies. He looks around the room and his gaze narrows on me. "What is the assassin doing here?"

Jenson shrugs. "She's doing more than you have. At least *she* was on time."

I choke back a laugh and then…

Did Jenson defend me?

"She's filling your heads with lies, Jenson," Ross retorts. "She can't be trusted. She hasn't even atoned for what she did to my daughter. Her presence here is like a slap in my face."

I fume in my seat.

I could make it literal.

"Natalie was barely injured," I argue, unable to keep my mouth shut. "You're being ridiculous."

He points a finger in my direction. "Don't talk to me, demon. You shouldn't be here."

Jax stands up. "Watch your mouth, Second."

"This is none of your concern, Forrester," Ross spits, before looking back at me. "You should call down your guard dog. Make him sit. Good God, what does he see in you?"

My blood is boiling.

"He's seen more than anyone ever has," I snap at Ross, "and he *chooses* to believe in me. I do not make him do anything."

"Then I suppose he is as much of a demon as you are."

I shoot to my feet and stop an inch in front of his face, fisting my hand around his shirt collar. "If you know what's good for you, Ross," I say, "you'll leave Jax out of our dispute."

His eyes are fire, but he doesn't say a word. My actions have sufficiently startled him.

I drop him and turn back to the table, trying to mask my irritation, but the scowl and murderous eyes show through my attempt at indifference. "When you are all ready to stop dwelling on the past and start focusing on the future, come find me. Until then, I have nothing more to say. Have a pleasant afternoon."

"Quinn," Jax tries again, but I am done. Done with Jenson, done with Ross, done with trying to help these worthless idiots. I'll save Haven myself. Guild knows that's the only way to get the job done, and done properly. I don't know why I bother...

No one tries to stop me as I dart around Ross and leave the room, closing the door quietly behind me. They probably wish I slammed it.

CHAPTER TWENTY-THREE

I stalk back to my room as fast and dangerous-looking as my leg will allow. I'm not even angry though, I'm...disappointed. Ross's reaction might have been on the extreme end of the spectrum, but Jenson was barely convinced even before he came in. Why can't they see we have to work together?

Look what happened with the Guild attack; I ran off and everything went to hell. I almost died, countless Resistance agents were slaughtered, and Sephtis slipped through our fingers. We can't beat him if we refuse to work together. The fact that I'm the one pressing that point shows I can be trusted. They are just too stupid to put the pieces together.

I reach my room then and am about to step inside when I notice something on the door. There's a note taped there, scribbled haphazardly, as if the person had been in a rush. I peel it off and read. Its contents freeze me to the spot.

Quinn,

I was thinking about what you said earlier and it made me think of something Anane said and, basically, I have a hunch. I've gone to the Barn to confirm my suspicions. I'll be gone for a few days. Don't come after me, no matter what. Tell Kuen not to worry too, though a fat lot of good that will do.

Be back as soon as I can,
Trey

There is a heart beside her signature and the words, "no matter what," are underlined twice.

Guild, Trey, couldn't it have waited?

"What's wrong?"

It's Jax.

He must've followed me from the Council room. I'm surprised I didn't notice. Either he's developed ninja skills or I'm losing my touch. Maybe a bit of both.

Still flustered, I hand him the note.

He reads it quickly and says, "Well, isn't that grand?"

"That's what I thought," I reply, finally finding my voice.

"What do you think she's up to?"

I sigh. "No idea, but if it involves Anane in any way, it can't be good."

"I was afraid you'd say that."

I purse my lips. "Let's go in and discuss it. I need to sit down."

His eyebrows shoot up. "Are you okay? I'm sorry. I should've—"

"I'm fine. Calm down, mom. I just know I should rest whenever I get the chance. Who knows when we'll be running or fighting for our lives again? I need to be ready and so I need to be healed. Come on." I open the door and he follows me in.

We sit side by side on the bed. I sigh when I take my right leg off the floor. Will I ever get used to it or will I be sitting here, ten years down the road, still waiting for normal?

"What do we do?" I ask Jax.

"That was my question. You usually have a plan."

I lean against him. "I know, but I'm tired. I'm tired of having all the answers, of being expected to have all the answers. I want someone to do the work for once, but at the same time, I don't want them to screw it up. All the while, I'm terrified *I'll* screw up." I put my face in my hands. "Ugh. It's a mess."

"I know, but every mess can be cleaned, right? I mean, you and Blake are talking again."

I give him a look. "If that was your attempt at trying to lighten the mood, it was the stupidest one I've ever heard."

He laughs. "Hey, a guy can't be perfect all the time."

"Right." I look down at my toes and he places a hand on my shoulder.

"Are you okay, Quinn? Are *we* okay?"

I look back up at him. "I think so," I reply, "and why wouldn't we be?"

He shrugs. "I don't know, you just seem...reserved lately. Thought I'd done something without realizing."

"No, it's not you. I'm on edge because I'm nervous and—to tell you the truth—scared. However, it's also the fact that Silent Night is gone. Her persona carried me for so long I'm not sure who I'm supposed to be now, let alone how to act or live my life. I'm a little lost. Then, that sense of loss makes me feel guilty, like I'm somehow missing who I used to be, but I don't want to go back, so I'm also confused. And..." I trail off, looking over at him again. "This isn't making any sense, is it?"

"No, I get it," he assures me. "You're still trying to piece your life back together, which is difficult to do when the rest of the world is falling apart."

I nod. "I don't have time to deal with my demons because I'm too busy dealing with everyone else's, mostly Sephtis'. How did I get stuck cleaning up his mess and trying to prevent more messes in the future?"

"You chose that path," he says, "the moment you decided not to swallow his lies anymore, let alone stomach his cruelty. You chose to fight back and now you have to follow through, but you're not alone. I'm walking the same path for my mother. Blake walks it for her parents. Trey and Kuen walk it for each other, and for you. We all do it for those who can't, to bring about a better future for everyone. We chose to be Haven's heroes and now we must save it."

I sigh. "I wish someone could tell us how to do it."

"Yes, but we can't be heroes if someone else does the work for us."

I let myself fall across his lap. "Why not?"

He pokes my cheek. "Because," he says. "Now stop whining and get your brain gears turning; we have a problem to solve."

I sigh again and sit up. "Fine," I say. I think for a moment before adding, "To start, Kuen and Jenson should be notified of Trey's departure. They need to be prepared for the results thereof. While we wait for confirmation or denial of whatever it is Trey's thought of, we need to get some work done here."

"Like what? Shoot."

"We need to prepare the base for possible attack. I can feel a storm coming and I want to be ready when it hits. We'll need a full inventory check of all weapons and supplies. Then I want our food stores doubled if possible and more weapons gathered if we can. We need to assess our abilities. I want reports on individual skills and then we can start assembling forces. What is the city like now? From what you saw the day you captured Anane?"

"It was still chaotic, sure, but the people have settled a bit. Maybe they can feel the storm too and have battened down their hatches."

"I wouldn't doubt it, but if you think it's feasible, I'm going to ask Kuen to take a trip to the Guild."

He frowns. "To what end?"

"One, to keep him busy while Trey is 'missing' so he doesn't snap and kill someone. Two, the assassins might've left clues behind as to their plans or where they've gone, and I also want to be certain they've abandoned that base."

"Good idea. Anything else?"

"Yes. What's up with the other assassin you caught?"

"Nothing as far as I know. Bast says he's been quiet."

"Has he been questioned at all?"

"Some, but the focus was on Anane."

I frown. "And maybe that was the Charger's plan. Use Anane as a distraction so the other one can slaughter us all. I want his guards tripled. Forget the straight jacket, but I want him chained like Anane. Tomorrow, I'm going to go talk to him myself."

He pokes me again, in the stomach this time. "See, that wasn't so hard. Look at the planning we've accomplished and it's been what, not even five minutes? We just have to keep pushing forward. How should we tell Jenson?"

"That, my love, will be your job," I reply, poking him in the nose.

He flinches back and then laughs. "All right, what do you want me to tell him?"

"Just what I've said, but make it out like it was your idea. I'll be the woman behind the scenes, for now. To avoid further conflict, Jenson can believe they're your ideas, and you'll definitely have input. I can't be doing *all* the work."

He rolls his eyes. "Uh huh."

I smack his arm. "Shush."

"Ow, I was kidding. Mostly."

I scowl.

"Oh lighten up, Quinn," he says. "So are we starting this now then?"

"Yeah," I reply. "You better go tell Jenson Trey's gone. I'll take on Kuen. Hopefully I come back alive."

"If he hurts you, I'll kill him." Jax's tone is light, but I can see the fire, the truth of the threat in his eyes.

"I know," I say softly. "I won't get hurt."

"You better not," he replies, pulling me into his chest. "I don't want to lose you." He kisses me once on the top of my head and we stay that way for a moment, wrapped against one another, lost in the second of bliss life affords us before it all comes rushing back.

It causes a great deal of agony, but eventually I make myself pull away and stand up.

"Let's get this over with," I say.

He sighs. "If we must. Promise you'll be careful?"

"I promise."

"Okay, then good luck."

"I'd like to say I won't need it, but…"

He nods.

Then without another word, we leave the room. He goes right and I go left.

Until we meet again…

• • •

I reach room 3672 with less hassle than the other day when I visited. My leg is doing much better, though still on the mend. I marvel at it every day, at my luck. I'm a miracle, and that's not my ego talking. I should be dead.

That fact hits me again.

I should be dead, yet here I am, going to talk to the brother I never knew and mentally ready to start another battle with the Charger, the father I never knew.

I shiver. The horrendous truth will never sit right with me, though denying it won't change a thing either.

The rooms around Kuen's still stand empty and it gives the hall an eerie feel. O'Reilly greets me at the door with a nod. "Ms. Ballinger," he says and I almost cringe.

Kuen has irrevocably altered him. He no longer stands straight and tall, proud of who he is. The harsh arrogance that surrounded him is gone, reduced to a timid acceptance. Kuen is now the alpha and O'Reilly will not even consider refusing to bow down. Kuen has *broken* him and my heart aches.

How many more souls will be shattered by this silent war? How many more people will turn victim to the monsters we cannot contain? Sure, O'Reilly was an ass, but he didn't deserve this. The guy can barely lift his head to me. He *fears* me. I never should've demanded he unchain the beast.

This is my fault.

He cocks his head at me. "Are you going to go in?" he asks.

I break out of my thoughts, realizing I've been staring at him wordlessly for a few minutes. "Yes, right, thank you."

He raises an eyebrow, further perplexed by my politeness.

Thank you? Why in the hell did I say that?

I'm falling apart. Sure, I've left the assassin behind, but that doesn't mean I need to have manners.

Awkwardly, I step forward and turn the doorknob. I don't give O'Reilly another glance, nor do I knock. I let myself in and shut the door behind me.

Again, the room is dark, but Kuen is sitting on the edge of the bed this time, sharpening a dagger. He holds it precariously in his still-healing hand.

Where the hell did he get that?

Every few seconds, sparks fly, illuminating his face and interrupting the heavy darkness.

"So they've decided it was wise to arm you then?" I ask. I didn't mean to say it aloud, but sometimes my thoughts slip out, unbidden. Hell, not sometimes, most of the time.

I can sense, more than see, his grin as he says, "Well, they didn't exactly decide. I made my own choice."

"You think that's the best route?"

"You think I'll get caught."

I don't answer.

"Quinn," he says, "the sooner you realize I know what I'm doing, the sooner we can all focus on more important things."

"It's not you I'm worried about," I mutter.

"What?"

Assassins below, he wasn't supposed to hear that.

I should never talk again. It would be so much easier.

"So what," he says, "you're worried I'll..." He stops and thinks for a moment, and then he laughs. "You're worried I'm going to use this," he holds up the knife, "and not on the 'enemy.' Glad you think so highly of me, sister. I could say the same about you. You're about as light-minded as I am and I'm almost as dark as they come."

My anger frees one claw and starts pacing the prison of my mind. "What happened to fighting the monster, brother?"

"Oh, I am, but sometimes it's fun to let him out to play, don't you think?"

My anger recoils inside me, replaced by disgust, and a touch of fear, though I hate to admit it. I came at the wrong time. I shouldn't be here, but I may not have the strength to come back. I meant to break it to him slowly, gently, but I don't have the patience for that.

I stand there in awkward silence for a moment before blurting out, "Trey's gone."

The crazed smile vanishes from his face. For once, I'm seeing real fear in Kuen's eyes. "What?" he chokes out. "What do you mean gone?"

I realize what he thinks has happened and throw my hands up. "No, no, she's not dead. She's just... Here, she left a note."

He relaxes as soon as I confirm she's still alive and takes the note I thrust into his hand. I can tell when he's done reading, because he crumples the piece of paper in his fist and lets it fall to the floor.

"Kuen…"

"For the love of…" he tries. "Damn, she can be so *frustrating*," he seethes. He clenches his fists again and puts his head in his hands. "She has a *hunch*? Why can't she tell us what it is? Why be so cryptic? If she doesn't die on this gods-damned 'mission,' I'm going to kill her myself. And what does she mean by 'tell Kuen not to worry?'" He looks up at me.

"You're not her keeper, Kuen," I say. "Just calm down. Please."

"Right," he snaps, "because that'll bring her back. How about you answer me this: how am I not supposed to worry when she disappears out of the blue, based on something *Anane* said? I'm going down there right now and I'm going to tell him exactly what—" He trails off when he sees the violence in my eyes.

"Touch him," I say coolly, "and you'll have your own cell before you feel my blade against your back, pushing you into it."

His eyes go cold, like a moonless night. "You'd kill me over him? I take it back; you still *are* the monster I once knew." His voice leaks disgust and I return the favour.

"You think that low of me? I wouldn't kill you to save him, but I'm sure as hell not going to let you hurt him with no evidence he's done anything wrong. Would a monster do *that*?"

"No evidence? His entire *existence* is wrong. The things he has done…"

"What about the things *you've* done?" I don't raise my voice, but my tone is deadly. "Guild, what about the things *I've* done?"

Finally, I've managed to shut him up. It's all he can do to look me in the eyes, let alone refute what I've said.

"Yet," I go on, "you and I are allowed to walk free. Somehow, we earned that right. Maybe he could too, if given the chance. Don't get me wrong, I hate him, but he's still a person and we all deserve a chance at something better, at something more. The real monsters are those that deny others' humanity. So ask yourself, where do you stand? Ask yourself: what am I? A monster fighting to be human or a human slowly succumbing to the monster within?"

"I… I don't know."

"Well you better decide, and decide quickly, because this war is escalating and I need to know which side you stand on before I take the first shot."

So I can decide whether or not the first bullet needs to go through his skull. I wouldn't kill him to save Anane, that much is true, but to save everyone?

I'd do it in a heartbeat.

CHAPTER TWENTY-FOUR

I shuffle through the halls, doing my best to take it easy.

I left Kuen's room without another word and without waiting for his reaction. I didn't so much as glance at Callum when I went; I was too afraid of what my guilt might bring to the surface, either my anger or the monster. The monster has made enough of an appearance today.

The one thing I *did* do before leaving was pick Trey's crumpled note up off the floor and stick it in my pocket. I'm not sure why I grabbed it exactly, but I think it can be attributed to the part of me that remains hopeless. The part of me that fears the note burning a hole in my pocket will be the last note Trey ever writes.

Don't think about that, I chide myself. *Think about your next steps.*

The plan to send Kuen on a scouting trip to the Guild has definitely gone down the drain. I can't let him out of the base right now; it would be too dangerous. What I *should* do is ask Jenson to assign more guards to him or, better yet, replace Callum entirely. That broken man would not be able to stop Kuen if he went rogue, but then again, would anyone? I'm not even sure I could stand against him, and that is a scary thought.

• • •

Jax finds me in my room later. I'm reading the book I found in the library a few days ago, the one with the assassin. Guild, has it only been a few days? It seems like it's been weeks since we caught Anane.

Jax doesn't bother to knock before entering. "I brought you dinner, seeing as you stood us all up," he says, holding up a plate of food.

"You know," I reply, "most people knock before entering someone else's room. What happened to your gentleman manners? You're lucky I was dressed."

He snorts. "I wouldn't call that lucky."

My cheeks burn. "Ajax Forrester!"

He laughs and then ducks.

"What the... Are you okay?" I ask him.

"Sorry, I'm used to daggers flying in this room."

It's my turn to laugh. "Oh my God, you actually ducked. I've got you that scared." I pause. "It's probably not a good thing, is it?"

He shrugs. "I don't know, but quit making fun of me."

"Oh come on, you're allowed to make fun of *me*."

"I am not."

"You do it all the time."

"Doesn't mean I don't fear your wrath for it," he points out.

"Am I that bad?"

"Not at all."

He walks over and sits down beside me, placing the plate of food on my lap.

I set my book aside and take a look at what he's brought me. Chicken, noodles, and, "Ooooh... Peas. My favourite."

He smiles. "I know, and I also got you this." He reaches into his jacket pocket and pulls out a chocolate chip cookie.

"Nice, but how clean is that pocket?"

"You don't want to know," he replies.

"Great." I ignore the hygienic mystery and dig in. Luckily, Jax also remembered a fork and knife.

When I'm done, I sigh and lean against him. "Thank you," I say.

He goes rigid. "Whoa, whoa, whoa," he exclaims. "Who are you and what have you done with my Quinn?"

"What?"

"You said thank you."

I slap him on the arm. "Oh, cut it out!"

He tries to push me away. "Ah! Help! I'm being attacked!"

"I'll attack you all right..."

I reach up, wrapping my arms around his neck, and trap him in a solid headlock.

He squirms and protests, but it doesn't take him long to fight back. He jabs me hard in the ribs with his elbow and I loosen my grip for a second, but it's enough. He slips out of my hold and wraps me in a bear hug before slamming me into the bed. It knocks the wind out of me and still, I try to laugh.

There's a crash as my plate and cutlery hit the floor.

"Whoops," Jax says.

I try to sit up, but he scrambles atop me and pins my wrists above my head with his hands. Then he stares at me, with that irresistible grin and damn handsome face...

Oh Gods, I'm in trouble.

"Oh no," I say, breathless, "you've caught me. Whatever will a poor girl do?"

"Perhaps a kiss?" Jax offers.

Oh, it's too precious. He thinks he's won.

However, I still have a few tricks up my sleeve.

He leans in and that's when I pull my secret weapon.

I jerk my right leg, letting out a little yell. "Ah, assassins below, my leg," I gasp. I furrow my eyebrows and clench my teeth to enhance the act.

Jax releases my wrists immediately and straightens up a little. "Gods, Quinn, I'm sorry," he says, guilt evident in his voice. "Are you okay? What should I—" He doesn't get to finish his sentence before I make my move.

I wrap my left leg around his torso and push, sending the both of us rolling. We nearly fall off the bed in the process, but he grabs hold of the frame.

"Jesus, Quinn," he breathes.

I can't help but smile. My plan worked; I'm on top now and he's subject to my mercy.

"Checkmate," I tell him.

He glares up at me. "Your leg was perfectly fine, wasn't it."

I grin and he shakes his head. "If I'd known what I was getting into when I first met you," he says, and I tense, anticipating the worst, "it wouldn't have changed a damn thing. I'd still have fallen for you just as hard, just as fast, just as irreversibly. I couldn't have stopped it if I wanted to."

I don't want to bring it up, but I feel like I have to. "What about... What about your mother?"

His expression changes, but remains soft. "I told you, Quinn, I've made peace with that, as much as one can. Being in such a high position as she was in the Resistance, she was always on the Guild's kill list. If you hadn't killed her, someone else would've, and besides, you're not the same girl who killed my mother, Quinn. Nor am I the same boy that watched that girl disappear into the night."

Why is he so good to me?

"You're sure you're okay?" I ask him.

"Positive," he replies. "I mean, not every day is easy. Sometimes I wake up and I just... I don't know. Memories hit me hard sometimes, but what's life without a little bit of difficulty? Acknowledging pain is half the battle. My mom, I think—no, I *know* she would be happy for me, *is* happy for me. She wouldn't hold it against you or condemn me for my choice to love you. She knows what this war has done to humanity and she'd be pleased I've found light amongst the darkness. You are my light, Quinn, and I will never, ever let the shadows of our past put you out. God, it might be selfish, but I *need* you."

He looks up at me just as one of my tears lands on his cheek.

"Hey," he says, reaching up and wiping away the rest with his thumb. "Don't you go crying on me because then I'll start and what a manly thing that would be."

I smile. "Don't worry, we all know you're a big baby."

"Oh shush."

I grin. "Make me."

He lunges up, wraps his hand around the back of my neck, and pulls me to him.

As soon as our lips meet, all tension drains from my body, all worries leave me. All that remains is his lips moving with mine and our bodies pressed against each other. I remember what he just said. He called me his light. He said he needs me. I kiss him harder, and the two of us come up for air for a second before plunging back in. He is a sea I would gladly drown in.

After what feels like lifetimes, we pull apart. I roll off him and the two of us lay side by side, breathing in sync with each other, hearts beating as one.

"God, I love you," Jax says.

"I love you too," I sigh. "It doesn't matter that the world is falling apart around us because *you* are my world, and as long as I have you, I'll be okay. I love you, and when this war is over, I'm never letting you go."

"Me neither," he replies, "me neither."

I shift over so I can lay my head on his chest. He runs his hand through my hair and I close my eyes.

"Are you going to start purring?" I hear him say.

"Maybe," I mumble.

A few minutes pass.

He sits up long enough to grab the blanket from the end of the bed and flings it over top of us.

I snuggle into him.

"So I guess we're staying like this?"

"Mmmm," I murmur, already half asleep.

He laughs softly. "Goodnight then. Sleep tight, beautiful."

"Don't let the bedbugs bite, handsome."

I don't open my eyes, but I know he's smiling. I yawn once and a few moments later, sleep takes me.

CHAPTER TWENTY-FIVE

The next morning dawns silent and still. Empty. My survival instincts kick in upon opening my eyes and I tense, one arm still slung over Jax's chest.

He stutters awake and would've sat up had I not held him back. "Quinn?" he asks softly.

"Can you feel that?" I whisper.

"No?"

"Something's wrong," I reply. "The air is too...still, like the calm before the storm or after. Either something's about to happen or it already has."

I whip off the blankets and roll to my feet, landing in a crouch. I reach under the mattress for my knife, when something catches my eye.

Across the room, my bedroom door stands ajar.

My fingers close around the hilt of my knife and I stand up. "We locked the door last night, didn't we?" I ask Jax.

"I know I at least closed it," he replies.

I don't dare turn my head to see the expression on his face. My insides are ice.

Something is wrong.

"I'm going to put my shoes on now," I tell him. "Don't take your eyes off the door."

"Got it."

I bend over and tug on my boots, skin prickling the whole time. "Okay your turn." I hear the bed creak as he eases to his feet and follows my lead.

He walks around the bed to stand beside me. "What now?"

"Did you bring any weapons with you at all?"

"No, but I suppose I could grab your utensils from last night if it'll make you feel better."

"It would."

He walks behind me to grab them off the nightstand.

"Watch my back," I say. Then I creep towards the door.

I reach for the doorknob when I get close enough but…

"Is that blood?" I breathe.

Jax joins me. "I wish I could say it wasn't."

There's a bloodstain on the knob and I follow my eyes down to a few drops on the floor. A trail leads out the open door.

I take a deep breath and pull it open the rest of the way with my foot, throwing my knife up in defense, but the hall is empty, just as the hollow feeling in my chest.

Empty except for the trail of blood that tracks along the right side of it and disappears around the corner.

Assassins below.

"Holy Gods..." Jax mutters. "Do you think it's a trap?"

"I think that somewhere there are a lot of bodies and maybe there are still people we can save. Come on." I tug on his arm.

"You mean to follow it?" Jax asks.

I simply nod and head off, not waiting to see if he's going to follow me.

I have an inkling of where this trail will lead, but I hope to God I'm wrong.

• • •

We follow the trail through the base, going a lot slower than I want. After my hall, the blood became harder to follow. A drop on the floor here, a smear on the wall there. Whoever did it, didn't want just anyone to find it. They wanted it to be me.

Several minutes later, we round a corner and enter the hall that houses the dungeon's entrance, just as I thought we would.

We come to a dead stop as we take in the severed head sitting in a pool of blood beside the archway.

George.

"Damn it all," I mutter. "I would suggest we get more weapons and go for back up, but it's clearly too late."

Jax doesn't answer.

I look over at him. "Are you... Jax?"

He's pale and trembling, though I can't tell if it's from fear or rage.

"What's wrong?" I curse the high pitch of my voice. Now is not the time to give in to my own fear.

"Bast was on the night watch," he chokes out finally. "Bast is down there." The pain in his eyes is unlike anything I've ever seen and my heart clenches in my chest.

Oh Gods. Oh Guild no.

"He..." I start, but Jax is no longer frozen. He's running for the stairs. "Jax, no!" I race after him, my heart in my throat.

Not Bast, I do not want to lose Bast, but if he's already gone... Hell if I'm going to lose Jax too. Over my dead and broken body.

The stairs are slick with what I can only assume is blood, given the darkness. I almost slip on the last step, but manage to catch myself.

The dungeon's lights are still on and they illuminate the carnage before us. Jax is on his knees in the blood that coats the floor, speechless. I stand on the bottom step, numb with disbelief.

You knew what they were capable of, my mind scolds me.

Yes, I did, but this...

There is blood everywhere. I didn't know that so few people could have so much. It's strewn around as if Anane and the other one were finger painting and, in fact,

I see a pair of red handprints on the far wall. The smell of iron and death coats the air, making it difficult to breathe, but I power through.

Of the six guards, not much remains. That is how brutally they were destroyed, that is how cruel and psychotic their assassins are. That is how completely and irrevocably Sephtis has wrested control of their minds. I only see three heads, one that seems to be speared with its own sword. Various other body parts litter the floor, broken and bloody. I notice a finger by my left boot and take a step back. I thought my monster was a nightmare, but this…

A shudder wracks through me.

This is something else entirely. This is inhuman. I've seen a lot in my short life, a lot of death and a lot of destruction, and I survived it. This is the first time in a long while that I feel nauseated.

My stomach heaves, but I tense and hold it back. I mustn't be weak; weakness is for those who will lose, and lose Sephtis shall.

I look away from the massacre and focus my attention on Jax, as if I could ever forget what I've seen. It's plastered on the back of my eyelids. Jax is still on his knees and I force myself to move, to walk over to him.

I place a hand on his shoulder. "I…"

"Don't talk," he says. "Don't you dare apologize for these people, these monsters. How can any person do this? How can someone justify this?" I can feel him shaking beneath my hand, the rage emanating from every muscle in his body.

"I wasn't going to apologize," I tell him.

"Good, because they don't deserve it. They should've been shot on sight." He shrugs my hand off his shoulder and stands up, clenching his fists. "We should go tell Jenson what happened. I don't suppose it would be worth it to round up a search party. The fiends have probably already crawled back into whatever dark hole they came from." He starts for the stairs.

"Wait," I call after him. "What about Bast?"

He stops dead.

"I can go...do it...if you want. I understand if it would be..."

He turns around. "I'll go. It's going to be difficult, but he is my best friend. I owe it to him to see for myself, to not be a coward. He wouldn't turn his back on me."

I nod. "Okay."

I hope to whatever god is out there that Bast isn't in the same shape as the others or rather, the same lack of shape. I hope his death was as quick and painless as it can be because anything else will destroy Jax. It will destroy me too.

We follow a thin trail of blood deeper into the dungeon, towards the cell of the second assassin. I knew it was a mistake to underestimate him. Sephtis sent someone he knew I wouldn't recognize, in order to bamboozle me. There was no way Anane could have escaped on his own, but the other guy could've done it with ease. In fact, that must've been what happened. He escaped, freed Anane, and the two of them tore the guards to pieces. Then they laid that trail of blood all the way to my room.

They could've killed Jax and me so easily.

Why didn't they?

I suppose they want me to feel like they hold all the power, that I owe them my life. They want me to be afraid.

Then another, more sinister question sneaks into my head.

How did they know where my room was?

We reach the cell then and my question is interrupted. The cell door hangs half off its hinges and the inside lays empty as a tomb, like the rest of the dungeon. The one guard lies in a broken, bloody mess beside the door, not as bad off as Anane's guards, but still unrecognizable. Something tells me it's not Bast. Yet, maybe that's the hope talking.

I'm almost too afraid to look at the other guard, to look at Bast, but fear won't change his fate. Nothing will.

I glance over and see...no one.

"Where is he?" Jax says, eyes flicking to meet mine.

"I...I don't know. He's not..." I bend my head towards the dead guard.

Jax shakes his head. "I specifically ordered two guards at this cell. He's not here."

"Then where..."

I look around the area, letting my feet carry me down a little further. I'm about to turn back when I see a pair of boots poking out from behind a corner.

"Jax... I think I found him."

He walks up behind me and I point my finger in the direction of the boots.

Jax takes a deep breath and together we walk the rest of the way.

My heart drops in my chest when I finally see the truth and unbidden tears run free.

Oh my God. Oh Gods...thank you. Thank you.

Bast is lying on his back on the stone floor, partially slouched against the wall. His legs are splayed out and one arm rests across his chest. The other is reaching towards a now smashed bottle of booze. Never have I been so happy to see someone drunk.

"You little shit," Jax mutters, shaking his head. He kicks Bast lightly in the ribs.

Bast groans and rolls over, curling in on himself. "Just five more minutes," he moans.

"Not today, bud," Jax replies. He reaches down and yanks off Bast's boot, pulling the rest of his body from the wall to the floor with a thud.

Bast's eyes fly open. "Okay, okay. I'm awake, now stop with the violence and give me back my shoe." He drags himself into a sitting position, holding his arms around his chest, and regards Jax and I. "What gives?"

"What *gives*?" I repeat. "You're the one who passed out drunk on the job, though—and you won't hear me say this again—I'm so glad you did, but you'd think a guy who just had a brush with death would show a little more...humility."

"A brush with...what?"

I don't answer and he looks back and forth between Jax and me. It takes him a minute, but then his eyes widen. As much as they can given his grogginess.

"What the hell happened to the two of you?" he asks, horrified, finally taking in Jax's blood-soaked jeans and the haunted looks in both our eyes.

"You tell us," I reply, "you were down here when it happened."

"When what happened? Can one of you please tell me what's going on?"

Jax sighs and the smile on his face from finding Bast alive and well vanishes. He drops Bast's boot and says, "The prisoner you were supposed to be guarding escaped."

Bast scrambles to his feet as fast as he can manage and stumbles back to his post. His face falls when he sees the mangled door and the body of his comrade. "No," he gasps. He turns back to us. "The others?"

I shake my head. "Whoever this assassin was, he freed Anane and the two of them slaughtered everyone else."

Bast can't find the words to speak and I don't blame him. I still feel sick to my stomach.

"We should go now," I suggest. "I don't think I can stay here much longer without having a mental breakdown."

"Agreed," Jax says.

We head for the main chamber, back towards the carnage.

Don't think about it, just don't...

The smell hits me again and I gag. Guild, it's been ages since I've been exposed to this level of suffering. I almost can't bear it.

I pause in the doorway and Bast barrels on ahead of me before coming to a halt. I watch him as he takes in the scene for the first time. Only moments later, he's on his knees, emptying the contents of his stomach. Then he's gasping, like he can't get enough air.

I rush towards him, and only then, crouching beside him, do I realize he's crying.

I grab his shoulder and shake him. "Bast. *Bast.*"

"It's all my fault," he gasps, fingers digging into his temples. "I am such an *idiot.* Why did I have to get drunk? Why can't I be fucking *normal?*" He takes in a shuddering breath, tears streaming down his face.

I don't think I've ever seen Bast cry before.

"I'm sorry," he whispers to the room and I know he's talking to the fallen, not to me.

I squeeze his shoulder. "It's not your fault, Bast. This would've happened even if you were sober. I know it's hard to hear, but you wouldn't have made a difference. You're lucky to be alive. The fact that you walked off and got drunk is what saved you."

"But do I deserve to be alive?" he asks me, finally meeting my gaze. His brown eyes are muddy from his tears.

"Of course you do. You are not a bad person, Bast. You are a good person in a bad situation and I will not let you lose yourself to this." I look up at Jax. "Neither of us will."

Jax nods. "Focus your hatred on the enemy, Bast, not yourself. Don't let them tarnish your innocence when they're the guilty ones."

Bast takes a deep breath and wipes his eyes with a clean section of sleeve. I notice the ends are dipped in blood from brushing across the floor.

Jax steps around me and holds out a hand to Bast. "Come on, man. Let's get out of here. The longer we linger, so will the pain." He helps Bast to his feet and I straighten, taking one last look around.

My eyes are drawn back to Anane's vacated cell where another horror awaits me.

"Assassins below," I breathe.

My legs take me into the cell of their own volition, the traitors. I don't want to get any closer; I've had enough. Yet, once my eyes have seen it clearly, there's no tearing them away from the crimson letters painted on the far brick wall of Anane's cell. Sephtis' favourite son has left us a sinister message:

Thanks for your time, sister.
I'll send Trey your regards, when we find her.

CHAPTER TWENTY-SIX

"Quinn?" Jax calls out. "Is something wrong?"

My blood is like ice. "They're after Trey," I tell him. "They're hunting her. Oh God, they know she's left and now... They're going to catch her, I know it. Jax, we have to—"

He regards me calmly, placing a hand on my elbow. I don't remember him joining me in the cell. "Slow down, Quinn," he says, "we'll figure it out. Okay?"

I force myself to nod, because it isn't okay. It'll never be okay. This whole life we lead is one disaster after another and it doesn't get better, no matter how hard we try. I don't know why we bother.

"Hey," Jax says, moving his hand to my face and turning my eyes to his. "It's going to be all right."

"How?" I ask, voice cracking as another unruly tear escapes.

"I don't know," he admits with a sullen face, "but it has to."

"Has to?" I repeat. "*Has to?* Nothing in this world has to do *anything*. The universe owes you nothing. It's not going to give you a break and it's certainly not going to say, 'Oh, I *have* to protect this girl Trey, just because!'"

"It's called having hope," Jax replies in a much calmer voice than mine.

"And what has hope ever done for us, Jax? I've tried to have hope, honestly I have, but I can't." Angry and desperate tears run down my face. I tried to be strong for Bast, but this...

Trey is all alone and she's being *hunted*.

"Hope is what brought Trey and Kuen to the two of us when we were drowning in that tank," Jax tells me. "They wouldn't have bothered to come if they hadn't thought there was a chance. Hope is what made the three of us decide to risk bringing you to the Resistance when you were dying from your leg wound. Hope is what keeps me sane whenever you have a brush with death, and hope, ultimately, is what brought us together, the faith that life won't always be this way and that love can save us. Hope has saved our lives more times than I can probably count, and that is why I still have it. We'll figure this out; we always do."

I rub my eyes with the back of my hand as I scowl up at him. "Why do you always ruin my reasoning with your logic?"

He smiles. "That's my job."

I shake my head. "I love you," I say softly.

"And I you."

He leads me out of the cell.

Bast is already at the stairs. "I thought we were going." His eyes are all puffy and red and there is an air of melancholy around him. It saddens me to see him like this—all his light snuffed out.

"We're coming," I assure him.

He starts heading up the stairs. Jax and I follow, not looking back this time.

Jax takes my hand in his and I feel safe. I can't wait to wash the residue of this place off me. I'm going to burn Jax's pants. Any physical reminder of the assassins' escape will go up in smoke and vanish into thin air. However, I don't think I'll ever rid myself of the memories.

Anane's message will forever haunt me, I'll never forget the smell, and I know the gruesome scene will visit me in my nightmares. Yet, one can try and maybe that's what life is about. Never giving up, even when you *know* it's hopeless. Maybe surviving is about living *despite*. Despite the horrors, despite the pain, despite the truth. It's about making the most of what you're given because, in the end, it's all you have.

● ● ●

The three of us look for the assassins' escape route before going to see Jenson, Bast giving Jax his spare gun in case of any trouble. We scour the connecting halls for five minutes in every direction, but find no other signs of blood. Shocked, we head back to my room and do the same in the opposite direction, checking any empty rooms on our way.

We find nothing. It is as if they dissolved into thin air. There isn't even a bloody footprint to give them away.

Jax slams his fist against a door. "How could they vanish without a trace?" he snaps. "The three of us left quite a trail with our own stained boots."

He's right. Whatever evidence is left has been tarnished now.

"It doesn't make sense," he sighs.

"Well, there isn't anything we can do about it now. We did our best. It's time to see Jenson."

Bast grimaces. "He's not going to be happy, is he?"

"No, he's not, and the longer we wait to tell him, the worse it will be."

Jax sighs again. "Better get it over with then."

• • •

Jenson yells at us all for a solid five minutes, blaming Bast for the escape, blaming Jax for catching them in the first place, and blaming me because of who I am.

"You knew this would happen, didn't you, Assassin?" he snaps at me.

I fold my arms across my chest. "I knew nothing of the sort, but I do recall telling you they were dangerous. None of you cared to listen to my warnings. Jax was merely following your orders, so there's no way in hell this is on his shoulders either. As for Bast, he's lucky to be alive, so I'd appreciate it if you stop making him wish he *was* dead. He feels bad enough already. We are not to be blamed for this. In fact, all the evidence points to you. This is your fault. You want someone to blame? Look in the mirror."

"You are severely testing my patience," Jenson tries, but I cut him off.

"No, you're testing *mine* and treading on treacherous ground, so I'd be more careful if I were you."

"I know perfectly well what you're capable of, Assassin, now if you would please…"

"Goddamn you!" I snap, slamming my hands against the table so hard it shakes. "My sister is in grave danger and all you can think about is yourself and your damn reputation! Here's a wake-up call, Jenson: no one gives a shit."

Silence descends upon the council room. Jenson is staring at me with wide eyes. Bast and Jax wait in tense anticipation for what will happen next.

None of us expect Jenson to say, "Trey is your sister?"
Seriously, that is the part he latches onto?
"She is."

Jenson's expression is unreadable. "So Kuen's your…?"

"Brother."

"So it's true then, what the dungeon guards were telling me."

The dungeon guards…?

"What did they tell you?" I ask, cautious.

"All four of you—Silent Night, Trey, Kuen, and Anane—are the Charger's children."

Well, shit.

I take a step back.

"How did you deduce that?" I ask Jenson, fighting to keep my voice neutral.

He leans back in his chair. "It wasn't all that hard to piece together, Ms. Ballinger, or is that even your last name?"

I clench my fists. "Don't you dare question my name. Tell me how you found out."

"Well, you revealed to us in our meeting, that the prisoner, Anane, was the Charger's son, his youngest, which led me to believe there were others. So, I asked around. The agents present on the day he was captured were able to tell me a very interesting story indeed. Kuen and Trey were also present when Anane woke up and when he saw the three of you, he called it a family reunion. They also told me Anane called Kuen big brother at one point, told Kuen to listen to his little sister when speaking of Trey, and to top it all off, addressed you as sister. So it was clear the four of you were all related, and when I pieced that together with the info you let slip... Well, it was like Christmas. I'm so happy to be able to confirm my suspicions." His smile lights his face up, but it's not bright. It's damning, like a funeral pyre.

"What do you plan to do with this knowledge?" I ask.

"I'm not sure yet," he replies, rubbing his chin. "We could use you and Kuen as bait, like you suggested we do with Anane."

"It won't work," I say. "The Charger doesn't care about us."

"Ah, but that's a lie. He cares about *you* or was Anane exaggerating when he said the Charger would give you the world?"

My heart drops into my stomach.

No. Jenson knows everything. We never should've let Anane talk…

He grins at me. "Caught in your lies, Assassin?"

"You can't," I breathe. "You can't give me to him; that's what he wants."

Dammit, my fear is showing, but I can't help it. I've never been more terrified. I can't go back to him. I won't.

"You think I would give you up to him that easily?" Jenson shakes his head. "You're the best pawn in this war; he's not going to take you, but he's going to try and when he does, he'll be sorry."

"You can't beat him," I argue, all but begging him to reconsider. "Your plan will fail and when it does, when he has me, he'll torture all of your secrets out of me. Even I can't withstand the kind of pain he can inflict."

It pains me to admit it, but it's true. I'd rather die than let Sephtis lay so much as a finger on me.

Jenson shrugs. "That's a chance I'm willing to take."

"Well, I'm not," Jax says. He pulls Bast's gun out of his coat and aims it at Jenson's head from across the table.

"Me neither," Bast agrees, knocking his bow and aiming it at Jenson's heart. "Take it back."

No.

Jenson's eyes are wide as he regards the two of them.

"Pledge to Quinn's safety or I won't hesitate to shoot," Jax adds. "I might not go for the head, but you'll be in a great deal of pain." His voice is calm but his eyes are dark.

Hell if I'm going to let the two of them become cold-blooded killers on my account.

"Stand down," I tell them.

Jax gives me a look. "But Quinn, he…"

"*Now.*"

Jax sets the gun on the table and Bast lowers his bow, though he keeps it ready.

"Put the arrow away, Bast," I urge.

"But…" His brown eyes are sad.

"Sebastian, don't make me ask you again."

He scowls at me, but returns the arrow to his quiver.

Jenson doesn't say a word. I don't know what to do next, don't know if I even have a plan, but I'm saved by a knock on the door.

"Jenson, sir?" a voice calls out. "Urgent message for you."

Jenson finds his voice and replies, "Come in."

The door opens and Bast, Jax, and I try desperately to erase any signs of the confrontation that just took place. I'm good at hiding my true emotions, them not so much. If we get the chance, I'm going to have to teach them a thing or two.

A rather nervous-looking man enters the room and stares warily at all of us.

"What is it, Lewis?" Jenson asks.

"It, um…"

"Out with it, man," Jenson barks. "Is it urgent or not?"

"Here," Lewis says, thrusting a crumpled piece of paper onto Jenson's lap.

Jenson frowns and picks it up, carefully flattening it out before reading. His eyebrows rise as he reads and the tension in the room grows to an agonizing crescendo, until Jenson swears and it shatters, bits of emotional shrapnel flying everywhere. I can't even describe the expression on Jenson's face.

"What is it?" Jax demands to know.

Jenson merely hands Jax the paper without saying a word, as if Jax didn't threaten his life only moments ago.

"Read it aloud," I urge him.

Jax takes a deep breath and begins.

Jenson,

I have reached the Barn and done some preliminary observations. It seems it is worse than I feared. My suspicions were right, and then some. I didn't want to consider it, didn't want to believe it, but it is nothing but the truth.

The Resistance East has been compromised. It's crawling with assassins; I believe they've been hiding out here since the "fall" of the Guild. I hope this message reaches you before it's too late. The Warehouse is in grave danger.

Don't let Anane escape.

I'm sending this message back to you and then I'm going in. If you don't hear from me within a day or so, I give you the right to assume the worst. Do not, under any circumstances, round up a search party. I'm not worth the lives you will lose.

Trey

P.S. If this is how it ends, tell Kuen and Quinn I am sorry, and I love them. Stay strong, guys.

Jax sets the note down on the table. All I can think about is that life is never fair, and how can one have hope after everything...

The assassins have the Resistance East.

We're done for.

"How did they manage to capture an entire base, without us knowing?" Jenson says.

"Because they always had it," I reply, several puzzle pieces falling into place at once in my mind.

Jenson looks over at me. "What?"

"The Barn was always theirs," I realize. "We've all been played for fools."

"I don't understand, Assassin," Jenson continues, "explain yourself."

I give him a look. "Do you know who the 'leader' of the Barn and the entire Resistance is?"

"Of course I do," Jenson scoffs. "Avery Norin."

"I'm afraid you're mistaken," I tell him, shaking my head. "That may be the name he uses now, but in truth he is Vyrin Aeron."

Jax gasps. "You're kidding."

I shake my head.

"What is so significant about his 'true' name?" Jenson questions, clearly irritated.

"The Master Assassin's true name is Sephtis Aeron," I reply, getting straight to the point.

Jenson's eyes widen to the size of tea saucers. "So you're saying...?"

I nod. "Avery and the Master Assassin are related. They're brothers, actually."

Jenson swears again.

Bast lets out a low whistle. "We're in deep trouble, aren't we?" he asks me.

"The deepest."

"How long have you known this, Assassin?" Jenson demands to know.

"Since just after the Guild attack. Trey confirmed it for me. She's known he was our uncle for years. She urged me to keep quiet because the truth would only cause panic, but I can see now she was as blind as the rest of us."

"So you're suggesting Avery and the Charger have been working together all these years," Jenson says, "thinking up an elaborate masquerade scheme, to...what? What's their end game?"

"I'm not sure yet," I admit. "I know Sephtis wants to annihilate everyone, but that doesn't mean Vyrin wants the same thing. We might be able to use that to our advantage. Other than that, I believe it's time to triple our defenses and assume all the Resistance East agents are dead, if they were even our agents in the first place."

Jenson shakes his head. "We lost so much manpower in the Guild attack, and now this. How can we win when we're at such a disadvantage?"

"By being more positive, Jenson. You're still alive, we know where the assassins are now, and we also know about Vyrin and Sephtis' ruse. It's not over yet."

"But..."

"Jenson, there's this thing called hope. I suggest you look it up, because you won't survive this war without it."

Jax smiles at me and Jenson says, "Fair enough, Assassin, and about those defenses..." He looks over at the messenger who has remained quiet throughout the entire exchange. "Lewis, call a council meeting. Ajax, I want you to go to the control room and put the base on lockdown, no one gets in or out. Understood?"

"Of course."

"Assassin, I want you to start doing some planning, keeping in mind that I will resort to *my* plan if you don't come up with something better. And Mr. Foster?"

Bast looks up. "Yes, sir?"

"I'll need your key to the Den."

Bast frowns. "My—"

"Yes, your key. I understand the bottle saved your life, but I can't have you impaired on the job. Next time, you might not be so lucky. Next time, it could cost someone else. You will get the key back, once I feel you've earned it, but for now, you have lost that privilege."

Bast swallows hard, but reaches into his shirt and pulls out his key chain. He unhooks the key and sets it in Jenson's outstretched hand.

Jenson closes his fist. "I will have a team see to the mess in the dungeons. We'll hold a memorial sometime this afternoon. All dismissed."

And that's that I guess.

Outside the council room, we run into a frantic Blake. Her eyes are red and her braid has come undone in places, wisps of hair sticking out in every direction.

"Oh my God," she gasps.

"Blake?" Jax says. "What's wrong?"

"I heard something happened in the dungeon and I… Well, I knew Bast was on night watch and then I couldn't find any of you and… Oh my God, I'm so glad you're all right." She throws herself at the three of us, wrapping us in a hug, and I feel some of the tension leave me.

She pulls away after a minute and the three of us explain everything that happened, including Trey's note.

"That's truly awful," she says when we're finished. She shakes her head at Bast. "I can't believe your drinking saved you."

He shrugs. "Yeah, well, Jenson confiscated my Den key, but it's for my own good. I can't trust that trauma will keep me from my bad habits."

"Let us know if the withdrawal starts getting to you though, okay?" she says. "It won't be easy."

Bast nods. "Thank you."

Jax claps his hands. "Well, I have to go before Jenson realizes I haven't dealt with his orders yet."

"I should change out of these clothes," Bast says.

"Do you want to grab some food after?" Blake asks him. "You can't be dealing well with everything on an empty stomach."

Bast smiles and it's good to see it on his face again, if only fleeting. "That would be great."

The two of them head off and Jax hugs me close before doing the same. "Be safe," he tells me.

"I'll try."

Once he's gone, I head for the armoury. I need the reassuring feel of cold steel in my hands and in every pocket. Also, I've been dying to try out my prosthetic sheath, to see how well it holds up. Jax really did think of everything when designing it. What I ever did to deserve someone like him, I'll never know.

It's a shame I lost my old weapons, but it was for the best. They represented the old me and she's gone now. Let them die in the Guild with her.

My thoughts are interrupted by a screeching sound, followed by static. I realize it's the PA system as Jenson's voice rings out. "Attention all Resistance members. I ask you to stop whatever you are doing right now and listen closely to this urgent message…"

I don't bother paying attention as Jenson lays out our current situation and what has happened at the Resistance

East. The PA system clicks off once I reach the armoury. Thankfully, I'm not the only one who's decided to rearm themselves, because I've realized I don't know the password to get in.

At least twenty people are already inside and I slip in, unnoticed. I go for the guns first, knowing that's likely the first thing we'll run out of. I grab a couple glocks, a pistol, and half a dozen cases of ammunition.

I choose an axe next, thinking of how proud Blake would be. It sucks that my old one got left behind, because it was my first Resistance weapon, but what's done is done.

I'm already having trouble carrying what I have, and I'm nowhere near finished.

One of the other agents must notice my struggle, for someone wordlessly hands me a bag.

I mumble a thank you, dump my arm contents into the bag, and go to town on the rest of the armoury.

I shove three swords in, all of them with grey handles that blend in with my Resistance uniform. One is a katana and just looking at it sends excited chills up my spine. I hold my bag up to a shelf with throwing knives and slide the entire pile into the bag.

I hover near a case with vials of poison, but eventually decide against it. I'm not going to end my life, no matter what happens, and I'm not going to subject anyone to that sort of ending either. If I die, I'm going down swinging, and I'll take whoever I can with me when I go, as many heartless assassins as I can manage.

Last, but not least, I grab myself a pair of wicked-looking daggers with hilts of dark blue. Now these might be my favourite. I stick one in my left boot, and slide the other into my prosthetic sheath. It fits perfectly.

Sweet.

I heave my bag up onto my shoulder and head for my room, mission accomplished.

• • •

Once in my room, I strap all my weapons into place. Two swords across my back, the third in the second prosthetic sheath, hilt resting against the outside of my calf, just below the knee. One glock at my hip, axe hanging from the other. The second glock goes into a case on my left thigh. I have three throwing knives on each sleeve, three more *in* each sleeve, and half a dozen more hanging from my belt. The pistol rests in the belt too, against my back.

I stand in front of the mirror when I'm done and admire my handiwork.

Guild, I look fierce.

I smile.

Quinn Marie Ballinger is ready for battle—may the best warrior win.

CHAPTER TWENTY-SEVEN

Outside my room, I nearly run into Kuen, and my muscles tense, bracing myself for the worst. I wonder how much he knows.

"So, our bastard father has taken the East headquarters then?" he asks.

I relax; so he doesn't know about the message in the dungeon. I pray he doesn't find out.

"It appears he has," I reply, "but I think Avery has been in league with him for years."

Kuen nods. "Oh, without a doubt. The Master Assassin was always the best actor, no surprise his brother is the same."

I narrow my eyes. "How did you know Avery and Sephtis are brothers? I never said, and Jenson certainly didn't tell you."

"Your buddy Bast told me. I had a little chat with him on the way here. Apparently *our* dear brother escaped the dungeons as well. As if this day isn't bad enough already..."

I let out a breath. "You're telling me. I was the one that discovered the carnage he left behind."

Kuen grimaces. "He always was a piece of work."

"And he will never be anything more than a monster," I reply. "I was going to give him a second chance and now... If I ever see him again, I'm going to shoot him. No questions asked."

Kuen grins. "Now that's the spirit!"

I head down the hall and he follows me. "One more thing you should know," I tell him, "Jenson knows Sephtis is our father, all four of us."

Kuen swears. "How?"

"He has eyes everywhere apparently, and he's prepared to use the two of us—well, *me* mostly—as bait if need be."

Kuen's expression darkens. "Over my dead body."

"Agreed. In fact, Bast and Jax both threatened to kill him when he mentioned it."

He raises an eyebrow. "Really?"

"Yeah, Jax was going to shoot him and Bast had an arrow aimed at his chest."

He shakes his head. "The level of loyalty you guys have astounds me."

I tilt my head. "How so?"

"You've known each other what, a few months?" he points out. "Yet, you're all prepared to sacrifice your lives and reputations for each other. Think about it. If one of them had come to the Guild and Sephtis had threatened *them* like that, would you ever have even considered holding a dagger to Sephtis' throat?"

"I…"

"Exactly. They risked a lot today in protecting you, they always do."

I frown. "Are you saying I don't deserve it?"

"No, I'm saying I'll never understand it. I'm jealous, Quinn. I'll never have friends like that of Bast and Blake, and I'll certainly never have someone look at me the way Jax looks at you."

It takes a great deal of effort to hide my blush and say, "I'm sure you'll find someone someday."

"Finding someone isn't the problem," he mumbles under his breath.

"Then what…" But I don't get time to finish my sentence. Someone is running at us, with frantic fear in their eyes.

Please no.

I can't take any more surprises today.

The person skids to a stop in front of us and half bows toward me. I don't recognize the scrawny man.

"Can I help you?" I ask him.

"Jenson asks that you come with me, immediately. It's of grave importance."

"Did he now?"

"What's happened?" Kuen asks him. I can feel the tension emanating from Kuen's frame.

The man swallows. "It's the assassins," he says. "They've sent us a message."

• • •

Kuen and I burst into the control room to find Jenson, Ross, Jax, and a handful of others gathered around one of the screens, immersed in intense conversation.

"You called for me?" I ask, raising my voice to be heard over the din.

Jenson straightens up. "Yes indeed, Assassin. What do you make of this?" He steps aside and turns the computer screen in my direction. It's showing a security camera feed. I recognize the building the camera is aimed at as the one directly across from this base's main entrance, but what's that on the wall...?

I squint to see and, as if reading my thoughts, Jenson zooms in on the section of interest. My heart drops into my toes when I finally see it clearly.

Holy Gods above.

Written in what is probably blood, are the words:

We have Trey.

If you ever want to see her again,

you'll give us Jenson.

The message is signed, Vyrin Aeron.

Well, I guess Avery's done pretending and Trey's suspicions were absolutely right. Trey is in dire straits, but at least she's alive, though I wouldn't put it past

Sephtis and Vyrin to kill her as soon as we hand over Jenson. Bastards.

"Well?" Jenson asks.

"Obviously, Trey was discovered and now our enemies have decided to beat us to the bait game."

"If that's the case," Jenson says, "they're doing it all wrong. I wouldn't sacrifice myself to save Trey's life."

I resist the urge to slap him.

"Which is why, Jenson," Kuen says, "the message wasn't aimed at you. You wouldn't give yourself up to save her, but I'd give you up, Quinn would, possibly even Jax, and Sephtis knows that all too well."

Jenson bites his lip. "And what would that get you?"

Kuen takes a step forward. "My sister back safe and sound for one…"

I take a deep breath and step in front of Jenson. "Kuen, we can't."

"What?" Kuen snaps. "Whose side are you on?"

I wince. "Whichever side ensures the survival of most. We can't give Jenson to Sephtis. That's what he wants. We have to deny him as much as possible. So, if he wants Jenson, he doesn't get him."

There is murder in Kuen's eyes. "So you're prepared to let Trey die for him?"

Stupid tears build up inside me, but I don't dare let them fall. "It's not to save him; it's to save us all. Besides Kuen, do you really think Sephtis will keep his promise? He'll kill her anyway. He only makes it seem like we have a choice, but he's already sealed her fate. We can't save her."

"To hell with that!" he explodes. "I can't believe you. You talk about hope, and loyalty, and protecting those you love, and now this? You disgust me! I take it back: your friends deserve so much more than your filth. If one of them were in Trey's shoes, you'd hand Jenson over in a heartbeat, wouldn't you?"

"I…"

"Don't you dare try to deny it!" He shakes his head. "You're such a hypocrite. Such a lying, two-faced *monster*! And to think, I saved your life. I should've let you die, you and Jax both. Nothing more than the two of you deserved. But Trey, Trey wanted you alive.

"Oh yeah, that's right, Trey saved your life too, but you're not willing to return the favour. You're going to let her die, because your poor, crippled frame can't handle father's retaliation."

Behind me, Jax stands up. "Watch it," he says darkly.

Kuen sneers at him. "You stay out of it, Forrester. This is a family thing." He laughs, but it's soulless. "So, sister," Kuen asks me, "what'll it be, Jenson or Trey?"

I stand tall and firm. "You already know my choice."

He takes a step toward me, so we're not even a foot apart. "You little *bitch*," he spits. "You think Trey will forgive you, you think she will be proud, that she'll understand?" Kuen is no longer merely angry; his monster has been let out. There is no shred of kindness left in his black eyes. No sliver of light. He raises his hands, bandages and all, and I expect him to hit me, but he grabs my arms instead. "If you won't stand aside," he growls, "I'll have to make you."

Before either of us can blink, Jax is by my side, his one hand latched around Kuen's wrist. The darkness in his eyes matches Kuen's as he says, "Get. Your. Hands. Off her." His tone could level cities and drown innocent men.

Kuen shifts his gaze from me to Jax. "I don't think I will," he replies, grinning, and then he squeezes my arms tighter, turning his hands as he does so.

I flinch.

Jax lunges.

Kuen dodges the first punch aimed at his face, but is unable to stop Jax from tearing his hands off my arms.

Jax pushes me back, out of the way, and I stumble into Jenson, though we both remain upright.

Kuen laughs, his entire attention now focused on Jax. "I've been waiting to have a piece of you."

"Likewise," Jax says.

Not another word is exchanged.

Jax aims another punch, but Kuen is expecting it. He reaches out and grabs Jax's fist with his good hand.

My heart leaps into my throat. I've seen the move enough times, *performed* it enough times to know…

But Jax doesn't end up on the floor. Somehow, Jax turns Kuen's power against him and it's Kuen who eats dust, though he's back on his feet in seconds and more livid than ever. He slams his fist into the side of Jax's jaw. Once, twice…

I wince with each blow, but Jax doesn't have time to dodge. He stumbles back a few steps and spits blood at Kuen's feet.

Jenson's men surge forward to help, but Jax holds up a hand. "Don't come any closer. He's mine."

They look to Jenson, who nods, and step out of the way.

Kuen grins. He takes a step closer and Jax mirrors him.

Kuen throws his fist, but Jax ducks at the last second, crouching low and aiming a kick at the side of Kuen's leg, just below the knee.

Kuen hits the floor again.

Jax doesn't give him time to get up. He slams his foot into Kuen's rib cage, all his hatred behind the action. Again. And again. And again…

Kuen lunges up, roaring his fury like a wild animal, and latches onto Jax's leg.

Jax can't catch himself in time and he topples onto Kuen.

Kuen flips them over and tries again to punch Jax in the face with his right hand, but Jax turns his head at the last second and Kuen's already broken fist slams into the concrete. He swears like a demon and Jax knees him in the gut while he's distracted.

Kuen rolls off and jumps to his feet again. Jax follows.

For a moment, they stare at each other, predators assessing each other, searching for weakness. That's when Kuen realizes they've switched sides. He can't see Jenson and I behind Jax anymore, which means Jax's biggest weakness is right behind Kuen.

Me.

He turns to face me and I press my gun against his forehead.

No one moves.

My hand is shaking ever so slightly and of course Kuen notices.

"You won't do it," he taunts. "Come on, sister, shoot me. Condemn me to death the same way you condemned Trey. Kill me like you killed Hai. Kill me and show your dear boyfriend the cold-blooded killer you really are. *Do it!*"

And that's when I realize he wants me to do it. He wants to be put out of his misery.

I lower the gun.

He sneers at me. "I knew you were too much of a coward. And now he will pay for it." Kuen pulls a dagger out of his boot and pivots, slashing at Jax who is now right behind him, having crept up while Kuen's attention was on my gun, but Kuen knew all too well what Jax had planned.

Kuen's blade slices across Jax's right cheek and blood flies.

I can't breathe.

Jax doesn't so much as flinch. His eyes betray no emotion as he lunges forward, wraps his arms around Kuen's side, and slams him into the wall.

Kuen didn't see *that* coming.

All the breath goes out of him in a whoosh and he crumples to the floor. While he's still trying to bring air back into his lungs, Jax kicks him in the side of the head.

Kuen goes limp. The rise and fall of his chest, which resumes a few seconds later, is the only sign he's still alive.

Jax crouches down and pries the bloody dagger out of Kuen's hand. He shoves it point first into the wall beside Kuen's head. Then he wipes the blood off his face with the back of his hand, which only serves to smear it, and stands up.

No one has said a word since the start of the fight and Jax regards us all with solemn eyes. "He needs to be taken to the dungeon," he says, looking at Jenson.

"Right," Jenson replies, "of course. Everett, Daniel, take the assassin to the dungeon. Make sure he's secure and watched at all times."

Two of Jenson's guards nod. "Yes, sir." They each grab one of Kuen's arms and drag him out the door. Three others follow, just in case.

When they're gone, Jenson looks at me. "Well, I guess that's that then. All dismissed. I would like a word alone with the assassin."

I can only nod. I'm still in shock.

Jax is the first one out the door, like he cannot find enough air to breathe in the room.

Ross lingers, giving me a dirty look, but finally follows the rest of the council members and other agents.

"You're not going to try to ransom me for Trey?" Jenson asks me when everyone is gone.

"No," I say. "Did you even pay attention to what happened?"

"Of course I did, but it doesn't hurt to confirm."

I sigh. "I suppose not." I pause and then I add, "He's going to need medical attention for his hand."

Jenson scrunches an eyebrow. "What?"

"Kuen. He's broken that hand twice in three days."

"So?"

"So, despite what he's done, he's still my brother and I don't wish him to suffer any more than he has to. This choice was not easy for me. I don't know if you have family, Jenson, but I might have lost two siblings today that I only just found. All I'm asking is that you try."

He takes a deep breath. "I will ask the nurses, see if anyone is willing to tend to him."

"Notify me if there are any other developments, but I'm going to go relax somewhere. This day has been too much already."

Jenson nods and I take my leave.

CHAPTER TWENTY-EIGHT

Jax is still hovering in the hall and I grab his elbow on my way out, coaxing him to come with me. He looks shell-shocked and I don't blame him. I can barely believe what happened, what he did. All for me.

We walk down the hall in silence for a bit and then I stop, turning to face him. "Are you...?"

He shakes his head.

"Right," I say. "Let's get you home."

I grab his elbow again and lead him through the base to his room. It's lucky I remembered the number. Otherwise, we'd have to find Bast or Blake. I don't want either of them to see Jax like this, and I doubt he wants that either.

I drag him to his bed and then lock the door. Jax is staring down at his feet when I look back at him and I take a moment to study the damage.

The blood on his face and hands has dried, and his cheek looks horrible. The gash runs on a curve from just below the eye down along his jaw to just before his chin. Almost three inches long. I know from experience that he's in a lot of pain. The cut will issue a stinging and burning all at once, not to mention the ache from the blows he received there, or was that the other cheek?

My heart clenches in distress at seeing my Jax in such a state and this is just what I can *see*. He's probably covered in bruises beneath his clothes and if not now, they'll colour him by morning.

"Jax," I say, "I'm sorry, and I know it's not my fault, but I don't know what else to say."

He's still silent.

I shuffle over and sink to my knees before him, as if he's a wild animal that needs to be approached carefully, and in a way, he is. It was the wild part of Jax that attacked Kuen and that part is still awake.

"Jax?" I ask, taking his hands in mine.

He flinches and tears his hands away. "Don't."

It's the first thing he's said to me since he told me to be safe earlier.

"Why not?" I ask.

"Because I'm in no shape to be allowed your touch right now."

I narrow my eyes. "What's that supposed to mean?"

"I... I just... Look at me." He holds out his bloodstained hands and grimaces.

Fury ignites in my chest. "Ajax Forrester, do you honestly think I could be ashamed of you right now, for this?"

He looks up, blue eyes full of pain. "Yes?"

"The fact that you could think that..." I take a shaky breath. "Why the hell would I be ashamed of you for defending me, and ultimately yourself?"

"I beat up your brother."

"He is no brother of mine. Not now. He tried to kill you. Look what he did to your beautiful face." My voice breaks as I reach up and place my hand on his wounded cheek.

He winces and turns his head.

"Jax, please," I say softly, "Look at me."

He turns back.

I stare right into his eyes as I tell him, "Kuen deserved everything he got."

"Still, I almost failed you," Jax replies, voice nearly a whisper.

I roll my eyes.

Not this bullshit again.

"No, you didn't," I snap. "I'm the one who didn't have enough guts to pull the damn trigger. You acted; you saw what was happening and did something about it. What did I do? I stood there and watched. You should be ashamed of *me*."

"Never."

"Then don't be so ridiculous and accept I do not feel any less towards you after what happened. In fact, I love you more. You took Kuen on, for me. The most dangerous assassin out there next to Sephtis most likely and you attacked him, just to save me. You could've died; by all accounts you *should've* died."

Finally, mercifully, he smiles. "One can accomplish anything with enough motivation. I tried to picture my life without you, tried to picture this *world* without you, and could only see darkness. I knew you were worth whatever consequence."

I blink back my tears and say, "Well, it appears the only consequences are this nasty cut and a slew of bruises. Come on, let's get that cleaned."

I stand up and Jax directs me to his dresser where I find a first aid kit. I clean the wound with antiseptic first, while Jax clenches the bed frame so hard I'm surprised it doesn't break. It's much easier to see without all the blood.

"I don't know, Jax," I tell him, "you might need stitches."

"Do what you can. I'll be fine."

"Jax…"

"Quinn, please."

I sigh. "Fine, but don't come crying to me when this won't heal or worse, it gets infected. I'm sure you remember what happened to me when I didn't adhere to medical treatment. Oh right, I almost died."

"Don't remind me," he mutters, "but this is just a cut."

"On your face," I point out, "near your brain. Not to mention it'll leave a nasty scar if left to heal on its own."

"Okay, fine," he groans. "You win, but can we hurry up about it?"

I smile. "Sure, let's go."

• • •

Shirley takes one look at Jax when he enters and clicks her tongue. "Has Ms. Ballinger been rubbing off on you, Mr. Forrester?"

Jax looks down at his feet. "I got into a fight."

"It would appear so. Lucky you decided to come here; that gash definitely needs stitches."

I elbow him in the ribs. "See?"

Jax looks up at Shirley and says, "Actually, it was Quinn's idea to come."

"Clever girl," Shirley replies, smiling, "you're lucky to have her."

"Oh, I know."

She steers Jax over to a bed without another word and gets to work, making him rinse his mouth out first.

He swigs and spits out a torrent of red.

I wince. I forgot about how many times Kuen's fists connected with his face.

Shirley stitches up the wound next, Jax flinching and gasping all the while.

After, she talks to us briefly about the current situation.

"It's a good thing you're healed, girl," Shirley says, "because the way things are going, we're going to need you in top shape."

"If Jenson doesn't try to sacrifice me first," I mumble, scowling.

"What? Why on earth would he do that?"

"It's complicated. Let's just say that today's fight might be the first of many Jax has for me, and that I'll be joining in on the next one."

"Wonderful," Shirley mutters. "Well, you two stay safe, Sebastian and Blake as well." She looks at me. "Don't exhaust yourself too much, a lot depends on you, and you," she turns to Jax, "I'll need to see you in four days to remove those stitches. Understood?"

Jax nods.

"Good. See you soon."

"Bye," I say and then Jax and I take our leave.

• • •

Jax and I go back to my room. He falls asleep on my bed and I don't blame him. He has to be exhausted. I lay beside him for an hour, until I decide there are better uses for my time, especially considering the situation we're all in. I strap all my weapons back on and leave Jax a note, telling him I've gone training. I hope he doesn't worry and that he sleeps a while longer. He certainly needs it.

The halls outside of the sleeping quarters are bustling with activity, everyone preparing for a possible attack. I find myself strangely calm. It's as if it's a normal day. Though I can sense the tension, I choose to ignore it.

I'm surprised to find the training room empty when I arrive. If the Guild had been threatened like this, the training rooms would've been filled to the brim with assassins vying for one last stab at improvement. They'd barely sleep. I almost feel like *not* training simply because that's what the assassins would do, but that's exactly why I should do it. I have to match them.

No, I have to surpass *them.*

I choose the best mat in the room and get to work.

CHAPTER TWENTY-NINE

Three days later, I'm back in the training room with Jax by my side. The two of us duel each other with a blade in each hand. We duck, dodge, parry, and stab. The wind of our motions buffets us and I can taste the sweat of our efforts. I'm winning, though Jax would say otherwise.

I haven't had much free time since the base was put on lockdown. Everyone is trying to distract me from the fact that Trey is still at the Guild. Jax keeps me occupied with frequent training sessions and Jenson even invites me to a few meetings, but I can't stop thinking about her. Whether or not she's still alive, what they're doing to her in the meantime... I've drawn up a dozen plans to get her back, but none of them are good enough and even if they were, no one is allowed to leave the base. I don't think Jenson will tolerate any more infractions from me.

I'm not the only one on edge. Everyone is waiting for the pin to drop, the creeping lion to attack. We all know it's coming and most wait nervously. Not me and not Jax. We're hard at work, honing our skills. Not to mention giving each other a good walloping.

I force a smile at Jax, which catches him off guard and he loses one of his blades in seconds.

He swears and grabs for a dagger—we're both fully armed as if engaged in actual battle—but I slap him on the arm with the flat of one of my blades and place my other blade against his throat.

"Checkmate," I say, grinning. He sighs and I lower my sword.

"I'll have you know I'm a lot better at fighting than you make me look," he replies.

"So you say."

"It's not my fault you're so…"

"Talented?"

"Distracting."

Blood rushes to my face. "I could say the same about you, love."

He shakes his head. "Oh, but if only we could all have such self-control."

"Again?" I ask, raising my sword.

"Of course, and this time, victory shall be mine."

Ten minutes later, Jax is at the end of my sword once more. "What was that you said again," I ask, "something about victory being yours?"

Jax scowls.

"Oh come on, Quinby, give the man a break. Let him win for once. You're wounding his honour."

I turn around and point my sword at Bast who's standing a few feet away. "*Let* him win?" I ask. "Now where would the fun be in that?"

He grins. "The fun is in knowing you let him win, and knowing he thinks he won on his own."

I smile and lower my sword.

Jax makes his move. He wraps one arm around my ribcage, holding me close to him and the other arm holds his sword against my throat.

I laugh. "Nicely done, boys," I say. "I'll admit; I didn't see that coming."

"You should make sure the enemy's dead before you turn your back on him," Jax whispers in my ear.

I turn my head towards him. "Thank you for the wise words, but you're not the enemy."

We lean towards each other.

As usual, Bast's voice breaks the spell. "Oh please, spare me the love making. It's appalling."

I pull away, but Jax plants a kiss on my head before doing the same.

Bast shakes his head.

"Jealous?" I ask him, searching for information.

"As if," he scoffs. "I can't get the ladies to leave me alone."

"Uh huh," I reply. "How come I never see any?"

"They're all very shy," he says. Jax bursts into laughter and Bast goes red. "It's not a joke, Jax man."

"Well, it's funny," Jax retorts, "and for the record, I don't believe you for a second."

Bast sighs. "Am I that dishonest?"

"It's hard to argue with the evidence," I tell him, "and you *are* the master tall tale teller."

He drags his shoe across the floor. "I guess."

Jax sheaths his sword and walks over to Bast. "Don't take it the wrong way," he says, clapping Bast on the shoulder. "We're just messing with you. You'll find someone. You're too awesome not to."

"Not to mention dangerously handsome," I add with a smile.

"Yeah, yeah, and someday pigs are going to fly too," Bast mutters.

"Don't say that, Bast," I reply, "there's someone out there for you, I know it," and in fact I *do*. That is, if Bast feels the same about Blake.

"The problem is, Quinn," Bast says, "that the person for you doesn't always feel the same and how the hell can you tell for certain? No man wants to assume and make a fool of himself either. So we stay silent and we wait."

I don't think I've ever heard Bast say so much in one go, with such seriousness.

"So you're saying...?"

"Nothing," Bast mutters. "It's not important." This makes me certain that it is, but I don't press further.

"So what are you up to?" I ask, changing the subject. "I never did thank you for standing up to Jenson for me the other day in the council room."

He waves a hand. "Oh it was nothing; the bastard had it coming, if you ask me."

I laugh.

"As for what I'm doing," he goes on, "well, I've come for advice."

"What kind of advice?"

"I was doing my rounds earlier when I came across something strange, more than strange actually. There's a storage room on the first floor that has blood on it."

I raise an eyebrow. "What's so strange about that?"

"It's still wet."

My eyes widen.

"What's more," Bast goes on, "the floor smells and looks as if it's been cleaned recently."

"Bast," I gasp, "why didn't you tell us as soon as you walked in here?"

He shrugs. "You guys were having fun. I didn't want to dampen the mood."

"Dampen the mood... Take us to where you found the blood. Now."

CHAPTER THIRTY

The hall Bast leads us to is quiet, eerily so. I feel as though I'm being watched, which I know is ridiculous, but I can't shake it off.

"This place gives me the creeps," I say.

"I know what you mean," Bast agrees. "Something feels off. That's why I came to get you guys instead of investigating on my own. It seemed like a recipe for disaster, and a slow death, if I went solo."

"You're probably right," Jax says, assuring him of his decision. It's times like these that I see their friendship, their brotherhood. It's not shown in big deeds, but in small ones, though the support is always there.

"Here," Bast says, pointing to a door at our left. "This is it, and as you can see, the floor from this door all the way down from where we came is shinier."

My brain gears start turning.

Why would someone clean the floor from this door back? The hall keeps going. It's like they've made a path or covered one up...

"Someone was dragged here."

"What?" Bast says.

"How do you know?" Jax asks.

"They were injured," I go on, "and left a trail of blood that had to be wiped away. That's why the floor is only cleaned up to this door. The victim must still be inside."

"And whoever did it," Jax finishes for me, "doesn't want that person to be found."

Bast looks at me in awe. "Holy shit, you're good."

I shrug. "I know from experience, except I would've cleaned the entire hall and I wouldn't have been so stupid as to leave blood on the door after all that work."

"Maybe it's a trap," Bast suggests.

"What?"

"All the leftover evidence," he says. "Maybe they *did* want it to be found."

I frown. "I guess that's possible."

"Well," Jax says, "there's only one way to find out." He backs up to the wall, and then rushes forward, slamming the side of his body against the door. The lock snaps. The door swings open, hits the inside wall, and swings back. It stays ajar about an inch.

I look at Jax. "You're lucky that worked."

He rolls his shoulder. "Storage room doors and locks are flimsy, everyone knows that."

I roll my eyes in return. "Come on; let's see if it's a trap or a person."

"Uh, guys...?" Bast says. "It's a person. At least, I think."

What?

I turn around and see Bast with one foot already in the storage room. The door is wide open and I catch a glimpse of what he's seeing.

Assassins below...

I step forward, as if in a trance, and push past Bast for a better look. Then I wish I hadn't. I understand now why Bast said he *thought* it was a person. The woman—and I know it's a woman only from the long hair—has clearly been tortured to within an inch of her life.

Her face is covered in lacerations and burns. Her nose is broken, the blood still on her face, though long dried now. From the way she's slumped against the wall, I can tell one arm is broken and the other one is hanging from a dislocated shoulder. Her neck is painted with small cuts, enough to sting while not puncturing her main arteries. I sense that she likely has several broken ribs and hasn't eaten or had water in days. She has no shoes and her feet are a crimson disaster. She might never walk comfortably again. I can't see her legs, but judging from the amount of blood on her pants, they have similar injuries to the rest of her body.

The worst part is that if it hadn't been for the black uniform and red cape that now lie in tatters, I never would've recognized her.

"Holy Gods above," I breathe. "Trey?"

Behind me, Jax swears, but I'm hardly listening.

Trey moans at the sound of her name and tries to sit up.

I fall to my knees in front of her. "No, no. Lie down," I tell her, "you'll only make it worse." I flash back to a similar scene when it was *her* telling *me* to lie down. That was after she and Kuen had saved Jax and I from drowning in that tank. Our roles weren't supposed to be reversed.

Silent tears fall fast and furious down my cheeks.

"Trey, what happened? How did you get here? Who did this to you?" My voice is frantic and enraged. This isn't happening. She shouldn't have had to endure…

"Quinn," she croaks, through her ravaged throat, likely rubbed raw from screaming.

I can barely hear her, but I bring my head closer. "What? Tell me what I can do. Please…"

"They're inside…the walls."

"What? Who?"

"The enemy," she gasps. Then she slumps back again, unconscious.

I try to piece together what she said. The enemy is inside the walls. The enemy…

I thought I knew fear, thought I'd conquered it long ago, but I've never felt so cold.

"Oh God," I gasp, "the assassins are here."

"What?" Jax gasps. "How?"

"I don't know, but if she's right, we're in serious trouble. We need—" I stop my sentence in my tracks as I hear a distant crack, almost as if…

"Was that a gunshot?" Jax asks.

"I desperately want to say no, but I'd be lying," I reply.

"So this is really happening?" Bast asks. "The assassins are here, in the base?" Somewhere, someone starts screaming and a shiver runs down my spine.

"It would seem so, and with the Warehouse on lockdown, we're all sitting ducks. We have to move. Trey needs to get to the hospital and then we have to find out for sure what's going on—" My words are interrupted again, this time by the screeching of the PA system followed by an eruption of loud gunfire.

Jenson's voice attempts to ring out through the static in the lines. "All agents to their posts. There has been a security breach. I repeat, everyone to arms. We are under attack. I repeat—" His voice cuts off, but we've heard everything we need to hear, at least for the moment. Jax, Bast, and I share a look.

Then Bast says, "I have to find Blake." He starts down the hall and I follow him out of the room.

"You can't go by yourself!" I call after him. "It's not safe!"

He gives me a look. "She's out there all alone. I promised her I wouldn't leave her by herself again. One of us needs to find her. You and Jax have your hands full."

"Okay, you're right, but please be careful."

He grins like a maniac. "Careful is my middle name." Then he races off without a backward glance.

Jax calls my name.

I turn to see him standing in the storage room's doorway, Trey's broken frame cradled in his arms. She looks so fragile.

"I've got her," Jax assures me. "Your job will be to keep the assassins off us until we reach the hospital."

I nod and draw my guns. "It would be my pleasure," I reply.

"Then lead the way."

CHAPTER THIRTY-ONE

The base is rife with chaos. Agents and assassins are engaged in duels everywhere you look. Jax and I sprint through the halls, pushing through the mobs. My guns smoke. Whoever gets too close receives a bullet in the head, no questions asked. I don't have time to stop and duel them properly. Trey is fading away.

The fighting gets thinner the closer we come to the hospital and I thank the heavens for that. At least something is going our way. Then we reach the hospital door and find it locked.

I bang on the door, sending it shaking. "Come on, open up!" I yell. "We have a seriously injured person and—"

The door opens a crack. "Name?" someone asks.

"If I was an assassin," I reply, "you'd already be dead. Let us in."

"Name?" they repeat.

I open my mouth to retort once again, but Jax says, "Quinn Ballinger and Ajax Forrester. We've brought Trey. She's in critical condition."

The door swings open all the way and we step inside. I should let Jax do all the talking in situations like this. We'd get things done a lot quicker, but I don't think it's possible for me to keep my mouth shut.

There are only a few other injured agents in here so far, but there'll be dozens once the battle's over. Some of the nurses are still in shock, shuffling around with dazed expressions on their faces.

"What's happened with you two now?" a familiar voice says. Shirley comes around the corner. "I thought I told you to be careful?"

"It's not us," I reply, "it's Trey."

Shirley takes one look at Trey and her hands fly to cover her mouth. "Holy mother of God," she gasps. "What...?"

"She was tortured, by the assassins, most likely the Charger himself," I tell her, though I have my suspicions that Sephtis handed her over to Anane so he could amuse himself. He knew Anane would want a piece of her and Sephtis wanted to watch the revenge unfold.

"She needs immediate attention," Shirley says. "I need three more nurses stat! Get me an intravenous apparatus too! And a strong drug, I suggest morphine." Shirley continues to call out orders and then directs Jax to a bed where he sets Trey down.

"The best thing you two can do for her now," Shirley says, "is to let us do our work."

"I won't argue with that," I reply. "Besides, there's a bit of an assassin problem we need to deal with."

"Too right," she says. "Good luck."

I nod and Jax and I head for the exit.

We run into Blake out in the hall.

"I was just looking for you guys," she exclaims. "Where's Bast?" Her voice turns from excited to apprehensive as she looks at the hospital door. "He's not...?"

"No," I assure her, "but we thought he was with you."

"I haven't seen him. Do you think he's okay? Why were you guys in the hospital?"

"We found Trey in a storage closet. She's barely hanging on to life."

Her eyes hold a dozen questions.

"It's a long story," I continue, "which we don't have time to explain. As for Bast, I'm sure he's holding his own."

Blake goes into game mode. "Right," she says. "What's the plan?"

"We have to find Jenson," Jax tells her. "Then we'll go after Bast."

She frowns. "Why Jenson?"

"That's who the assassins are after," I reply, "the reason for this attack. Vyrin asked us 'politely' to hand Jenson over and since we refused, he's going to take him by force. We can't let that happen. Jax, do you have any idea where Jenson could be?"

"He's in the control room," Jax replies. "I'm certain of it."

"Then let's go." I draw my swords this time.

Blake raises her axe and Jax loads his rifle. They follow me down the hall.

CHAPTER THIRTY-TWO

Pandemonium. That's the only word I have to explain what's going on as Jax, Blake, and I cut people down like stalks of wheat amid the flashing lights and wailing sirens of the base. All around us people are either fleeing or fighting and it's impossible to tell who is friend and who is foe. Everyone is wearing a grey Resistance uniform—agents and assassins alike—but there's no time to wonder what that means.

I duck and dodge and lunge, all the while trying to move forward. Blake is a blur by my side and Jax's rifle fire is a near-constant sound in my ear, on top of the clash of metal, screams, and the sound of flesh being torn. The cloying smell of blood and gore threatens to choke me, but I bite back on it.

You've endured worse, I tell myself.

I press on, ignoring the pressure in my limbs as the exertion starts to gnaw away at them. My arms and legs smoulder in the beginnings of protest, but remain strong. My right leg doesn't falter as I cut a path toward Jenson.

You want him, Vyrin? Well, you'll have to go through me first.

· · ·

Ten minutes later, the three of us break through the main block of fighting and find ourselves in an empty, silent hall. Well, not exactly empty. Bodies line the tiles, collapsed at odd angles, and blood decorates the walls, floor, and ceiling. Everywhere, weapons lay discarded, never again to be picked up by the person who left them. So much death. It doesn't matter what we do. It always came back to this—a hallway full of corpses, a sinister portrait that will haunt our gallery of memories.

Blake lays a hand on my shoulder. "Hey, don't let it get to you."

"It's just... When will it end? When will the past stay buried along with all the people we've lost?"

"When we end the ones who dig those graves. Come on, Jenson's still in danger, and we're not helping him by dawdling here."

I sigh. "You're right."

Not so distantly, a scream rings out.

Jax straightens up. "That was Jenson."

"Are you sure?"

He doesn't answer, only runs off down the hall.

Blake and I race after him, nimbly dodging the bodies while trying not to think too much about the action.

A few halls later, Jax rounds a corner and skids to a stop.

Blake and I nearly run into him.

"You!" Jax spits out.

I follow his gaze and a part of me is not surprised in the least by what I see. Amongst a slew of bodies, stands Nicholas Ross, holding a gun to the back of Jenson's head.

Jenson is on his knees at Ross' feet and when his eyes meet mine, all I can see is cold, unadulterated fear. Jenson's ego is gone, shattered.

And Ross, Ross is finally showing his true nature.

I should've known.

CHAPTER THIRTY-THREE

"So we meet again, Ross," I say, "and my, what an interesting turn of events."

He smiles at me, but there is no kindness in his dark eyes. "Call me Ruse," he replies. "I'm sure you've heard of me, Silent Night."

My stomach drops.

No. It can't be.

"You're lying. Ruse is just..."

"A legend?" He laughs. "Dear girl, I thought you of all people would know better than that. Ruse *became* a legend, because that's what Sephtis wanted all of you to believe. He's always pulling the strings."

"And you're totally okay with being a puppet?" I counter. "Wait... How do you know the Charger's name?"

"Aside from the fact that Jenson told me a few days ago?"

"Yes, aside from that," I reply, waving a hand. "You say it as though you're comfortable with it."

He shrugs. "Well, brothers should be comfortable saying each other's names, don't you think?"

If my jaw wasn't attached, it would've hit the floor. "What?"

He grins maniacally. "Surprise! I bet you thought the revelations were over. Who would've thought? Nicolas Ross, the third Aeron brother? But it is nothing but the truth. Who else would Sephtis charge with such a task? I am paramount to his success."

"It was you," I say. "You were the one who told Anane where my room was."

He smiles. "Good, you're starting to catch on."

"But why? Why bother?" I demand to know.

He shrugs. "Why not? It was fun, toying with you, trying to break you. This entire organization has been nothing but a game for years, and you, dear Jenson, were but a willing pawn."

Ross—I refuse to call him anything else—looks down at Jenson, patting him on the head. Jenson tries to jerk away, but winces as if the action brings him pain. Ross strokes the side of Jenson's face and I fight the urge to vomit.

"Shhh... It'll all be over soon," Ross croons.

"Don't touch me, you traitorous wretch!" Jenson spits. Again he attempts to move away. Again he clenches his eyes tight in agony.

Ross clicks his tongue. "Touchy."

"Let him go," I say.

"Or what?" Ross counters. "Are you going to continue your bloody tirade and kill another uncle?"

My blood turns to ice. "What did you say?"

He smiles. "You heard me; you just don't want to believe it."

How would he know about Lincoln? How would he know he was actually Jean Ballinger, my uncle?

"Stop with the games!" I snap. "Tell us why you're really here."

"I'm here to tear the Resistance apart from the inside out," he spits, "to kill Jenson, and to eradicate any hope of ever beating the Guild. You will all lose. Don't you see? You never had a chance. Avery was a lie. I was a lie. A third of the agents here are actually mine. Whatever good you thought you accomplished, well, it was all a *ruse*." He laughs at his own joke, but I'm done listening to him.

I pull my own gun out of its holster. "Step away from Jenson."

He shakes his head. "Put that away or he'll be dead before you can pull the trigger."

I obey, seething with rage the entire time. I don't want to follow this madman's orders and I'm certainly not happy to be saving Jenson's sorry ass, again.

He better be worth this.

"He misses you, you know," Ross says softly.

"Who?"

"Your father."

"He's not my father," I scoff, "and if you think playing at that is going to bring me over to your side... You're more stupid than I thought."

"He wants you to come home."

"*This* is my home," I spit, "and I don't give a damn what he wants."

"Good to know that Silent Night still has her fire."

"That is not my name!"

"Leave her alone!" Jax growls.

"And what will you do, Forrester, that she can't? You're pathetic, the both of you. All this talk of love…" He turns back to me. "Yet, Sephtis is willing to forget all that, if you return."

"I'm not going back to his enslavement," I snap, "so you can save your breath."

He shrugs. "It was worth a try. Well, chatting was fun, but I have a job to do. Jenson? Shall we?" He slings one arm around Jenson's throat and presses the barrel of his gun harder into Jenson's skull. His finger tightens on the trigger.

I take an involuntary step forward. "No!"

A gunshot rings out, cold and clear, but it is not Jenson who slumps to the floor, dead.

Ross lurches to the side, his eyes rolling back in his head. He hits the ground with a sickening thump and doesn't stir. Jenson falls forward onto his face without Ross to hold him up.

Behind them stands Natalie, gun still raised, her entire body quivering.

I look at Jax and Blake. Both of them are in shock and I don't blame them. I certainly never would've seen this coming.

I take a step toward her. "Natalie?" I ask softly.

"You... You don't understand," she gasps. "I h-had to. You were right, Assassin, I *do* care. And he..." She starts to cry. "He killed them all!" Her legs go out then and she collapses to the ground, heaving with sobs, gun still clutched in her hand.

I take a few more steps. "Hey, it's going to be all right," I tell her. "No one blames you. He—"

"Thank God!" a voice shouts behind me.

I turn to see Bast running our way, and an assassin creeping up behind him, club raised.

The world starts to move in slow motion.

"There you guys are," Bast gasps out, stopping to catch his breath. "I thought I'd never—"

"*Bast!*" Blake yells. "Look out!"

Blake and Bast's eyes meet for a fraction of a second.

My heart leaps into my throat as Bast dodges, but not enough.

The club smashes into his shoulder and he goes flying, hitting the wall with a booming sound that echoes in the small space. He collapses to the floor, unmoving.

Blake screams his name and throws her axe at the assassin. It lands square in his face, going in a good two inches. Blood sprays and the assassin drops like a stone.

Time speeds up again as Blake runs over to Bast, falling to her knees beside his lifeless form. Not only can I hear her sobs, but I can feel them.

Behind me, Natalie falls silent.

I can't move; I can't think. All I can do is listen as Blake starts to speak.

"No," she gasps through the tears. "No, Bast, you can't go. There are so many things...I never got to say. I shouldn't have held them back, but I was afraid, so horribly afraid. I always have been. You were the one who taught me courage. You've never been afraid of anything. Bast the fearless... I always wished I could be like that. Maybe that's why I fell for you, but I was too afraid to let it show and now it's too late… I'll never know what we could've had, if you liked me enough to have anything. God, I'm such an idiot for not saying anything."

She stops and looks to the ceiling.

"Is this my punishment?" she screams, voice raw. "I love you, Bast. God, I love you so much and I'm sorry… I'm so sorry for staying silent... I'm sorry…"

Her voice cuts off as she slumps against his body, sobbing.

I sink to the floor, my legs unable to support me in the face of such tragedy.

No. No, it's not fair! Not after everything…

Silent, unbidden tears blur my vision.

Why is there no mercy in this Godforsaken world?

And then…

Then Bast coughs.

My lungs take in a shattered breath.

Blake sits up.

Oh my God.

Bast's eyes flutter open and he grins weakly at Blake. "Aw, Blakey," he rasps. "I'm touched; never knew you cared. Oh, and for the record, the feeling's mutual."

I can almost hear Blake's heart stuttering as it tries to keep up with the influx of emotions running through her. For a moment, she just stares at him.

I hear Jax crying as his best friend returns to the land of the living, but I can't tear my eyes away from the scene in front of me to comfort him.

Finally, Blake finds her voice. "You..." she gasps. "You *idiot*." Then she brings her tear-streaked face to his and kisses him.

I've never smiled so wide in all my life.

Bast wraps one hand around the back of her neck and kisses her back with the enthusiasm of a love-starved man. It's like they've never seen each other before. I feel like I'm intruding, like I shouldn't be witnessing this moment, but I don't think they care, let alone remember that the rest of us are here.

Bast pulls her closer and sits up so that Blake is practically in his lap. I'm going to tease him about that later, but right now I'll give them their moment, God knows they've earned it.

Apparently, Jax doesn't have the same idea because a few seconds later he coughs and says, "Oh honestly, get a room if you're going to go at it like that."

Bast pulls away with a sigh and glares at Jax. "Way to ruin the mood," he mutters.

"You're one to talk, bud," Jax retorts. "After the amount of times you've interrupted me, you had it coming."

Bast rolls his eyes, but he smiles.

Blake peels herself away from him long enough to stand and help him to his feet as well.

He reaches out and wipes beneath her eyes with his thumb. "There," he says, "no more tears."

She wraps an arm around his good side. "I'll feel much better when we get you looked at."

"How's the shoulder?" I ask him.

"Never been better."

"Oh, I'm sure…" I reply, knowing full well he's putting on a brave face for Blake. His shoulder must be on fire and he would probably collapse without Blake's support. His condition reminds me of the other two.

I look behind me. Jenson is in shock; he literally dodged a bullet. A few feet back from him, Natalie lies unconscious.

"We have to get everyone to the hospital," I say, "without any more near-death experiences."

"Agreed," Jax replies. "I'll get Natalie." He turns to me. "You good with Jenson?"

I nod.

"And Blake has Bast, so that's everyone covered," he finishes.

"I can walk just fine on my own," Bast protests.

Blake elbows him in the ribs lightly and says, "You try it, and I'll make sure you're laid up in the hospital for a week."

"Okay, okay," Bast says, "please don't hurt me." He gives Jax a look. "So, this is what it's like?"

"Oh, it gets better," Jax assures him, "and by better, I mean worse."

"You watch it there, Ajax," I retort.

"See?"

"Come on, don't we have a hospital to get to?" Blake urges.

Jax walks over to Natalie and pries the gun out of her hand before lifting her into his arms. A spark of jealousy flares inside me, but I stamp it out. Natalie doesn't even stir.

I help Jenson to his feet and pull his one arm over my left shoulder.

"What about Ross?" Jenson mumbles.

"We leave him," I reply.

"Ross?" Bast asks.

"We'll explain later," I reply. "Right now, getting to the hospital is more important. You guys lead the way."

Blake nods and our little procession begins its trek.

CHAPTER THIRTY-FOUR

The hospital is a complete mess compared to how Jax and I left it earlier. There are people everywhere—injured, healthy, nurses... Almost all the beds are full. There are agents with gunshot wounds, missing legs, and gashes that reach bone. The place reeks of iron and misery and I gag as I drag Jenson through the doors, followed by Bast, Blake, and Jax with Natalie.

The six of us aren't noticed at first in the chaos and then I recognize one of the nurses who rush by. I reach out and grab her arm. "Lana?"

She turns and her eyes light up in surprise and worry as she sees me. "Ms. Ballinger, what happened?"

"Bast, Natalie, and Jenson need attending."

Her eyes widen at Jenson's name and that's when she finally notices the man I'm supporting. "Right this way," she says and she heads off.

Lana leads us to a more secluded section of the hospital, with actual rooms, and assures us she will send a troop of nurses right away. Blake, Jax, and I deposit our charges on the beds, each in their own rooms, and close the doors.

Blake kisses Bast once on the forehead before leaving. He smiles, but is mostly asleep.

"We're going back out there, aren't we?" Blake asks me.

"We have to," I tell her. "Those still able to stand on their own have to fight until there are no assassins left."

"Let's not waste any time then," Jax says.

We march back through the hospital, trying to ignore the cries of grief and pain tugging at our heartstrings. The old me would've laughed and relished at their sufferings, but now I just wish to disappear. I'm not sure which is worse: welcoming pain or ignoring it.

CHAPTER THIRTY-FIVE

Blake, Jax, and I are doing well despite our fatigue until the lights go out. One minute I'm going sword to sword with an assassin—a sour-faced lady with dreadlocks—and the next, the hallway is plunged into darkness. The gunshots around us cease as everyone takes a moment to recover. The ever-present sirens continue their steady rhythm and my heartbeat rises, echoing their din.

Then the emergency lights kick in, bathing everything in a red glow, and I see the woman lunging at me. Her sword is aimed right for my exposed chest.

I sidestep at the last second and she rushes past me, stumbling from the lack of resistance. I turn and plunge my sword into her back.

She stills and collapses to the floor when I remove my sword.

I flick the blade to the side, dislodging some of the blood, and scan the area for my next opponent. Blake and

Jax are still engaged in combat and a group of loyal agents has set up a barricade on one end of the hall where they're using bows and rifles to snipe enemy agents.

I check the other end of the hall, to make sure no one is sneaking up on us, relishing the short moment to catch my breath. My heart is working overtime. Blood and sweat stick to my skin and my leg aches. Nothing major, just a dull weariness in my bones.

My eyes spot new movement at the intersection behind us and I go to meet it, jumping over bodies and dodging puddles of blood on my way. I slip into a shadowed doorway at the end, sheathing my sword in favour of a pistol.

I know the person is there, but I can't hear their feet. Either they've stopped moving or they're an assassin.

I jump out of my hiding spot, raising my gun in front of me, and am about to shoot when I recognize the face under the pulsing red lights.

I lower my gun. "Kuen? What are you—"

His eyes light up in fear and he raises an axe in his hands. "Duck!"

I don't think. I just trust him and drop to the ground, smearing new blood on my clothes and skin.

I hear the crunch of bone as his axe connects with someone behind me, then the thud as that someone hits the floor. They died instantly, before they could scream.

I jump back to my feet and turn in a slow circle with my gun, heart racing.

Kuen's axe is two inches deep into a fallen assassin's skull and my stomach turns at the sight.

I look back at him. "Weren't you in the dungeon?"

He shrugs. "Broke out." He walks over and pries the axe out of the man's head, using his body for leverage. I notice that his good hand is in a full arm cast now, but that it doesn't seem to impede him much.

I remember the confrontation in the council room, our argument, Jax and his fight. My expression darkens. "Why did you save me?"

"A simple thank you would suffice."

I scowl.

He hefts the axe onto his shoulder. "Look, Quinn, I realized we can't keep going on like this, constantly at war with one another. If we want to beat our father, we have to work together. Let's leave it at that. Now are we going to kill these bastards or what?"

I sigh. He's right. I don't want my last words to him to be ones of anger, like they might be with Trey.

I give him a grin. "You're welcome to tag along, if you can keep up."

His eyes flash with excitement at the challenge and we race each other back into the battle.

Blake and Jax don't bat an eye at his presence and we carve a thick swath through the remaining assassins, weeding them out one by one.

• • •

The battle is long and arduous, but finally, mercifully, comes to a close. The four of us are covered in blood, some of it our own. The body-strewn halls of the base echo with the enormity of what has happened.

CHAPTER THIRTY-SIX

We don't talk on our way back to the hospital. Kuen parts ways with us before we reach it, saying something about doing one last check for survivors.

The three of us are heavy with the reality of what has happened. Ross was a double agent and the people we killed today had been our fellow agents just yesterday or at least, we thought they had. Like Ross, they were assassins all along, putting on quite the show as they waited for the right time to strike, as they waited for Sephtis, the master puppeteer, to give them the go-ahead.

I shake my head in disgust. What else has been a lie? Is anything real in this cruel war of masquerades? At least Jenson is still alive and Ross is dead. Strangely, we have Natalie to thank for that. I may have underestimated her and been a little too harsh in my decision to break her spirit, but time will tell.

We come upon Bast's room first. The door is ajar and a pair of nurses bustles around him. Blake hesitates and looks at us.

Jax smiles. "You go," he says, "Quinn and I are going to check on Jenson."

She hangs her head. "I don't know…"

I place a hand on her shoulder. "You'll be fine. Lead with your heart and everything else will follow."

"Right."

"If you're worried it was all a dream," Jax says, "the rest of us saw it too, a bit more than we wanted to see, if I'm being honest."

Blake finally smiles. "Shut up," she replies, but her smile takes away any seriousness in her voice.

"Now get in there before Bast drives himself crazy wondering if you're still alive," I tell her.

"Okay, okay," she replies.

I give her a little push and she finally steps into the room. The nurses pause as she enters and Bast looks up. The smile he gives her looks much better on him than the sly grin he always hides behind.

"Hello, beautiful," he says.

"You're not looking too shabby yourself," she replies.

Jax and I share a look. Then we leave the two "lovebirds" be, not that they ever gave us the same peace and quiet.

The next room over is Jenson's. He's sitting on the edge of the bed when we enter, engaged in a heated argument with the nurses attending him.

"Don't touch me," he snaps. "I told you I'm fine. I don't need..." He trails off as he notices Jax and me in the doorway.

The nurses sense the shift and stop hovering.

Jenson looks at them. "Wait in the hall. You too, Mr. Forrester."

Jax gives me a look and I nod. Jenson doesn't want to hurt me this time.

The nurses follow Jax out and he closes the door behind them.

Jenson regards me with a neutral expression. "Well, Assassin," he says, "this is the second time you've tried to save me." There's no anger or disgust in his voice, not even when he says the word assassin. In fact, I sense a tone of apology.

"Don't expect it to happen again," I reply, but my voice too is devoid of tension.

What I'm really telling him is that I'm going to try to forgive him. We've both made mistakes and treated each other awfully, our egos constantly clashing. That changed today. For the first time, we stand on the same level.

"I may have underestimated you," he says. "I may have been too harsh. I was...wary of your recklessness, your arrogance. You reminded me of myself and I didn't like the reflection I saw. That's why I condemned you." He wrings his hands. "You came in here, barely more than a child, and had a better idea to end the Guild than I've come up with in years, than this organization has ever come up with. It seemed too easy. I didn't want to trust you, to hope things were going to change for the better."

I smile sadly. "I didn't want to trust you either."

He shrugs. "You had no reason to. We held your life in our hands; you *let* us do that and still, I could not believe your intentions were true. Then later, when you attacked Natalie…"

I wince.

"I may seem like a stuffy, tired old man to you," he says, "but I had a family once. I used to smile, but then my wife and daughter disappeared, taken right from our house in the middle of the day. No witnesses, no explanation."

Oh.

He hunches over, as if wanting to curl in on himself. "They were returned two days later. I found them discarded on the front steps, tortured beyond recognition and I… I haven't been the same since." He looks up at me, tears glistening in his eyes. "She would be your age now."

"Who?"

"My daughter."

And it all makes sense. He sees his daughter every time he looks at me. He sees what should've been and he sees the people who took that away. I represent the Guild in his eyes and every time he looks at me, he sees what he lost because of them.

"Jenson, I'm—"

He holds up a hand. "I wasn't finished. I vowed to never let a crime like that go unpunished, that I would protect each child of the Resistance with my life. So, when you attacked Natalie… I had no choice. You broke a sacred rule, regardless of what she did to provoke it. I imagined what would've happened if you'd gone too far, what her father would have had to live with…but I'm glad I didn't go through with your sentence. I was wrong about you…Quinn. You are dedicated and loyal and the Resistance needs you. It needs people like you."

I look at him in shock. "Did you hit your head?"

He laughs. "Very funny. No, I didn't. I simply opened my eyes. Ross…opened my eyes. There are enemies all around us and I shouldn't be wasting time condemning my allies."

I give him a soft smile. "I am sorry…about your family. We have all lost loved ones to this war and it needs to stop. Do you know who killed them?"

"Yes," he says. "The list you gave us upon your arrival brought closure in that regard. It was an assassin named Hai."

My heart clenches.

Those poor women…

"Then your vengeance has been served," I tell him.

He narrows his eyes, trying to contain his surprise. "How do you know?"

I smile. "I put him out of his misery during the Guild attack. It was not as slow and painful as you probably would've liked, but he is gone and Haven is better for it."

He smiles at me. "Thank you."

I wave a hand. "Oh, don't thank me yet, Jenson. We still have a lot of work to do."

Jenson shakes his head. "I can't believe Nicholas was an assassin all this time. I never thought…"

"None of us did," I tell him. "I was fooled as easily as you were, but that was always his specialty. He's an expert actor. He spoke more ill of the Guild on a daily basis than you did, but he also had Avery to promote and support him all these years. My relatives have been playing a skilled and careful game, but the game is up. Ross is dead, Avery's cover has been blown, and Sephtis didn't get what he wanted. You're alive and unharmed and if I have anything to say about it, you'll remain that way."

He smiles. "What of the traitors?"

"Dead. Kuen is rounding up the last of them as we speak."

He raises an eyebrow. "You let him out of the dungeons?"

I shrug. "He broke out. Then he saved my life and, well, the rest is history. He was a force to be reckoned with in battle, even with one broken hand."

Jenson nods. "I suppose I underestimated him as well." He takes a breath. "How many of ours left standing?"

"I'm not sure, but they'll have to be enough."

"Do you have a plan?"

"I'm working up to one."

"As long as it involves retaliation and a certain Master Assassin dead," Jenson says, "consider it approved."

I grin. "That's the idea."

He nods. "Then lead on, Quinn, and tell anyone who questions you to come straight to me. You're a full-fledged Resistance agent now. Use that position wisely."

I smile, butterflies dancing in my stomach at the sudden promotion. "Thank you."

He grins. "Don't thank me yet."

CHAPTER THIRTY-SEVEN

I rejoin Jax in the hall and the nurses bustle back in to check on Jenson.

"So, how'd it go?" Jax asks.

"Well," I reply. "We had the most civilized conversation we've ever had. We...forgave each other for past missteps and we're finally focused on moving forward. He says I'm a proper Resistance agent now and he gave me authority, I think?"

Jax frowns. "Did he hit his head?"

I laugh. "That's what I said."

His frown turns into a smile. "That's great to hear, Quinn. I told you he would come around someday."

"Too bad it took a betrayal for it to happen though."

"Yeah," he says. "Natalie next?"

I nod.

We approach Natalie's room with caution. I'm no longer sure what to expect when it comes to her, but I'm surprised when Blake joins us. She doesn't say a word and I wonder at her motives.

There are three nurses attending Natalie when we walk in and they seem to be trying to calm her. One nurse grabs a syringe.

"No," I say, lunging forward. My voice is serious, though not raised.

The nurse turns to face me. "Why don't you let me do my job, *Assassin*?"

I raise an eyebrow at her tone, but bite back on a menacing retort. "My name is Quinn, actually," I reply. "My friends and I would like to speak to the patient."

The woman scowls. "Can't it wait? She's not in any shape to…"

I glance past her to Natalie and can see she is right. Natalie is awake now, but comatose. She stares at nothing as her body quakes and silent tears stream down her face.

"Ready or not," I tell the nurse, "we have to speak to her now. It'll be better to get it over with, so she can be left to forget instead of prodded for answers after she's partially recovered."

The nurse sighs. "Fine, but make it quick." She and the others leave the room and close the door.

Jax, Blake, and I regard Natalie's broken expression.

I'm the first to speak. "Natalie?" I try my best to sound approachable, but comforting people has never been one of my strong suits. "Natalie, can you hear us?"

She doesn't reply, but she flinches at the sound of her name.

Well, that's something *at least.*

I open my mouth to try again when Blake touches my arm. "Let me try," she says.

My eyes narrow. Blake can't stand Natalie. "Why?"

"Just... trust me."

"Okay." I doubt Natalie could get any worse than she is, but I'll probably end up eating my own words.

Blake takes a step forward. "Natalie? It's Blake. I know you're upset and scared, but we're not going to hurt you. Just please, talk to us."

We wait for a few minutes that feel like forever while I wonder what horrors are playing in her head. She stares at us without seeing, her eyes unfocused and glassy with tears. Then she blinks and her eyes focus on Blake. She takes a deep breath, stretching out her clenched fingers, and says, "I'm sorry."

The words are barely above a whisper and I'm not sure I heard her right. Blake's expression is unreadable as Natalie goes on.

"I'm sorry, Blake. I was young and stupid; I'm sure you can agree we both were."

My eyes widen. She's talking about when Blake's ex died. When Blake killed him in a fit of rage and Natalie witnessed it all. His murder was attributed to a rogue assassin. Only Blake, Natalie, and I know the truth.

"You made a mistake," Natalie continues, "and I *had* to drag you through the dirt for it, when I knew full well all the lies *I* was living. Your secret was always safe with me; father taught me how to hide things." Her voice is tinged with regret and hatred. "I want you to know, that while I'm ready to spill his secrets, yours will forever be safe. I'm not going to use it against you anymore. I'm tired of being the…"

"Spoiled brat with a massive attitude problem?" Blake offers.

I raise my eyebrows, expecting retaliation, but Natalie merely smiles ruefully.

"Yeah, that," she agrees, wiping her eyes with her sleeve. "The 'Princess' is denouncing her throne. I'm done with that side of me."

"I'll make sure her highness stays good and buried," I assure Natalie with a hint of my wicked smile.

She turns her attention to me. "Assassin," she says with a nod.

"Roseanne," I reply. "That was quite the deed you did back there." I can still hear the echo of the gunshot and see Ross's body crumpling to the ground where he stood; I'm sure she can too.

She looks at her feet. "I did what I had to."

I shrug. "No one blames you, but we do want to know why, if you're up to telling us."

There's still ice between us, neither one of us forgetting the words we've exchanged, not to mention the fact that I attacked her in a fit of rage.

"He was a difficult man to call father," she says.

I realize the two of us are quite similar, though she grew up knowing her father to be a tyrant and I... I didn't think I had a father.

"He always expected perfection," she goes on, "and I always did my best to please, to obey. He was an assassin through and through, ruthless, and there were often days where he had trouble hiding his true nature. Those days were the worst. He had a temper unlike any I've ever seen, but he never once laid a finger on me. I never understood why.

"I felt useless to him, like I didn't belong. I was never taught how to fight and I never understood that either. He clearly didn't want an assassin for a daughter, though he made sure Ash, Jeremy, and Luke followed in his deadly footsteps."

She pauses then, taking a deep, agonized breath, and not because of any physical injury. She looks at me, all her pain reflected in her eyes, which are starting to fill with tears again.

"He killed them—his own sons, every last one of them—when we invaded the Guild, and when he came back... He told me every detail of their gruesome demise. He called them weak, disappointments. He said they ruined the Aeron family name... That was the day I first considered killing him, but I wanted to slit his throat or better yet, repeat the horrible things he did to my brothers while they begged for his mercy. That was the day I realized my father was a monster and the day I wondered if maybe I was too."

She looks at me with dead eyes and for a minute, I'm lost for words.

Finally, I say, "We're all monsters."

I'm not going to sugar-coat it for her. The world is a cruel place with even crueller people and we all have a part to play in the hierarchy of evil. If the Guild taught me anything useful, it's that.

"But," I go on, "we can choose whether or not we let the monster control us. You showed us who you truly are today. Yes, you killed a man, and yes, that man was your father, but if I can tell you anything with any certainty, it's that blood means nothing. He was no more your father than Sephtis is mine. They don't own us, Natalie. We are free to make our own choices, free to rid the world of their monstrosities.

"You didn't kill your father today, that man has been dead a long time. No, you killed a power-hungry assassin poised to end us all. You saved Jenson's life and possibly the entire Resistance. You did well, so don't beat yourself up over what you didn't accomplish or run yourself ragged wondering if you could've done it differently. It won't do you any good. Trust me, I know. Don't let the dead tear you apart, leave them where they lie."

She does her best to look strong as she says, "I'll do my best."

"It won't get better overnight, Natalie, but it will get better."

She smiles. "Thank you."

I smile back. "Thank *you*."

I shake my head in disbelief as I leave the room. That was the nicest conversation the two of us have ever had.

Jax and Blake follow me into the hall. The nurses push past us, the one with the syringe giving me a nasty glare. I resist the urge to return the favour.

"That was quite the speech you gave, Quinn," Blake says.

"I've been known to say the right things sometimes," I reply. "That was quite the apology she gave you. What do you make of it?"

"I believe her," she replies, "but that doesn't mean I trust or forgive her, yet."

I nod. "That's to be expected."

"I'm confused," Jax says, the first words he's spoken in a few minutes. "Why did she apologize? What mistake did you make, Blake?"

She hangs her head. "It's a long story, one I'm not sure I'm ready to tell yet."

It's evident from his gaze that he wants to protest, but he says nothing more. Instead, he looks at me. "What now?"

"I have to see Trey. You guys don't have to come, but..."

Blake and Jax share a look. "We're coming."

"All right."

CHAPTER THIRTY-EIGHT

We reach Trey's hospital room without a fuss, but there's not much to see and I regret coming. Only one nurse hovers around Trey's still-unconscious form. There aren't enough to go around, given the situation, and there's probably not much they can do for Trey anyway.

From a distance, I can make out countless tubes running in and around her body. A monitor against the far wall shows the struggle of her heart. My own heart jumps in my chest at the sight of Trey so broken. She was always so strong, full of life and now... Now she'll never be the same.

If she lives, a dark and unwelcome voice adds.

I tell it to shut up; I can't afford to think like that.

"Oh, Quinn," Blake breathes when she sees Trey, "I'm so sorry."

"Yeah, well, sorry won't change a thing," I mutter. I curse my sudden anger, but it's the only way to cope with my emotions. The other option is to succumb to tears, but I've done enough crying. I'm tired of it.

Blake tries to place a hand on my shoulder, but I shake it off. "Don't. Just...don't."

"Ms. Ballinger," a voice calls and Shirley comes up behind us. This time, her presence doesn't comfort me.

"What do you want?" I ask, struggling to keep the edge out of my voice. She doesn't notice.

"Good to see you're alive and well," she says. "I heard you were paramount to our victory today. How is your leg holding up?"

"It's fine," which is the truth.

"Good," she replies. "Listen, I have news, regarding Trey here." Her voice loses some of its joy. Whatever she's going to tell me, I know I'm not going to like it.

Just get it over with.

"She's not doing so well," Shirley tells me and though I try to ignore the grief in her tone, I can't. "The burns and lacerations are severe, and she's lost a significant amount of blood. Her left arm is broken and the right shoulder has been left dislocated, probably for days. We put it back in place, but there's no guarantee it'll stay where it should. Ideally, a dislocated shoulder should be put back within hours, not days."

I'm having trouble breathing. "Anything else?"

"Four of her ribs have been broken, one puncturing her lung, which we started treating immediately."

Breathe.

"Her feet have been cut up beyond repair, and her legs..." Shirley eyes me warily.

"Just tell me," I snap. "How can it possibly make things any worse?"

"Both legs have been broken, in multiple places. She won't likely walk again."

I can't.

I can't breathe.

"Oh, is that all?" I ask.

Shirley eyes me warily, but the sorrow in her eyes is genuine as she says, "I'm sorry."

"Hell of a lot of good being sorry will do. Will she live?"

"What?"

"Will. She. Live."

"I don't know," Shirley answers, and I can see in her eyes that it's the truth.

I have to go. I have to get out of here because my monster is clawing away at her chains and I'm dangerously close to unleashing her.

CHAPTER THIRTY-NINE

I turn and run. I hear Blake calling out to me and Jax telling her to let me go.

No one should be within fifteen feet of me right now. I don't know what I'll do, but it won't be pretty.

I run faster, the people around me blurring to nothing as my tears finally start to fall. I push them back again.

No.

I will not give in. I will not be weak.

I wipe the tears away as I leave the hospital behind, as I leave the rational world behind.

I reach for my knife. I need cold steel in my hands, to comfort me, to focus my anger to a lethal point. I need... and it's at that moment I realize I don't *know* what I need—only what I want.

I want to rip throats out and tear innocent men to shreds. I want death, horror, blood. I want a massacre, to lose myself to bloodlust so I don't have to think. I want to free myself from this nightmare, even if I'm only caging myself in a different prison, one ruled by the monster, but I can't let that happen…

I can't have what I want. Because to have what I want would mean bringing her back, and ruining everything I've accomplished over the last few months. It would be another relapse, one I'm not sure I could recover from. If I let Silent Night out to play, she'll lock Quinn away for good. She'll destroy me.

Yet, some part of me wishes to be destroyed.

As the battle between good and evil rages in my head, my body is still running. I'm always running, from my past, away from my future, running from who I am, because I don't know who I'm supposed to be. And now… Now Trey is dying and the last thing I said to her was a threat. The last thing we did was argue.

I skid to a stop, spinning on my heel and flinging my knife into the wall. I reach for another and another.

The pain doesn't stop, the unrelenting anger doesn't quiet. The monster claws and claws, and…

Someone comes around the corner.

Stay away. Turn around. I'm not safe.

"Quinn?"

I hurl the next dagger at the person's head.

They dodge.

I growl in frustration and unsheathe my sword.

"Whoa…"

I'm not seeing straight, let alone thinking straight, and I lunge for the unlucky bypasser. Yet, they catch me against them, deflecting the blow with a blade of their own. I struggle against them, but in seconds they've wrenched the sword out of my hand.

"Quinn."

Strong arms have hold of me now, pressing my arms into my sides so I can't reach for more weapons. I kick and scream against them.

"Quinn, stop…"

I scream.

"Let it go, just let it go."

Without warning, the mask of anger slips and falls. My screams morph into sobs and soon I'm crying into the chest of the man I tried to kill. Everything comes crashing down and slowly, I let it go.

When I finally draw away, I see who my saviour is. Kuen stares at me with an anxious expression.

"I'm sorry I tried to kill you," I say.

He smiles ruefully. "Well, we're even now I guess."

"I suppose so. Did you find any stragglers?"

"A few, but they didn't make it far." He pauses and then says, "Will you quit stalling and tell me what happened?"

I bite the corner of my lip. "It's Trey,"

His eyes turn twice as worried, but his tone is excited as he says, "What? She's here?"

"In the hospital wing," I reply. "She's…" My tears start to fall again and I let them. "Oh God, Kuen, they don't think she's going to make it." My voice breaks, but my pain is nothing compared to the agony that unfolds in the depths of Kuen's blue eyes.

"No..." he whispers.

"And if she *does* survive," I go on, "the nurses say she'll never walk again. They... They broke her, in so many places. It's like looking at a stranger and I blame myself..."

"Who broke her?" he interrupts me.

"I don't..."

"Who was it, Quinn?" His tone is dangerous.

"I can't be sure," I relent, "but my instincts tell me Sephtis gave Anane full reign."

Kuen whirls and punches the wall with his bad hand. Drywall dust flies, along with chunks of his cast. Blood drips from his fingers again and I wonder if that hand is ever going to heal.

He doesn't blink at it. His internal agony far outweighs whatever pain the blow dealt him. In fact, knowing Kuen, he's probably using the new pain as a distraction.

"If I ever see that demon again, I'm going to kill him."

"If *I* ever see him again, I'll let you. Now go," I urge him, "Trey needs you."

"What are you going to do?"

I grin malevolently. "I'm going to write our father a message."

Kuen returns my smile. "Tell the bastard I said hi and that I hope his last few weeks of living are worth it."

"Oh, I will."

Kuen nods once and then heads off down the hall, all but running to Trey's bedside, bloodied axe bouncing against his hip. I hope she's still alive when he gets there. If she dies...my wrath will know no bounds, and neither will Kuen's monster. She has to be okay, for all our sakes. She *has* to.

CHAPTER FORTY

I shuffle to my room, mulling over my ideas in my head. It's paramount Sephtis doesn't find out Jenson is still alive. He has to believe the Resistance is without leadership, that we are broken and beaten down. That is our only advantage. As far as Sephtis is going to know, both Jenson and Ross are dead and I... I am now leading the Resistance.

It's the only way.

I'm not sure how long we'll be able to keep up the charade, but it will be crucial to our success. Sephtis loves his games and his pawns.

Well, guess what, father? *We're playing my game now.*

I enter my room and it takes all of five seconds for all my plans, not to mention my calm bravado, to fly out the window. At first glance, the room doesn't look any different, but the immediate change is in how it feels—rifled through by an expert hand, tainted. The air tastes of poison, but I know it is only a trick of my mind, triggered by my unease as my eyes settle on the bed.

My bed. My sanctuary. My safe haven.

All sense of protection is gone as I study the sword embedded in the pillow, pinning a note to the white surface. A few stray feathers brush across the floor as I stand frozen in the doorway. I fight the flashbacks with every ounce of will I can muster, but I still catch a brief glimpse of my mother's face and deep crimson blood on a once-pristine carpet before I wrest control of my mind once more.

He wanted this, wanted me broken, and he knows exactly how to do that. I shudder. He knows me too well.

At first glance, it could've been anyone who entered my room and triggered visions of my mother's horrific death, but I recognize the sword in the pillow. I left that sword behind during the attack on the Guild. There is only one person who could have it.

Sephtis Aeron is a clever man and not too long ago he was in the base, in my room, and he slipped through my fingers once again. I don't know whether I should scream or cry, or both, but I shove my emotions down inside as I march over to the bed, rip the note out from under the sword, and begin reading.

My dearest Silent Night,

I hope by now you have accepted Ruse's offer, but I am writing this in case you do not, though I don't believe you to be that stupid.

But I digress. Have you ever been to the opera? I hear it's lovely this time of year. That's where I shall be waiting, if you wish to see me. There is so much we need to discuss. You must come alone, I'm sure you understand. You keep lovely company, but they don't agree with my nature, so to speak. The boy should be killed for drinking on the job. I can only guarantee their safety if you leave them behind.

Nothing would please me more than to see your precious face again. Please consider my offer, but decide fast. I shall only wait until midnight.

I left a present for you in the closet on the first level. I hope it pleases you.

Hope to see you soon, daughter,
Your father,
Black Death

P. S. Tell Kuen I said hi, that is, if you ever let him out of the dungeons.

My blood is glacial. So many thoughts are racing through my mind and I don't know what to focus on. He knows Bast was drinking that night. He left Bast alive on purpose and I was foolish enough to think Bast had saved himself.

No.

Sephtis wants my friends alive so I can watch them all die one by one when he wins.

If he wins, I correct myself.

The most unsettling part of the letter was the postscript and the mention of his gift. He was the one that abandoned Trey in that supply closet and he knew Kuen was in the dungeons. How long has he been lurking around, snooping? It will be impossible to deduce the limits of his knowledge. So much for this being *my* game. Sephtis is sitting at the other end of the table, grinning at me as he says, "checkmate."

Then there's the matter of his invitation, but there's no question about that. I have to go. It's likely a trap, but at this point, I'll take whatever chance I can to get close to him; because if I can get close to him, I can kill him, and I want nothing more than to spill his blackened blood. For my mother, for Trey, and for all the other people whose lives were torn apart by his regime.

I'm tired of waiting. It's time to end this, and this time I won't fail. This time I have a clear head and I won't have Jax's life hanging over me because this time I'm going alone. Jax will probably hate me for it, especially if I don't come back, but I don't plan on failing.

"I'm sorry, Jax," I whisper to the empty room.

There's no other way. I have to do this.

I've made up my mind and I shed no tears as I get to work. I have to be on my way before anyone comes to see how I'm doing.

I crumple Sephtis' note up into a ball and chuck it in the garbage. I can't have any of my friends following me. They'll only get hurt and I can't watch anyone else die or see any of them turn out like Trey. I have to protect them.

I stash my old sword in my closet, refusing to take it with me. Sephtis wants me to wield it again, to become

Silent Night once more, but that girl is dead. He will have to deal with the disappointment.

I throw the ruptured pillow under the bed as a final touch and then I sit down to write the others a note. I outline all my plans, underlining the importance of Jenson being "dead," and putting Jax "in charge." Then I explain what I'm going to go do, asking them to please not try to follow me. I tell Bast and Blake to be strong, to support each other through whatever is coming. I tell Kuen to look after Trey, and himself. When I get to Jax, my vision starts to blur and a couple tears land on the page. It's difficult to get the words out.

....What do you say to someone who means so much to you? Take care? I'll be back? I'm sorry? I've never been much good at this, saying goodbye, but then again, I never let myself get attached. I don't regret it. And this won't be goodbye, not if I have any say in it. I'll be home soon, Jax. I love you.

Quinn

I set the note on my nightstand and, after checking that all my weapons are secure, I leave the room. No one notices the dark figure slipping out into the streets, by the fading light of the setting sun.

CHAPTER FORTY-ONE

The city is miraculously quiet. Fires smoulder here and there, but they are unattended. Either the citizens have grown tired of rioting all hours of the day or they know the assassins have been on the hunt. They seem to have an uncanny knack for discovering the unknown.

I creep through the streets, silent and slow. There is no reason to rush and call attention to myself, not to mention stress my leg any more than I need to. Sephtis said he would wait until midnight and the sun has only just sunk below the horizon. I have plenty of time, but that doesn't mean I'm not eager to get it over with. The sooner Sephtis is dead, the better. The sooner Sephtis is dead, the sooner I can breathe freely for the first time in thirteen years. The sooner everyone can.

• • •

It doesn't take me long to reach the theatre where Sephtis waits. There is no opera, hasn't been in decades. All that remains is the dilapidated building where a grand opera house once stood. It can barely be called a theatre anymore. The place is abandoned—boarded up windows and a layer of neglect slowly suffocating the remaining life from its walls.

I'm not surprised to find the front door ajar. I'm also not stupid enough to go in that way. I slip around to the back of the building, combing the walls for other entry points. One of the windows on the second story has gaps in its boards. I pull my easy-grip gloves out of my pockets and put them on. It doesn't take as much time or effort to scale the wall as I expected. Jax was right about my prosthetic at least. It *has* to be the best grip available.

I pull myself up onto the windowsill and perch precariously on its three-inch width as I pry off a few more boards. They come away with ease, which is lucky. I don't feel like losing my balance and plummeting to my death today. Only one Aeron will die tonight and it won't be me. I'll make sure of that.

I crawl carefully through the hole I made in the window and drop to a crouch. The inside of the theatre is dark and cold, like a tomb. Dead. It has sat empty for too long and now its only company is the dust cloaking everything in a thick layer of decay. I resist the urge to cough as its damp smell reaches my nostrils. I won't let a little bit of must break my cover.

I stick to the wall as I creep through the yawning halls in search of a staircase. I don't know why, but something tells me Sephtis will be on the main floor. He likes a show, so what better place to meet than the stage?

I try to ignore the feeling of unease that crawls into me as I near my enemy. What will he attempt this time?

Last time you faced him, I remind myself, *you ended up losing your leg and nearly drowning in a glass tank. This time Trey won't be coming to save you. Sephtis made sure of that.*

I won't need to be saved. I can handle this.

Sure you can, alone and unprepared.

I tell the voice to shut up and grit my teeth against the nagging thoughts that still circulate.

A few moments later, I come across the grand staircase. It beckons me down into the depths, to my possible death.

Shut up.

Sephtis is waiting at the bottom.

I can do this. I must. No one else will.

I take a deep breath and descend towards the beast, towards Sephtis, and a battle that will haunt me until my dying day.

CHAPTER FORTY-TWO

It gets brighter as I go down. Sephtis must've figured out how to turn the lights on after years of disuse. Good for him, but it won't provide much cover for me. Then again... Do I *want* to lurk in the shadows? That was Silent Night's trick and a lot of good it did me when I faced Sephtis at the Guild. No. This time, I'll walk in plain view. If Sephtis wants a show, I'll give him one.

Put him off guard, make him think he can predict your every move, and then show him how well you can disguise your intentions, even without darkness.

Confident in my plan, I pick up my stride.

The staircase brings me to the double doors that lead straight to the auditorium. I pluck up my courage, step forward, and fling open both doors. I stalk inside with the calculated grace of a panther and the doors bang shut behind me. My demeanour is immediately thrown off by the audience I discover.

"You," I seethe.

Avery grins at me from centre stage, Vyrin rather. "Hello, Silent Night," he says, "long time no see."

I take a few steps toward him. "Likewise, Avery, or would you prefer Vyrin?"

He shrugs. "Whatever helps you sleep at night."

I scowl. This wasn't in the plan. He's not supposed to be here.

"Upset, are you?" Avery goes on. "Expecting your dear father? He's tied up at the moment, but he'll be along shortly. He figured I could keep you company and we both trust killing one uncle was enough for you."

I flinch. Ross had said almost the same thing before he died. "How do you know about Lincoln?"

"Jean, you mean?"

It's impossible. They shouldn't have this information. *What is going on?*

"We know about it the same way we know everything," Avery says, "because he was our puppet and he played his part perfectly."

"What?"

Avery laughs. "Oh, it's too precious... You thought it was all a coincidence? Ha! You think it was a happenstance that the man you were sent to kill was your uncle, that it was chance that *he* of all people came into possession of that master list of kills? Did you ever ask yourself where he could get such a list, where the Resistance could've gotten it?"

No...

"Sephtis," I answer.

"Clever girl," Avery replies, "that's exactly right. Sephtis gave it to me and I wove quite the tale, enough to convince your uncle that he must sacrifice himself for you and the good of all. He believed it so wholeheartedly and followed the plan to a T. Alas, his sacrifice was in vain. I may rule the Resistance, but it is as much of a sham as Avery is. The Barn, the Resistance East..." He scoffs. "More like the Northeast Guild. All of the agents there are assassins and have been since I took my rightful place as leader."

I can't breathe. All the realizations are choking me, starving me of oxygen as my brain tries to grapple with the truth. Sephtis has been pulling the strings all along. He made me kill my uncle, and for what?

"What's the point?" I ask Avery. "There has to be a point to this, right?"

"Other than our amusement? Possibly. Come, join me. My brother wants me to show you something." He gestures for me to go to him, but I shrink back.

"I don't think so."

He smiles. "Oh, darling, I was hoping you'd say that." His eyes gaze past me and he nods.

Before I can turn my head, strong arms are on me, lifting me off my feet. I resist the urge to scream, and focus.

I wrestle my right arm free and elbow one of my attackers in the face.

He swears and his grip slips, just enough.

I manage to grab one of my daggers and in seconds it's buried to the hilt in his ribcage.

His eyes bulge and his grip goes slack as blood starts dribbling from his chest and open mouth. He coughs, choking on his own blood, and I fall towards the floor, pulling my second attacker down with me.

He lands on top of me and our eyes lock for a moment before he jumps to his feet. He aims a kick, but I roll away, drawing my gun in the same motion.

I roll to a crouch, aim, and fire.

My second attacker crumples to the ground, bullet in his skull. Blood stains the once-pristine opera house carpets a different shade of red.

I stand up and find myself surrounded by men, all pointing guns at me.

Assassins below…

I'm out of breath, but I manage to look defiant as I drop my gun to the floor and raise my hands above my head in surrender.

"That's it, Silent," Avery says and I flinch at Jax's old name for me. Avery has no right to say it. "I'd hate to kill you before you enjoy the show. I did give you the chance to come quietly, but you had to make a scene."

I refuse to stand still as a pair of men comes up to me with a rope. I don't make it easy for them as they tie my wrists together behind my back, getting in a few kicks to the shin and digging my nails into one guy's arm enough that he bleeds.

He hisses in pain and retaliates by tying the rope even tighter. I don't give him the pleasure of seeing me wince.

Then they yank me around to face Avery.

"Put her in the front row. Best seat in the house," he tells them.

They start dragging me down the aisle.

I rip my arms from their hold and give them a glare that could shatter steel. "I can walk perfectly fine on my own, thank you very much," I snap.

They look to Avery and he shrugs. "There's no harm in it."

They escort me to the seat Avery mentioned and sit down on either side with one empty seat between me and them. The others fan out around me, guns still trained on the back of my head.

The two assassins I killed lie forgotten. This is the coveted world of the Guild assassins. From deadly to dust in seconds, and no one to remember your name.

I sit down grudgingly, without aid despite my tied arms. I didn't forget my training during my time at the Resistance, but it seems my assailants did. They didn't remove any of my weapons. They probably figure I can't reach them with my hands tied the way they are. I guess none of them realize how low the two swords on my back hang, how easy it will be to saw through the ropes binding me.

I resist the urge to grin and face Avery. Let him put on his show. Let him think he's won. Then let all hell break loose.

Checkmate.

"Now that I have your attention," Avery calls dramatically, "may I present to you a demonstration of my latest invention, or concoction, I might say." He raises his arms for added effect and the curtains are swept away, revealing a glass...cage I guess, though it is completely closed off.

What in the world?

"Bring them up," Avery orders.

There must have been a lift system built into the floor of the cage because two people appear, armed to the teeth. A tall man faces off against a reed-thin woman who doesn't look like she stands a chance against him.

Avery looks over at me and grins maniacally. "You're going to enjoy this, Silent Night."

I doubt that, but I stay silent as I watch the horror unfold.

The woman flies at the man before I can blink, and he barely gets his sword up in time to block her attack. Soon the two are a blur as they slash, dodge, and block. It's clear from the beginning that despite the size difference, the girl has the edge. The man doesn't stand a chance against her ferocity.

However, just when I think it's over, the man pulls a gun out of his back pocket and shoots the woman in the leg.

The woman stutters for a moment, a mere second, and then keeps stalking calmly toward the man.

What?

The man panics and keeps shooting until he's emptied the entire round into the woman's shoulder, legs, and lower abdomen.

This time, she doesn't so much as flinch.

The look of horror never once leaves the man's face as the woman runs him through with her sword. The man falls limp and I want to look away, but my eyes are frozen as the woman hacks him to pieces, tearing him apart until the remaining fragments don't resemble anything close to human. All the while the woman's blood seeps from her countless wounds and then…

She crumples to the ground and I know she's finally dead.

The resounding silence in the auditorium could slice glass.

I shift my gaze to Avery. "What the hell did I just witness?" My tone is unforgiving. I want answers.

"That, Silent Night darling, was the fruition of all my long labours of the past decade."

"Your…? You… What have you done?"

He reaches into his pocket and pulls out a syringe filled with an orange liquid. "I call it Black Death 2.0 or Demon's Breath," he says. "It's a virus, one that was difficult to perfect. It's not contagious, but it doesn't have to be."

I'm trying to remain calm, but I can already feel my hands shaking behind my back, quivering against my swords. "What does it do?" I ask him.

He grins. "Glad you asked. Send this lovely little liquid into the bloodstream and you create a fine-tuned killing machine, as shown in our demonstration. Essentially, the virus eradicates all emotions, save for anger and a taste for blood. Your brain no longer recognizes fear, love, sadness, or pain. Wounds won't stop you unless fatal, because your brain simply becomes unaware that they exist. A victim of Demon's Breath will not rest until their opponent is dead and sometimes not even then, because there's one last concept of this wonderful concoction." He sets the virus down on the table beside him.

"And what is that?"

"It sets your inner demon free and allows it full reign to play. It takes different amounts of time for different people, but the demon eats away at you until it's the only one at home and your concept of right and wrong is eliminated. All you know is violence." Avery's eyes shine with his pride and clear insanity.

The world is falling apart before my eyes. He's created an abomination.

"And what exactly do you plan on doing with this virus?"

"Sephtis and I are going to create an army of humans-turned-demons and then, Haven City shall be ours."

"You're crazy," I reply. "Unleash this virus and there won't be a city left to have! Am I the only one seeing sense here? Gods above, you're going to kill us all."

If that virus is set loose in someone like Kuen... Haven would not be able to handle his monster. Kuen can barely handle it now while it still has a leash.

"Hush," Avery says, "I've thought of the repercussions. That's why my next project will be working on finding a cure, in case everything goes wrong."

I have to get out of here. I have to warn the others. I....
I have to destroy that virus.

"How much of the virus have you made?" I ask, trying to sound casual.

"Just the one dose for now, but it can be used to make more, rest assured."

Rest assured?

He's mad. Yet, if I can get that syringe, I can stop all of this before things go horribly wrong.

My thoughts are interrupted by a familiar voice that sends terror-driven goose bumps down my spine.

"Oh, my *dear* little brother, there will be no need for more."

I turn and see Sephtis standing in the centre aisle, gun in hand, eyes trained on Avery.

"And a cure would be horribly tragic." Sephtis raises his gun and shoots his brother in the head.

As Avery topples from the stage, I make my move.

CHAPTER FORTY-THREE

I jump out of my chair, drawing my swords as I do so. A piece of rope still hangs from my right wrist, but I ignore it as I rush into battle.

You can taste the guards' shock when they see me up and swinging, and this moment of confusion allows me to kill two before they can blink. A few raise their guns, but someone must've ordered me alive, because they drop those in favour of cold steel.

I grin.

Bring it on, but my blood will not be spilt tonight.

I slip into assassin mode and gunfire echoes behind me as I dance.

My blades are a blur of silver, and then crimson. Dodge, parry, strike, slash, stab, slice... Limbs are lost; lives are forfeited. Chaos reigns, but I am its queen.

In moments, six more bodies lay in various stages of deformity at my feet. I breathe, heavy but sure. Not once did my leg falter. One more gunshot goes off before silence invades.

I turn slowly to face my father.

"Hello, Silent Night," he says softly. He's standing on the stage now, no weapons in sight, but his right sleeve is splattered in scarlet and bodies litter the floor around him.

"So we meet again, Sephtis," I reply evenly.

He doesn't flinch at my use of his real name and we study each other, two monsters stalking their prey. He moves first, picking up the syringe from the table and glancing at his brother's lifeless body.

"Pity he had to die, but I couldn't have him ruining my plans." He sounds so detached, like he couldn't care less.

"Pity that you're the only one left," I retort.

He looks at me in what can only be described as cold confusion.

"Ross is dead," I say simply.

His eyes flash red for a moment before returning to his calm facade. "Pity," he replies, "but I can't say I'm surprised. Jesper was always the weak one."

"Both of your brothers are dead!" I snap. "Don't you care? Don't you *understand*? You are alone."

"I've always been alone; I wouldn't get anything done otherwise."

"Stop spewing your emotionless garbage," I counter. "I know you are not made of stone. Your heart might be a shard of ice, but it's there. Can you honestly stand there and tell me you feel no remorse for shooting Avery in the head, that you truly don't give a damn Ross was shot by his own daughter, or that *your* daughter, Trey, is slowly dying, because of *you*? As for Kuen and I, you are dead to us. Face it, Father, the only family member still loyal to you, not to mention still alive, is Anane, and he is lost in the head. What's the point of ruling this city if there is no one left by your side?"

He smiles at me, and that, more than anything, strikes fear into my heart. "That's just it, daughter," he says. "I don't want to rule Haven; I want to *destroy* it."

My heart skips a beat, though I shouldn't be surprised.

He regards me coolly and I can almost see the gears shifting in his head as he waits for me to figure it out, but I can't.

"Why? How does destroying Haven better your life? I don't understand."

"Once upon a time, I did wish to rule this city," he admits.

"What changed?"

His eyes become fire. "You."

I shiver.

"You with your petty hopes of something more, something better..." He laughs. "Guild, I don't know what I saw in you, why I expected such great things when you were always destined to fail me. I would've given you the world, the world I would rule, the world you would inherit, but you threw it away, spit in my face." He pauses and I don't dare say a word. "I'm sure Vyrin told you about Jean?"

I nod.

"Not everything, I'm afraid. You see, he was a test. You killed him, which didn't exactly show loyalty, only that you feared me. The real tell was the list. Would you take it and what would you do with that information? I was never so enraged as when I found you gone, Silent Night. You betrayed me just like that," he snaps his fingers once, "and you never looked back. For what?"

I hold my head high as I reply, "I did it for my mother."

"Ah yes, that damn woman…" His eyes hold fire, but his voice carries an anguish I've never heard in him before. "She may be your cause, Silent Night, your driving force, but before she was yours, she was mine."

I frown. "I'm not sure I follow."

"All this?" He gestures to the bodies and flicks the syringe in his hand. "All this destruction is for her. You keep asking what the point is and the point is that I killed her to get to you, to raise a successor to my dynasty, and you scorched it all to ashes. Killing her was pointless because you failed me; you failed both of us. She died in vain.

"There's not a night that goes by that I don't wake up in a cold sweat with the image of her blue eyes the last time I kissed her… I keep seeing the moment when the pillow exploded. I can still feel her blood on my hands. And there's not a goddamn second that goes by now where I don't wish I'd put a bullet through your traitorous forehead instead." His hand twitches as if looking for a trigger. "I've always been alone, Silent Night, and your mother was the one good thing…"

It dawns on me.

Gods above.

"You loved her," I breathe.

"With every fibre of my body," he says. "Why do you think I didn't kill her after taking Trey, like I did with Kuen and Hai's mothers? Why do you think I let her live for five *years* after she refused to hand you over, when I only gave Anane's mother a single day? Our love wasn't perfect, but it gave my heart something to live for. Now… Now there is nothing. And it's your fault, my 'perfect' assassin."

I take a step back. "I didn't shoot her."

"True, but you ensured her death was as pointless as an unloaded gun. She died for nothing, all because you decided you wanted to save this city. Well, guess what, daughter? Haven is beyond saving and I will put an end to whatever hope is left, with your help of course."

He smiles at me and my brain screams at me to run, but I can't move my legs.

"I always had a plan B, Silent Night. Your skills can be used for two things, authority or destruction. This time, you don't get to choose." He waves the syringe in his hand and I stop breathing.

No.

I pivot and sprint up the aisle to the doors.

No.

They seem so far away.

No.

I slam into them and wrench them open, or try to.

Oh Gods, they're locked. Oh Gods, oh Gods...

I turn and find Sephtis right in front of me.

No!

"There's nowhere to run to, Silent Night, no shadows to slip behind, and as for your friends..." He laughs. "They won't be coming to save you this time. It's the end of the line. Say goodnight, because the monster is about to tear free and when it does, no one will be safe.

"You will hunt everyone down and no one will see or hear you coming. You will be a plague upon this city, a Black Death, until no one is left standing, let alone those who remember your name, and when it is all over, I will stand and laugh atop your broken-minded body. Then, perhaps, I will kill you, but not until you've watched all your friends die, not until you've personally slit all their throats, if not something much more gruesome.

"Make no mistake, Silent Night, you will destroy this city, but not before you've destroyed yourself and everything you love." He holds up the syringe.

No.

I try to duck under his arm, not knowing what I plan on doing, just that I can't stand and watch as he ruins everything... But he grabs me and slams me into the doorframe. All the breath goes out of me in a whoosh.

"You're not going anywhere," he growls.

I try to stand and the fingers of his right hand wrap around my wrist. He forces me to my feet.

I reach for a knife at my belt.

In a movement too quick to follow, he wrenches it from my hand, and drives it into my left arm, pinning me to the door.

I scream.

Nothing could have prepared me for this—the sense of helplessness. I try to fight back, try to kick and claw at him, but all I can focus on is the pain…

His fingers close around my throat and I fall still. I can feel the blood running down my arm, can imagine hearing droplets hit the floor.

Our eyes meet.

There is nothing human in his gaze and nothing but fear and agony in mine, I'm sure.

Please God…

Don't let this be the end.

"Say goodnight, Quinn," he says softly.

Then he plunges the syringe into my neck.

To be continued in…

Solemn Vow

AUTHOR'S NOTE

Thank you so much for reading!

If you liked *Sacred Ruse,* it would mean the world to me if you could leave a review where you purchased the book and/or on a review app like Goodreads. Reviews are essential to a book's long-term success. Even a rating by itself or a single sentence can help boost rankings. Oh, and don't forget to tell your friends!

If you are interested in more content from yours truly, please subscribe to my newsletter! Subscription gives you access to exclusive promos, three Fidalian Chronicles short stories, first look at cover reveals, first dibs for ARC & beta reading opportunities for future publications, and other content not shared anywhere else.

You can sign up on my website which I have left below. I can't wait to share more with you!

www.emmacouetteauthor.com

ACKNOWLEDGEMENTS

First, I want to say thank you to my significant other, Allan who urged me on when imposter syndrome was crippling me, when I was worried that I wasn't meant to be a writer and that book one would be my only novel. I'm glad I listened to you and not my anxiety.

Second, to my parents: to my dad for buying more copies than I have and to my mom for spreading the word among her coworkers and Facebook friends.

Third to my amazing Critique Partner, Taylor who helped make this book was it is today. This book wouldn't be anywhere near as good without her feedback and guidance.

Thank you as well to my Beta Readers: Rachel Cole, Ashley K W, James Matthews, Mickey Miles, and Karen Sproxton. I can't wait for you guys to see the finished version!

Big thanks to the members of my Street Team for spreading the word about the cover, pre-order, giveaway, and for reading and reviewing ARCs: Rachel Cole, Ashley K W, Kimberly Swartz, and Stephanie Whitson

Thank you to Miblart for creating this third edition cover.

Huge thank you to Nicki Richards for editing the book. She taught me so much with book 1, but there will still lots of missing commas and emdashes that needed fixing. Those pesky emdashes.

Shoutout to the writing community over on Instagram who always inspire me and motivate me to keep going no matter what. I want to give a special thank you to Pagan Malcolm for her marketing and launching expertise, Bethany Atazadeh for her well of self-publishing knowledge, The Indigo Book for her support of indie authors, and Lydia Srofe for her writing sprints last fall.

Last but not least, thank you to my readers for returning to the world of Haven City for book 2. I am still blown away by the audience I received with *Silent Night* and I can't wait for you guys to see how it all ends in book 3. Thank you for supporting me and my ever growing imagination.

EMMA K. C. COUETTE
BOOK CATALOGUE

ABOUT THE AUTHOR

Emma K. C. Couette is a Canadian wordsmith from a small, Ontario town. She has written a few award-winning short stories and dabbles in poetry when the inspiration strikes her. Her dreams include travelling the world, being a mom, and owning a small library. *Sacred Ruse* is her second novel, the sequel to *Silent Night*.

Website: www.emmacouetteauthor.com
Instagram: @emmacouetteauthor
TikTok: @emmacouetteauthor
Goodreads: Emma Couette